POSSE
WHIPPED

by

Paul K. Metheney

Edited by Karen T. Newman

Copyright © 2022 Left Hand Publishers, LLC
5753 Hwy 85 North #6092 Crestview, FL 32536
All rights reserved. ISBN: 978-1-949241-25-9

https://LeftHandPublishers.com
Twitter.com/LeftHandPublish
Facebook.com/LeftHandPublishers
editor@LeftHandPublishers.com
Cover design by Paul Metheney, pmetheney@gmail.com

Author's Dedication

Many thanks go to Karen T. Newman, and her company, Newmanuscripts.net, for her hours of dedicated editing and insight. Thank you to the men and women of law enforcement who keep us safe every day. Kudos to the town of Taylorsville, KY, and the Spencer County Sheriff's Department for their information and inspiration. And special thanks go out to my loving wife for making the writing of this possible.
To the readers who purchased this book, thank you.

Table of Contents

A Mine is a Terrible Thing to Waste

January 11, 8:12 A.M., Mounton, KY

"You're killing her, Dusty!" Sheriff MacDowell growled.

"Your Honor," Judge Stemple said coolly.

"What?!"

"In this room, you will refer to me as 'Your Honor,'" said the judge, his wrinkled face a hardened chunk of marble.

"Fine. You're killing my granddaughter, *Your Honor*!" the sheriff snarled the last two words.

"Point of fact, Mac, I am not. Even though the community medical center closed only a month or so ago, it's still private property and despite your badge, you have no legal right to remove equipment. I am sorry for Naomi's misfortune."

"Dust—*Your Honor*, if you don't allow us access to that dialysis machine, you are killing her as surely as pulling a trigger."

"Naomi is at the top of the transplant list, I've heard," Judge Stemple commented. "Has the blizzard closed the roads between here and any out-of-town medical facilities?"

"Naomi is NOT at the top. A hundred thousand people nationwide are waiting for a kidney transplants, but on the Kentucky lists, and in particular, the University of Kentucky, she's close enough. But with the roads the way they are, we can't get her there." Sheriff MacDowell was pleading for his granddaughter's life. "Her mama, Beth, was a nurse at the medical center. She can run the machine. We just need your permission to get it.

"I've known you and your family for nearly thirty years now," the sheriff continued. "You and my wife, Hannah, are even kin, fourth cousins or something. Hell, your grandkids, Jasper and Mindy, babysat Naomi since Jeb and Beth brought her home from the hospital."

Overcoming his shock at the length the normally stoic sheriff spoke, Judge Stemple wouldn't relent.

"I'm sorry, Mac, but the law is the law. Not even the *great* Sheriff MacDowell can break the law anytime he sees fit or his family has a need. Despite what you may think, you do NOT own this town. The dialysis machine is the property of Dawson Medical Enterprises. Unless they give you permission, it's grand theft, and that's all there is to it. I pray the Good Lord takes care of you and yours." Without another word, Judge Stemple rose, chair creaking, shrugged on his heavy leather, wool-lined coat, and strode out the door of his office.

Sheriff Jacob MacDowell fell back into one of the few chairs in the room, numb in disbelief. He sat alone in the judge's office in the courthouse building which pulled extra duty as the town hall, city council, and county commission meeting room. Since the impromptu meeting was to be short, they hadn't even turned on the heat, as evidenced by the steam of his breath as he spoke. The big brick building with its two-story antebellum columns was empty due to the inclement weather.

This ain't over. Naomi ain't over. Not by a long shot, Mac thought with an angry edge he wasn't aware he possessed. Setting his worn, brown Stetson low on his graying head, he launched his lean frame into the tempest outside.

#

Mac's ire cooled to a simmer as he trudged through the dirty, coal-tinted snow drifts in the street and eyed each storm-closed storefront. Like a red-hot iron turns to steel, his rage tempered to an unbreakable resolve. Walking through this town, his town, always helped him gain perspective.

He stomped toward *Ginny's Diner*, down the snow-buried Main Street, past the dozen or so red brick buildings of "downtown" Mounton. *Ginny's Diner* looked like an oversized Airstream trailer, covered in windows and burnished aluminum sides gleaming in the January sun. Snow piled up on the diner, but fell off the curved sides, drifting high around the sides of the restaurant. His son, Jeb, waited at the diner after parking Mac's battered old Bronco out front. Jeb inherited his father's lean frame and full, thick hair, but his good looks, lighter complexion, sprinkle of freckles, and piercing green eyes came directly from his mother. Mac hated to admit it, but Jeb was in better shape. His son didn't have the limp Mac picked up in the Marines, thank God. While still athletically thin and slightly shorter, Jeb was more upper body muscular, whereas Mac leaned toward lanky and raw leather tough. Mac watched enough TV to know stubbly chins are "sexy" right now, but years in the Marine Corps and Hannah hating the scratchiness of it was enough for him. Jeb favored his father's clean-shaven look but did have a fuller head of hair, which he kept slightly longer than Mac's lifelong crew cut. Mac's face indicated a life lived outdoors and Jeb couldn't match with it his mother's fairer skin tone. While the two men didn't look like brothers because of the difference in age, it didn't take much imagination at all to place them as father and son.

When it would be time to head home, the accumulated snow would make it nearly impossible and take forty minutes or so, but his old four-wheel drive Bronco would navigate the half dozen miles down the hill to sit in his farmhouse's circular drive.

The mountain hamlet boasted a population of 691, or will soon, once Laney Emerson has her twins in a few months. It only technically qualified as a town when they put the post office in a half dozen generations ago, which still resides in *Duncan's General Store & Mercantile*. The Emerson twins will push Mounton County into the second least populated county in all of Kentucky, with a population of 2,077. Somewhere along the line, the town of Mounton became the county seat. The county consisted of a hundred square miles made up of the couple of mountains encompassing the town, the surrounding horse and dairy farms, and the Stemple coal mines. The Mounton volunteer fire truck attached a heavy blade during the winter to double as the county's snowplow to clean off the main streets. The sheriff's department traditionally volunteered to help salt Main Street and the single side street during the winter. Deicing the two roads required less paperwork than winter fender benders. The blizzard in the last twenty-four hours had dumped more snow on the local roads than the volunteer fire truck could plow and snow was sitting waist high in the middle of the small town. The outlying roads into and out of the county were in worse shape and completely undrivable, even by a four-wheel drive with chains.

Mounton's only industry wasn't the judge's family coal mines, which for the last ninety years, plundered the mountain for whatever deposits remained, but the dozen businesses in the area were all dependent on residents making their living at the mines. While it was the largest employer, Stemple's great-grandfather started the mine as a two-man operation and it soon became the black lifeblood of Mounton. Stemple's great-great-great-grandparents, along with his wife's ancestors, were smart enough to claim and homestead parcels of rolling hills of land off the mountain to start ranches and farms. Stemple's family made fortunes in the horse and dairy business, started the mines, and then slowly but surely bought or started most of the town's businesses. To this day, the mine still relied on manual labor for ore extraction, exactly as it had ninety years ago. Settlers, who discovered the terrain just too damned difficult to traverse in winter, founded the town several hundred years ago. Their wagons broke down, so they decided this was a good place to settle. Nobody knows if the name is short for Mountain Town or if they just couldn't spell worth a damn and were a little on the simple side. Mac leaned toward the latter. *The only mountains poking up in all of central Kentucky and they managed to get stuck.* It tended to back up the "simple" theory. Regardless of its origin, or what the judge might say, Mac didn't think of it as *his* town, but he did consider himself its sole guardian. Every person here was under his personal protection and the same went triple for his family. Mac knew it was egotistical to consider himself the *shield* of Mounton, but after all these years, he just didn't trust anyone else to do it properly. Heaven help the man, or judge, who prevented him from carrying out his duty as its, or his granddaughter's, protector.

#

The bell above the door at Ginny's jangled welcomingly as Mac stepped in and shuffled his feet on the soggy door mat, kicking off excess snow from his boots. A rush of warm, fragrant air carried the promise of fresh coffee and crisp bacon.

"Constable," Ginny acknowledged Mac's nod.

Ginny was actually the son of the previous proprietor, Virginia, and

4

quite a few years younger than Mac. Virginia bequeathed her son the diner, and though he was the current Ginny, of a long line of Ginnys, he looked more like a biker gang enforcer than a restauranteur. A shaggy, brown mane, tucked neatly up under a translucent shower cap, framed a short-bearded face only a mother grizzly could love. Muscular, tattooed arms, as big as Mac's thighs, bulged out of the faded Lynyrd Skynyrd tee shirt. Ginny claimed the once-white apron, displaying stains Mac guessed dated back to the founding of Mounton, was the secret of his culinary mystique. Mac figured the apron was a violation of at least three health codes. But nobody could argue with Ginny's ability in the kitchen. The man was more than a chef. Unheard of in the diner business. The man was an artist and every woman in the county, including Mac's own wife, had tried, at one time or another, to weasel the secret of his pie crust. Some claimed he did time and learned to cook in a federal prison kitchen. Mac was the sole individual who knew his giant friend's real name was Merle. He had worked in his momma's restaurant until the age of seventeen two decades ago when he left town for puzzling reasons of his own. Nobody but Mac knows why, but when he came back to Mounton, his vocabulary had taken a curious upswing.

Ginny's Diner remained open during the snowstorm and even its parking lot hosted only a couple of trucks, probably here from the night before since it was almost impossible to traverse the snow-bound streets. *Duncan's General Store & Mercantile* closed because very few people could get into town to buy anything left. The townsfolk had just about ravaged the shelves before the snowstorm hit anyway. Why the town purchased all the Jiffy Pop nobody may ever know. *Darlene's Beauty Emporium/Barbershop/Tanning Salon*, consisting of a singular tanning bed with two ultraviolet bulbs burnt out, was as dark as the mine itself. The half dozen brick storefronts packed in tight in the town's center were dark and snow piled high in front of them. Mac couldn't tell if *The New Texaco* at the other end of town was open. Folks around here still called it *The New Texaco*, even though it had been there for nearly twenty-five years. The townsfolk had only accepted the gas station because a distant cousin of Hannah's opened it. The town of Mounton rarely received change well.

Mac himself moved here twenty-seven years earlier but the people of Mounton more readily accepted him because his wife was born and raised here. She insisted on being here for the birth of their only son and to be close to her family. Mac, fresh out of the Marines, had no better suggestions. He still didn't. A couple of years after the MacDowells moved into town, Orville Gray, the sheriff of Mounton County for as long as anyone could remember, suffered a fatal heart attack while digging a post hole. With Dusty Stemple's surprise endorsement and Hannah's family connections, Mac ran unopposed, became the new sheriff in town, and ran unopposed every term since then. Mac tried to tell them his entire military experience consisted of boot camp, walking guard duty, and a couple of simple investigations. Evidently, just being IN the military was all the qualifications the people of Mounton County required. Then there was the fact the night fry cook down at *Ginny's* didn't really want the job. It might have been a cut in pay.

Mac collapsed into the cracked red vinyl booth across from his son.

"And…?" Jeb, implored. Naomi was the only child of Mac's daughter-in-law, Beth, and Jeb. Worry poured off Jeb in waves.

"The judge responded negatively to your request," Ginny growled in his deep bear voice, guessing correctly as he poured Mac's coffee.

"Yepper," Mac mumbled raising the steaming cup to his lips.

Ginny said, "He remained adamant to the letter of the law."

"Yepper."

"What are we gonna do? What'll I tell Beth?" Jeb's eyes were frantic. "Dad, I am not gonna let our baby die just because old Dusty Stemple's head's up his ass."

"You mind your manners. *Judge* Stemple may have inherited those mines and half this county, but he earned that law degree, looks out after this town, and he IS your elder. Your momma would skin us both if she heard you bad mouth your elders. Which is exactly why I made you stay here while I talked to *His Honor.*" Mac chastised him, knowing the boy had inherited his momma's good looks and Mac's temper.

"And, pray tell, what morally ambiguous action are you contemplating, my laconic friend?" Ginny queried, suspecting the answer.

"Jeb and I are going to go back to the station to get in touch with Frankfort, Louisville, or Lexington. I need to do everything in my power to do this the legal way," the sheriff declared. "Speaking of which, this is for you," handing Jeb a badge.

The twenty-six-year-old looked down at the offered shield for a long moment and then shook his head, pushing it back towards his dad.

"I'm sorry, Dad. My whole life I wanted to be your deputy, help protect this town, and uphold the law. But the law doesn't seem to care about what's right or wrong, and for what I think we are going to have to do, I don't want to hide behind a badge and do it an injustice."

Mac could barely hide his grin as he slid the shield across the chipped linoleum tabletop back toward his boy.

"Jebediah, I'm real proud of you for feeling that way son, but this ain't about hiding behind a badge. This is about *me* saying my *employee* was following orders when all this comes to the light of day. Frankly, I may be protecting you, but I intend to be hiding behind the biggest, baddest lawyer I can find. But no matter what happens, Naomi is going to have two parents to raise her. So… Put. On. The. Damn Badge."

This was the most Ginny had ever heard Mac utter in a single paragraph in public. Feces was getting pretty real if the sheriff was using swear words.

Mac reached into his pocket to pay for the coffee and Ginny gave him a look fierce enough to regret it.

"Mac, if you gentlemen are going to endeavor as I think you may, you will require a strong back and a weak mind to assist you." The diner owner raised an eyebrow as he spoke.

"Yeah, Ginny, but you got a diner to run and it may not be very good for business afterward," Mac objected, looking around at the few miners eating breakfast.

"Dad's right. Stemple owns the mines, most of the town, and damn near everyone working here," Jeb said. "Besides, you have customers right now."

"These misanthropes?" Ripping off his stained apron, the giant cook roared, "GENTLEMEN! Diner's closed. Breakfast is courtesy of Judge Stemple. Get out. Now."

Shirley, sitting at the cash register, every day of eighty years old, didn't even look up from her knitting.

"You are one crazy sonnuvabitch," Jeb smiled at the big man.

Ginny looked him in the eye and laughed, "Yeah. Like I never heard *that* before. Or today. Mac, do you have another badge handy? I have always fancied a career in law enforcement."

Mac looked at Jeb. "Get him a badge."

Jeb laughed. "I'm always telling you we need more help. I guess this counts. Sort of."

#

January 11, 9:32 A.M., Mounton, KY

Mac and Jeb straddled snowdrift after snowdrift to get to the two-story, clapboard sheriff's office just two blocks away.

"How's the knee?" his son inquired.

"It's fine," Mac replied. "This weather isn't doing it any good, but nothing a couple of Tylenol can't handle."

Jasper Stemple's new yellow Dodge Challenger skewed all over the icy street as they struggled; his sister, Mindy, in the seat beside him, laughed psychotically. Jasper grinned just like his grandfather and waved as he slid sideways in the snow past the father and son.

"Those spoiled fools ain't gonna live to see seventeen," Jeb commented as they struggled toward the sheriff's office. Mac didn't even nod as he watched the judge's grandkids slide down the icy snow-covered street.

Nestled in behind Darlene's Beauty Emporium/Barbershop/Tanning Salon, the little wood frame sheriff's station had been there since the early days of moonshining. Mac had made few changes to the station, but the main improvement was allowing Jeb the installation of a computer with Internet access. Jeb claimed if sixty percent of the county had broadband Internet, the sheriff's office should too.

"Jeb, the cell tower's down. You try the phone and the Internet again, I'll try to get the short-wave up."

Jeb sat down at the desk, while Mac fussed over the radio on the bookshelf. In a day when most jail holding cells were made up of chain-link wire, the solitary cell in the Mounton station still had the original cell bars from back when wanted posters featured Jesse James. Sheriff Gray had installed the short-wave radio early in his tenure and Mac figured it was older than he was and twice as cranky. As the internal vacuum tubes warmed up, Mac could smell the dust burning, just like he did every day. He fiddled with the dials to try to get a response from memorized frequencies.

"This is Stat Flight One, University of Louisville Hospital. What is the nature of your emergency?" came the static-covered voice from the short wave. Mac snatched the mic from its clip in near disbelief.

"Harlan? Is that you?"

"Mac? What the hell are you doing on this frequency?"

Mac breathed slowly to calm himself. Jeb abandoned the dead phone and computer to stand closer to the small speaker in the radio. Jeb brought Harlan up to speed.

"How can we help, boys?" Harlan was the lead pilot for the University of Louisville's medivac helicopter and the numerous emergencies, cave-ins, and mine-related fatalities had treated him to more than his share of flights up the mountain. Between emergencies, he backed up Louisville Metro's air patrol.

"The staties are working to clear the roads, but it could take days. Maybe more. A landslide buried Highway 55 coming up the mountain. We can't even make it down to the Bluegrass Parkway," Mac moaned. "I got a sick little girl up here and she needs dialysis now. Bardstown Hospital has dialysis, but we need to get to the University of Kentucky's transplant unit if possible." After a decisive pause, Mac continued. "Harlan ... it's my granddaughter, Naomi." Defeat pressed in on him like the snow outside.

"Damn, Mac. I am so sorry. At top speed, I can be down there in thirty minutes once we get clearance. The problem is the storm is now covering this whole section of the state and has turned into a complete whiteout. The FAA has grounded everything from here to Lexington. Probably will be for quite a while."

"Harlan, there has to be some way to get the chopper down here." Mac had met Harlan in the military when Harlan came back from flying tours in the Middle East and Mac policed Camp Le Jeune. Despite over thirty years of friendship, Mac knew he was emotionally blackmailing his friend into risking his helicopter, license, career, and life on a flight he knew was just too dangerous. With Naomi's life at stake, he would risk all that and more.

"Mac, the problem isn't just clearance. This ice storm has all but eliminated every place I could put down on your side of the avalanche. We normally set down at the school ballfield or up at the mines and the storm has probably both of those buried in a ton of snow. Anything on the mountain flat enough to put down on is covered in drifts, telephone wires, ice, or trees."

"Dad?" Jeb grabbed Mac's arm. "Dawson."

Mac's eyes lit with a new fire. He nodded.

"Harlan, can you do us a favor?" Jeb begged.

"Name it."

"Track down and get a hold of a Dawson Medical Enterprises. We would, but our phones and Internet are down. They're out of New Jersey, I think. Give them our situation. They had a dialysis machine here when their medical center closed down. We need permission to use it. Can you find them?" Jeb was nearly begging at this point.

"My guys are already dialing, Mac. It may take some time, but we'll find them."

"Thanks, Harlan. I'll radio back in two hours to check in." Mac hung the mic back on the clip. Naomi had been getting dialysis at the community medical center where Beth worked up until they closed and then she and Hannah were taking turns driving the five-year-old to Lexington to get treatments. She had been on the transplant list for over a year. For most of her life, all Naomi knew was being sick.

if we had a *real* sheriff?"

Stemple glared at Mac, daring him to deny any of it, confirming to himself what he was going to do. What he had to do.

"Did you get all of that?" Mac asked.

"What are you going on about?" Stemple snapped.

"Yeah, we heard it all. *Everyone* heard it all," Jeb's tinny voice came from Mac's belt.

"What in the hell's going on here, Mac?" Stemple demanded, unbuttoning his leather coat.

"I can't believe you enticed him to do an actual villain monologue!" Ginny's normally thundering voice squawked from the ether. "Vintage Dr. Doom."

Mac held up a tiny lapel mic, hidden in his left sleeve and attached to his belt radio. He double-tapped the talk button signaling them to approach from the wood line. He pointed out Jeb, Ginny, and a handful of newly unarmed miners to the judge.

"You know Ginny and my boy, Jeb. You remember him. You tried to kill his daughter today," Mac spoke solemnly. "Well, Jeb was out there in the woods. He and Ginny found your boys and after what I can only imagine was an interesting moment or two, let your miners listen to you tell all about how you and your family have been letting these 'moronic, inbred hillbillies' die so your grandson can drive a new car and screw his sister."

Judge Stemple stared at the approaching men in shock.

"Oh, and Dusty? It's 'Sheriff,'" Mac said coolly.

"What?" the judge snarled, whirling back to face Mac, confused, anger building with every second.

"You will refer to me as 'Sheriff' when I'm wearing this badge. Only my friends can call me Mac."

"NO! No witless jarhead is going to ruin my town!" the judge screamed, reaching inside his coat, leveling an automatic at Mac.

Mac heard the explosion simultaneously as a blast of bloody mist sprayed across his face. As the judge fell forward, he focused past the falling body to see Ginny lowering the smoking rifle he had removed from a miner, as Stemple slumped to the ground.

"Mac, this is Stat Flight One on final approach. I tried you on the short-wave but got no answer, so I just took off. We were about to radio in when your little soap opera started transmitting. Nice use of our frequency by the way. What are your instructions? Is Naomi ready for transport? What the hell is going on down there?" Harlan's voice booming from his radio.

"Harlan, new plan. Naomi is already getting dialysis, but the Judge's been shot and needs immediate evac. You can land the chopper in my driveway. By the time you can get here, we will have the flagpole in the driveway circle down. Do you remember how to get here?" Mac barked into the lapel mic in his sleeve. Mac caught Jeb's eye and tipped his head toward the front of the house.

"On our way," Jeb told him.

Jeb drafted the miners and hustled them around to the front of the house. Jeb pull-started the snow blower from the shed as the miners took down the flagpole. After blowing the waist-deep snow from the circle in the middle of the drive, he plowed a path from the garage to the middle of the circle, well aware he was decimating the flowers his mom had planted around the flagpole.

Ginny ran to Mac and helped apply pressure to the judge's chest to staunch the flow of blood.

"We gotta keep him alive," Ginny whispered as they worked on the prone man.

"Ginny, it wasn't your fault."

"I know. But this sonnavabitch hasn't paid his tab at the diner for breakfast today."

#

January 13, 11:21 A.M., Lexington, KY

"Did his honor survive?" Ginny asked as he entered the waiting room. He wrinkled his nose at the antiseptic smell every hospital bathed in. A far cry from his usual aromas of flour and deep fat frying.

"Not all of him," Jeb replied drily.

Mac, Jeb, and Beth had flown into Lexington with Stemple and

18

Naomi. There was plenty of room for them and the medics as they worked to keep Stemple alive. Ginny and Hannah were just arriving twenty-six hours later, after the state road crews had made the road down to the Bluegrass Parkway semi-passable enough for Mac's four-wheel drive Bronco. Ginny had put chains on the tires and loaded the rear cargo area with bags of salt to weigh it down for extra traction. Cut off from any updates regarding her grandchild for the last day or so, Hannah rushed to Naomi's first floor room leaving Ginny in the hall with Jeb.

Ginny gave Jeb a puzzled look.

"Stemple only lasted for about an hour after they got him on the operating table. Turns out though, the old bastard had an organ donor card." Jeb said tiredly.

"You must be kidding me! You mean ..." Ginny exclaimed incredulously.

"Yeah, we're just waiting now to see if Naomi rejects it. They have her on all kinds of anti-rejection protocols, but Dusty seemed to be a pretty good match. Beth hasn't slept since long before we 'borrowed' the machine, but she won't leave Naomi's side."

"Jeb, my lad, those are exceptional tidings. At least the old greedy blackheart did *something* positive before he shed this mortal coil." Ginny queried as he looked around, "Where's Mac? Is he with Naomi?"

"No. After spending the better part of the day trying to get Harlan out of trouble for flying without clearance, he said he had something to do," Jeb declared.

"How did he coerce the late judge into a verbal confession?" Ginny inquired.

"Dad just figured if the judge thought he had the upper hand, he would blab about his master plan," Jeb explained. "I think he was counting on Stemple's ego. The fact the judge thought he was smarter than everyone else and he probably planned to kill Dad, helped a bit too."

"Uh, did Mac happen to elucidate in regards to my fate? I mean, Stemple may have been an avaricious old cutthroat, but I DID just shoot a county judge in the back," Ginny said. "Some lesser evolved citizens may frown on that kind of behavior."

"I don't think he brought it up to the staties yet. He told the hospital it was a 'gun-related-mishap,' which I guess, technically, it was. He told me there were more than enough witnesses you needn't worry. I think some of the 'in-bred hillbillies' are mad enough to back anything we say," Jeb said, grinning like only a father of a healthy baby can. "Don't give it a thought. You saved my dad and my baby. Besides, weren't you just deputized?"

Ginny looked at Jeb and just shook his head, amazed at how crazy parenthood can make a guy.

"Hey," Jeb continued. "I need to go check on Beth and Naomi. C'mon man, you're family now. Screw the rules."

"You should get that inscribed on your family crest."

As they peeked into Naomi's room, Hannah was tucking a blanket around Naomi as Beth snored softly in a chair by her bedside. Ginny tapped Jeb on the arm and pointed out the window.

A remarkably accurate, seven-foot-tall snow sculpture of a giant fist holding a gavel straight up, loomed right outside Naomi's window.

#

Pay No Attention to that Man Behind the Curtain

January 17, 12:08 A.M., Frankfort, KY

The man sat in shadows of a well-appointed den. The French doors looked out over an expansive estate covered in a deep blanket of snow. Large books line the walls more for the ambience it gave the den than the occupant's reading pleasure. The room carried faint scents of leather, polished mahogany, and fine tobacco smoke. A single green desk lamp illuminated the desk and left much of the room in darkness. Expensive electronic communications equipment replaced several volumes on several bookshelves. Next to the multi-line phone on his desk sat a black box with lines plugged into the phone as well as adapters to connect to mobile phones.

He leaned back in his swivel chair as he surveyed his snow-buried kingdom out the window. The chair was Italian leather, hand rubbed to looked distressed, wrapped around a polished mahogany frame. The chair cost him forty-five hundred dollars at *Scully & Scully's* in New York and he considered it a bargain. He even enjoyed the fact they called it "a director's chair."

The plan was coming together. I have procured several mentally aberrant individuals who have no issues in executing some of the more gruesome corrections if needed. They would actually enjoy it. I even found a convict whose sexual proclivities lean toward some of the more distasteful tasks, should the need arise. They are not suitable for the more critical and mundane activities. I may not even utilize their services. They are too volatile, but they will keep the minor pieces in line, while those knights and bishops will keep the pawns from straying.

He glanced at the marble chessboard set up at a small table at the side of the room. Two polished wooden chairs flanked either side of the table. The inlaid and unused chessboard, like the books, sat there for their aesthetic value. The man played all his chess games on a mental board.

As planned, I must next recruit my minor pieces and pawns from my opponent's side of the table.

Once I set the board, it will be relatively easy for me to not only remove all his pieces, leaving him open for checkmate but to recapture my queen.

A new storm front moved in from the southeast and a fresh torrent of snow fell outside his window. The chill on the glass panes did not match the glare in his eyes.

#

Dead of Winter

"That is about as dead as they come," Jeb told his dad.

"Yepper," Jacob MacDowell, sheriff of Mounton County, Kentucky, replied. "I've seen dead before and it looks just like that. Maybe a little warmer."

They stood over the corpse of a gigantic frozen body, face down, half in and half out of Lake Mounton. The heavy snow the night before mostly covered the frozen mountain of flesh. They could tell by the impact dent on the ground next to the body someone rolled the deceased over onto his face.

"Let's get him turned over and see if it's really Wilbur," Mac told his son. "You can't really tell who this is, with all this snow on the body." Jeb, long used to following his father's lead, stayed on as a full-time deputy only recently.

With a strain, they wrestled the gargantuan corpse loose from the frozen edge of the lake and rolled it over on its back. "Damn! I bet he weighs three hundred and seventy-five pounds soaking wet, no pun intended," Jeb grunted.

Mac stood back while Jeb kept kneeling, dusting the frost and snow off the face. "Guess Neville was right. Definitely looks like Wilbur Clay, don't it?"

"He's looked better," Mac said while looking up the hill they just descended and the surrounding area. Snowflakes pelted his face and melted immediately, leaving cold, wet drops. The flakes landing on his Stetson survived longer and tended to accumulate. Mac glanced at Jeb and saw the snow land and cling to his heavy winter coat. The branches of the trees and shrubs on either side of the hillside sparkled with snow and ice. The steep hill sloping down to the lake was an unbroken field of weeds peeking up through last night's snow fall all the way up to the roadside. It had let up for a few days, but at about 11:00 last night the storm, literally, dumped a mountain of snow on Mounton County. Mac and Jeb arrived in Mac's rust and primer colored excuse for a Bronco. Only Mac and Jeb's footprints disrupted the snowy field coming down the hill. The clouds let loose before midnight last night covering this part of the mountain in a thick blanket of white. Further down the road, they only got about half as much, but here the snow was already a foot deep. Mac hated that his and Jeb's footprints marred the pristine whiteness of the hill. Otherwise, the snowy scene would have been fit for a postcard. Minus the dead body of course.

Jeb checked the body's pockets.

"It's Wilbur all right. Wallet's got seventeen dollars, so robbery is out. Even has his truck keys," Jeb said, examining the wallet and pocket contents.

"Wilbur was the union leader up at the mines," Mac remembered.

"Before you closed them down," Jeb finished. But quickly added, "For some really gross labor and health violations. There're also some rumors about him being a mean drunk and wife beater. And by 'rumors,' I mean, almost certainly, a fact."

"None of which are good reasons to end up dead, frozen halfway in a lake."

"Kind of looks like he slipped down the hill and cracked his head on the way down and froze to death. He's frozen solid. Takes more than a couple of hours, even in last night's snow and temperatures. Bad way to go," Jeb mused.

"Can't really think of a good way right this minute," Mac said.

"Let's call KSP," Jeb suggested. He knew how his father thought. "Let's get *them* to haul his enormous frozen ass up the hill. We'll use *their* medical examiner and see if we can get a rush on it. I'll get plenty of pictures and let's wait in the truck. No point in freezing our hind ends off till they get here. Wilbur sure as heck ain't going nowhere."

Mac, not looking forward to digging Wilbur out of the ice and dragging his immense carcass up the hill with his bad knee, silently thanked his son's judgment.

"Yepper."

After photographing the scene thoroughly, Mac and Jeb climbed back up the hill and sat in Mac's Bronco with the heater on full. Once the Kentucky State Police arrived, Mac described the situation, while Jeb stretched yellow crime scene tape across the top of the hill. After he lit road flares to protect the law enforcement vehicles, ambulance, and required fire truck, he started a log sheet of people who had entered the crime scene. At this moment, it contained only himself and his father. Unlike TV detectives, KSP sent a single crime scene investigator, not an entire team. The CSI took more photos and looked for forensic evidence on the scene, made all but impossible by last night's snowfall. Given the likelihood Wilbur died from the fall down the hill, the CSI determined it wouldn't be necessary to bring in heated blowers to melt the snow to look for forensic evidence. Mac and Jeb walked the top of the hill beyond the tape, securing the scene as the KSP detectives, officers, and EMTs traveled down the hill towards the body. The state's ME supervised the removal of the body, on a stretcher and sealed in the ME's biggest body bag, but it took the winch from the firetruck to drag Wilbur Clay, up the slope. Mac silently mourned the trampling of the near pristine snow on the steep hillside.

#

One hour earlier

Mac and Jeb walk into the Mounton County Sheriff's Office, handing Dawe, the night shift deputy, a steaming hot cup of fresh coffee from *Ginny's Diner*. He traded Mac the few pages of his nightly report for the cup.

"Was a pretty slow night. There was a scuffle at *The Digger's Hole Saloon*. You know, the bar way out in the sticks. No injuries, no arrests. Two drunks too intoxicated to throw a punch. The little guy was too drunk to walk, let alone drive, so I got his address from his driver's license, drove him back home, and dumped him in his recliner. It started really snowing hard on my way back. An hour or so later, I was back here when a motorist came in and reported a truck with Kentucky plates, hitting what they thought was a deer on Lakeside Road. So, I drove all the way back out there. Couldn't find the carcass by the road, so I just came back."

"Did the motorist ID the truck?" Jeb asked.

Dawe handed Mac the motorist's statement. "No. Too dark with no streetlights out there and snowing like crazy. Just big. Pretty new. They probably could ID it if they saw it, but they couldn't tell me precisely which model. No truck owners reported an incident. I figure it was a just a close call. Another deer bites the dust. No harm, no foul. After the snow started, it quieted down."

The front door to the office slammed open. Neville Jarvis, wearing rubber waders and a single sweatshirt and no cap, stood in the doorway.

"I want to report finding a body."

#

"Slow down, Neville," Mac said. "Come over here, sit down, have some coffee, and tell us about it."

Neville Jarvis was a big man, tow-headed, and the current acting mayor pro tem for Mounton until the elections in the spring. The last mayor ended his term prematurely with the assistance of some undiagnosed pancreatic cancer. Rumor has it Jarvis was the front runner in a landslide to be the mayor full time. The former safety officer for the Stemple Mines, known all over the county for his size, blonde hair, disdain for outdoor sportsmen, and extremely enormous political signs, ran nearly unopposed. Word around town is he is so cheap, he plants the big four-by-eight-foot signs himself. He seems to think if he plants enough of the monster signs, it will compensate for his attitude towards hunters and outdoorsmen. In central Kentucky. As if.

"I was going ice-fishing over to the lake when I saw him." Neville's teeth chattered, his hands shook as he tried to sip the hot coffee.

"Since when do you ice-fish?" Jeb wondered. "Never mind. What'd ya see?"

"Wilbur Clay," Neville said. "Dead as dead can be. Down by the lake's edge. Frozen stiff."

Dawe looked at Mac.

"What?"

Dawe stared at his boss. "Wilbur was the guy in the bar fight last night."

#

After Neville described how to get to the edge of the lake where he saw Wilbur's body, Mac and Jeb bundled up for the trip out to the edge of the county. Dawe stayed back at the station with Neville and took his written statement and documented the events so far. As the two men walked outside past the mayor's Super Duty truck, they glanced at the gigantic signs and tools in the bed. "Nice truck," Jeb noted.

"Yepper."

#

January 17, 11:15 A.M., Mounton, KY

"I guess you're right," Jeb told Mac. "We have to cover every base. It's a crying shame some of these bases are so far out of town. Good thing Patty-Jane could get off from the phone company to get the kids off to school so Dawe could pull a double shift." Looking out the Bronco window, Jeb shook his head. "Are we even *in* Mounton County anymore?"

"Yeah, even though it's the closest bar to Mounton, *Digger's Hole Saloon* is about only about two miles inside the county line. The county line curves wide around the lake. This is the last place you can get a legal drink for two more counties."

"Think Wilbur was walking home last night?" Jeb questioned his dad, looking toward the road and the lake.

"'D be my guess."

"At least he wasn't driving drunk," Jeb admitted. "We might have had more folks headed to the Frankfort ME than just him."

Inside *Digger's Hole*, the bar was empty, but warm, out of the snow and wind. The saloon smelled of spilled beer and stale nuts. A leprechaun of a man sat on one of the bar stools.

"Howdy, Sheriff," the man greeted Mac and nodded at Jeb. A shock of red hair crested an enormous head. Had he been standing, he *may* have topped out at a hair over five-foot tall and a hundred pounds. The bright green shirt and suspenders completed the leprechaun image.

"Joint's really jumping, huh" Jeb joked.

"Naw. It's too early to be open. I'm here 'cause the owner called and said you wanted to talk to the bartender on duty last night and since I was here anyway, what the hell. It worked out. I already volunteered for the day shift last night. I slept in the little room above the bar. It's barely more than a twin bed and a shower. I don't start for a couple more hours, but gives me time to get this placed spruced up a might."

"Okay. What's your name?" Jeb queried, his notepad out and ready to take notes.

"Howdy."

"Uh, hi. What's your name?"

"Howdy."

"Listen, sir, we're here on official business. We don't have time for this—"

"Sorry, Deputy. My name is Howdy. Howdy Barnes. I'm just messin' with ya' is all."

Jeb looked at his father, exasperated.

"Mr. Barnes," Mac spoke for the first time since entering the bar. "Have you seen this man?" holding up an enlarged photo from Wilbur's driver's license.

Howdy squinted at the photo. "Oh, sure. That'd be Willy. Don't know his last name. Big fat sonnuvabitchin' bohunk of a miner." Looking at Mac, "I mean former miner. Union rep or sumpin'. I had to call you guys on him last night. He was in here buying some folks a few rounds all afternoon and half the night."

"How was Wilbur Clay able to buy rounds of drinks for anyone?" Jeb questioned. "Wasn't he unemployed?"

"On credit. We don't do credit, but to be real honest, a shit-faced drunkard with probably two hundred and fifty pounds on me, I might have been just a tad intimidated. We haven't had a real bouncer here in ages. Can't find anybody to take the job. Some of these unemployed miners are rough trade. He insisted I give him credit. Claimed he was about to come into some serious foldin' money.

Figured I never see the cash, but at cost, the liquor was cheaper than reconstructive surgery. Once I called the cops on him, I was sure that was money I'd never see again."

"What time did you call the sheriff's office?" Mac wondered.

"'Xactly 10:03. Some little runt of a bald guy took exception to the fact Willy didn't buy a round for his table. Seemed to know Willy and not in the let's-be-besties-sort-of-way. Both of 'em drunk as skunks. Could barely stand up, let alone fight. I called you boys 'cause without a bouncer and Willy's more than three times my size. I figured I could make him your problem."

"What happened afterward?" Jeb urged, writing furiously in his notepad.

"Aw, like most bar ruckuses, it petered out to nothin'. The deputy showed up in about twenty minutes, separated them. The deputy gave them choice of a ride home or to jail. Willy looked at his watch and took the third option of walking home. Guess he wanted to cool off in the snow. Your guy drove the little feller off, but since he didn't cuff him or nothin' I guess he weren't in no trouble."

"Do you know which way Willy headed?"

"Yeah, he headed off towards the lake."

Jeb had another question for the little leprechaun of a bartender. "No offense, but how small does a guy have to be in order for YOU to call him a runt?"

#

29

January 17, 10:48 A.M., Mounton, KY

"Well, as expected, thirty minutes of our lives we'll never get back. A hammered Wilbur. Call the media. I'm guessing he spent most of his time blasted," Jeb studied his dad on the drive back from the bar.

"Sounds like he was celebratin' a tad extra, though," Mac said.

"Why aren't we looking where we both know we should be?" Jeb demanded.

"Son, our job is to investigate every lead. We have to be able to not only prove what we think we know 'beyond a shadow of doubt,' but also, we looked at every other possible angle. Besides, I have Dawe looking into some other things. You and I just go where the evidence leads. Speaking of which, let's swing by the lake on our way home. I wanna take another look at the hill Wilbur fell down."

"Isn't Joe on overtime? We should be following up the hot leads."

"Jeb, Dawe is doing what I requested because he has a few connections *neither* of us does. Besides, it's January in Kentucky. All the leads are cold."

#

January 17, 4:00 P.M., Mounton, KY

"Doc, can you see us?" Mac spoke loudly into the computer during the Zoom call to the KSP's medical examiner in Frankfort. "Jeb is here with me. What have you got for us?" Jeb, who normally worked a few hours in the morning with Mac, then came back for the evening shift, had decided to come in early while they investigated the Wilbur Clay case. He initiated the Zoom call for his dad.

"Well, Mac, I won't bother you with the identification info, you seem to know all about him anyway. Him being the first death of the day, he was lucky enough to go to the head of the list. If you can call that luck. I'll just give you the highlights. You rarely bring me anything, but when you do, it's always unique. The tox screen shows his blood alcohol ratio was enough to kill most men. But it wasn't what killed him."

"Despite the cold, it wasn't from exposure. He had enough alcohol in him to keep him from freezing to death in the short term. Seems someone or something pummeled Shrek here one time too many.

Once to be exact. Blunt force trauma. From the impression it left on the skull, his head impacted with something with a convex surface about eight inches wide with a tapering hollow indent up the middle. The impact runs horizontal across the back of his skull. Left almost a perfect dent. Must have been helluva fall. With considerable force. Even though rigor mortis hadn't resolved yet, the arctic temperatures had nearly frozen the body stiff. After he died, no amount of alcohol would keep him from freezing. No defensive wounds. No hair and fibers other than his own. Other injuries are consistent with a fall down a hill. Could have fallen and on the way down cracked his head on something, but he didn't die immediately when he fell. It's weird. The impact came from something impacting the back of the head. Drove pieces of his skull directly into his cranium. The brain trauma killed him, but AFTER the fall. We couldn't do a time of death based on liver temperature because of the body and environmental temperature, but we did ascertain he died right before 11:00 P.M., give or take a few. My initial thoughts on Cause of Death are accidental death by misadventure. But there are some serious discrepancies. The lividity indicates he died face down. I'll have a detailed report emailed over to you in the morning."

"Doc," Mac requested. "Hold off on the final COD for a bit. I think I know what the convex surface might be."

"Care to share?"

"Not till I know more. I'll call you tomorrow. Thanks for the rush."

"No worries. Give Hannah my love."

#

January 17, 5:47 P.M., Mounton, KY

After getting his name from Dawe's incident report, Mac and Jeb drove back across the county to interview ...

"Harold Calvin?" Jeb bellowed loudly, hammering the front door of a run-down house trailer. "Open up, Mounton County Sheriff's Office."

"I heard ya. All a Kentucky heard ya. Hold on, will ya'? Criminy," a voice from inside the house moaned.

Calvin's house was a rusting double-wide, permanently parked a good thirty-minute drive, in good weather, from *Digger's Hole Saloon*. Black streaks from years of rain ran down the faded, dull white sides of the trailer. Weeds poked through the snow. A piece of cardboard and fiberglass insulation showed in a duct taped to a broken back window. No vehicles parked in the snow-covered gravel drive, but a broken-down John Deere sat next to the trailer, covered up to its hood in a snow drift. The whole scenario did not scream "Wayne Manor."

A few seconds later, a bleary eyed, balding man about four foot nine opened the door and allowed them to enter. He stumbled back to his La-Z-Boy and collapsed his ninety-eight-pound frame into it. To Mac, Jeb said quietly, "Boy, Howdy wasn't kiddin' about his size."

"Have a seat boys. What can I do for you fine gentlemen this day? It's still morning, right?"

"Are you Harold Calvin?" Jeb demanded in his most official voice.

"What's left of him."

"Mr. Calvin, can we ask where you were between 10:00 P.M. and 6:00 A.M. last night?" Jeb questioned Harold as Mac walked around the shack, almost distracted.

"Sure. Ask."

Jeb looked at his dad. "Two thousand and seventy-seven people in this county and I get every friggin' comedian today." Turning to Harold, "Fine. Mr. Calvin, where were you between 10 o'clock last night and 6 o'clock this morning?"

"Damned if I know."

"Excuse me?"

Mac picked up an empty whisky bottle and examined it as Harold answered.

"I don't remember shit about last night. Hell, what time is it now anyway? I was at the *Hole* last night with a few friends. I vaguely remember standing up to an enormous drunk asshole and woke up in this chair right here, when you started with all the bangin' and yellin'. I'm not exactly sure, but I may have been overserved. Can I sue them?"

"Mr. Calvin, do you know this man?" Mac asked holding up his photo of Clay.

"That's him! I remember him now. Will Claymore, or Clayton, or something. He was a gigantic douchebag when we worked at the mines," glancing at Mac. "He ruled the unions with an iron fist. Nobody liked him. Complete dick. He and I got into it a few times over paid time off or some shit back in the day."

"Can we take look around, sir? Especially out in the shed?" Mac appealed to Harold.

"Yeah, go ahead. As long as I can just sit here. But you gotta tell me."

"Tell you what, sir?"

"How bad did I kick his ass in the bar fight? I bet I knocked him cold."

January 18, 9:30 A.M., Mounton, KY

"I'm dreading this," Jeb said.

"Yeah, me too. Peggy Clay's waitressed at *Ginny's Diner* since before her having her first kid. I hate even the idea of questioning her about this," Mac lamented. Mac took off his old Stetson and Jeb did the same with his Louisville Cardinals' ball cap.

They stood in front of her mobile home door for a few silent seconds before Mac solemnly knocked. Faded primer spotted the trailer's aluminum sides in places. Drifts of snow cover the lawn with patches of weeds popping through the dirty snow. The snow barely hides the lump that vaguely resembles a broken Big Wheel. Large rust spots and vertical black steaks running down the sides reminded Mac of Calvin's double-wide. The two mobile homes could be interchangeable. Unfortunately, the same could be said about many of the residences in Mounton County. Even from outside the mobile home, the air reeked of mildew, desperation, and broken promises. Mac had once dropped Peggy off home from the diner a while back when Wilbur had failed to show to pick her up. The place hadn't improved a bit since then. Peggy's mother usually watched the kids during her shifts at the diner, driving in from Harrodsburg. Peggy answered the door after a few moments wearing a long-sleeved hoodie sweatshirt and sunglasses.

"Peggy."

"Sheriff. Come on in."

Peggy Clay had once been a very attractive woman, back before she made her last name Clay. Even the birth of two boys did not add the weight some women pack on after pregnancy. Her hair having once been luscious strawberry blonde, full and thick, now hung limply and straight. Mac knew even before she needed the sunglasses to cover her face, she had dark circles forming under eyes. She was in her early twenties and looked twice her age today.

"I suppose you've heard about Wilbur," Jeb inquired as they step inside the dark double-wide. The lights were off, but from the doorway, Mac could see a sink full of dishes and broken toys scattered all over the floor.

"Yeah, Dawe came by to notify me ysterday morning and the mayor stopped by yesterday afternoon to check in on me," Peggy stated without a drop of emotion in her voice. "The mayor offered to stay and watch the kids if I needed some time to myself to just go off for a bit. Mighty kind of him, but I'm fine."

"I'm sorry I haven't been by sooner, Peggy. We've been busy looking into this thing," Mac said. "No excuse, but it's the truth."

"Do you know what happened?"

"Well, it seems it–" Jeb began.

"We don't have all the facts right now Peggy," Mac interrupted his son with a glance. The interruption was strange in itself, as Mac usually let Jeb do most of the talking. "We're still digging up all the details."

"The mayor said he fell down a hill by the lake, hit his head on the way down and frozed to death."

"The mayor said that, did he?" Mac raised an eyebrow. "Well, as I mentioned, we don't have all the facts just yet, but as soon as we do, we'll let you know."

Jeb gestured to Peggy's sweatshirt and glasses. "A little cool in here, huh? And bright."

Peggy rubbed her sleeved arm tenderly.

"Yeah, Wilbur didn't like the thermostat set too high. Said it wasted money. I guess we can turn it up a few degrees now."

Mac looked down the hall and the two little boys standing in the bedroom's doorway. The oldest had a black eye and the other had gigantic hand-shaped bruises on his arm. Big bruises. Mac knew the youngest, a line of snot drooped from his nose, was no more than three years old.

Mac mused, "I imagine there'll be a few changes around here now."

Peggy followed his gaze. "BOYS! Get back in your room! This is grown-up talk. Sorry, Sheriff, they're just a bit confused about everything right now."

Mac looked at the partially covered, fading yellow and purple bruise on her once attractive face. "I'm guessing things will get easier ... for everyone."

Peggy quickly turned to the kitchen area of the mobile home. "Can I fix you a cup of coffee or something? Sweet tea?"

"No, thank you. We have to be going," Jeb said. "Peggy, we know this is horrible timing and we hate to mention this, but we need to know. Where were you two nights ago?"

"No, I understand. I watch all the police shows. It's almost always the spouse. Don't give it a thought, Jeb. I was right here with the boys like I am every night. Waiting for Will to come home. Jes' like I do every night. I guess that's one of those things about to change as well."

"Anyone come by?"

"Not really. I did talk to Mama on the phone a little before 10:30. She calls in once a week just to talk and find out about my schedule for the next week so she knows when to come by and watch the boys. She only calls when Wilbur's out drinkin', which is most every night, and the kids are in bed. We chatted for quite a bit."

"Was there any change with Wilbur or anything different going on?"

"Yeah. A day or two before ... the accident, Wilbur was in a better mood than he usually is. He even said he was sorry for the way he treated me and the boys and everything was 'bout to change. He promised things was gonna be different. But then, he promised a lot of things."

"Did he mention why he was in a better mood?"

"No. But even though he was drinking more those coupla days, he didn't come home sore. He just came home and pretty much passed out."

"Well, Peggy, we won't take up any more of your time." Mac looked down the empty hall, before he and Jeb step toward the door. "If there's anything you or the kids need, you don't hesitate to call me or Hannah, y' hear?"

"Sheriff, there is something thing I'd like to know, if you don't mind?"

"Sure, Peggy, name it."

"Did he suffer?"

"I'm sorry?" Jeb sputtered, genuinely thrown off.

"Was Wilbur in much pain at the end?"

Mac understood why she wanted to know and lowered his head. Jeb spoke up.

"No, Peggy, he didn't suffer at the end. It came quick and it seems he was pretty well intoxicated, so he felt no pain, probably none at all."

"Dammit," she said quietly and closed the door behind them.

#

On the drive back to the station, Mac picked up the radio handset. "Dawe, come in."

"Dawe here," his voice playing out of the radio speakers. "What's up, Sheriff?"

"I have a few more things I need you to do."

"Whatever I can do to help."

"First of all, tell Patty-Jane you're getting three days in a row off real soon. I promise."

Mac explained what he wanted.

"Better make those three days damn soon, Sheriff. Shorthanded, double shifts, and now this? I am one lowered toilet seat away from divorce papers."

"Be thankful," Jeb grabbed the mic. "Mom doesn't believe in divorce, but she is a firm advocate of the 30-ought six."

#

January 19, 11:40 A.M., Mounton, KY

Neville came by for an update, since he did find the body and is the current, and likely next, mayor. No longer in his ice-fishing gear, but in slacks and a warm jacket. Just as he entered, Dawe stepped out of the sheriff's office, wearing a parka and gloves. "Sheriff, I'll be back in a flash."

"What can you tell me about Wilbur's accident, Mac?" the mayor demanded.

After a nod from Mac, Jeb updates Neville on some of the details they had agreed on earlier.

"Well, that settles that," Neville pronounced. "Sounds like an accident. Wilbur gets roarin' drunk, slips down the hill, hits his head, rolls over, and dies of exposure. Good work, Sheriff."

"Well, Neville, it wasn't exactly an accident," Mac told Neville in a flat voice.

"I don't understand. How could it be anything else?"

"Jeb." Mac nodded to his son.

"Well, first, the body was found face down in the frozen mud. When a half-conscious body falls into a lake's edge, they roll over face up, not face down. Too easy to suffocate. It's human nature to roll face up to try to get more air. The fall didn't kill him on the way down the hill and the ground next to him showed an indentation next to where he landed. Somehow, he ended up on his face. It is possible he rolled over after the fall, but the smart money says somebody rolled Wilbur over."

"Why would anyone even touch him?" the mayor asked.

"Maybe they didn't want to look Wilbur in the face," Jeb wondered. "Maybe Wilbur was still alive."

"What about this fight at the bar?" Neville blustered angrily.

"News of his drunken fracas is all over town this morning."

"We talked to Harold Calvin," Jeb said flatly. "Passed out drunk, delivered to his home across the county by the night deputy, Dawe, at 10:45 P.M. So, he has a bit of an alibi."

"He coulda been faking bein' drunk and after your deputy left, raced across the county and finished his fight with Wilbur."

"Yes, that's a theory," Jeb agreed. "But his car was still at *Digger's Hole* and even if he borrowed or stole a vehicle, raced across the county, found Wilbur laying at the bottom of the hill, it seems unlikely a four-foot nine-inch man weighing a hair less than a hundred pounds rolled over a limp 350-pound man to finish the job. In less than fifteen minutes. You can't drive from his place to where Wilbur was found in twenty minutes. Definitely not in that weather."

"Why did he have to *find* Wilbur? Maybe he knocked him down the hill from the roadside?"

"Because Dawe delivered Calvin to his home at 10:45," Jeb continued after sharing a look with his father. "In fifteen minutes, Wilbur would have gotten farther down the road than where he was found, even walking. By the time Calvin could have driven back across the county, Wilbur would have been home. No. The simplest answer is Calvin passed out right in his La-Z-Boy where Dawe delivered him and stayed there all night until we woke him the next afternoon to question him."

"What about the wife?" Neville urged. "She had motive enough if Wilbur was beating her and the kids."

"The wife, *Peggy*," Mac said curtly, "does have a motive, but she also has something of an alibi. The Clays' trailer is way out in the boondocks, out past *Digger's Hole* and the lake. Who would have watched her kids while she ran off to murder her abusive husband? I don't see her taking the kids with her to do the deed."

"Well, Dad, maybe the mayor has a point," Jeb admitted as if reading from a script. "Maybe she left her kids at home alone asleep. Anyone dark enough to murder someone in cold blood certainly wouldn't hesitate to leave her kids home alone for a while."

The mayor vigorously nodded in agreement.

"You're right there, son," Mac said in a mock voice. "But Peggy's mom called her at 10:24 P.M. long distance and they spoke on the phone for an hour and seventeen and a half minutes. Dawe's wife, Patty-Jane, confirmed the phone records at the phone company. I owe Dawe some time off to repay her for all her work, by the way. And even if Peggy knew exactly when he would be coming home and where he would be at 11:00 P.M. and had time to walk to where Wilbur was on the road, she's about a third his size. How could she have rolled him over? Besides, if she wanted him dead, there are plenty of other ways a woman cooking your meals could do it. And there is another item ... neither she nor Calvin have access to a truck."

"What's a truck got to do with it?" the mayor roared.

Mac turned to Jeb.

"A motorist claimed a big truck clipped a buck or something off the edge of Lakeside Road about 10:40 P.M. *Before* the snow started. Exactly up the hill from where you found Wilbur. Our guess is the aforementioned buck was Wilbur."

"Then we're back to the accident again," the mayor smiled. "You boys are talking in circles. A tourist vehicle runs Wilbur off the road and he falls down the hill. Probably some tourist. At least you're thorough."

"Good theory. Problem being, there are no eight-inch convex-shaped rocks on Wilbur's hillside," Mac pointed out. "We looked. In fact, except for ours, there were no footprints at all in the snow leading down to the body Wednesday morning. Jeb has pictures to confirm it."

"Well, it snowed all night covering any footprints."

"Yeah, Mayor, about that. When you came to us the next morning, how did you know it was Wilbur Clay if you never came down the hill? There were no footprints in the morning snow. Only mine and Jeb's. How is it possible to know without leaving two sets of footprints in the snow? You would have had to go down, then back up the hill, the morning AFTER it snowed. If you discovered the body when you went to go ice-fishing in the morning, then rushed over to tell us you found Wilbur, how did you know who it was from way up on the road? We couldn't tell who it was until we turned him over and brushed off the snow and ice on his face. Unless, of course, you *already knew* who it was down there?"

"Mayor, don't you own a big Ford Super Duty?" Jeb smiled. "You know Dad, when you used to take me ice-fishing and we didn't have a bore to drill into the ice with, you would take a post-hole digger to dig a hole in the ice with. You said ice bores cost too much danged money."

"I didn't say 'danged.' But, yes. Yes, I did son. We used a post hole digger more than a few times," Mac reminisced. "Mayor, let me tell you a theory *I've* got cooking in my noggin. Ya gotta minute?" Mac sat in his office chair and leaned back without waiting for a response. "A former union rep blackmails an upcoming politician with information about a time when the politician received a paycheck as the safety officer for the mines. The same mines closed down for being death traps. The union leader might have had access to some info could put the politician in a bad light."

"I get it," Jeb jumped in. "The 'politician' decides with a campaign to finance, it's too expensive to pay off the former union leader and arranges to meet the drunken blackmailer, only to run him off the road and down a hill."

The mayor looked from father to son. Dawe stepped back into the station and nodded at Mac.

"Yeah, I can see it now," Jeb hypothesized. "The drunken former union rep gets swiped by a big truck about 10:40, falls down the hill, and when our politician gets down there, sees he's not quite dead, rolls him over and bashes him smack in the back of the head with what I would guess to be the biggest tool in the back of his truck, probably a post-hole digger the politician uses to plant huge campaign signs. Very likely he didn't have the stomach to bash someone he knows face first. Which would leave an eight-inch convex-shaped dent with a space for the handle in the middle in the back of his head. I'll bet if someone could find said post-hole digger, it would match the same shape and size and have some serious DNA on it. DNA that this cold weather would help preserve."

"You boys don't know what you're blathering about. You have no proof of anything," the mayor stammered as he edged toward the door.

Finally, Mac spoke up.

"Actually, Mayor, we do. You can stop where you're at. The post-hole digger normally used to plant your oversized political signs. You don't need to go fetch it from the back of your truck. Dawe just retrieved it. It now sits in the trunk of his cruiser, and if I know him, wrapped in clean paper."

"You had no warrant. It'll be completely inadmissible in court. You just searched my vehicle illegally."

"Actually, Mr. Jarvis, it was laying right in the bed of your truck with some of your humongous signs, where anyone could see it. We didn't need a warrant," Dawe said.

"What we needed was for you to react exactly the way you did," Mac continued. "I'm guessing the motorist who reported the accident can ID your truck somewhat reliably, and we already know, from Patty-Jane Dawe's research, your phone records show a call, or six, from our victim. Dawe's search of Wilbur's home, which his not-so-grieving widow was happy to allow before you showed up later, turned up the documents he was blackmailing you with. Not hidden terribly well, Clay not related to a Mensa candidate and all."

Mac pulled a card out of his wallet, handing it to his son.

The mayor stared from father to son, mouth open.

"Jeb, could you please read the mayor his rights? Him being familiar with search and seizure laws and all, may not need it, but let's do it anyway."

#

January 19, 3:20 P.M., Mounton, KY

"Okay," Dawe addressed Mac after the Kentucky State Police hauled Neville Jarvis off. "I see how all the pieces fit together, but when did you first suspect the mayor?"

"Jeb, you wanna take this?" replied Mac. To Joe, he smiled, "He's been dying to go there for two days."

"Sure," Jeb smirked. "We suspected him the moment he walked in to report finding the body. Dad thought he was bent for ages. Neville was the safety officer at the mines. He had to know about the conditions there, but we could never prove anything. But when he came in claiming he had gone ice-fishing, we knew he was lying. First, Neville has probably never been ice-fishing in his life. He wasn't even dressed for the part. Everybody in Mounton County would know not to approach the lake from such a steep hill. The mayor lived here most of his life. Had he been ice-fishing before, he would have known better. When it snowed all night, it would be too darn slippery."

"Especially with no hat and in rubber waders," Mac smiled.

"Waders?" Dawe asked.

Jeb answered, "Nobody wears waders to ice-fish. With ice-fishing, you sit above the water. In the dead of winter, the object is to stay out of the water. You could say ... those waders got him into hot water."

#

Gimme Twelve Steps

"Hello, my name is Hannah. And I'm an alcoholic."

"Hello, Hannah!"

The basement of the Mounton First Baptist Church was nearly full. Someone had placed an old pulpit at the far end away from the outer door and stairs. They positioned the pulpit opposite the steps and door intentionally so shy guests could enter easily, without drawing attention.

"Well, truthfully, I may not be an alcoholic. I don't believe I am. I hope I'm not, but God will judge me someday and I'll leave it up to Him. I'm going to tell you my story and you can decide for yourself. I see some new faces here and I get up and tell this tired old story about once a year or so, in the hopes it may help someone else.

"I've only drank two times. Both of them a little less than thirty years ago. I was in college and the first time was at a party. I had never been away from home before. Drinking and dating and dancing just seemed so ... rebellious. I drank too much at the party and was sick for days. Alcohol is like poison to me, I guess. The second time was when I was on a date with a guy I was going out with, just before graduation. He sort of pushed me into drinking more than I should have. I'm not blaming him for my drinking. I was responsible for my own actions. Even then, nobody could make me do something I didn't want to do."

A small titter of laughter from the audience members familiar with her.

"Or so I thought. Before I knew it, I was three sheets to the wind and this boy, a man really —I was seeing, from a really good family, starts to get more ... physically ... aggressive than I was comfortable with. I tried to fight him off, but as drunk as I was, he just overpowered me. Next thing I knew, I am stumbling down the sidewalk with my torn clothes covering me as best as I could hold them. Did he violate me? Absolutely. Should he have been punished for it? I guess he should have. Someday he will be. But he is not the only person to blame here. I put myself in a bad position. I drank too much. I allowed myself to get in a situation I shouldn't have been in. He violated me, but I wasn't blameless.

"I guess I am telling you all this as a cautionary tale. Drinking enables you to do things you know you shouldn't, but do anyway. Besides hindering your ability to see right from wrong, it reduces you physically so you can't handle yourself. To you ladies, I am also cautioning against putting yourself in compromising positions. The combination of alcohol, lack of common sense, and a man who didn't accept 'no meaning no' got me raped. I don't want something similar happening to you. Except for the people who have been in this room and the man who did this, nobody knows this story. I appreciate the Anonymous part of this gathering and given he never received any punishment by the law for what he did, I assume he never told anyone. I only hope he never did it again. He's been in the public eye quite a bit and I've kept an eye on the papers, and it seems he didn't. But then again, my story was never in the papers, so it isn't much of an indicator.

"It's been over twenty-eight years since I've had a drink and not a day goes by I don't thank God. I come here not so much because I need it to stay sober, but I feel God taught me a lesson back then and it's His will for me to help wherever I can. I hope my story helped you."

The audience applauded a little longer than usual after someone shared their story. Many had heard this story before and it never failed to touch them. Several young women wiped away a tear. Hannah believed those tears were more for their own experiences.

A newcomer in the back never took his eyes off Hannah. After quietly applauding, he folded his enormous, tattooed biceps across his Lynyrd Skynyrd tee shirt. As Hannah looked over the room, she spotted him and her mouth opened in shock and fear.

"Salutations, Hannah."

"Hello, Ginny. I didn't expect to see you here," she said as she accepted a cup of coffee from the muscular chef.

"I dare say you didn't," Ginny replied. "An exceptional share. Very personal."

"But not what I meant," Hannah explained. "I just never thought I would see you at a meeting."

"Oh. I've been attending meetings in one location or another for nearly twenty years. First, it was the pressure of ... well, let's just say, getting an education. Then my mother's passing. Then the pressures of running the diner and building a business. It all seemed overwhelming. I haven't partaken in a particularly long time, but occasionally, I find a meeting helpful in reinforcing why I should never imbibe the demon rum. This is the first I attended in Mounton. In the past, I traveled to Louisville or Lexington. I didn't think Mounton was large enough to have its own meeting."

"Yes," Hannah said, "it seems drunks are everywhere."

"If it's any consolation, based on what you conveyed, I don't think you can claim the title. I do find it a leap of faith that in a hamlet this minuscule the anonymous portion of the sobriquet lives up to its name. I wouldn't care to have my private demons reiterated all over Darlene's. Given your share, I imagine it may hold doubly true for you."

"Yes. Well, I have faith ... and more. As you may have heard, I have told my story for years and not a word has ever left this building, so I think my reputation is safe."

"Hannah," Ginny beseeched, "if you don't mind me inquiring, and if you do, please just tell me to mind my own bee's wax, but does Mac know?"

"No, Mac doesn't know anything about the assault. It happened just before he and I started seriously dating. All he knows is I had a couple of bad drinking experiences in college and never touch the stuff. If I had ever told him, he would have tracked the man down and killed him. And as much as I wished for his demise back then, I have come to realize I have some responsibility in putting myself in a bad situation."

"My dear, if you don't mind an unsolicited opinion, you have no culpability in the scenario you described. Any man who would act in such a fashion deserved what Mac would have done to him."

"Be that as it may, Ginny," Hannah said. "But I would greatly appreciate it if you NOT tell Mac. It is ancient history. I have come to terms with it and I'd hate to see Mac go to jail for something done so long ago. It helped me find my calling to help others."

"My dear, I would never betray your trust," Ginny acknowledged in a quiet voice. "But, again, completely unsolicited, if you ask me, YOU should tell Mac. Everything. He won't think less of you and I think he may surprise you."

"By understanding?"

"No. By not getting caught."

#

Posse Whipped

The town is dying. There are no two ways around it.

Mounton is nearly the smallest backwoods community in Kentucky, which is saying something. It's also the county seat for Mounton County, perched atop one of the few mountains and surrounding farmland that made up the whole county. Mac's wife, Hannah, was not only born and raised here, but her great-great-great grandparents helped found Mounton. Well, not so much "founded" as crashed their wagons here.

The town itself was barely more than two streets. Old red brick buildings jammed close together lined Main Street, many of them closed and boarded up. Smaller shops populated The Side Street, the locals have called it that for so long, the original name of the street has been forgotten. The Side Street consists mostly of wood-framed buildings, some still dating back a couple hundred years. A *Dairy Queen*-like ice cream parlor opened a few years ago, down Main Street, not far from the end of town where *The New Texaco* sat, but recently closed. Not unusual for an ice cream shop in February, but the mines closing prompted the plywood on the windows and the for-sale sign posted. Several concerns were still very much alive. *Ginny's Diner* always did a brisk business, as did *Duncan's Mercantile and General Store. Duncan's* carried everything from clothes to foodstuffs, but their big sellers were typically hardware. While not actually commercial, the three churches in the area were standing room only every Sunday morning. Mac figured if people couldn't turn to their paychecks, they would turn to God. The community medical center had shut down back in December before the mines closed, but the local doctors' office expanded to handle the extra patients. *Darlene's Beauty Emporium/Barbershop/Tanning Salon* catered to all the locals and despite a reduction in population, was still doing well. Born and raised in Mounton, many of her older customers intended on dying here. And with a nice hairdo.

All of which, doesn't change the fact that Mounton is dying. Most of the town folk hold to the idea it was Mac's fault. Mac thought it a bit himself. He initiated the investigation which led to the mines' closures.

The truth is, a corrupt judge, the patriarch of the Stemple family, had been forcing the locals into dangerous, and nearly slave-like, labor in the Stemple family mines when Mac stumbled across the working conditions while trying to save his granddaughter. Since the judge's death, the Stemples couldn't afford to run the mine safely and profitably, so OSHA shut it down. The mines directly, or indirectly, impacted most of the town's economy. Accurately or not, Mac holds himself responsible for the death of the town he swore to protect.

In a town meeting he called, a good portion of what remained of Mounton's sparse population gathered in the town church. Mac had considered doing the meeting in the big courthouse in town but wanted the meeting to have a sense of community. Many people subconsciously think of courthouses as Big Brother Government and a church as a place to gather with common beliefs. Mac wanted them to come together. As reduced as the town's population was, the church was standing room only. After the minister's prayer, Mac stood at the pulpit and addressed the town. His town.

"Howdy. Most of y'all know me. For those few I've never met in person, my name is Jacob MacDowell. I'm the sheriff of Mounton County. Back here," turning and pointing to a man, not much younger than Mac himself, sitting in the deacons' pews behind the pulpit, "is Adrian Stemple. I know you're all aware he owns the mines. Next to him, is my son, Jebediah, who I am happy to say, has become a full-time deputy sheriff.

Mac hated speaking in public. Hell, he hated speaking to anybody but friends and family. But sometimes, you just gotta bite the bullet. Nobody said being sheriff would be easy. But at moments like these, he wondered what a career in landscaping would be like. He tried the trick of imagining his audience naked and the first person he spotted was Shirley, the ancient crone who cashiered down at Ginny's Diner. *Great. Now I'll never get THAT image out of my head.*

"I'm gonna cut to the chase. I figure nobody wants to sit and hear me yap any more than I want to do it."

An enormous, biker-looking, bodybuilder, in the back of the room, massive arms folded in a ZZ Top tee shirt, barely held back a snort of laughter. Mac looked right at him and closed his eyes in exasperation.

"Mounton is dying. We all know it's 'cause the mines shut down."

A low grumble of anger spreads throughout the pews. A lot of eyes shifted from Adrian Stemple to Mac himself.

Jeb stepped up quietly to defend his father. "Now, hold on. This ain't gonna turn into a lynch mob or a blame game. We've just been through the worst winter since the founding of this town, but we are here to talk about the future of our town, not the past. Adrian ain't his daddy. It's taken a lot of guts for him to sit up here, and he ain't here for window dressin'. He's putting his money where his mouth is and is planning on helping any way he can."

"How 'bout giving us our jobs back?" a faceless voice shouted from the crowd. Mac nodded to Jeb. Mac backed up as Jeb stepped up to the pulpit mic.

"Well, you're just gonna have to get over it," Jeb said without any inflection. "The mines played out years ago. Adrian's daddy kept 'em going by having you folks working for slave wages and deadly working conditions. Lotta folks died in those mines. OSHA wouldn't let him re-open 'em the same way, even if'n he wanted to. And he don't. Dad shared with him an idea he had, and Mr. Stemple's willing to back it up with the money his family made from this town over the last century."

Mac continued, "If you're willing to listen, we'd like to share an idea with you, and if'n we all work together, I'm bettin' we can save Mounton."

They listened.

#

February 12, 9:14 A.M., Mounton, KY

Not everyone accepted Mac's idea overnight. But it did catch on.

Many families abandoned their homes and left town, seeking work in Louisville, Frankfort, and Lexington. Relinquished to the banks,

Adrian Stemple quietly assumed the foreclosure notes for pennies on the dollar. Hannah and her Bible study group swarmed each abandoned house, cleaning, refurbishing, and redecorating each into a cozy B&B. Men, out of work from the mines, did the same, repairing and painting the outsides of the abandoned houses. Others worked in one of the mines, making it a more tourist-friendly attraction. Due to the costs, only one of the shafts would be modified for tourists. Mac put some of the unemployed miners to work developing The Side Street, where cars will traverse and park. Men used to the hard labor of the mines had no problems clearing land and paving a road. Mac cajoled state and federal officials into subsidizing the road work and some of the municipal repairs.

Prior to the "town hall" meeting at the church, Jeb traveled to various tourist towns throughout the Appalachians, learning all he could about using pan mining as a tourist attraction. After the town meeting, he ordered the necessary equipment online, using Adrian Stemple's credit card.

The populace stashed from view any computers in town. A verbal agreement circulated among the townsfolk kept cell phones out of plain sight. They barely got a signal on the mountain anyway.

Duncan embraced the spirit of the transformation, but it didn't take much. His store had barely changed its look in the last few hundred years. The wooden porch and steps lead through a squeaky screen door to the original hardwood floors. Duncan's concession to the new Mounton was to add a gift shop section with low-priced trinkets and tourist tee shirts he printed himself.

The Emersons borrowed enough money from Adrian Stemple to put in an old-time photo shop in an abandoned storefront in the downtown area. You can get prints, or for a minimal surcharge, get digital copies, all sepia-toned via a back-room computer. Ephraim Emerson worked the photography tourist shop twelve hours a day in the summer, sold and delivered firewood scraps from the lumber yard, in the winter, as well performed part-time computer repair work. Next year, after her newborn twins are a little bigger, Laney will help in the shop.

Adrian Stemple will still make a fair amount from the new tourism industry, but the whole town implemented an equitable profit-sharing plan, based on the amount of labor and property each household invested. Adrian loaned money, interest-free, to any household who needed it, enough to keep them in groceries and essentials until revenue from tourism begins.

Not everyone accepted the turn of the century change. The town council ratified an ordinance to gentrify the "downtown" Mounton area to look turn of the century. Small Historic Mounton flags went up on the light poles downtown, as well as large concrete planters in which Hannah's church ladies delighted in planting perennials. There are three churches in Mounton and Hannah had managed to guilt all three women's study groups into a single group everyone just called "The Church Ladies." The town council granted *Ginny's Diner* an exception since the decor is old enough to be "retro-chic." Some of it actually hails from the '30s and '40s. Not a hundred years old, but close enough to give the diner a "historical landmark" deferral. Nobody really wants to cross Ginny on this. The place is a tradition.

Darlene's Beauty Emporium/Barbershop/Tanning Salon and *The New Texaco* are on the side road behind Main Street, but even Darlene had a new coat of paint applied and installed a swirling barber pole, all while continuing to operate. The town may have gone back a century in time, but once a week, if the ladies from church don't get their hair done, time could come to a stop.

#

March 24, 9:09 A.M., Mounton, KY

Mac and Jeb stood next to the pretty news reporter as she waved a microphone in Mac's face, while her videographer stepped back to better frame the shot. The reporter dabbed a drop of sweat from her brow. Between the panels set up to reflect the outdoor lighting and the unseasonably warm spring weather, keeping her cool was a challenge.

"I'm here with Sheriff Jacob MacDowell and his son, Deputy Jebediah MacDowell, of Mounton County, Kentucky. In less than a month, the small rural town of Mounton had completely reinvented itself. You may remember, Mounton made the news several months ago when it came to light a corrupt mine owner was exploiting the locals with dangerous working conditions to turn a profit. There was also a mention of an incestuous affair between his grandchildren.

"Sheriff, is it true it was you who exposed this criminal conspiracy and the alleged incestuous goings-on?"

Mac, clearly uncomfortable in the spotlight, said, "There were a few people who helped."

"Is it true Adrian Stemple, son of the corrupt judge and who owns the mines now, is financing this whole 'rejuvenation' we're hearing so much about? Interest-free? His way of making reparations to the folks of Mounton for the decades his family endangered them."

"Uh ... yepper."

"Tell us about what's going on here." Her too-white smile dazzling, as she thrust the microphone back at a nervous and sweating Mac. Mac wasn't bothered by the heat nearly as much as public speaking.

"Well, you know, it's like this—" Mac turned to Jeb.

"Since the mine isn't viable to work anymore, the Stemple family," Jeb took over, rescuing his father, "hell, the whole town, has pitched in and turned Mounton into a highlight of Kentucky tourist destinations. Folks wanting the whole frontier experience can come to Mounton and step back in time. Families looking to work in, or just see, a coal mine from a hundred years ago, can come, explore, and learn. We have plenty of homes converted into bed and breakfasts, souvenir shops, and even a creek where kids of all ages can pan for gold or precious stones."

The reporter thrust the mic back into Mac's face. "Is it true you don't allow modern vehicles on the town's main street?"

"Yepper." Mac nodded to Jeb to take over again.

"We have plenty of parking and a side street folks can drive and park the family car on," Jeb explains, "but Main Street is strictly horses, mules, wagons, carriage rides, and the occasional old-timey bicycle. No modern vehicles whatsoever."

"There you have it. A town where visitors can step back in time, mine coal, pan for gold, and experience life a century past. All watched over by the only sheriff in Kentucky to not carry a gun and who doesn't work on Sundays. Back to you, Sheryl."

"And cut," the cameraman said.

"Miss?" Mac wondered, "What was the last bit about not carrying a gun and Sundays?"

"I just threw those in on the spot. I thought it was a nice hook. You know, the whole Mayberry angle. You don't carry a gun, do you?"

"Nah, but I don't necessarily want to advertise the fact. I really just want this to be about the town."

"Don't worry about it, Sheriff. This is going to our local affiliate. No one will see it."

Turns out, they did.

#

March 30, 12:10 P.M., Chicago, IL

"Turn dat shit down. I want to hear this," Sly said in a heavy Latino accent.

The pounding bass from the speakers faded dramatically.

The local affiliate station had forwarded Mac's clip to Louisville, who, in turn, passed it on to the national news. Turns out greed, corruption, incest, and a happy ending are newsworthy.

USA Today and a national magazine featured stories on the small town, detailing its comeback, and its lurid history. A sheriff with no gun was almost as interesting as a destination into the past. Two major celebrities had publicity teams take pictures of them mining coal by hand. Publicity photos taken, the celebs quickly escaped back to the twenty-first century via helicopter and jet back to L.A.

Couples and families from all over America flocked to Mounton to experience history and take selfies at key locations in the notorious town. Mounton becomes the "in" spot to vacation. It had become a destination. Especially for three men in Chicago, needing a safe place to refuel on their way to Atlanta.

Sly spent a great deal of time and effort figuring ways to keep his crew and their families ahead of the system. Rent, utilities, gas for their cars, there never seemed to be enough money to cover it all. Sly had a mother still living in a shitty little house in Pilsen. Grady's little sister wore Goodwill clothes to school. His boys and his family were all he had and he would do anything to provide for them.

"Pack up, hermanos. We going on a road trip."

#

April 15, 8:23 A.M., Mounton, KY

"You see 'em too?" Ginny asked.

"Yeah." Sheriff MacDowell didn't look up at the giant of a man named Ginny, as the big cook poured Jeb, another glass of sweet iced tea. The sheriff didn't turn around to look at the corner booth of the diner Ginny is referring to, either. He just sipped his coffee, despite the heat, staring straight ahead. A sphinx in a world of cracked red vinyl benches and laminated tables.

"They've patronized my establishment every few days for the last couple of weeks. Eat breakfast, pay cash, and evacuate. Same three gentlemen, same dirty old van."

Jeb looked over Mac's shoulder at the booth. "Illinois plates. Three males: one Hispanic, two African American. Two of 'em six foot to six-two. One about five-foot-eight. Weight, one-eighty. The big one tops out at about two-eighty. Just like the BOLO from the staties said. Do you want to pick them up now, Dad?" Jeb had just ended his morning two-hour patrol with his dad and after breakfast, prepared to head home to catch a few hours of sleep till he had to pick up his daughter from pre-school.

"Calm down, son. What do you want to arrest them for? Surviving Ginny's bacon and eggs? Seems like punishment enough. Besides, we have no evidence or even probable cause. It's just a 'Be On the Look Out,' not 'Shoot It Out at the Local Diner.'"

"And I, for one, am not mopping up the blood," Shirley, the ancient cashier stated. "Again. Today."

Father and son were enjoying breakfast at Ginny's Diner and Jeb had changed out of his uniform and into cargo shorts and tee shirt at the station before breakfast. Despite the unseasonably hot weather,

Mac's standard ensemble remained a tan, short-sleeved sheriff's uniform shirt, a well-worn pair of Wranglers, his ancient brown Stetson hat, and twenty-year-old Dingo cowboy boots. As noted in the news, a sidearm was notoriously absent. *It's more important people respect the man than the uniform ... or the gun,* he told Jeb time and again. Mac doesn't wear a Sam Brown belt or a firearm. He's the sheriff in a small Kentucky town where the entire population totals six hundred, two, and one-third, Jeb's wife, Beth, is three months pregnant with their second child. A gun just doesn't seem necessary. Then there is the matter of his wife, Hannah, being firmly against him carrying one. And cigars. Every time Mac slipped one into his shirt pocket, she seems to know and slipped it out.

"Hey! What's the matter with my bacon and eggs? Hasn't hurt your scrawny ass and you've been digesting them for as long as I can remember," Ginny feigned insult.

"I've built up a resistance. It's a known fact any poison consumed in small amounts, over time, will build up a certain immunity. Not everyone has my iron constitution." Mac looked at Jeb, and spoke in a low voice, "Son, I'm gonna need you to work a few more hours today. Slip out the back and try not to let those fellas get a look at you. Meet me at the station in a bit. If I don't show up in fifteen minutes or so, call the staties and tell 'em what we have. I'm gonna go over and have a chat while Ginny goes and gets me a piece of pie."

"Do you want me to stay to back you up? There's three of them and the BOLO said they're armed."

"No, I have something else in mind I need you to do. If things get out of hand, Ginny's here." Mac smiled up at the diner owner. The muscular giant looks more like a long-haired, tattooed biker than a chef and proprietor. Some town folk think the bear of a man learned his legendary cooking skills as a cook for the Hell's Angels.

"And pray tell, what compels you to speculate I would 'have your back' after you so callously besmirched my culinary efforts?" Ginny demanded.

"Oh, I didn't figure you'd fight them. I thought we'd just make them eat more of your cooking."

Mac waited a few minutes after Jeb left, put on his Stetson, tilted the brim up, hoisted his lean frame out of his booth, and approached the three men.

"Howdy, fellas. How's the grub?"

The biggest of the three at the booth half spit up his orange juice.

"Uh, good. Is anything the matter, Sheriff?" the shortest thug blustered. Mac checked out the man's appearance: light-mocha skin tone and slicked-back, dark hair. He wore a dark sports coat over a black tee shirt. Mac guessed the slicked back hair, oversized diamond stud earring, and sports coat were attempts to foster an appearance of sophistication his compatriots lacked. Establishing an air of dominance. But even seated at the table, Mac could spot the low-hanging, baggy jeans and tennis shoes so white, they were almost painful to look at. Gangsta chic.

"Nope, just wanted to introduce myself and welcome you to Mounton. I'm Sheriff MacDowell and the unofficial welcoming committee. You fellas enjoying our fair metropolis?"

"Yessir, we are. We was jes' saying these is some of the best bacon and eggs we ever ate," the shorter Hispanic man said. One African American was the biggest of the bunch, as big as King Kong and twice as muscular. Ginny may have a couple of inches on him and more lean muscle, but pound for pound, it was a toss-up. His skin was so dark he could have been a photo negative. Ebony tattoos were barely visible on his dark-skinned arms. His hair, a close-cropped Afro, barely a half-inch long. An old Chicago Bulls tee shirt stretched across his broad chest and ample arms. Brand-new, steel-toed workman's boots punctuated his long thick legs clad in sagging jeans just like his companions. Mac wondered if they bought the jeans bulk at O.G.s R' Us. The middle thug sported a longer Afro. The BOLO named him as Grady Noble. His size and complexion must have been chosen by Goldilocks as he was not as dark or as large as Kong, nor as light-skinned or short as the Hispanic leader. His sweatshirt hood was down off his head and Mac could see at least two eyebrow piercings and just as many on his lips. Very Dennis Rodman. Under the collar of the sweatshirt, Mac could see a couple of gold chains. Below the obligatory baggy jeans were bright red high-top sneakers. *A sweatshirt in this heat? Clearly not the brains of the operation. But you have to give him credit for dressing the stereotype.*

"Don't tell Ginny. He'll get a big head. Bigger than what he has now, I mean. You boys visiting? We have a great new coal mine tour."

"Nah. We just passing through. We were thinking about checking out your souvenir shop though. Need to fill up the tank at the gas station too. We may do your mine thing some other time," Shorty said.

"Souvenir shop? Oh. You mean *Duncan's Mercantile.*"

"Uh, yeah, Duncan's," Shorty agreed, clearly not knowing what a mercantile was.

"Well, you fellas have great a trip and travel safe. Stay out of the heat, if you can," Mac smiled genially.

"Peace out," Kong's deep voice followed Mac back to his table.

"Peace out?" Shorty snapped at Kong. "Shut up, dumbass."

"Just trying to be friendly, like you said," Mac heard Kong's reply, as he sat down back at his booth. He smiled. Friendly is good.

Ginny ambled up to Mac's table to refill his nearly full coffee cup. "Wore your Stetson inside?"

"Wanted to look taller, pushed it back to be more easy-going, and reinforce the image of a uniform. Too much?" Mac asked the diner owner.

"Nope. If you were shooting for small-town hick sheriff, you really nailed it."

"Good to know all those years at Julliard did not go to waste." Mac smiled up.

"Closest you been to Julliard is Lexington. What's the point of your little thespian session?"

"Just wanted to get a good look at 'em and size 'em up," Mac said, taking a bite of his pie. "Seem a bit *urban* for a regular breakfast in Mounton, huh?"

"Profile much?" Ginny joshed his best friend.

"I hope not. But mostly, we get young families with too much money trying to experience the frontier from the front seat of their hybrid cars," Mac said. "These fellas looked like they just stepped out of a stereotypical ad in 'Gangbangers Quarterly.'"

"Nah. We get gangbangers in here all the time. Just last week, the Kentucky chapter of the Crips rolled up on some hotcakes. Was a massacre. We barely had just enough syrup to go around."

"You know, Ginny, good thing you're a good cook because your humor is just sad."

"Says Andy Taylor from Mayberry. And did you seriously call my culinary efforts 'grub'?"

Mac noticed the trio rising and paying the cashier for their meal. He casually stood and moved past Ginny toward the cashier.

"How much do I owe you, Shirley?" Mac asked.

"Susie, you know damned well Ginny hasn't ever taken any of your liberal, pacifist family's money. Danged if I know why not." She peers over the top of cats-eye glasses older than Mac. "'Sides, you barely even touched your pie. You know how sensitive Ginny is 'bout his cookin'.'"

"Fine. Can you give me change for a fifty?"

"Since when do you carry a fifty-dollar bill around?"

"Daddy always said to keep a fifty pinned to my shirt for a rainy day. It's practically pouring," Mac deadpanned.

"Jacob McDowell, there ain't been a cloud in the sky in weeks and it's every bit of eighty-five degrees already this morning." Not known for a sunny disposition, Shirley was the cashier here before Ginny's mom owned the place. "Here's your change."

Mac held out his hand with a paper napkin on it to accept the money. When Shirley gave him a sample of her infamous glares, he shrugged. "Twenties are unlucky."

"Not if you have enough of them," the cashier replied as she resumed her knitting.

#

April 15, 10:36 A.M., Mounton, KY

"What'd ya find?" Mac asked Jeb back at the station.

"I dusted the twenties and sent the fingerprints to the staties, but I can tell you now, there were too many prints on those things to give us anything conclusive."

"Well," Mac sighed, "it was worth a shot. Nothing was lost apart from a little bit of time and Shirley's opinion of me."

"I can't help you with Shirley, but moments from now, you will be saying how you have the Best Son Ever."

"I say you are already. What do *you* think you did to earn the honor ... *this time?*"

"Figurin' the prints wouldn't give us anything, I scanned the twenties and sent the scans to Dave over at the FBI. Turned out the Feds used those exact serial numbers in a failed sting operation on the very gentlemen listed in the BOLO. Dave called me back immediately. Our federal friends are very anxious to talk to these boys and recover their lost sting money."

"Damned if you really ain't the Best Son Ever. If it wasn't for Naomi, you could be in the running for Best Kid Ever." Mac dotes on Jeb's daughter, Naomi. It was obvious to everyone the little girl has her *Pappaw* wrapped around her finger. To Jeb and Beth's credit and a good portion to "*Mammaw* Hannah," the child's good nature does not take advantage of it. Much.

Jeb smiled. "You best watch out. I'm campaigning with Naomi to dethrone you as Best Dad Ever."

"Not a problem," Mac said. "It's gonna be decades before you're in the running for 'Best Pappaw.' And I got that bad boy locked down. Now, about these fellas from Chicago. I've been givin' that some ponderin'. Here's what I want you to do and we're gonna need to hurry."

#

Twenty minutes later, the old van pulled out a parking spot in front of *Duncan's Mercantile* just as Ginny's motorcycle pulled into the space they vacated. The van drove down a few blocks on The Side Street to what the locals still refer to as *The New Texaco*, Mounton's sole gas station. It had been in town for over two decades.

"Help you, fellers?" the young attendant grinned, wiping his hands on a dirty rag. The spot where his name tag had been was the rare clean patch on his greasy coveralls. His Texaco cap was pulled low to block the morning sun.

"Nah, amigo, we just gonna fill up before we blaze through those mountains. I can't imagine there are many gas stations till you get to the state line, huh?" Shorty said.

"Quite a few actually, but you're smart not to chance it. I can fill it for ya. We're still a full-service station."

"You gonna pump our gas too? Man, this *is* Mayberry," Shorty guffawed as he walked around the van to look at the tires.

"Want me to check your radiator while I'm at it?" the attendant asked. "Hot day like today, you'd hate to overheat."

"For no extra charge? Shit, yeah."

The attendant fiddled with the pump handle to set the gas to pumping while he opened the short hood of the van. Before locking the hood bar into place, he saw the largest of the two hoods still in the van squeezing into a brand-new "Mounton, Kentucky" tee shirt just purchased at *Duncan's*.

"You gotta head in this place?" Shorty asked.

"Sorry. What?" the attendant grunted from behind the hood of the van.

"Baño. You know, a shitter?"

"Oh, yeah. Over on the left side of the building. You don't need a key or nothin'. It's unlocked," the voice behind the hood muttered.

"No key," Shorty snickered. "I bet they ain't a locked door for fifty miles around."

As Shorty sauntered back to the van, pants hung low around his hips, the attendant closed the van's hood with a thunk.

"Your radiator is good to go," he looked at the gas pump readout as he pulled the nozzle from the tank. "Comes to $44.75."

"Here you go. Keep the change." Shorty hands the attendant forty-five dollars.

"Grassy-ass amigo."

"Denada," Shorty said, climbed into the driver's seat, and sprayed gravel as he burned away from the station.

"*Oh. No. YOU'RE welcome, amigo,*" the attendant thought with a smile.

#

April 15, 11:28 A.M., 5 miles outside of Mounton, KY

"What the hell?" Shorty slammed the steering wheel. A whisper of white smoke unfurls from under the hood of the van, even as the vehicle sputtered to a jerking stop. "Get out and see what's up," he snapped at the two larger men in the van.

"Why us?" Kong whined. "I don't know nothing about no motors. I don't even own a car."

"Just get out a take a look."

Both men grumbled as they climbed out the sliding door of the van towards the front of the old van.

"Ow! Shit!" Kong flapped his left hand in the air in front of the van's open hood. "It's hot."

"You fellas need a hand?" a voice called from the way they had just driven.

The three van occupants looked to see Mac and a young deputy walking down the road toward them from Jeb's pickup.

"Uh ... hey, Sheriff. Naw, we good," Short stammered.

"Really? Cuz it looks as if your van is having a speck of trouble," Mac smiled as his deputy walked further away from him, toward the back of the van.

"I know him," Kong said to no one in particular, staring at Jeb.

"Naw, man, we all good. We'll just call AAA and be on our way in a jiffy."

"Well, more's the pity. There is next to no cell service in these hills, and even if you could get a call through, AAA is two hours away to the next town where they have someone that can fix all that. Jeb has a way with cars, whataya say we just give it a look-see?" Mac continued to walk toward the front of the van.

"I *said*," Shorty pulled his Glock from the waistband of his jeans

61

and aimed it directly at Mac's chest, "we be good."

"How'd you know where to find us? There's a lot of road between your punk-ass little town and the state line." Shorty demanded as the third man relieved Jeb of his firearm.

"Truth be told, it wasn't exactly an accident. Jeb started part-time at *The New Texaco* today. Turns out he might have seen your radiator was bone dry, how low you were on oil, and noticed some of our famous coal dust found its way into your gas tank."

"Aw, man! He did all that shit," Shorty shook his head.

"Hey," Jeb smiled as he polished imaginary dust off his badge. "You can trust your car to the man who wears the star."

"I tol' you I seen him before," Kong declared triumphantly.

"Well, if it's any consolation, Bernie fired me," Jeb said. "Won't look good on my résumé. Turns out I *do* have a way with cars, it's just not a very good way. But between the coal dust, the empty radiator, the oil, this heat, and the effort of this old van strainin' on this steep mountain, we figured you'd be just about here somewhere. Certainly, not in the next county."

Shorty lifted the nose of his pistol at Mac. "You so smart, how come we got the guns, and you standing there smiling like a big, unarmed dummy?"

"Yeah. You fellas know pointing weapons at officers of the law is a felony, right?" Mac inquired.

"Don't 'aw shucks' me, Sheriff. You know what's going down here. But it don't matter. We got three guns, two of which we are pointing at Barney over there, and you ain't even carrying," Shorty smiled. "We saw you on TV. You walk around Mayberry with no piece at all."

"All true. But you see, Sylvester—may I call you Sylvester?" Mac used Shorty's first name from the BOLO. "I don't need to carry a gun. I got one of these," as he showed his Motorola radio. "And with one of these, I can aim twenty guns. Why would I carry just a single gun?"

"You lyin'. I checked this town out. It's just you and two Barneys."

"You did do your homework, I will give you credit. May I?" Mac lifted the radio. When no comment came, he held the radio to his mouth, without ever taking his eyes off Shorty, he whispered, "A demonstration may be in order."

A rifle shot cracked the summer air and almost simultaneously, the front left tire of the van exploded.

All three Chicagoans jump, startled by the shot. Jeb smirked.

"So, you got a sniper on the ridge?" Shorty/Sylvester accused.

Mac smiled even broader. "Actually, I have a whole posse spread out across the ridge behind me."

"You lying'," Shorty's, and his compatriot's, eyes scanned the ridge line nervously.

"Nope. You may have seen on TV we are trying to turn Mounton into a tourist town and when I recruited our visitors if they would like to be a part of a real-live posse and help bring in some drug-muling desperadoes, we had more volunteers than we needed."

"No way you would put guns in the hands of a bunch of turistas. How do we know you got more than a solitary shooter up there? We still got you outnumbered." The conviction was starting to bleed out of Shorty's voice. Sweat poured from Kong. And not just from the heat.

Mac clicked the talk button the walkie-talkie, "Convince them."

A dozen red laser dots wavered on the chest and heads of the Chicagoans. They stared at each other for a moment and then reluctantly looked at their own torsos. "Shit."

Jeb stepped forward. "This may be the point when you hand me the guns."

Jeb, pistols tucked in his belt, took pictures with his phone of the back of the van with its cargo load of OxyContin. Mac sat on the lowered tailgate of his truck, his back turned to the three Chicagoans, laid out, face down and zip-tied, in the hot, metal bed of Jeb's truck. He pulled a cigar from his shirt pocket and unwrapped it.

Ginny sauntered down the road from the ridge and when he got close enough, tossed Mac a small object. "Here. Figured you might want one of these for your trophy case."

"I don't have a trophy case," Mac replied.

"You do now."

"What you got?" Shorty questioned Mac as he twisted sideways to get a look.

Mac inhales the aroma along the length of the unlit cigar. "Turns out you were right about something. I *wouldn't* give guns to a bunch of tourists, but the souvenir shop had a whole box of these cat-toy, laser pointers."

Ginny smiled, "Yeah, the whole bunch of them are up there on the ridge, hootin' and hollerin' and high-fivin'. They had so much fun, we may have to add this 'Posse Experience' to the town's tourist activities."

"Ain't you the cook from the diner?" Shorty/Sylvester groaned from the back of the truck.

In his best Rodney Dangerfield imitation, Ginny quipped, "I get no respect." Ginny stuck a thumb under the collar of his Lynyrd Skynyrd tank shirt, proudly displaying his badge pinned there. "I will have you know, today I am the 'Assistant Deputy in Charge of Posses, Tourism, and Baked Goods for Mounton County.'" Looking at Mac, "But, I *do* need to get back to the diner. You got this?"

"Yeah, the staties should be along in a few, Jeb is busy collecting and cataloging evidence. Why don't you take the 'posse' back to your place and treat 'em all to lunch on the Mounton County Sheriff's Office."

"Thanks. I can use the business after taking the morning off," the giant admitted.

"And Ginny," Mac caught his friend's eye, "thanks."

Ginny looked at the three men cuffed in the truck, "Denada."

As Ginny walked back toward the ridge, Mac cut the tip off the cigar. *Hannah would probably shoot me if she saw me lightin' this thing up.* He stared at the stogey for a few seconds and tossed it in the weeds beside the roadway. *I bet she's watching me in her danged rifle scope right now.*

#

April 16, 10:47 A.M., Mounton, KY

"What'll ya being needin' now, ya bloody tourist?" Looking up from his sweeping the floor, Duncan barked as Mac entered *Duncan's General Store and Mercantile*. Duncan called anyone not born and raised on the mountain and whose family had not lived there fifty years prior, a *tourist*. His family was some of the original settlers of Mounton. They had originally immigrated to South Carolina in the 1700s, but found it "too tame" and migrated west with the settlers who ended up in Mounton, Kentucky. Aside from Ginny, he was Mac's oldest and dearest friend in the small town.

"Common courtesy, but since you're obviously out, I'll take a pint of good manners," Mac replied.

"Aye, ye be needin' more than a pint," Duncan smiled behind his red-going-to blondish-gray beard. A plaid shirt barely stretched across his barrel chest. He was husky, bordering on portly, and a new pair of bib overalls stretched across his prodigious belly. He was all-in on the town of Mounton reinventing itself as a turn-of-the-century mining town/tourist trap. Alastair Duncan looked the part of a 1900s storekeeper without even trying. The store itself hadn't changed for the last few hundred years, except for adding some metal display racks and expanding into the next empty storefront. The wood plank floors worn smooth and shiny from centuries of wear. "If some half-blind countryman named MacDowell hadn't pitied a deformed wretch of a foreigner somewhere in your past, I wouldn't be given ya the time of day, let alone a pint of good manners. Now that we're done talking about your piss-poor ancestry, how's your pretty bride?"

"My bride of the last twenty-seven years is prettier than ever and you better keep your distance, you old reprobate."

"Och, if she ever took a fancy to a true Scotsman instead of some mongrel with a good name, no distance could keep her away," Duncan grinned, puffing out his chest. "What're bothering' me now about, laddie?"

"I came in to pay for the toy laser pointers Ginny 'commandeered' yesterday," Mac told his friend.

"Aye, and it's about time too," Duncan said. "I'll give 'em to ye at a discounted rate seein' as how you're a government man and it was a for a good cause. I can give ye five—nay! On account of Hannah, I'll give ye ten percent off."

Mac smiled, knowing Duncan couldn't give the things away at half the price to his regular customers. Duncan was living proof the Scottish stereotype for thrift was alive and well. Mac paid the storeowner and pocketed the receipt for petty cash.

"Will ye be having a wee nip with me this bonnie morning, laddie?"

"Duncan, it's 11:00 A.M.."

"Aye, but it's 4:00 P.M. in Glasgow, which is close enough to happy hour for a good Scot's purpose."

Mac smile widened even broader. Another Scottish stereotype reinforced. A fascinating aspect of the Duncan charm is the more agitated or excited he became, the more his heavy Scottish brogue emerged. Sometimes to the point of not being understandable.

"I've been aching to ask you all these years, how is it you haven't lost your Scottish accent? Your family has been here since the 1700s," Mac quizzed his friend as he pulled a Red Vine from a candy jar and leaned against the stout wooden counter.

"As simple as ye are, ye daft dunderheid. First of all, my kin have always had the good sense to speak like civilized people and thrice a year or so, I go back to the motherland and check on my relatives there. The way I see it, I don't have an accent, but you all sound like a bunch of hillbillies."

"I hate to break it to you Duncan, but we ARE hillbillies. Comes down to it, so are you."

"Aye, but I have the good graces to be a *Scottish* hillbilly."

"Let me ask *you* something Mac," Duncan began.

Mac nodded as he jumped up to sit on the counter chewing his Red Vine.

"What exactly happened with those laser pointers?"

"I used 'em to collar a bunch of bad boys who were running drugs through Mounton," Mac responded.

"So ye did, eh?"

"It's my job."

"So, let me be askin' a final question then, Bucko. If ye captured them eijits, all by yer lonesome, why'd ye need so many lasers?" Duncan needled with a wry smile.

Mac just stared at his friend as he digested the question. Duncan went back to his sweeping.

"Sometimes, I truly believe ye may be a daft dunderheid."

#

Meet Cute

"*Is this Betta Washington?*" the mechanical voice asked over the phone.

"Yeah, who's this?" Betta demanded. A typed note had arrived at her rundown motel room door instructing her to call a telephone number from a payphone far from her room. It had taken her half a day to find a working payphone. Despite the vocal distorter, Betta could tell it was a white male voice on the other end of the phone.

"My identity is not important right this minute," the distorted voice explained. "What is important is if you are the same Betta Washington, former anesthesiologist, convicted of anesthetizing a patient during a heart operation while under the influence. The patient subsequently died. The AMA, the criminal, and civil courts all found Betta Washington negligent, stripping her of her career, income, home, and reputation. Are you that Betta Washington?"

"WHO IS THIS?"

"I will take your outburst and the fact you called this specific number as acknowledgment, Ms. Washington. The important question should not be who I am, but what I can do for you."

Betta took a calming breath. Her mind was racing. Her mama always told her to beware of white men offering something too good to be true. It was one of the few times her mama told her the truth. Not that her mama would have been able to recognize her, even had she been alive. Tattoos ran up and down both arms, her face, and neck. Her once beautiful Afro now shaved down to stubble and her eyebrow was the only piercing visible to the public. Yep. Mama would be proud. Screw Mama.

"Fine. What can you do for me?"

"I can make you exceedingly rich," the disguised voice promised, "using the skills and training you worked so hard for."

"Would it be illegal?" Betta challenged.

68

"My understanding is that your participation in any medical procedure would be a violation of your parole. So, doing any medical procedures, would, by definition, be illegal. Still a problem?"

"Not really. It just adds a zero to my paycheck," Betta replied.

"Do not try to be clever, Ms. Washington. Someone in your position has no money, no prospects, and very few scruples. Forbidden to work in your chosen profession. No hospital would hire you to clean bed pans, let alone perform anesthesiology. You are in no position to negotiate compensation. How accurate am I?"

"All right. You can't blame a girl for trying. As you said, at this point, I have very few options available to me. There are very few things I would not do and a few I would enjoy very much."

"As long as we understand each other," the digitally distorted voice explained. "Rest assured your compensation will more than compensate you for your efforts. A package will arrive at your present residence with a number of burner phones with instructions to allow us to communicate more easily. Also, be thinking about what you will need, and what it would cost, to capture and sedate five people for at least a week. The girl will be a child. We will discuss this in more detail once the phones have arrived. And a single last thing. Betta Washington is not a proper name for a bishop in this game. I shall call you 'Anesthesia.'"

"If the money's right, I don't give a rat's ass what you call me. What are—" Betta started, but realized the voice on the phone had disconnected.

Welcome to Crazy Town, girl, Betta thought as she looked at the closed pawn shop and discount liquor store across the trash-filled street. But what are my options? He wouldn't be the first white man to give me orders. Who knows? It could be fun. And if not, well, I already offed one cracker. What's one more?

April 17, 11:19 P.M., Lexington, KY

Joshua May was well on his way to intoxicated. Drinking at a local Lexington dive under a fake I.D., the gangly teenager was emulating what he saw in movies. The lonely hero, down on his luck, "drinking the blues away." The reality was, Joshua was lonely mostly due to some poor life choices, bad hygiene, and the bad luck of being born into the family of an alcoholic father and a mother who had mentally checked out years ago. Joshua knew he had about thirty dollars left in his pocket and a rusted-out 1989 Toyota Corolla to his name. He had run away from home three days ago and nobody had noticed. For the last three days, he had ditched school and been sleeping in his car. Future bad life choices would come as a complete surprise.

Joshua sat sulking over the raw deal life had handed him when he heard the two men sitting a few stools down talking about their future with gusto.

"I'm telling ya, Mitch, we need to blow this town and find us some greener pastures," the larger of the two was saying. Both men were larger than Joshua, but then almost everyone was. The speaker had the thick arms of someone used to hard work, but the gut of someone who had pushed it up against a bar too many times. His swagger and attitude indicated someone used to being in charge. "There's a whole state—hell! There's a whole country out there we ain't explored or made our mark on yet."

The other man was wiry and lean. His short-cropped hair and squinty eyes gave Joshua the impression of a weasel or a rat.

"All well and good, Ralphie, but the bank repossessed your truck and my ex-wife took mine, the kids, and the mechanic she rode in on, when she blew town. Well, not the whole town, just the ones who had ten dollars. How exactly are we gonna move to those greener pastures with no wheels?" Mitch the Rat demanded.

"There was no sense in me makin' those truck payments. The damned bank was jes' gonna take it back anyway," Ralph explained in a logic only Michelob Ultra and Wild Turkey could explain. "If it ain't some bank, it's the friggin' government. Ain't no way for a hard-working soul to get ahead in this ole world."

Joshua was at a crossroads he was unaware of. He could clean up his act, go back to school, get a job, find a place to live, and become the best Joshua May he could become. Or ... he could continue a lifelong habit of making piss-poor choices in search of a father figure, family, and sense of belonging he had wanted his whole life.

"I have a car!"

"Well, howdy-do, son. My name is Ralph Hickman and this here hombre is Mitch Northrop. Who do we have the pleasure of meeting?"

"Uh, my name is Josh. Josh May."

"May or May Not, heh?" A joke Josh had heard a hundred times and never once thought it was funny.

"Yeah, good one, Mr. Hickman," Joshua conceded with a smile.

"Well, John May or May Not, what brings you to this fine establishment?"

"It's Josh. I guess, Mr. Hickman, you could say I was sitting here looking for an opportunity. Sort of seeing what life could have in store for me," Joshua admitted.

"Call me Ralph, John. Opportunity is a wonderful thing, son. But it almost always requires an investment." Ralph leaned with an elbow on the bar, as much to hold himself up as to look cool while talking to the teenager. While not a particularly educated man, Hickman had an instinctive insight into what other people desired. Without even realizing it, he changed his posture, speech, and attitude to get people to do as he wanted. It was how he "befriended" Mitch. Mitch needed to be led. John here, needs a daddy figure to look up to.

"Me and ole Mitch here is about to set sail for fun and adventure and to make our fortunes," Ralph blustered. Then sensing Josh's desire for a father figure, "I got me a daughter in a private school right here in Lexington and that ain't cheap. You got any kin here, son?"

Josh thought about it, "Not really."

"You got anything to invest, Mr. John May or May Not?" Mitch the Rat asked.

"It's Josh, sir. I'm sorry to say all I have is about thirty bucks and a vintage 1989 Toyota Corolla."

Ralph stood a little bit taller and patted Josh on the shoulder.

"Well, John, you got more than a few bucks and an old car. You got a can-do attitude. Combined now with the two new best buddies you can count on, you are practically Rockefeller. Why, if we were to pool your resources with ours, add in all our intelligence and spirit, hell! Stick with me kid. We're going places. Maybe even as far as Memphis!"

#

An Offer You Can't Refuse

April 18, 10:14 A.M., Mounton, KY

"We'd like you to think it over Mac," Statton Mills said. He headed up the biggest coal industry committee in the Commonwealth of Kentucky. "We've looked at what you have started here in Mounton and would like you to do the same in Frankfort. Kentucky desperately needs big changes. In four more years, Governor Jaspers will retire and we want you to take his office."

Four men stood in the sheriff's office in Mounton as Mac leaned a hip against his desk, arms folded, a wry smile on his face. The men stood because there weren't enough chairs for them to sit, so Mac stood to both be sociable and to maintain eye level and not have them looming over him.

"And don't you worry about raising enough money, son," Samuel Jearns of Altria stated, looking around at the other men. "We'll more than take care of the funding. All you've got to do is be yourself and do what our campaign manager says." The Altria Group didn't even hide the fact their funding came from Phillip Morris tobacco.

"We like your style, Mac. We think your homespun earnestness is exactly what this state needs," Statton continued. "We believe there may be only one single serious challenger for the office and your lack of high-level political experience may actually give you an advantage here. Your wife and family couldn't be better if we cast them ourselves."

"I think what Mr. Mills is trying to say is your personal life and the image it creates is an important component of your political viability," explained Jesse Farmer with the Kentucky Healthcare Coalition. Healthcare organizations were a significant portion of the lobbyists in Kentucky.

"Mac, you may already know it, but Kentucky is dying, just like Mounton was. Coal and energy were our lifeblood and we are bleeding to death. We're among the lowest in average annual income and highest in unemployment. Kentucky is fiftieth in the national economic ranking. We can turn Kentucky around with some out-of-the-box thinking," claimed John Washington from the Kentucky Chamber of Commerce. His voice was practically pleading. Of the other power brokers here, his was the smallest salary by far, but the Chamber was a powerful voice in Kentucky.

"A sheriff with your record and doesn't carry a gun is right out of Mayberry and as good as money in the bank," Jearns added. "Cleaning up corruption, reviving a dying Kentucky mining town, plus all the national media publicity you've been getting lately is political gold."

"Give it some thought, Sheriff," said Farmer. "We know your granddaughter just had a double kidney transplant, and even though her daddy's insurance covered a great deal of it, there were a lot of extra costs. Taking the 'big seat' would mean considerably more money than you're making now. We know making a farm profitable in Kentucky is difficult these days."

Obviously, the power players planned this assault. These four men had strategized on how to get Mac to see their point of view. They sounded like they knew more about the MacDowells' financials than he did. They probably did. It angered him they were using Naomi's needs as a lever. It bothered him even more, he himself had used money as an excuse to get Jeb, Beth, and Naomi to move back in.

"Take your time. Governor Jaspers has just started his last term and we need some time to put out some feelers and vet you a little deeper. Talk it over with your family," Statton soothed. "Take as much time as you need. We need to put some bugs in the right people's ears, do a little opposition research, and see what kind of money they can raise. This state needs you, son. Think of all the good you can do."

As Mac showed his guests to the door, he deliberately amped up his drawl, "I'll give 'er some thought and get back to you fellers after a bit."

After closing the door behind the men, Mac smiled and just shook his head, amused, as he meandered back to his desk.

\#

"Governor? These daft eijits want to make you governor?"

74

Duncan gasped in disbelief.

"I don't think they actually said 'make,'" Mac smiled, forking a bite of Ginny's apple pie toward his mouth. "They said 'run.'"

Duncan, Mac, and Jeb sat in *Ginny's Diner* to discuss the meeting Mac had just come from. Ginny refilled the men's coffee and sweet iced tea as he hovered above the conversation. He had a standing rule that he would personally serve Mac and his family, while his waitress, Peggy, took care of the other diners. Since Ginny was the only day cook, it sometimes impacted Mac and his clan from getting their meals in a timely manner, but the personal attention, occasional bits of gossip/intel, and quality of cuisine more than made up for it. Currently, Duncan and Jeb were having lunch, with Mac just having a piece of pie, at *Ginny's* so the four men could discuss the idea.

Mac had just relayed the gist of the meeting with the Kentucky power brokers, much to the surprise of his friends and son, both in the content of the message, and that he actually spoke for five minutes non-stop.

"Regardless of the actual words they used, these dunderheads want to put you in the governor's chair in Frankfort?" Duncan asked incredulously.

"Yepper."

Jeb stared at his father quietly.

"Will ye be takin' them up on this boggin' offer?" Duncan queried, still in shock over the proposition.

"Eh," Mac answered in his usual taciturn method, pushing his empty pie plate aside.

A few moments of silence reigned as each of the men considered the idea.

Ginny let out a small laugh. "I'm just imagining you driving your old beater of a Bronco up to the governor's mansion."

"I think he'd make a great governor," Jeb blurted out. "He's honest and fair and is looking out for everyone."

"Aye, I hate to say it, laddie, and pardon my bluntness Mac, but are those qualities of a good politician?" Duncan threw out to the small group. "I agree, even for a tourist, Mac here is less annoying than ninety-nine percent of the eijits sitting in office, but all those things ye think may be sterling qualities in a sheriff may not make for a good statesman. You're just a wee bit *TOO* honest. A bit *TOO* much of a straight shooter."

Again, the group of friends pondered Duncan's statement.

"There's something more important than if Mac would make a good governor," Ginny began.

"What're be blathering about, lad?"

The diner owner looked Mac in the eyes and put forward, "Why do they want *YOU* so bad? What's in it for them?"

#

April 18, 5:12 P.M., Mounton, KY

"I don't think you should do it, honey," Hannah told Mac after he had retold the story of the meeting. He had also replayed the questions and feedback from Duncan, Jeb, and Ginny when they discussed it over lunch.

They sat across the empty dining room table at their farmhouse to discuss the offer. Hannah knew it was something big and was already worried because Mac rarely pulled her aside for a sit-down to talk. It just wasn't his style. Mac arched an eyebrow at his wife of nearly thirty years, curious to hear her thoughts.

"First, I agree with Ginny," she started. "There must be some ulterior motives for them wanting you so badly. There must be dozens of possible candidates more qualified and experienced. No offense, honey. But why did they pick you? Secondly, what would Mounton do without you? This town is our home and as much as I am loathing to agree with those men, they were right in saying it was *your* idea that saved this town and transformed it. Besides, who would want your job? It's not like people are standing in line to be underpaid and overworked.

"I know things are not as good as we would like them to be." Hannah was on a roll. "Try as I might, the farm barely pays for itself at times. I have to struggle to make payroll some weeks, with all the upkeep, maintenance, utilities, and taxes. Mama and Daddy left us this place free and clear in their will, but the insurance money barely covered the back taxes. I love this place, but it's an old farm. If it wasn't for your salary, I know there are some months, we would come up short.

"I know all those reasons sound like good reasons to take them up on their offer, but ...

With a deep breath to calm herself, she added, "... I do not want to move to Frankfort and be away from my grandbabies. Beth will need help with the new baby and Naomi, and Frankfort is just too far away!"

Mac eyed his beautiful wife. Of all the reasons she may not want him to accept this offer, he suspected the last was the most important. There was no doubt in his mind Hannah would gladly lay down her life without a second's thought in protection of her granddaughter and upcoming sibling, let alone the babies' father and mother, Jeb and Beth.

Mac reached across the table and covered Hannah's hand on the table and smiled. Hannah stared at her husband with a microscopic quiver in her lip only Mac would have noticed. Her lip quiver spoke more to him than all the conversations he had all day.

#

Never Bring A Wife to a Gunfight

May 1, 6:37 A.M., Mounton, KY

"I wish you would keep that thing put away." Mac's wife, Hannah, complained.

"Am I interrupting something?" Jeb asked, barging into the kitchen from the back door leading to the mud room. He, his wife, Beth, and their daughter, Naomi, had moved into one of the town's newly renovated B&Bs a few months earlier. Naomi was well on her way to healing from a kidney transplant five months prior. Their moving back into Mac and Hanna's was an ongoing discussion. Well, mostly Hannah was discussing it.

"Not a thing. Your mother's just complaining about me having my weapon out again." Sheriff MacDowell tells his son with a wink. "When you get to be our age, you like to keep it handy. You never know when you might need it."

"Well, as long as you keep it clean and don't go shooting it off half-cocked, I guess it's okay," Jeb smiled at his dad as he joins him at the kitchen table.

"Ha and ha. If it wasn't for the gutter, you boys would be homeless. Now, get your holster and oily gun parts off my table, so I can serve breakfast," she said, turning off the gas burners. "Jeb, you want me to fix you a plate?"

"No, ma'am. Thanks, though. Beth and I ate before she headed off to the doctor's office. She wanted to go in early to get ahead of the day. She's taking Naomi to work for a few hours before dropping her off at school.

"What's the deal with the Colt, Dad?"

Mac couldn't answer with his mouth full of eggs, so Hannah chimed in, "Your father got it into his fool head to get in some target practice with his antique weapon this morning. Before breakfast. Good thing our closest neighbors are miles away, or he'd woke up the whole town."

"Just because something's old, doesn't mean it can't get the job done, honey," Mac smiled at his wife of twenty-eight years, as he wipes his chin with a paper napkin. "You didn't seem to mind when it woke *you* up this morning."

"I hope, for the sake of any therapy bills, you two are talking about your old Peacemaker." Jeb looked at his father, snatching a piece of bacon from his dad's plate, "Why haven't you ever taken me shooting? All these years and I have never seen you shoot."

"I reckon I don't want you pickin' up my bad habits. Just figured you'd learn down at the Academy." Prior to officially becoming a deputy, Mac insisted Jeb go to the Police Academy in Louisville. Before accepting the job, Jeb had spent a couple years working on a criminology degree in Lexington which he continues to study for online. A source of pride for Mac, and dread for Hannah.

"You boys and your handguns. One of these days, those things will get you into trouble and even with the good Lord's help, I won't be able to get you out of it," Hannah said.

"Now I know why you won't let Dad wear a weapon to work!" Jeb claimed. Mounton's population is just a biscuit over six hundred residents. The need for a sidearm was pretty rare. Mac has developed quite a reputation over the years for maintaining law and order without a gun, even though, to Hannah's dismay, he doesn't discourage his deputies from doing so.

"It's not she won't *let* me," Mac grinned. "She simply convinced me I had a great idea to never strap on a sidearm. I'm smart that way. Besides, it's more important people respect the man—"

"—than the uniform ... or the gun," Jeb finished for him with a grin. "Yeah. Like I've never heard that before."

Mac sopped up a bit of egg yolk with a biscuit when Jeb asked, "You any good?"

"Well, I can say I ain't improving. If you ask your mother, she'll tell you I can't hit the broad side of a barn."

"Jacob Andrew MacDowell, you are outright fibbing. I never once said you can't *hit* a barn," Hannah declared, snatching up his plate before he finished eating. "I just think of you wearing a handgun is like a monkey with a mandolin. No good will come from it. Now, if you two have finished with your dirty talk and lies, I'll clean up this kitchen."

Mac looked longingly over at the counter at his half-full plate, "I reckon I'm done eating. Let's go, son. This town ain't gone police itself."

"And Jacob, you leave your old cannon right there. I will finish cleaning it, put it back in its case, and then in the safe," Hannah ordered, pecking him on the cheek. "The last thing you need is a new way to find trouble."

#

May 1, 10:25 A.M., Mounton, KY

"Spence, you 'bout got them boxes filled to full capacitor?"

"Hold your horses, Syrus," Spencer Stamper snapped. "This shine won't make us a plumb nickel if'n we bust all the jars."

"Sonny, you find them guns, and get 'em loaded in front of the truck?" Syrus asked his youngest brother.

"Uh-huh."

The Stamper family earned a reputation far and wide throughout Mounton County. And not in a good way. Hygiene, education, and an immaculate gene pool were not their strong points. Syrus, the eldest brother, was the schemer and planner, which comes in handy since much of the Stampers' lives revolved around avoiding honest labor and borderline criminal activity. Syrus's leadership made sense, as he was the eldest, and the one with the longest educational record, graduating the fifth grade, with less than stellar marks.

Grease and dirt covered all of the Stamper brothers. They sported oily black hair, wore dirty clothes, and anyone standing close enough could attest to their aversion to soap and water. Being raised in the back woods with no maternal influence and an alcoholic pappy builds a certain amount of character. Not necessarily GOOD character, but ... they simply weren't aware of their appearance and its effect. It was just life in the holler. Syrus, and by his gospel, his brothers saw their activities as a way to alleviate some of the worries of the under-employed and downtrodden citizens of Atlanta. Syrus saw them more like good Samaritans than moonshiners. Of course, if those good Samaritans was to make a few coins in the process ...

Syrus was known for wearing long-sleeved work shirts, buttoned to the neck, even in the summer months. He fancied the buttoned collars gave him an air of sophistication. Spence typically wore oversized flannel shirts which he ripped the sleeves off of before he handed them down to his "little" brother. Sonny, too big to button his older brother's hand-me-downs, wore the shirts unbuttoned over a greasy white tee shirt, the short sleeves of the tee shirt hanging past the ripped-off selves of the flannel shirt. All three wore dirty jeans their family had always referred to as dungarees.

Spencer, the middle son, bridled at Syrus's tone but recognized his superior intellect. There seemed to be a direct ratio of body mass and laziness to intelligence and orneriness in the Stamper family. Syrus the eldest, was the shortest and leanest, with the family's stock bushy head of hair. He avoided any physical labor he could get his brothers to handle, claiming his due as the mastermind. Spencer was about three inches taller than Syrus, but not quite as bright. What Spencer lacked in brains, he made up for with a mean streak and his pappy's racial biases. Syrus wasn't necessarily *mean*, but he had cornered the market on conniving.

Sonny, the youngest son, and second cousin (don't ask), rarely speaks in sentences of more than a few words, but makes up for his lack of eloquence in sheer size and strength. No one knows if his reticence to speak is a lack of education, a natural shyness, or his brothers never let him get a word in edgewise. Bear-shaped and round-jawed, the gigantic baby brother of the clan sported a thick waist and arms knotted like oak branches. Likely the hairiest man in Mounton County, his beard grows down his neck to merge with his chest hair and up onto his face nearly to his eyes, reinforcing the ursine resemblance. A long mane of wild, black hair bushes out in all directions. Arms, like baby oak trees, covered in a dense matte of hair, knot out of his stretched tight tee shirt sleeves. Of the three brothers, Sonny was the simplest and most childlike. No one ever implied Sonny wasn't capable of great violence, but it was almost always at Syrus's direction. Of all of Mounton County, only Ginny surpassed his size and strength. Sonny could easily be confused with a black-haired grizzly bear in dirty clothes. But not a bodybuilder. Nobody ever confused Sonny with a bodybuilder. Thick-waisted, but solid muscle, not fat. An unsatisfied shine customer once swung a two by-four at Syrus and Sonny stepped in the way to shield him. The assailant ended up busting the two-by-four across Sonny's torso and was later treated for a cracked occipital bone and four broken ribs. While Ginny carried a minimum of body fat, a mass of lean muscle, and a strength born from decades of weightlifting, he and Sonny could look at each other eye-to-eye. Granted, Sonny's eyes may not be quite as focused, but still.

"I cain't figure what you're in an all-fired hurried for," Spence nagged. "It's gonna take us half the dad-gummed day to load this truck and we sure cain't drive this rig up them hills after dark."

Syrus looked at the middle brother. "Yeah, you're absolutely co-rrect. Ain't no way we can navigate the holler with this big ole monster in the pitch black, which is why we are leaving at the butt-crack of dawn tomorrow."

"Gas," Sonny grunted.

"Yep. You're right as rain there, Sonny Boy. Actually, diesel fuel, but we're gonna have to amble on in to Mounton and procure enough for this thing to make it to Atlanta."

"Mounton's got law, Syrus, what're ya gonna do about them?" Spence demands of his oldest brother.

Syrus cuffs the back of Spencer's head. "Why you always so negative? I got a plan. Mounton's only got three lawmen. That skinny feller works nights and will be off duty in the morning. The sheriff and his boy will be attendin' church tomorrow morning, so the town will be wide open. We get the juice and skedaddle on down the road 'fore they is even out of Sunday school."

"An' what if'n they ain't in church?" Spence asks, rubbing his head.

Syrus picks up a semi-automatic off of the cab's seat, pops out the clip, and inspects the unloaded weapon. "Well, I reckon I got plan B too."

\#

May 1, 12:12 P.M., Mounton, KY

Mac and Jeb relieved Dawe, the night shift deputy, at 7:00 A.M. and then climbed into separate vehicles to drive around the county on patrol. Earlier this year, Jeb set up an online relay system to forward any 911 calls to their cell phones and radios. Jeb headed home at 9:00 A.M. for a few hours sleep, then met his dad at *Ginny's Diner* for lunch.

Dawe prefers the night shift as he has two boys in elementary school. He catches up on his sleep while they are in school. He's able to spend time with them and his plump, but well-loved, wife after they get home from school and she gets home from her day shift at the phone company.

"The MacDowell Boys," as the old-timers call them, met back at Ginny's Diner for lunch as they do most days to catch up.

"Mac. Jeb. Missed you this morning. Saturday breakfast with 'The MacDowell Boys' has gotten to be a bit of a ritual," Ginny said.

"I woke up early and wanted to do a bit of shooting," Mac explained.

"Yeah, Mom offered to clean his gun," Jeb joked. Mac turned to glare at his son. Innuendoes such as this did not impress Hannah. Ginny was smart enough and knew well enough to not take the bait.

"Pray tell what tidings hail from the exotic world of law enforcement," Ginny asked, as he turns to get Jeb's sweet tea and Mac's usual cup of coffee.

"Pretty much more of the same," Mac said, setting his Stetson on the table, brim up, and sitting at their usual booth.

"Yeah, not exactly what I signed up for," Jeb scowled.

"So, no car chases, exploding buildings, or kidnappings, huh?" Ginny asked with a smirk behind his grizzled face.

"What's the special today?" Mac asked.

"Does it matter?" Ginny smiled at his oldest friend.

"Kinda. Jeb just rescued the Morris's cat a couple of days ago and I would hate to think she's today's Blue Plate Special," Mac poked at Ginny, who towered next to their booth, hands on his hips.

"Nope. Cat was yesterday. Today is Spaniel Béarnaise with asparagus and baby potatoes."

"We'll take two. Make Dad's rare," Jeb quipped. "He's not a big fan of overcooked canine." Mac watched with a grin as a tourist overhearing the conversation, stared at, and then pushed his plate back.

When Ginny came back with their plates, Jeb asked, "So, what's the latest?" Ginny was a prime source of information in Mounton County. More people told Ginny gossip than the bartender at the local watering hole or Darlene at *Darlene's Beauty Emporium/Barbershop/Tanning Salon*. Ginny was Mounton's answer to Google.

"A singular item of interest to you may be the Stamper Brothers went and got themselves a tractor-trailer."

"They bought themselves a semi?" Jeb asked.

"I never said they *bought* it. You know the Stampers. They're about the only fools in the county to find a truck that fell off of the back of a truck," Ginny speculated, shaking his head.

Mac finished chewing and wiped his mouth. "The question is not *how* the Stampers got a truck, but *why* those boys would need a semi."

"There's no market for hot rigs in this area," Jeb continued the thought. "And they certainly don't need it to haul their Mensa certificates around in."

Ginny refilled Mac's coffee cup. "Ha! If cerebellums were dynamite, those boys would be screen doors on a submarine."

"Any word on what they have in mind?" Mac wondered.

"Negative. Some crony of theirs from the local drinking establishment slurred words to the effect of Syrus would be 'taking care of the skinny-ass sheriff if'n he gets in the way.' You, being the skinny-ass sheriff in question, I assume."

"Yeah. I get it. Maybe we'll take a drive up the holler Monday or so, and see if the brothers are up to something," Mac said.

"Like they're never up to something," Jeb said. "Be nice to lock those inbreds in a very small box for a while."

"Easy, cowpoke. Rein it in there. All we got is an unsubstantiated rumor from an unreliable source," Mac looked at Ginny. "No law against having a truck, despite questions of how they obtained it, or their plans for it."

"Mac," Ginny whispered in a serious tone, "you may want to reconsider carrying a sidearm for the nonce. Even an ignorant canine can get rabies and bite."

"Ginny, you, of all people, should know: sometimes a dog is just a ... blue plate special waiting to happen."

#

May 2, 9:38 A.M., Mounton, KY

"Rumor has it the Stampers may be gunning for you," Hannah stated, out of nowhere.

Mac and Hannah were parking her Jeep Wrangler in the church parking lot. Like the majority of vehicles in the lot full of pick-ups, Hannah had her deer rifle on the rack in the rear window. It never even occurred to them to lock the doors as they got out. This was Mounton. And the sheriff's wife's Jeep. At church. If there were ever an unlikely target for theft, this was it.

"Where'd you pick up such a fool notion?" Mac asked, carrying the hot casserole for the potluck luncheon after services, careful to not spill anything on his good sport coat.

"Never you mind where. Is it true?" Hannah asked. Mac thought about it. Hannah was at her Bible study class yesterday, and as small as Mounton was, if it was a rumor concerning Mac, odds were: Hannah knew before Ginny did.

"Hard tellin' what to believe when it comes to the Stamper family," Mac reassured her. "Half the time, the old bitties in this town are talking to hear themselves talk, half the time the Stampers are doing the same thing, and the other half the time, it's coming straight from a Mason jar. Don't give it a thought. Anything comes up, Jeb and I can handle it."

Hannah grabbed him by the elbow of his sport coat, just as they reach the door. Mac struggled to keep a grip on the casserole. "Jacob Andrew MacDowell, you promise me if there even *looks* like there will be trouble, you will call the State Highway Patrol in to deal with those fools."

"Honey, you know me. If I thought there was a chance in hell those inbreds were a threat, I'd have my gun with me." Mac looked down at his own waist to show Hannah there was nothing there but Wrangler jeans and his dressier belt buckle under his sport coat.

"You better NEVER carry a weapon into the House of God," looking down at his belt. "And that is not what I would call a promise, Jacob MacDowell."

"No ma'am," looking down at his own waist. "Well, depends on what you're looking at. It ain't a promise, but it's promising. And shame on you for looking at my crotch in front of the Lord's House. Now, let's get this casserole inside before I burn myself."

Hannah looked up at the sky and stepped back.

"What're you looking for baby?" Mac asked his wife as he struggled to open the front door of the church with his hands occupied.

"Lightning. If you are going to be smut-talking on the stoop of the Lord's house, it'll be coming soon and I just don't want to be standing too close when it hits."

#

May 2, 10:12 A.M., Mounton, KY

Hannah turned to watch Jeb, Beth and Naomi come from the back of the church to the MacDowells' usual pew.

Five-and-three-quarter-year-old Naomi jumped into her Pappaw's lap, pushing his old brown Stetson to the side. Beth slid in next to Hannah, but Jeb stayed in the aisle and whispered into Mac's ear, "Dad, you better come with me."

Mac looked up into his son's serious-as-a-heart-attack face, kissed Naomi on the cheek, handed her to Hannah to prevent his wife from getting up, picked up his Stetson hat, and whispered, "I'll be back in a jiffy."

As Naomi searched Hannah's purse for the butterscotch candy she knew she'd find, Hannah studied Beth's face.

"Don't look at me," her daughter-in-law protested, "he didn't say a word to me. We drove by the gas station twice and came here."

Explains why we're late."

#

"The semi just pulled into *The New Texaco* as we were driving in. I could see Sonny and Syrus outside the rig, but Spence's got to be around somewhere," Jeb told Mac on the steps of the church. "You can see the truck from here, parked at the pumps."

"Yepper. I reckon it's them alright. Okay, give me a minute and we'll take a walk down there and have a chat."

Mac stepped back into the church for a moment, then walked over to the driver's side of Hannah's Jeep and opened the door for a minute or two. He stepped around the car and walked back to Jeb, who was now holding his Ruger. Mac glanced at the pistol.

"Best put it away, son. Let's talk first and see what we can find out. Plus, you don't want your mama catching you carrying on Sunday. She'll skin both of us."

#

"Far enough, Sheriff," Syrus yelled out from about twenty yards away, positioned right in the middle of Main Street

"Jeez. Cliché much?" Jeb said to Mac under his breath.

Without taking his eyes off Syrus, Mac motioned quietly to Jeb, "Step over to the front of the old ice cream shop. Gives us some angles and separates their targets."

Sonny Stamper had a shotgun down behind his massive leg, and while Syrus's hands were free, Mac didn't figure he was unarmed.

"Sonny." Mac nodded to the youngest brother.

"Sheriff Mac."

"So, Syrus, you gonna make me stand out here all morning or you gonna tell me why you need a big ole semi?" Mac asked the elder Stamper. From behind him, Mac heard the quiet thunk of a car door shutting just over the choir singing "How Great Thou Art."

"T'ain't none of your beeswax, Sheriff. We gonna drive this here truck down to Atlanta. Ain't no law agin it."

"No, but there is such a thing as a bill of lading. Do you have one of those? What about a manifest? Interstate travel documents?" Mac asked. "Do any of you even *know* what a CDL is?"

Confused and out of his depth, Syrus pulled the revolver from the back of his jeans and tucked it into his front waistband. "No, Sheriff, but I got one of these. Folks say you don't never carry a gun."

Mac pulled back the right side of his sport coat and tucked it behind the grip of the Colt Peacemaker, strapped to his leg. "Never say never, Syrus."

The Stampers just stared at Mac for a few beats. "Dang. I was hopin' it weren't gonna come to this, Sheriff, but ..."

Syrus started to reach for the automatic at his waist, as Sonny's left hand reached for the barrel of the shotgun, moving it up from his leg. Like sleight of hand magic, Mac had drawn in the blink of an eye and the holstered gun appeared in Mac's hand, pointed straight at Syrus. Both Stamper brothers froze. Their weapons hadn't moved an inch.

Jeb smiled, "Was *that* fast? It seemed fast. Syrus, do you think that was fast?"

"Throw down your gun, Sheriff," a voice boomed from behind Jeb. Jeb half turned to see the third Stamper brother with a 1911 .45 caliber pistol aimed at his back.

"Spencer." Mac acknowledged, never taking his eyes from Syrus. His pistol's aim never wavered.

"You heard Spence, Sheriff," Syrus laughed. "Drop it."

"Syrus, this is an original 1873 Colt Peacemaker Single Action Army revolver. This handgun is a certifiable antique. A true collector's item, similar to the ones owned and made famous by Buffalo Bill Cody, Wyatt Earp, Pat Garrett, and Billy the Kid, just to name a few. I would no more 'drop' this gun onto hard pavement and scratch it all up than cut off my own arm."

"Why're you even jawing about some dumb old gun when Spence is standin' over there with a .45 aimed at yore boy's back?" Syrus taunted.

"Sorry. In all honesty, Syrus, I don't give a fig about educating you on the finer points of antique firearms, as much as I was stalling to let Hannah get lined up."

"What the ..."

The crack of the rifle simultaneously snapped as Spencer spun around, his shoulder a mist of blood. Jeb, already half turned, snagged the sidearm from Spence's hand, and in a single motion, pushed the already off-balance Stamper to the ground. Spencer looked up from his wounded shoulder to see Jeb with his own gun aimed at him.

Mac still hadn't moved or taken his eyes off Syrus. The Peacemaker had not wavered an iota.

"Sonny. Since I have Syrus dead to rights, I imagine Hannah now has her sights leveled somewhere between your crotch and your forehead," Mac explained. "What do you think you ought to do now?"

Sonny looked at Syrus, then the sheriff, and then his own crotch. The shotgun clanked to the pavement with a clatter.

"Good boy. Syrus, up to you now, son. Do you think you can clear your weapon, get lined up on me, and fire before I pull this trigger? Did I mention this was a single-action revolver?"

Syrus used two fingers to withdraw the pistol from his waistband and lower it to the ground.

"Now, that didn't hurt did it?" Mac said. "Well, I imagine it hurt Spencer quite a bit, but he'll get over it. Jeb, please call Beth for some medical attention before he bleeds all over our sidewalk. Boys, if you will, lay face down on the road for a bit with your fingers laced behind your head. We will scrape up handcuffs big enough to fit Sonny here in no time. Let's take a look at this truck now, shall we?"

#

After descending from the church steeple, Hannah strolled down the street, deer rifle cradled in her arms.

"Sheriff," Syrus asked from the ground, "you let your wife do all yore fightin' for ya?"

Mac smiled down at the eldest Stamper brother, "I don't *let* her do anything. She's just making sure I am not skipping out of church."

Hannah walked over to Jeb and made sure he was alright. She handed him the rifle and knelt next to Spencer to take a look at his wound.

"You barely managed to crease him, Mom," Jeb smiled mischievously. "Was it God's will for you to miss?"

"I didn't miss. If God had wanted him dead, I would have aimed two and an eighth inches down and eleven and a half inches to the left," Hannah declared without a bit of hubris while pressing a cloth to Spencer's arm to stanch the flow. "Oh bother. I got some of his blood on my best dress. Mac!"

"I heard. We'll bill the dry cleaning to the county," her husband yelled from the back doors of the tractor-trailer. "Still cheaper than Kevlar."

"You might not think so after you talk to the pastor," Hannah said. "My shot echoed all over the church and interrupted the choir and his sermon."

"So, what you're saying is," Mac smirked, "I might have to do my apologizing via the offering plate."

"Dad," Jeb asked, as he met his dad at the back of the truck, "did you go back into the church to get Mom to play sniper for you?"

"Nope. I slipped in before the choir got going to give her a kiss just in case this thing turned pear-shaped."

"So, she went out to the Jeep and got her rifle all on her own?" Jeb asked. "Doesn't she trust you?"

"Son, you should know better. Your mama trusts me. She also knows without a doubt where she is going in the next life. She's just not too sure about me and until she is, she doesn't intend for me to go anywhere. When I heard the car door close, I had a fairly good idea what was going on. Besides, anybody walking out of Pastor Allen's services best be armed."

"Hey! I thought you told me you weren't any good with a gun?" Jeb asked.

"I never said I wasn't any good. What I said was, 'I wasn't getting any better.' Didn't lie. I ain't a bit faster than I was twenty-six years ago ... when your mama taught me to shoot."

"You know I love your daddy to pieces, Jeb," Hannah slipped her arm inside Jeb's as he cradles the rifle. "But when it comes to his old hog leg, he can't hit a hill of beans more'n seventy yards away."

90

Mac thought, Between the dry cleaners, the church disruption, and Hannah never letting him live it down, it might have been easier to just have gotten shot.

#

May 5, 7:47 A.M., Mounton, KY

At the sheriff's office, Mac retrieved the keys from the desk and started to open the cell the Stamper boys were in.

"Dad! What are you doing?" Jeb asked. "You gonna let them go?"

"Jeb, do you think doing hard time in a state penitentiary will teach these idjits the error of their ways and turn them into model citizens? If anything, it will just teach them how to be better criminals."

"But they threatened to kill an officer of the law. Me, as a matter of fact."

"Technically, they didn't actually say as much. They requested I drop my gun, but they never said a word about killin' you."

"Dad, they pulled guns on us," Jeb demanded. "AND what about bootlegging moonshine out of state."

"Son, I figure if you ask Spencer right now if he was sorry he had his gun out, I'd imagine he'd say he was. Your mama skipped a shot off the side of his arm, and while it won't do any permanent harm, I reckon it smarts like the devil. I figure aside from the humiliation of being taken down in the middle of the street by a woman, the Stamper boys feel plenty punished as it is," Mac explained. "As for the truck, all I saw was a truckload of paint thinner. Right, Syrus?"

From the open cell door, Syrus looked first at Jeb and then at Mac. "Huh?"

Mac shook his head, disgusted.

"Boys, I am going to make you a one-time offer. You have exactly a single minute to ponder it, then consider it rescinded."

At the confused look on Stampers boys' faces, Jeb explained, "It means 'withdrawn.' Jeez!"

"What's the deal, Sheriff?" Syrus spoke up.

"For now, we're going to call the little scuffle in the street a 'misunderstanding.' Spencer will have a nice scar to show off at the bar. For now. I'm even going to let you keep your load of the 'liquid' you have in the back of your truck, AND the truck, providing you can prove to me you acquired the vehicle legally," Mac paused, looking at each of the brothers.

"You're letting them keep the moonshine?" Jeb asked.

"Are those boxes filled with moonshine, Syrus?"

"Uh, no?" Syrus was not quite sure what's going on but thought it better to play along with Mac at this point. He assumed no good could come from him admitting the truth. His relationship with the truth had always been tenuous at best.

"As a matter of fact, I spoke with the district judge on the matter, and he is releasing you into the custody of Adrian Stemple. He appointed Adrian to assist you boys in the marketing, branding, and shelf placement for Stamper Family Paint Thinner."

"What?" Jeb stammered.

"Turns out there is no law against manufacturing paint thinner or even transporting it across state lines, provided you have the right paperwork and a commercial driver's license. Good thing we never saw anyone actually driving a truck."

A smile crept across Syrus's face, "Yeah, Sheriff, paint thinner."

An equal, but somewhat less sincere smile, emerged on Mac's face, "Here's the thing, Syrus. If a single person ever takes a sip of your 'paint thinner,' whether you encourage them to or not, one, or more, of three things is going to happen. First, I am going to arrest you for the little misunderstanding out on the road today. Plenty of witnesses saw you fellas draw down on us when we approached. Some may have even seen Spencer aim a weapon at a duly authorized officer of the law. Two, I am going to turn the three of you over to ATF and let the United States Federal Government maintain your room and board for the next twenty years or so."

"What's the third thing?" Syrus asks.

"Oh, Syrus. Bless your heart. I'm going to tell my wife. You aimed a gun at her baby boy today. Do you believe she will aim for a sleeve the next time? Let me ask you boys something, of those three things, which do you figure is the worst option?"

#

Daughter & Law

"Beth get Naomi picked up?" Mac asked Hannah as he hung his hat up on a hook on the wall of their mud room. He was just coming home from work and his next stop was kissing his wife of nearly three decades.

"Yes," Hannah replied. "Jeb was with them. He wanted to spend a bit of time with his family before the second part of his shift starts."

"Boy takes good care of them."

"Honey," Hannah said, "you don't know the half of it."

"Oh, and what don't I know?" Mac wondered.

"For a person who makes his living observing people, you can be blind about some things. Our boy's face absolutely lights up when Beth is in the room. His vocal tone softens and you can hear his smile in it. Even his movements are slower like he is afraid of scaring a skittish doe. The funny part is Beth is a hundred times smarter and tougher than Jeb gives her credit for. And it looks like Naomi is going to be smarter than both of them put together someday."

"If not already. I keep trying to find time to talk with Beth, but things just keep getting in the way," Mac told his wife.

"Find the time. When their new baby gets here, she won't have five waking moments to herself, let alone to talk to your fool self."

May 7, 5:32 P.M., Mounton, KY

"SweetPea! Your momma's here. Get your stuff," Mac called out the back kitchen door to his granddaughter.

"Thanks for watching her, Dad," Beth sighed. "You don't know how much we appreciate you guys watching her between Jeb starting his afternoon shift and me getting off work. I know you have a lot more going on than babysitting Naomi."

"Nothing more important. Hannah would have loved to do it as usual, but she had to run into Louisville for a dentist appointment and to get some prescriptions filled," the sheriff told his lovely daughter-in-law. "How's the new job coming?"

"Fine. A lot of hours and a lot less pay, but I'm just happy to find a job here," Beth said. "Hannah told me you'd be happy to watch Naomi. I just want you to know Jeb and I really appreciate it, between the weird early mornings and in between when I get off and Jeb leaves for work. I got here as soon as I could. I hope she wasn't a bother."

"Watching our little angel is never a bother. I'm up before dawn anyway. Once a jarhead, always a jarhead."

"Well, just another way Naomi certainly takes after you."

Mac stared out the window at Naomi trying to squeeze the last few minutes of enjoyment out of the swing set before she has to go home.

"You guys sure make a great-looking family."

"We had good genes to work with," Beth replied.

The two sat in the kitchen watching Naomi outside.

"Did I ever tell you about how Jeb and I met?" Beth questioned her father-in-law.

"Jeb said it was at a college mixer or something if I recall."

"Of course, he could boil the whole story down to two words. Just like his daddy."

"So, what's the real story?" Mac urged.

"Well, he wasn't wrong." Beth started. "Some friends shamed me into going to a party on campus. I had one more year of nursing school and I have to admit, I was a bit on the overzealous side. I was overcompensating for starting so young, I guess. I studied around the clock. So, in order to save me from myself, my girlfriends dragged me to this frat party. I didn't want to be there. I sat in the corner and nursed a beer—don't tell Hannah—and a gaggle of frat boys circled me like a piece of meat needing to be devoured."

"I bet," Mac smiled. "And I won't say a word to Hannah."

"Anyway, I had just about discouraged half of them when this good ole boy in a black tee shirt and Cardinals baseball cap worked his way to the front of the pack. I thought he was just about the prettiest thing I had ever seen but then figured him to be just the redneck version of the misogynistic cavemen trying to get into my pants. Then he took his cap off, held it with both hands, and asked if I would care to dance. Just as we walked off, a two-step came on and a football frat boy tapped Jeb on the shoulder and then shoved him out of the way. He practically carried me to the dance floor. He was so big I couldn't see over his shoulders, but when he whirled me around, I could see Jeb standing there. At first, he was so mad, he just clenched his fists like he does. Even his ears got red."

"He didn't punch him, did he?" Mac surmised.

"No. He looked me in the eye and realized I wasn't some damsel in distress needing saving," Beth recalled. After a pause, "I think right then was when I fell in love with him."

"What happened next?" Mac asked, totally engrossed in the story.

"I might have kneed the frat monster in the groin."

"You—?"

"Just as hard as I possibly could. Jeb and I actually had to dance around him as he writhed on the floor."

"Do you know how much you are like his mama?"

"Well, I think he learned how to treat women from you," Beth said. "I see how you let Hannah be so strong. Be her own person."

"Oh, honey. No one *lets* Hannah do *anything*. The best a body can do is avoid being a target and occasionally aim her in the general direction of someone who deserves her 'strength.'"

"Regardless, I hope someday to have half the strength she has," Beth maintained.

"Half? I have my sights set a tad lower and hope to live long enough to get there."

"Beth, can I ask *you* something?" Mac slid her a cup of coffee across the kitchen table next to the window.

"Sure, Dad."

"It occurs to me with everything been going on, I haven't asked you what you think about all of this," Mac apologized to his daughter-in-law.

"All what?"

"The judge, the changes to the town, the little dust-up on Main Street, the governor offer, all of it. You're about the smartest person I know. Probably THE smartest person I know next to Hannah; the way you paid your own way through nursing school. Telling Jeb you wouldn't get married and start a family until you graduated. I wish I had talked to you sooner about your thoughts on all this."

Beth sat for a moment, following his gaze out the window at her daughter playing.

"Dad, first of all, if I am one of the smartest people you know, you need to expand your social circle, A LOT," Beth said. "What you are doing with this town is inspired. In just a few months, you have instituted a complete transformation turning this from a dying little postage stamp to a thriving tourist town. I have to admit it doesn't excite me too much about some of the situations Jeb seems to find himself in. Even in this town, I am dreading getting *that* phone call. But I have never seen him happier or more excited to go to work."

"I will allow we've had a few more interesting moments lately," Mac commented with a grin. Then, more seriously, and quietly, "Beth, it would never be a phone call."

"I know. As for the governor offer, nobody can tell you what to do there. You and Hannah will have to decide for yourselves. The job will be completely different from what you do now. I, personally, would hate to see you two move to Frankfort, but you need to do what is best for you."

"Gotta tell you, Beth, I was hoping for a little more opinionated direction."

"You probably shouldn't ask a pregnant woman for more opinion. She'll more than likely rip you a new one for daring to have male chromosomes, demand a gallon of raspberry Häagen-Dazs, and start crying about the way her hair feels. Chromosomes aside, would you like a bit of hormonal wisdom?"

"Yepper."

Beth stood up as she spied Naomi out the window, finally giving up the swing set.

"You are not in this alone. Mounton is more than just a place for you to protect all by your lonesome. Don't think you can do all this by yourself. You are not the Lone Ranger. You are a part of the Mounton family. Don't forget: family takes care of each other. Just like you and Mom take care of Jeb, Naomi, and me."

Right then, Naomi came bursting into the kitchen. Beth collected her daughter's backpack. Mac picked up Naomi for a goodbye hug and a kiss before he swung her around and landed her on her feet. Beth patted her daughter on the back, as Naomi ran for the car, her mom close behind.

Mac held the front door for her as they walked toward their car. "Beth? Thanks."

"Anytime, Dad. But next time, have that raspberry Häagen-Dazs or things will get ugly."

#

How Quickly They Grow Up

"How're ya doing, Adrian?" Mac asked. "We haven't had much of a chance to visit with everything goin' on." Both men were coming to lunch at *Ginny's Diner* and without discussing it, sat at the same booth to catch up. Mac's usual booth. Ginny was already bringing a cup and a pot of coffee for Mac, and a sweet tea for Adrian. Without asking for their orders, the big cook ran off to get two daily specials.

"Doing well, Mac," Adrian Stemple said. "Been busy. All the foreclosures, loans, construction projects, this is the busiest I can ever remember."

"Things have definitely picked up around here."

"Hey, what's this I hear about you running for governor?" Adrian asked. "What can I say? Small town. News travels fast. I'll bet you five dollars The Church Ladies could tell you what I had for breakfast."

Mac grinned at him and shrugged. "Haven't decided yet. Obviously, my household has some mixed opinions. I think I've got some time to mull it over."

"Well, if you ask me—and you haven't—I would say you would make a damned fine governor," Adrian said. "I think this state needs some new blood and common sense in Frankfort, and you'd be great at the job. You know my father wanted to run, but was afraid those fool kids would come out in the vetting."

"How the kids doing?" Mac asked.

"Oh, there's a fun story. They blame you personally for the destruction of their family empire, the killing of their granddad, the neutering of their grandfather's biggest failure, and their present imprisonment in schools across the country from each other."

"So, I probably shouldn't be expecting Christmas cards from them, is what you're saying?" Mac smiled.

"No, I dare say you shouldn't," Adrian laughed. "I've got Jasper at a military academy on the East Coast. 'A structured environment specializing in high-spirited young adults from good families.' More colloquially referred to as 'Camp Fuck-Up.' Mindy is at a private school on the West Coast she calls the 'Sacred Heart of the Immaculate Whores.' They barely speak to me, but I notice they cash their allowance checks as fast as possible. Speaking of which, I got a call from an attorney wanting me to be a witness. Turns out, he's where their allowance checks were going. Seems my sweet children are filing a wrongful death suit ... against you. And Ginny."

As if on cue, Ginny appeared with their plates.

"Thanks, Ginny," Mac said as the diner owner walked away.

"Interesting name he's got," Adrian said. "Guess his momma was a big Haggard fan."

"How'd you know about that?" Mac asked. He thought he was one of the very few that knew of the giant's real first name.

"Oh. It was in the transcripts of the inquest of dear old Dad's death."

"Oh yeah, right.

Mac was anxious to get off the topic of Ginny's name. Talking about it in his own diner was just asking for trouble. He was thankful his friend wasn't serving their table for that part of the conversation.

"So the kids are suing us? Really?"

"Yeah, I turned the lawyer down since I was busy keeping an eye on the businesses when it all went down. Seems I wasn't keeping a very good eye on them or I might have seen some of the shenanigans dear old Dad was pulling. You know he was always disappointed in me that after two years of law school, I went after a business degree. I guess he wanted me to follow in his footsteps."

"Probably better that you didn't. It looked like he hid the shadier parts of his mining practices and business from you," Mac said.

"Yeah, but I still should have seen it coming. Shifty old bastard never played straight with anyone," Adrian told Mac. "Based on everything I can see, I don't think they will have a snowball's chance," Adrian said. "I get the impression their attorney wanted them to go after the county, deeper pockets and all, but the kids didn't want him to. It doesn't make sense, you were on duty and Ginny was deputized. That alone affords you a certain amount of protection. Yeah, he was shot on your land, but the only reason to not go after the county is they want you and Ginny to go broke paying for attorneys and not using the legal team the county would supply for a defense. I don't really think their attorney thinks they have a chance, otherwise, he would be working for a contingency fee and not cash up front, but if they do file, it could cost you, Hannah, and Ginny a fortune to fight it. I think their goal is to have you spend so much on attorneys, it costs you your farm"

"Boy, will Hannah be excited about *that*," Mac said sarcastically. "The farm's been in her family for centuries."

"Well, if it's any consolation, I have cut off their allowance and told their attorney I would be providing your attorneys all of the business and mine records I can get my hands on. I don't think he's counting on my testimony anymore."

"I appreciate your help and heads up, Adrian," Mac said. "If you hear any more about it, let me know. So far nobody's been in touch with us and I haven't been served, so who knows? Maybe their attorney will convince them it's a dead end. Especially after their allowance dries up."

"I got the feeling somebody is feeding this attorney some info which may not be in the public domain. He seemed awfully knowledgeable about the details of the case."

"Well, I have made a few enemies over the years," Mac smiled weakly. "This is my first time getting sued, but then again I never killed anybody before. Come to think of it, I didn't this time either."

"Leave it up to my two hellspawn to try and destroy a man's life for an imagined slight," Adrian said. "You need to watch out for these two, Mac. They take after their grandpa in too many ways. Eh, but what can you do? Hey, I'll tell you what. I will swap you both of my two demons for Jeb, straight up."

"Think I'll pass. But, what *are* you gonna do? Jasper will be eighteen in less than a year or so and Mindy is right behind him. How're you gonna keep them out of trouble when they graduate?" Mac studied his friend.

"Eh, I've been giving it some thought. I cut them out of the will.

Working for a living is probably the best thing that could happen to those two little hellions. I may be able to lock them away, separated in colleges on either side of the country. I'll try to pay some schools to be extra stern. If not, I'll pay whatever law enforcement they're around to watch them. Sooner or later, they'll do something stupid and get sent to prison, only to find out the Stemple money won't buy decent criminal attorneys. A few years of hard time may be good for them."

"Hope it works out for you," Mac sympathized.

"Yeah, but whatever happens, I deserve it. I raised those hellions. Their momma was no help and if anything, their grandfather made them even more spoiled than they were going to be anyway. I turned a blind eye to his antics and never really put those kids in check. Whatever comes of them is my fault and I've earned what I get. This suit could come up in the campaign. I just hate they're lashing out at you and yours."

"Adrian, I can't speak to what went on in the past, but what you are doing now is stepping up in ways your family never did. You're doing everything you can to make things right in your family and in your town, and that's all a man can do."

"Yeah, but I'm doing it alone."

#

Of Playahs & Pawns

"Jefe, you have a package," Grady said as he handed Sylvester a Fed Ex box. Sly looked at the young hood and took the box.

"Wonder who knows we're at this address?" Sylvester asked nobody in particular. No return address. Flipping open a knife, he opened the box.

"Cellphones? Who the hell would send me cellphones?" Sylvester, or Sly as he preferred, looked at the various phones. He noticed one out of the bubble pack and it had registered a missed call. While he held it and stared at it, it vibrated in his hand, startling him.

"Uh ... Hola?"

"Señor Ortiz?"

"Si. Yeah." From the accent and pronunciation, Sly guessed the person on the other end of the phone was Anglo. It was more difficult to tell since the caller was using a voice distorter.

"This is the person responsible for you and your compatriots' freedom. These are burner phones. After each use, you will remove the chip, and crush and burn both the phone and chip. Do not use the phone for any other calls or texts. Do you understand?"

"Yes. I know how a burner works."

"I can help you and your friends make a great deal of money as well as get revenge on the people responsible for your recent legal problems. But you must do exactly as I instruct. Are you interested? If not, destroy this phone, and all the others, and you will never hear from me again."

Sly thought long and hard about what The Voice had told him. He had dreamed long of getting his *venganza* on the hillbilly *alguacil* who did not even carry a piece. Making a lot of money, legally or illegally, was always a positive. The only concern Sly had was working with, or more accurately *for*, someone he didn't know. Especially a *white* someone he didn't know. But a lot of money AND revenge on Sheriff Mayberry.

"I'm in."

"As I thought. Destroy this phone and keep the others nearby. I will contact you with further instructions. In the meantime, locate suppliers for Oxy in large quantities. I will provide you with the funds to procure it."

"Or I could just call you on the number you are calling from now," Sly smirked into the phone.

"Doubtful. I am also calling from burners I destroy after each use. Do not try to outsmart me, Ortiz. You cannot. Find the drugs. Await instructions."

'Await instructions.' Who says that?

"Yeah man, 'awaiting.'"

"Mr. Ortiz, if for a single moment, you consider taking off with my drugs, money, or both, think about this: I know your names. I know where you live. I know where your families live. I know where they work and go to school. I know who all your neighbors are. I know your parole officers. And their families. I have access to a wood chipper. Do you understand what I am saying, Mr. Ortiz?"

Sly blinked. This pendejo meant business.

"Yeah, I feel ya."

"Follow my instructions to the letter and all will be well and you will be very rich." Click.

I got your instructions right here, puto!

Former mayor, Neville Jarvis, also received a large box of burner phones at his home in Mounton. A UPS delivery truck dropped off the box and hours later, a distorted voice had offered him an opportunity.

"So, you understand how to dispose of the phones after each use?" Continued the altered voice on the first call.

"I get it," Neville groused. "I'm in. Want do you need me to do?"

"I suspected it would interest you to make a great deal of money and get revenge on the sheriff," the electronically distorted voice over the cell phone said. **"Mr. Jarvis, when God considers chess, do you know what the first thing he does?"**

"I can't say I do."

"He selects a Grandmaster to play His side of the board. Do you know what the first thing that Grandmaster does? Of course not. How could you know the mind of God or of His Chosen? The first thing a Grandmaster does is to place his pieces on the board in all the right positions."

"Pardon my asking, but what has chess got to do with revenge on MacDowell?"

"Just suffice it to say, I need you to find a few loyal pawns WITHOUT mentioning our relationship. With these helpers, I need you to obtain at least four garbage trucks and clean the interiors thoroughly. Leave the outside and the cabs dirty. Do not get them from anywhere near Mounton. Communicate with these helpers only via the burner phones I have supplied."

"Garbage trucks? What do we need garbage trucks for? And why clean them?"

"The outsides and the cabs must look like dirty, used garbage trucks. Other than that, you do not need to know anything else at this time. I will let you know all you need to know when the time is right. Do not question my orders. Remember I enabled you to retain your freedom. Once you have the trucks, I need you to store them surreptitiously for several weeks."

"I know why this all interests me. First, that big oaf, Wilbur Clay, ruined my life and chances to be mayor, then that pencil-necked sheriff trumps up a bunch of fake charges," Neville whined. "But what's your angle in all this?"

After a moment's silence, **"Mr. Jarvis, my interest is getting back what once was mine, securing my proper place, and seeing that Sheriff MacDowell gets his due."**

"I guess that puts us on the same page then." Neville thought for a few seconds. "I think I can come up with a few good ole boys to fit the bill perfectly."

"Excellent. Make sure they know nothing of these calls. As far as they must know, YOU are the mastermind."

"No worries there. These boys don't tend to overthink things."

"Very well. I will be in touch in a few weeks to check on your progress."

"I'll be here," Neville replied as he hung up. What a douche! But the money's good and he made good on getting me off on my murder rap. But revenge on MacDowell is the real icing on the cake.

After pressing the red button to disconnect, Neville grabbed a few of the marked phones and headed out to his truck. It wasn't a long drive, but it would be a slow ride through the holler. His Super Duty truck would make it, but at the last second, he turned toward his shed to grab his tire chains. He would need them to get through the muddy trails through the woods, and especially down in the holler.

"Syrus, we got company," Spencer yelled out.

"I see 'em. Sonny, grab a rifle and head into the woods. Keep an eye on things. If I raise my hand, you pop anybody in the truck," Syrus Stamper told his gigantic younger brother. "Spence, work your way over to the stills and make sure they cain't be seen from here. Then hightail it back here from a different direction. No point in anyone knowing where the moneymakers is at. And keep your trap shut. You need to be all stealth-like."

The big truck pulled up to Syrus, leaning against his own battered and rusted Jeep. The chains on the tires clanked as it pulled alongside. Both vehicles sat next to a ramshackle old farmhouse that hadn't seen a fresh coat of paint in ... well ... ever. The graying boards were dry rotted and curling away from the walls. Oversized tractor tires and chicken wire crates littered the area around the shack the Stampers referred to as their front yard.

"Mayor."

"You may not have heard, Syrus, but I am not the mayor any longer," Neville Jarvis said coolly.

"Oh, yeah. I heard something 'bout you. Din' choo irradiate big ole Will Clay over some mining business?" Syrus pressed slyly. "Why ain't you incarcerated?"

"I think the word you are abusing is *eradicate,* not irradiate. I stand acquitted. All charges dropped," Neville replied. "Seems there was some misconduct in the sheriff's department."

"Yeah, Sheriff Mac runs a pretty loose ship up there. But I will say he gave me and my brothers a fair shake. Coulda run us in for shine but instead set us up with this legal paint thinner business," Syrus boasted. "But I gotta tell ya, it ain't proper havin' his woman do all his shootin' for him."

"Word has it," Neville paraphrased, "he set you up with a legal business where you make a tiny fraction of the money you would have running shine down to those fancy Atlanta bars. Isn't Judge Stemple's boy your boss now?"

"We ain't got no damned boss! We is entremanures!" Syrus clearly rankled at working legally under Adrian Stemple's watchful eye.

Neville, the ultimate small-town politician, knew he had hit upon the right nerve.

"Yeah, it would piss me off, having to answer to a rich boy who never worked a day in his life. Guess it don't bother you boys to work for pennies on the dollar, while Uncle Sam and Adrian Stemple takes the lion's share. Then, after all is said and done, you have to split your part three ways."

Syrus flinched a little. He was splitting their part of the paint thinner proceeds four ways, and he was taking two of those, with Sonny and Spence none the wiser. His anger was cooling as he thought over what Neville said.

"Danged if you right there. After taxes and fees and bizness expenses and Stemple's piece o' the pie, they ain't much left to split. Not like when we wuz in the shine business," Syrus complained, almost to himself, the wheels turning.

As Spence made his way back to the shack, Neville mimicked Syrus leaning form against the Stampers' rust bucket. Psychologically, he was putting himself on Syrus's side.

"What if there was a way you boys could make a LOT more money, get out from under Stemple's thumb, and get over on the MacDowells?"

"Well, I reckon I'd have to give it a great deal of thought."

Syrus signaled Sonny and Spencer to come out of the woods and Neville Jarvis explained what he needed: at least four garbage trucks "acquired" from outside Mounton County, best if out of state, and the backs cleaned thoroughly.

Syrus, the least intellectually challenged of the three Stamper brothers, spoke, "I don't think there is four garbage trucks in all of Mounton anyway. What do we need these trucks for and why clean 'em?"

Unable to answer those very questions, Neville responded as he handed Syrus a handful of cellular phones, "I'll tell you when you need to know. And right now, you don't need to know."

"What are these for?" Syrus asked.

"These are burner phones. They are nearly untraceable. Do NOT make phone calls on these. They are for communicating with my phones only. I will call you occasionally to give you instructions. If you need to call me, my number is here." Writing down his burner number. "Use them once, then completely smash them with a hammer and burn them so nobody can trace them."

"Must be why they is called 'burners,'" Spencer deduced.

Sonny Stamper nodded. Syrus looked blankly at the phones, and Neville winced.

#

*"**Señor Ortiz? Did you get the money I sent you?**"* demanded the electronically distorted voice over the burner phone.

"Si. But I still want to know who—" Sylvester demanded.

"My name is not relevant. The delivered money should have proven my sincerity. Did you procure the Oxy as instructed?"

"Si. Yes." Sylvester seethed, but held his tongue. The weird voice DID deliver on the money as promised. Sly and his crew did get the drugs as instructed. And there were a LOT of drugs. If this played out as smoothly as the money delivery, he and his compadres could make some serious coin. Maybe enough to move his *mamacita* out of Pilsen. He didn't like taking orders, especially from someone he didn't know, but understood why The Voice was keeping his anonymity. He just didn't like it. He liked being *el jefe*, not some *secuaz*.

"**Excellent. You and your compatriots will procure three untraceable vans and transport the product to Mounton, KY. You will transfer your cargo to several vehicles which will be provided. You will receive further instructions then.**"

"Mounton? Why on earth would we go there? Kentucky was where dat *hijo de puta* sheriff and his *familia* busted us. His punk ass burg is nothing but trouble for us."

"**We discussed revenge on the sheriff and his family as part of the arrangement. If you want to catch a fish, you must put your line in the right hole,**" The Voice on the phone restated.

"And exactly how are we going to 'fish in the right hole'?" Sly snarled.

"**A grandmaster does not need to discuss his strategy with a knight. He simply directs the pieces to move as they are able.**" Click.

Sly stared at the disconnected burner with pure fury. A knight? Does this puto think I am some sort of *empeñar* he can push around to do his scut work without question?

#

The man sitting in the darkened room disconnected the voice distorter from the burner phone. As he destroyed the phone and its SIM card, he considered the conversation. *Ortiz will bear watching. He has delusions of being a player, and not a piece on the board.*

#

All Buckle

Someone was following Mac. They were close. He could feel it. His instincts as a cop kicked into high gear. His every step felt copied and every move imitated. His shadow duplicated its prey inch by inch. Crouching down as he walked was murder on his knee.

Without turning his head or giving any indication of making a move, Mac whirled suddenly to confront his stalker, fell to the floor, whipping out an imitation gun in the form of a pointed index fingered and fired. "Bang!"

His would-be pursuer collapsed in a boneless pile on the living room carpet.

"Aw, Pappaw! You got the drop on me again," Naomi said, getting to her feet.

"How?" Mac smiled at the recently turned six-year-old.

Naomi thought about the scene. "I din't move from cover to cover so I was protected 'fore you drew on me."

"And you followed too close," the sheriff of Mounton County told his granddaughter. "The best tail is a tail they never know is there. Unless you want them to."

"But I'm getting better, right?" the little girl giggled, flinging herself into her grandfather's arms.

"Yepper. SweetPea, in a few years, you'll be able to sneak up on a baby deer," Mac said, kissing her on the cheek. "And I won't be able to pick you up like this." He laid on his back and held her an arm's length above him, mindful of her well-healed scars at her waist.

"Oh, Pappaw, I'll never get too big for you to hug me. Even when I'm big like you."

"Hug? Never. Hold up in my arms? Not for a while. Get the drop on you? I don't know. You're getting pretty tricky."

Hannah, watched the scene from the kitchen entryway while drying a breakfast plate. She smiled at the relationship her husband shared with their granddaughter. The child loved her Mammaw, but

absolutely doted on her Pappaw. Every move Mac made, Naomi
struggled to copy. She was even an early riser like him. She dressed
and talked like him. Mac doesn't say much, and imitating him may
not always be a good thing, especially when he loses his temper. She
may have her grandmother's and father's dimples, but Naomi has
eyes only for her Pappaw. None of the MacDowells had broached
the Frankfort offer with Naomi yet. Mac and Hannah were enjoying
their granddaughter with no thought of the future. All that mattered
to Mac and Hannah was, the baby-shampoo smell of her hair, the
glow of her smile, and the warmth of her hugs.

Mac looked up from the floor to see his wife watching them from
the kitchen entryway. He marveled for the millionth time how
gorgeous she was. When they first met, she was just out of her teens,
studying agriculture at Bowling Green, and her beauty rivaled any
movie starlet. It was a very different sort of look than she has now,
he thought. She was innocent and delicate then, almost other-
worldly. Today, she still hadn't the salt and pepper Mac sports in his
short-cropped hair, but she has a few seasoned lines around her eyes
and mouth telling a tale of years and smiles, while the glint in her eyes
and self-assuredness spoke of love and an inner strength. While some
women age gracefully, Hannah seemed to grow more beautiful and
stronger every year. He couldn't figure out what she ever saw in the
skinny jarhead she had met decades ago.

They met while she was on her first Spring Break in Myrtle Beach,
even though she was in her last year of college. He was on liberty
from Ft. Bragg with a few of his Marine brothers, doing what young
Marines do in their off time: drinking and chasing girls. The first time
he saw her, he knew he was done chasing girls. The first time she told
him she didn't approve of alcohol, he knew he was done drinking. To
spend time with her, he delightfully gave up both. They dated
numerous times during their brief Myrtle Beach vacation, but he
never dredged up enough nerve to do more than kiss her goodnight.
His confidence and cockiness went out the window. His awe for her
made him completely forget he trained as a combat soldier. They

wrote often. She finished her bachelor's degree. He earned a promotion to sergeant and a few commendations as a military police officer. Just at the end of his first hitch, he injured his knee tackling a thief at the PX. One lump sum severance package, an honorable discharge, and a lifetime of VA benefits later, Mac was out of the Marines with a mostly repaired knee and no training except his military background. Hannah's college friends had pushed her into dating men with bigger prospects right up till the time she and Mac got married. He later found out, from her father, she had turned down numerous marriage proposals ... while waiting for him. Some came from very solid prospects: a handsome weatherman who would later become a national network, a slightly older law student from a very well-to-do family who eventually became a state big-wig, a young politician who would later become Secretary of Agriculture for Kentucky, and an up-and-coming rodeo star. Few of them took the let-down well, even though Hannah did her best to gently let them know her interest lay elsewhere. No matter how stubbornly they pestered her to continue seeing them, she couldn't be mean when rejecting their advances. It just wasn't in her. Mac and Hannah visited each other a couple of times, wrote often, and as soon as his hitch ended, they tied the knot. Hannah wanted to live in Kentucky with her parents and since Mac had no better ideas, vocation, or prospects, he agreed. The Agri-Sciences she had studied at Bowling Green she applied to make her parents' farm/ranch as profitable as possible. Mac helped her, sometimes not so successfully, as much as he could, until the community surprised him by electing him sheriff. It was probably for the best. Even Mac admitted when it came to being a farmer, he was an excellent sheriff. He could ride and manage livestock well enough but had absolutely no green thumb. Plants just seemed to die when he was close by. If it ever sold, the family land would bring a small fortune, but as a working farm, it barely paid its way. The surprise election results could not have come at a better time, as Hannah had just told him the happy news she was expecting. Flash forward twenty-seven years and Mac is playing with his beautiful granddaughter on the living room floor of the very house they moved into not long after he married the most beautiful woman he had ever seen.

His granddaughter, Naomi, had him wrapped around her little finger, but Hannah still had him wrapped around her heart.

#

May 14, 6:45 A.M., Mounton, KY

Mac's only son and senior deputy, Jeb, pulled his personal truck into the parking lot of the Mounton County Sheriff's Office, fifteen minutes before their shift began. Both men occasionally used their own vehicles for work, enabling them to take tax deductions as well as allowances for certain expenses. From the county's perspective, it was considerably cheaper than buying more department SUVs. The two MacDowell men walked to the door together.

"Beth get Naomi dropped off at the house okay this morning?" Jeb asked his father.

"Yepper," Mac said.

"Mom gonna drop her off at school?"

"Yepper."

"You guys sure you don't mind taking her some mornings?" Jeb studied his dad for any signs of stress. "Sorry we drop her off so early. Ever since Beth went back to work, you guys watching Naomi sure has been a help."

"Are you kidding? That little angel is the highlight of our day," Mac smiled.

"Well," Jeb reiterated, "we're sure obliged."

"Hannah asks on a regular basis why you three don't move back in."

"For starters, we need to start a life of our own, just like you and Mom did. Secondly, you don't even know if you'll be living here or in Frankfort. And lastly, it's not 'us three,' it's about to be 'us four' shortly."

"Even more reason. Beth will need even more help with two babies. We have more than enough room at the farm and it would let you tuck a few more bucks away," Mac paused before they reached the door. "Ya know, two babies are a lot more expensive than one."

112

"Wow! Pulling out the big guns already? You must really want us to move back in."

"We do. But to be honest, your momma made me promise I would hit you with the money thing. You know Hannah's motto: 'Never use a .38 when a deer rifle is handy.'"

"Here's the really sad part," Jeb disclosed with a smile, while stepping into the office, "Mom's not who we're worried about Naomi taking after."

#

"How's the MacDowell family this morning?" the night deputy, Joseph Dawe, greeted as the pair entered the sheriff's office. Dawe worked the night shift as Mounton's only representative of the law between the hours of 11:00 P.M. and 7:00 A.M.

Joseph Dawe would never be in a 'men of law enforcement' calendar. Tall, thin, and gangly, the Ichabod-like deputy was a sharp contrast to his plump, smiling spouse. Dark-haired and self-confident, the night deputy was deceptively intelligent and utterly devoted to his family. Patty-Jane worked part-time at the Kentucky Telephone Company's substation.

Life was slow in Mounton, the pay low, and the town remote, and the Dawes would not have it any other way. Born and raised a local boy, Joseph married his high school sweetheart and immediately began increasing the population number on the *Welcome to Mounton* sign at the edge of town.

Jeb helped his dad with the morning patrols to get the day started and then came back at 5:00 P.M. to work till 11:00. It gave him a few hours to stay with Naomi, and before Beth started these new, longer shifts at the doctor's office, a bit of time with his wife. Now, they mostly just see each other at breakfast at 5:00 A.M. They managed to coordinate their schedules so they could have a day off together. Such is the life of a two-income family in Kentucky.

"Just fine," Jeb answered. "How's yours?"

"Fat and sassy. Well, one of those anyway," Dawe looked down. "Speaking of which, Patty-Jane's been asking when you might be thinking about getting an extra body or two 'round here? Not that we don't appreciate the overtime, but she don't want our boys thinking their Poppa is just 'the nice man who visits between naps.'"

Mac looked up. "Soon."

Jeb jumped in, "Tell Patty-Jane we're down to the last few names and should have a coupla warm bodies in here in a few days. Once they get trained, we'll let you pick your days." *Days* being an inside joke since Dawe preferred the night shifts to let him see his family and help his wife take care of the boys. "Beth would like me to get back to a regular schedule myself."

"Patty-Jane'll be happy to hear it, fellas," the night deputy said jovially as he headed toward the door. "It'll be nice to have a couple of solid days with the boys again too. See you gents this evening."

Once the night deputy stepped out, Mac turned to his son.

"Who's left?"

"We got the guy from D.C., the hotshot from the academy in West Virginia, and the kid from Leitchfield. I like the guy from Washington, but the hotshot was top of his class. Marksmanship, criminal investigation, legal. This kid is the goods."

"And probably just a few years younger than you and he actually *graduated* the academy," Mac kidded his son. "And what do any of those things have to do with maintaining law and order in Mounton?"

"Well, it wouldn't suck to be a little more like a *real* sheriff's office," Jeb smiled.

"What about Leitchfield?" Mac inquired.

"Twenty-three, did a couple semesters in Lexington for criminal science but had to drop out to go back to Leitchfield to take care of his folks and their farm. Baling hay, tending to the animals, managing the farm, et cetera. I guess money got a bit tight and he couldn't afford to stay in school. Good grades. On paper, he seems about as physically fit as a Kentucky-bred farm boy can be. Looks like a hard worker."

"Why Mounton?" the sheriff queried.

"Wrote that he applied all over and is looking to make some money to send back home." Jeb shuffled some papers. "Lord knows why. There sure ain't no money in law enforcement."

"Tell me about D.C.," Mac insisted as he held up the resume.

"A little older than the other two. Distinguished career in Washington, but wants to raise a family in the country away from the gunfire. Been a cop for a while and knows his business."

"Okay, call in whichever two you want and let's get 'em in here on a probationary basis. We can start 'em as soon as they get here," Mac stated as he headed for the door and his morning patrol.

"Right after patrol, I'll probably call the hotshot from the academy and the kid from Leitchfield. He sounds like he could really use the work."

"A lousy reason to give him the opportunity, Jeb. Just because he's hungry, doesn't make him a good deputy."

"Yeah, I know. I think with the two younger guys, we have a better chance of teaching them the right way to do things as opposed to breaking them of any bad habits—" Jeb said, looking down at the resumes. "Oh crap!"

"What?"

"I think the guy from D.C. may be black," Jeb explained. "We could get in trouble for some discrimination thing."

"Did you know he was black when you picked the other two?"

"No."

"Are the other two as qualified in their own ways as he is?" Mac quizzed his son.

"They don't have the street experience, but they are just as well-trained and athletic as hell. Plus, they're young and single."

"Then don't worry about it. He's still working in D.C. and I know we can't offer him anywhere near what they are paying him. You're probably doing him a favor of not having to turn us down."

"Dad, can I ask you something?"

"Yepper."

"Did you give me the responsibility of the deputy search for a reason?"

"Well, son, let's just say anything can be a teaching moment if you look at it the right way."

#

May 15, 3:02 P.M., Mounton, KY

There was only a day or two left until the regular school in Mounton was let out for the summer, but the teachers found the preschoolers and daycare children preferred to think of themselves as grown up enough to be "in school." The kids didn't even mind they stayed in school all summer long. The working parents definitely didn't mind.

The town, as small as it was, had a single building for all grades up to high school. Mounton bussed its high schoolers to Louisville or Bardstown, depending on what part of the county they were in. Since the Mounton building contained most grades and was the only school in town, most people just called it The School. There just weren't enough students to justify, or taxes to pay for, a separate middle school building. The middle school football team had six players on it, who played both offense and defense. They had a hard time finding schools with small enough teams to play against.

Beth MacDowell strolled painfully to the only schoolhouse in Mounton to walk her daughter home from her pre-school class. Being her day off, she wanted to enjoy the fresh air. Too much of her week was ten-hour days on her feet in the stuffy confines of the town's only doctor's office. Plus, Beth wanted to spend a few extra minutes with Naomi walking on such a lovely day. Even if her feet already hurt from work the day before. Beth forgot all about her sore feet and long working hours when she saw Naomi emerge from the front of the building with the other pre-school students. The kids all ran to their respective mothers, most of whom sat in working-farm pickup trucks or rusted four-wheel drives.

"How was your day, Honey?" Beth inquired of her precocious six-year-old, who seemed to be going on thirty. She was mimicking her grandfather more and more every day.

"Bad." Clearly taking after the stoic Mac.

"Why was it 'bad,' baby?" Beth only now noticed the rip in a knee of her daughter's bib overalls.

"Johnny Smith."

116

"What about Johnny Smith?" Beth dusted off Naomi's overalls. It was like pulling teeth to get the youngest MacDowell to explain things.

"He's crazier than a bag full of bat-shit," the six-year-old explained.

"Naomi! Language!"

"Sorry. He crazier than a bag full of bat-*poop*."

"Honey? Are you repeating something you heard your Pappaw say?"

Naomi hesitated, torn between always telling the truth and being fairly certain she was getting her Pappaw in trouble.

"Uh ... yepper."

#

May 17, 7:07 A.M., Mounton, KY

Jeb contacted Lawrence Patricks, originally from West Virginia, and Mason Wheeler from Leitchfield, Kentucky, about coming on board the Mounton County Sheriff's Office. Mac insisted it be on a probationary basis until they got to know them better. Both reported for work at 7:00 A.M. sharp the following Monday. Lawrence showed up in a Camaro more than two dozen years old and Mason parked a shiny, brand-new Dodge RAM 350, four-door pickup at the curb outside the station. Pieces of Scotch tape still clung to the window from where the new vehicle sticker had been taped.

Lawrence's deputy's uniform had been ironed and starched so crisply, it looked like it would snap if bent. The night deputy, Dawe, comfortable in his faded Wranglers and well-worn deputy's khaki short-sleeved shirt, looked up at the new recruits from the single desk the deputies shared and his nightly summary report, "He'll get over that soon enough."

"Jeb, take Lawrence out on the morning patrol and give him the nickel tour," Mac instructed.

"Sure, Dad," Jeb replied, grabbing his cap from the hat tree by the door.

"Dad?" Lawrence prodded as they closed the door. "A little 'informal,' isn't it?"

"Yeah," Jeb agreed, "he tried to make me call him 'Sheriff' when I first started, but I just couldn't pull it off."

"You serve under your father?" Lawrence asked as they got into the official sheriff's truck. "How does that work?"

"Better than working for my mom."

#

May 17, 8:44 A.M., Mounton, KY

Jeb spent the morning showing Probationary Deputy Lawrence Patricks around the small town of Mounton but also studying him. The new deputy practically oozed regulations out of his pores. His bodybuilder physique fit his crewcut haircut perfectly and he barely squeezed into his new uniform shirt. He had filed all his personnel paperwork and picked up his uniform the Friday before. He even wore the uniform's Smokey the Bear hat. Jeb wore a faded Cardinals baseball cap.

"The first thing you need to know is: Always be early for your shift. 'If you're not fifteen minutes early, you're—'" Jeb started.

"Late," Lawrence finished.

"I was gonna say 'fired', but 'late's' good too." Jeb smiled at the new recruit. "Dad's a stickler for being early. He considers protecting this town a personal responsibility and expects the same from all of us."

Lawrence scribbled furiously in his notebook. Jeb watched from the corner of his eye while driving the only county-purchased SUV.

"So, there are two streets in town: Main Street, which is restricted from vehicular traffic, and what everybody calls The Side Street, which parallels Main and where everybody parks. They both connect with 55 and 44, but only Main Street and The Side Street lead into town," Jeb explained to Lawrence. "Most of the businesses are on Main Street and have adapted the 19th Century style we use to attract tourists. It didn't take much. Many of these storefronts are identical to what they looked like two hundred years ago. At the south end of Main Street is the First Baptist Church of Mounton. By the way, I don't know what your personal religious beliefs are, but joining a church will fast-track your acceptance here in town. May cut five or ten years off it.

"Main Street converges with The Side Street, and *The New Texaco*, which has been here as long as I can remember. The other end of The Side Street is *Ginny's Diner*, *Duncan's General Store & Mercantile*, and *Darlene's Beauty Emporium/Barbershop/Tanning Salon* is in the middle with the sheriff's station just behind it."

"There's really no cars allowed on Main Street?" Lawrence conjectured. "What do you do if a car goes in there? Write them a ticket? Arrest them?"

"Mostly just laugh at 'em," Jeb smiled. "There are concrete and steel poles at each end of Main and they just trapped themselves on a two-block-long street with no exits."

#

While Jeb showed Lawrence the ins and outs of patrolling the metropolis of Mounton, Kentucky, Mac took Mason along with him on a similar tour of the town. Mason was a tall, gangly kid compared to Lawrence's bodybuilder physique. While not fat, the deputy was definitely not in the same physical shape as Lawrence. His skin tone was pale with a sprinkle of freckles across his nose. *Any amount of sun would fry this kid to a crisp.*

Mac drove them around the county in his battered old Bronco. Like Mac himself, the vehicle was getting on in years, but unlike himself, he had taken exemplary care of the aged Bronco. Mac paid cash for the used vehicle as a young Marine and babied it like a child. Originally green and tan, the 1992 4x4 featured the original Eddie Bauer buckets seats. While it didn't look like much, the engine practically purred. Hannah took care of her family. Mac took care of the Bronco. To each their strengths.

Mac and Mason drove down the mountain that the town crested and back. While there were few roads to lead into town from various farms and homesteads, there were only two roads of any note up and down the mountain.

"Mounton is the county seat," Mac explained. "The county only encompasses a couple of mountains and a bunch of gorgeous farmland. Some of the early settlers couldn't get their wagons any further in the snow-covered mountain, so they founded the town right here."

"So much for the pioneer spirit," Mason joked.

"Yeah, turns out my wife's family was some of those pioneers,'" Mac stated deadpan.

"Ow. Sorry."

"No worries. But you do have to wonder at how bad a place they were coming from to think this snow-buried mountain in central Kentucky was better."

#

May 17, 11:04 A.M., Mounton, KY

Jeb and Lawrence patrolled most of the morning. Lawrence scribbled furiously in his small notebook.

"It's not a very big town," Jeb kidded him. "You can't have a whole bunch of notes."

"Just jotting down a few thoughts," Lawrence replied.

"Jeb, you there? Come in."

"Go ahead Dad," Jeb spoke into the handheld mike.

"We've a got a 10-54 on Route 3, about two miles outside of town. May need a cleanup."

"Roger, Dad. On our way," Jeb hung up the mic on the dashboard clip.

"10-54? A 'possible dead body'?" Lawrence asked incredulously.

"I guess you could say."

"Don't we need to call for backup?" Lawrence looked at Jeb.

"I kinda doubt it."

#

The dead body turned out to be a deer carcass some driver had hit and left by the side of the road.

"Still think we need backup?" Jeb kidded, pulling on a windbreaker, despite the May heat.

"Your dad called this a 'possible dead body'?" Lawrence snorted.

"Well, this job doesn't have a lot of excitement. You kinda have to make your fun where you can find it. And from the way its innards are spread out over the road, I would say 'dead' is more than a possibility."

"You knew about this?" Lawrence accused.

"Let's just say I had a fair idea based on my dad's tone of voice," Jeb replied. "Plus, we've only had a single murder here in about twenty years. I thought the odds were pretty good on roadkill. Shame it ain't possum, though."

"Why?"

"Easier to clean up," Jeb said straight-faced. "Hey, grab a shovel out of the back. Some trucker knocked the guts outta this baby."

By the time they finished loading the carcass into the back of Jeb's truck, Lawrence's new uniform shirt was covered in viscera and blood. Jeb peeled off his windbreaker and gloves, tucking them into a plastic garbage bag in the back of the pickup.

"A little hydrogen peroxide or lemon juice will take that right out," Jeb said, indicating Mason's three-day-old shirt covered in blood.

"You think so?"

"Oh, hell no! It's ruined. It had a good life and can go to a better place now. Don't you worry about it, we'll get you a new shirt. At cost."

\#

May 17, 1:02 P.M., Mounton, KY

"So, how'd your first morning go?" Mac asked Lawrence. It was midday and Mac assigned Lawrence to cover the office since his shirt was ruined.

Lawrence and Jeb had dumped the deer carcass off at the landfill and returned to the station. It was very likely that bears and coyotes would get to it before it became landfill. Lawrence changed into a black tee shirt and Jeb left to return later for the evening split shift. Mason would return at the same time as Jeb to get a feel for the evening shift. Mac and Lawrence were sitting at the two desks in the station. Lawrence was filling out forms reporting the disposal of the deer, while Mac studied his newest employee.

"It went fine, sir," Lawrence stood. "I hated ruining my uniform on my first day, and I have some questions about the use of the 10-

54 code over official radio channels for roadkill, but all-in-all, I thought it was a good day. I can see places where I can be of service to the county."

"Relax, son," Mac said. "This ain't the academy. Didn't cotton to the 10-54 bit, huh?"

"If I may speak freely, sir: No, sir. It was a flagrant disregard for police radio protocol, sir."

"Well, just don't report me yet," Mac drawled. "And you know you don't have to fill out all those forms for just pickin' a deer offa the side of the road, right?"

"They're required by the state, sir."

"Then, you know what, Lawrence? Knock yourself out." Mac hefted his lean frame out of his chair and headed for the door and the diner for lunch.

#

May 17, 4:14 P.M., Mounton, KY

"So, what'd think of Lawrence?" Mac asked his son. Jeb had stopped by before starting his shift, knowing his dad would want his first impression. Once during the week, Beth, Jeb, and Naomi usually joined Mac and Hannah for Thursday night supper. And Sunday dinner. A fact Hannah assumed without saying.

"Other than he could probably give Ginny a run for the money on a bench press, he seems okay. A little by-the-book. I bet he could recite the Kentucky penal code word for word. Not much of a sense of humor and is definitely not a people person. Takes notes on everything. Seems like a stand-up guy. What'd you think of Mason?"

Mac pondered for a minute.

"Jury's still out."

Jeb smirked. Years ago, his father had told him the old saw about "the reason God gave you two ears and one mouth is you should listen more than talk." His dad saying the "jury's still out." means Mac is keeping his opinion to himself and has reservations about the Kentucky-born probationary deputy. Over the years, Jeb had learned to translate Dad-Speak fluently. Mac would sometimes talk at length in front of family, and occasionally Ginny or Duncan, but in a certain mood, it took a crowbar and a stick of dynamite to get more than ten words from him. Or Jeb's mother, whichever was closest.

#

May 18, 11:38 A.M., Mounton, KY

"Little early for you isn't it, Sheriff?" Ginny probed as he set a cup of coffee in front of Mac. Today, he was just looking forward to sitting and relaxing with a good cup of coffee and a great piece of pie. The biker-sized owner and head chef at *Ginny's Diner* didn't bother taking his order. Mac would eat what was put in front of him. It was usually excellent, but Mac wouldn't complain if it wasn't. Ginny refused to take his or Jeb's money. It had something to do with saving Ginny's life once, knowing the secret of Ginny's culinary background, or some pictures involving sheep. Nobody knows for sure except Mac and Ginny.

Typically, Mac would cruise around town about midday and eat lunch at the diner, but today he opted to let Lawrence make the afternoon patrol. It was only his second day, but after all, it was Mounton and the town's population was just a biscuit under 600. *How much trouble could he get into?*

The call came in from Darlene herself, proprietor of *Darlene's Beauty Emporium/Barbershop/Tanning Salon*, just after noon. Jeb had rigged a system to forward all calls to the station to the officer-on-duty's cell phone.

"Sheriff's office."

"Sheriff, you best get your scrawny ass down here right soon," Darlene whined into the phone. "GQ out there is stirring up all sorts of trouble."

Mac put the phone back in his pocket, looking up at Ginny, just as the gigantic cook and proprietor was about to sit Mac's lunch in front of him.

"The good news: I am spared from today's blue plate special."

"Call the governor back," Ginny said. "You don't merit a reprieve."

"It was Darlene," Mac told him.

"Ow. I'd sooner squabble with the governor. All he can do is summon the National Guard. Darlene could get rougher than the National Guard on a good day."

Mac put on his old brown Stetson and walked out the jangling door, wondering how Lawrence could have gotten on the fightin' side of Darlene in just an hour.

#

Darlene rushed out to meet Mac's Bronco as it pulled up to the *Beauty Emporium/Barbershop/Tanning Salon*. No small feat for a woman who probably packed over three hundred pounds into a five-foot-three frame. *Well, 'rushed' may qualify as a bit of an exaggeration, but 'purposeful waddling' meant Darlene was PISSED.* Mac had only seen her power-waddle once before, years earlier when a kid tried to steal some products from her shop. *Beauty products for Christ's sake!* It impressed everyone how fast the proprietress could move when motivated. It especially impressed the would-be thief so much that when he grew older, he moved out of Mounton and went to seminary school. He may still have her fingerprints on his upper arm.

"So, Mac, what are you gonna do about this situation?" Darlene's voice rumbled. Darlene had smoked Pall Malls for nearly thirty years. It's living proof of God's hand at work that she never got lung cancer, but her voice rumbled like it could grind rock into fine gravel. Rumor has it she wears about three nicotine patches simultaneously and is in a permanently bad mood as the result of a constant need of a tobacco fix. At least, everyone hopes the bad mood is about tobacco.

Beside her stood the oldest man Mac knew: Ezekiel Thompson. Ezekiel stood ramrod straight, had barely enough hair to support a thinned-out crewcut, skinny to the point of being ropy, and toughened like a five-foot nine-inch length of beef jerky. He wore dark gray trousers, old and worn, but pressed and clean. He kept his light gray shirt buttoned to the neck. A pair of lace-up boots as old as Mac himself looked scuffed but glistened from a shine in the last week or two.

"Situation?" Mac invited the outburst he knew was coming.

"Yeah, situation! The Terminator over there is giving parking tickets to some of my best customers and driving off business," Darlene growled. It's hard to tell the difference between Darlene's normal speaking voice and her angry growl, but Mac got the gist of it. He wondered if Mr. Darlene could tell the difference between her growl and pillow talk. *Great. Now I have to get THAT image out of my head. On the upside, I am now no longer hungry for lunch.*

"Lawrence."

"Sheriff. I was in the process of citing these vehicles for parking violations when this ... person practically assaulted me. I'm glad you're here. I'd like to charge her with obstruction of justice, interfering with a police officer, and public nuisance," Lawrence stated in a calm, confident voice.

"No." With a sigh, Mac took the tickets from Lawrence's hand and looked them over.

"What? You're going to let her interfere with me doing my job?"

"Uh ... yepper. Apologize."

"WHAT! You can't be serious?" Lawrence stood dumbfounded. "She practically accosted me, threatened me, and made it near impossible to do my job."

"Apologize."

Red-faced and looking like he may have a stroke, Lawrence walked over to Darlene, who had stood close enough to hear the entire conversation. Her thick arms were barely able to fold around her prodigious chest. At this point, Lawrence may have been praying for a stroke.

"Ma'am, I ... apologize," Lawrence conceded through gritted teeth all the while looking at Mac.

"For?" Mac prompted.

"For inconveniencing you and your customers." Lawrence stared at Mac to see if his apology was sufficient.

"Darlene." Mac tipped his hat and got back into his truck.

#

May 19, 7:19 A.M., Mounton, KY

Jeb laughed so hard he had to pull the office SUV over to the side of the road to keep from hitting something.

"So ... you ... you ..." another bout of laughter racked the younger MacDowell so hard he couldn't continue.

"I don't see what's so funny," Lawrence burned. "Your father ignored multiple traffic violations and a mid-level felony yesterday."

With tears of laughter running down his face, Jeb explained, "Dad showed me the tickets. First of all, you wrote up Ezekiel Thompson, who is 103 years old and has fought in three wars. Except for his time overseas, he has been a resident here for all of his life."

"So, it's okay for him to park illegally on the street?" Lawrence vented.

"No, but he has an artificial leg from the one he lost in Viet Nam and refuses to get a handicap sticker because he said those are for the 'pansies who really need them.' A hundred and three. So, given he still drives and has gotten his haircut every other Tuesday at Darlene's for the last thirty years, Dad cuts him a little slack."

"What about the obstruction of justice charge?" Lawrence refused to let it go.

"Well, Darlene has been at the current location and a business owner for longer than I have been alive. She stayed open when the mine closed down and things were pretty grim around here. Besides being a successful proprietor and employer in a town in desperate need of those, she supported the town's reinvention of itself into a tourist destination when a lot of other people were resistant to the change. She's a keeper and we try to help those out who help out the town."

"So, we just look the other way here when people break the law?"

"No, but consider the situation mostly exacerbated by your lack of knowledge of the local citizenry," Jeb grinned. "Those weren't so much crimes as they were misunderstandings."

"Uh-huh," Lawrence looked dubious.

"Hey," Jeb joshed the new recruit. "Think of it as a win. You tangled with Darlene on your second day and survived."

Lawrence scribbled furiously in his notebook.

#

May 20, 2:34 P.M., Mounton, KY

Given the Darlene incident, Mac decided to swap rookies with Jeb and partner with Lawrence on the afternoon patrol. The sheriff's cell phone rang about midafternoon.

"Sheriff's office."

"Mac, this is Ginny. You may opt to swing by. The Skinner boy is here and is conducting himself a tad erratically."

"On our way." Mac pressed the red button on his phone to disconnect.

"What's up?" Lawrence asked from the passenger seat.

"Not sure. But Ginny wouldn't call in 'nothing,'" Mac told him as he swung the Bronco in a U-turn to head toward the diner.

#

"Most expeditious," Ginny greeted them at the door of the diner.

"We were close by."

"Young Mr. Skinner over there is on his fifth helping, and shows no signs of abating. As exquisite as my culinary skills are, this emaciated little popcorn fart shouldn't be able to ingest more than a plate or three of breakfast," Ginny explained. "I would have handled it, the young man seems harmless enough, but I have a thigh bigger than he is. I am loathed to be litigated against regarding evicting a young scullion for consuming too much."

Mac and Lawrence ambled over to the booth.

"Hola, Theriff," the Skinner boy mumbled through mouthfuls of food. "Want thome pancaketh?"

"Hey, Alvin. Hungry much?"

"Man," Alvin Skinner grinned up at the two law enforcement officers, swallowing a huge mouthful. "I can't get enough to eat. These hotcakes are tasty!"

"Sheriff, a word?" Lawrence nodded his head away from the booth.

Once the two were away from the table, "You know he's baked, right?"

"Baked?"

"Yeah, 'barbecued,' 'blazed,' 'gorked,'" Lawrence whispered to his boss.

"Blazed?" Mac asked.

Lawrence shook his head. "You know, chopped."

"Oh. You mean 'stoned.'"

"Yeah, and the '70s called and they want their dictionary back. His eyes are dilated to the point I doubt he can see us clearly. Slurred speech. And throughout our approach, the little stoner never stopped eating."

Mac turned back to the booth. "Alvin, pay your bill. Let's go."

"Uh, Theriff. I may have overethtimated my current cash flow," Alvin slurred with a mouthful of food.

"How short are you?"

"About 100 percent."

"You didn't even check your pockets," Lawrence interjected. "Sort of makes this 'dine and dash' premeditated."

"What does 'premeditated' mean?" Alvin asked.

"You planned this, dumbass," Lawrence replied as he reached behind his back for his handcuffs.

Mac held his hand in front of Lawrence to stop him.

"Alvin, up," the sheriff said.

As the Skinner boy climbed out of the booth, somewhat clumsily, Lawrence asked, "I suppose you're not going to arrest him either?"

"No."

"Sheriff, do you ever arrest *anyone* in this town?"

"Not underage kids, no matter how 'blazed' they are," Mac explained. "His dad will pay Ginny and punish Alvin way more than ten days in lockup will."

At the mention of his dad, Alvin perked up. "Wait, you're gonna call my dad? I think I'd prefer to go to jail."

"See? The punishment fits the crime," Mac explained to Lawrence. Turning to Skinner, "Alvin, you ever hear the story of the Great

Porno Robbery?" Looking at Lawrence, "Damn shame. Cuz you're not gonna hear it today either."

#

May 21, 6:45 A.M., Mounton, KY

"How was your shift with Mason?" Mac asked his son.

"It was good. Kid's a quick study. Doesn't make waves. Even bought my supper as a way to kiss up," Jeb said. "I heard you had a call from Ginny about Alvin Skinner yesterday."

"Yepper."

"Ginny said Lawrence wanted to arrest him and you just turned him over to his dad."

"Yepper. When did you talk to Ginny?"

"When Mason took me to dinner. Ginny had just *baked* some fresh pies," Jeb smiled. "It was pretty *tasty* after some *chopped barbecue.*'"

"You know," Mac told his son. "Your mother wanted a girl twenty-eight years ago."

#

May 22, 2:45 P.M., Mounton, KY

"What are you doing here?"

"Oh, hi, Sheriff," Mason looked up from the filing cabinet. "I know I have the evening shift with Jeb today, but I thought I would come in early and familiarize myself with the files and filing system. Okay?"

After a little thought, Mac agreed, "Yepper."

"I figured you would still be out on your afternoon patrol and wouldn't mind an extra body around the place for an hour or two," Mason surmised.

"Things're slow, so I thought I'd come in, finish up some paperwork, and wait for you and Jeb to come on duty," Mac replied.

"If you want, I can stay and wait for him," Mason said. "You could head home early if you like."

"'Preciate it, but nope. County's paying me. Might as well earn it."

"Okay, just let me know if I can help out. I'm just going through some old case files. For a small county, you sure have had some interesting cases."

"We do what we can."

#

May 23, 11:15 A.M., Mounton, KY

"It's about time you checked in," The Voice on the phone snapped as he picked up. Even the snap in his voice sounded like a robot's mechanical voice box.

"It couldn't be helped," the voice from Mounton replied. "Cell phone service is barely a rumor here and the sheriff's station is so small, I can't call from there. I had to wait till I could get to a private landline. What's with the voice distorter? I called *you*."

"I'm staying in character. It takes a bit of practice to make this work properly. What have you found?"

"Not too much so far, but I've only been on the job for a week. I'm still on probation and don't have full access to everything, but I've got a lot of notes jotted down."

"You better get what I need," the dark voice on the phone snarled. **"I'm paying you good money to get it and I would take failure very … poorly."**

"I'll get it. And I'm not doing this for the money. Well, not ONLY the money. This sheriff is bent. It's just like you said. Favoritism, neglect, nepotism. I'm telling you, he needs to be behind bars. Besides what I'm learning in town, I just need some time with the files to get the goods."

"See that you do. Unlike some undercover operations, this is time-sensitive. I need the information in those files now."

"I'll send you my notes via email as soon as I can get some private time with a computer and have something substantial to report."

#

May 24, 11:25 P.M., Mounton, KY

"Sheriff, you better come quick," Dawe's voice yelled over the phone.

"What's up, Dawes?" Mac answered his landline phone at home.

"I'm looking out the window at a fire in town. A big one."

"Where? You call Lexington and Louisville Fire Departments?"

"Already done. Plus, I called in all the boys," Dawes paused. "It's at *Darlene's.*"

"Damn. On my way." Sheriff MacDowell hung up as he grabbed his hat. Hannah was shrugging on her jacket. He knew better than to try and get her to not go along. Besides, he may need help with Darlene.

Jeb was pulling on a fireman's coat as Mac and Hannah pulled up. He tossed a coat to Mac and then Mason when he pulled up right behind Mac in his shiny new Dodge RAM truck. Patricks and Dawes were already there and dressed in heavy pants, coats, and helmets, awaiting orders from Mac. Beth and Naomi were off to the side, Beth waiting for any injuries resulting from the fire. Naomi sat in the passenger side of Jeb's truck, watching and absorbing everything, particularly in the direction of her Pappaw.

"Jeb, you and Lawrence see if you can help the Volunteer Fire Brigade. Mason, come with me. We have to find out if anyone is still in there," Mac directed his team.

"On it," Jeb said, as he and Lawrence dashed off toward Mounton's lone fire truck.

"Sheriff, I'm down with tickets, chases, even an occasional B&E, but running into a burning building wasn't exactly in the job description," Mason stammered grabbing the sheriff's elbow.

"Yeah, it is," Mac looked him in the eye. "Protect and serve."

"I am not getting paid enough for this," as he reluctantly followed Mac toward the burning business front.

Four hours later, the combined efforts of the Louisville, Lexington, and Mounton Volunteer Fire Departments finally contained the fire. *Darlene's Beauty Emporium/Barbershop/Tanning Salon* and the building next door were complete losses. Only the antique, red and white barber pole survived. The buildings to either side suffered some smoke and water damage. The sheriff's station, in the alley behind *Darlene's,* sat completely untouched.

Hannah sat with her arm around Darlene, or as far around as it would go anyway, comforting the sniffling woman. Mr. Darlene sprayed a garden hose impotently at the remains of their shop. Beth treated a few firemen for smoke inhalation, while Naomi continued to watch every move her Pappaw made. Jeb and Lawrence sat on the ground, leaning against Jeb's truck tires, drinking bottled water. Mason sat in the front of his truck, staring out the window, his face, sooty, gaunt, and haunted. Mac wandered among the various fire departments, seeing if he could lend a hand in any way.

Mac stepped up to his son. "Jeb, given the hour, you and Mason sleep in and take the morning off. Come in for your evening shift. I'll take the day shift and Lawrence can do the afternoon shift. Dawes will do his usual night shift. If anything comes up, I'll call."

"I doubt it's going to get more lively than this," Jeb said.

#

May 25, 2:25 P.M., Mounton, KY

"So, what's the latest?" Jeb questioned his dad as he stepped into the sheriff's station. "I'm still wired up from all the excitement last night and wanted to stop by to see if we heard anything."

"I'm on the phone with the Lexington fire chief right now," as he pushed the speakerphone button.

"Hey, Jeb. I have some interesting news for you guys. The investigators just finished up the preliminary on your fire last night. We rushed it as much as we could, but at first blush, it looks like it was an accident, not intentional arson."

"Great. Darlene can file her insurance claim now," Jeb said.

"And no DB's. But thus ends the good news. The bad news is ..." the fire chief drawled. "The fire started in the shop adjoining Darlene's and it looks to have been a meth lab gone bad. We found a scattering of Oxy all over the place and all the chemicals needed to cook up enough meth to fry all of Mounton County."

"I *unofficially* reviewed their business license myself," Mac remembered. "The paperwork implied some sort of homemade candy store."

"I even helped them carry in some venting fans and big cookers.

Oh. Crap," Jeb realizes.

"Isn't there usually some atrocious smell associated with cooking meth?" Mac asked.

"Seems like they never got a chance to use most of the equipment. Probably their first batch," the fire chief conjectured.

"Doesn't sound like it went very well, huh?" Jeb inferred.

"I'll keep you informed," the chief said as he hung up.

"So, are you tellin' Darlene, or is Mom?"

"I'll just write it up and file it," Mac told his son.

"Everything?"

"Yepper."

Mason was already in the station when Jeb arrived fifteen minutes early for their evening shift later in the day.

"What's up, Mason?" Jeb greeted the rookie, hanging his cap on the hook by the wall.

"Not much. Your dad and Patricks must be out on their last rounds and I just filed my report on last night's fire. Been reading some of these old files. Pretty interesting stuff."

"Probably reads more exciting than the actual reality of life in Mounton," Jeb replied.

"Oh, I don't know," Mason chuckled. "Seems pretty active. Drug runners, meth labs, shootouts on Main Street. Some serious Wild West shit, if you ask me."

"Well, don't tell Patricks. He's just getting over having to throw out his brand-new, gut-stained work shirt."

#

May 27, 7:15 A.M., Mounton, KY

"Sheriff's office. Sheriff MacDowell speaking."

"Mac? Read the paper."

"Dave? What—" but the FBI agent had already hung up, leaving nothing but a click, a dial tone, and confusion in his wake.

From *The State Journal* (Frankfort's daily newspaper front page):

MOUNTON COUNTY CORRUPTION

SHERIFF'S OFFICE UNDER INVESTIGATION

The sheriff's office in Mounton County, headed by Sheriff Jacob MacDowell, is under investigation by the Commonwealth's District Attorney's office, and possibly the Kentucky Bureau of Investigation, as well as the Federal Bureau of Investigation. Allegations of misconduct and malfeasance have been forwarded to The State Journal and rumors of criminal activities abound. The Commonwealth's Attorney's office has no comment, and both bureaus stated flatly they don't comment regarding ongoing investigations, which adds credence to the rumors.

Copies of official reports and files have come to The State Journal to substantiate the purported criminal activities by the sheriff's office. The activities in question include breaking and entering without a warrant, grand theft of medical equipment, police brutality, evidence tampering, and political favoritism. Other questions surrounding the sheriff include a variety of procedural and investigative infractions, nepotism, racist hiring practices, and his inclusion in the conspiracy to murder a local circuit court judge who may have been looking into the sheriff's actions. The most damning of the evidence is his approval of a business license in the center of the town of Mounton, just steps away from the sheriff's office. When the meth lab, approved by Sheriff MacDowell, burned to the ground a few nights ago, the sheriff was the last person in the building, according to a variety of professional firefighters from Frankfort and Lexington. Reports inside the sheriff's office itself details the sheriff's senior deputy, Jebediah MacDowell (son), assisting the owners of the meth lab carrying in cooking and venting equipment into the business several weeks ago.

When we contacted the sheriff's office for comment two nights ago, Sheriff MacDowell was unavailable for comment, but the senior deputy on duty, Jebediah MacDowell, told us "What happens in Mounton County stays none of your damned business." See page 3 for more ...

#

Mac set the paper down on the table at *Ginny's Diner* after reading the entire article.

"Well, at least the photo is flattering," Ginny suggested from over his shoulder.

"Dad, we have to do something about this," Jeb snarled from his side of the booth. His own newspaper crumbled into a ball. "I never talked to any newspaper."

"Yepper."

"What do you think we should do first?"

"The first thing is ..." Mac looked at his son in all earnestness, "we should hide your mother's deer rifle."

#

Turns out Hannah had nothing to say about the article after Mac showed it to her. Jeb watched as her only reaction was the narrowing of her eyes to mere slits, much like he had seen mother wolves do on the *Nature Channel*. Just before they disemboweled a threat to their cubs. Jeb suddenly felt a small amount of pity for whoever was responsible for the article.

Jeb, Ginny, Duncan, and Mac stood in the MacDowells' kitchen, as they watched Hannah put down the paper. Jeb had privately requested Duncan and Ginny to come over in the hopes of containing Hannah. Turns out she did not need contained as much as aimed.

After a few moments' pause, Hannah turned to her husband, "Jeb wasn't even in town two nights ago. He took Naomi for a doctor's appointment in Lexington and they stayed over to visit the Kentucky Castle in Versailles the next morning. Jacob Andrew, what do you intend to do about this?" Jeb had never understood the expression 'deadly calm' until right this second.

Mac looked at his wife. Not 'Sweetheart.' Not 'Honey.' 'Jacob Andrew.' In her serious tone of voice. This was not looking good for someone. Despite the severity of the situation, Jeb gave silent thanks Hannah had not directed her wrath at him. This time. His dad had better put the figurative pin back in the grenade quickly before his mom made the expression quite literal.

"I have a few ideas," Mac said as he laid out his plans and suspicions. An unintended perk of his scheme was it would keep Hannah contained on the farm. This would be the second thing today *The State Journal* would owe him for.

#

May 29, 12:12 P.M., Mounton, KY

"Naomi, would you like to tell Mommy why the principal called me to come pick you up in the middle of the day?" Beth already knew some of the highlights after her brief conversation with Naomi's principal. She used her best Mommy Voice to try and have a calm conversation with her daughter while driving her to her

135

grandmother's house for the rest of the afternoon.

"No."

"No what?" Beth insisted, confused at her daughter's refusal.

"No ... ma'am?"

"Naomi," Beth started again, trying to contain her amusement. "First, you're not supposed to tell me or Daddy no. Second of all, I am not looking for a 'ma'am.' I am looking for the explanation of what went on today at school."

"Oh."

"NAOMI MACDOWELL!"

"You asked me if I would like to tell you why Principal Parton called you to pick me up. I don't. You want me to tell the truth, don't you?"

Beth gritted her teeth. Is six years old too old to put a girl up for adoption?

Then calmly, "Naomi, what happened?"

"Johnny Smith said his dad called Pappaw a crook," Naomi conveyed matter-of-factly.

"So, then what happened next? You didn't hit him, did you? You know violence is not the way to solve anything. You're supposed to use your words."

"I did, Mom. I used my words. I told Connie Pinkerton Johnny got beat up by a girl. By lunchtime, she had spread it all over the school."

Well, at least she's not taking after her grandfather's temper.

"And then I made it true."

There it is.

"You don't want me to be a fibber, do you?"

Beth spent the rest of the drive to her mother-in-law's house in silence, afraid of either laughing or sighing.

#

Beth took her daughter into her in-laws' house and sent Naomi to the backyard to play.

A quick explanation as to why they were both at the MacDowell farm in the middle of the day, and Hannah leaned back in her chair and looked out the window at Naomi playing on the swing set.

"You get on back to work and I'll take care of Naomi," Hannah reassured her daughter-in-law.

"Thanks, Hannah. They don't exactly cover 'Johnny Smiths' in the *Parenting for Dummies* book."

"Well, just buying a book with such a title is an admission of guilt," Hannah joked. "Everybody's a dummy when comes to parenting although they eventually grow out of it and figure it all out, and by then, they're grandparents."

"Ha!" Beth laughed and headed for the door. "Jeb or I'll be back to pick her up after work. You're a lifesaver."

After Beth headed to her car, Hannah whispered to herself, "Nope. Just a Mammaw."

"Naomi!" Hannah yelled out the back mud room door. "You play for a bit more and then come in and then Mammaw will make you some lunch."

"I'm sorry about Johnny, Mammaw. Am I in trouble?"

"Yes, SweetPea. And as punishment, you only get one cookie after your lunch."

Hannah closed the back door and walked to the pale yellow landline telephone hanging on the kitchen wall and the thin phone book on the small desk next to it.

"Mrs. Smith, is your husband home?" Hannah spoke into the receiver. "I need to have a word with him."

#

June 1, 7:05 P.M., Mounton, KY

"Lawrence, could you join us for a minute?" Jeb opened the door to Mac's office for the probationary deputy.

"Yessir, no problem."

Mac was already sitting at the desk Jeb leaned on. Patricks took the only chair.

"You have no doubt heard or read the *State Journal* article about the department," Jeb started. "You have any questions or concerns? We understand if you have reservations about signing up with a department with such dark shadows cast over it."

Lawrence looked at the two men.

"No sir. I have no doubt this is all some misunderstanding."

"Glad to hear it," Jeb shared. "Now, we want to give you some insight into some of this on the condition it doesn't leave this office."

"Absolutely."

Jeb spent ten minutes outlining some details of the events laid out in the newspaper.

"Lawrence, do us a favor and send in Mason on your way out. We need to give him the update and gauge his reaction as well."

Lawrence motioned Mason into the office as he walked out. Mason looked puzzled as he stepped into the small room the senior officers waited in. Lawrence Patrick headed out the front door as his shift had just ended.

Ten minutes later, Mac, Jeb, and Mason all walked out of the office at the same time.

"We'll fill in Dawe when his shift starts tonight," Jeb explained to Mason as he forwarded the 911 calls to their mobile phones.

"Roger wilco," Mason said, as he headed out to the department SUV.

"So far so good," Jeb told his father after everyone had left the station. "Did you make those calls?"

"Yepper."

"Guess all we have to do now is wait and see what happens."

"And keep your momma cool for a day or so. I can't figure out why everyone thinks I have the temper in the family."

Turned out they had to wait two days.

From The State Journal:

SUSPECT SHERIFF STINGS
MOUNTON COUNTY SHERIFF'S OFFICE COMMENTS

Jebediah MacDowell, spokesman for the Mounton County Sheriff's Office, and son of suspected Sheriff Jacob MacDowell contacted The State Journal yesterday. Deputy MacDowell stated the items mentioned in the earlier article regarding the Mounton County Sheriff's alleged improprieties, were part of a multi-level sting operation the FBI was conducting to flush out ongoing local corruption and criminal activities. Deputy MacDowell promised to provide The State Journal more information once the operation had concluded. In an effort to ensure the veracity of the Deputy's comments, we traced back the call as originating from the Mounton County Sheriff's Office. See page 4 for more ...

#

"It looks like you got your answer," Hannah told her husband as she folded up the paper.

"Yepper."

"Can I have my deer rifle back now?"

"Not quite yet," Mac told his wife. "Let me and Jeb wrap up a few things and then I'll get it for you myself."

#

June 5, 2:15 P.M., Mounton, KY

Mason, Jeb, and Mac once again crowded into Mac's small office at the sheriff's station.

"Mason, Dad, and I wanted to pull you aside and let you know your services are no longer required at the Mounton County Sheriff's Office."

"WHAT?"

"We'll need you to turn in your service weapon, badge, and equipment. You're done."

"Why are you doing this?" Mason demanded, looking at Mac.

"Because you're the mole feeding information out of this office," Jeb answered.

"Tell him why, Jeb," Mac said.

"Well, first of all, Dad noticed you were driving a brand-new, awfully expensive truck for someone who had to quit college due to lack of money. You were making a lot of money from someone. Secondly, your story of helping your folks on the farm when it's clear from your complexion and build, you haven't spent a day in the sun working hard. In the third place, you were the only person on duty, besidesdad, when *The State Journal* spoke with 'Deputy Jeb' at the station. You spent a great deal of time looking through the old files. Finally, we fed you the story about the FBI sting operation and gave

Lawrence a completely different story. It was the sting story 'Deputy Jeb' fed to the paper. The only question that remains is who you were working for when you infiltrated the office."

Mason sat in the wooden chair in front of Mac's desk, his face reddened more with every sentence Jeb spoke.

"You two don't know what you're talking about." Mason took his badge off his shirt and his handgun from his holster. When he did this, Jeb tensed slightly and Mac didn't move an inch. Slamming both his gun and badge on the desk, Mason stared venom at the two MacDowells.

"I wouldn't work in this podunk cesspool anyway. Everything I did was completely legal. I was working undercover to expose you for the incompetent crooks you are. You two are finished in the law business with all the shenanigans on file. I'll ship you the rest of my gear!"

With a slam, Mason stormed out of the station, climbed into his big Dodge RAM, and burned rubber all the way down the secondary street of Mounton. Just past *The New Texaco*, he pulled out his cell phone and glancing at the minimal bars on the top, placed a call.

"They burned me," Mason barked into the phone as soon as The Voice picked up on the other end. "I told you the newspaper stuff was too much. We should have just turned the stuff over to the feds and been done with it."

"Where are you now?" the mechanically altered voice demanded.

"I'm headed back to my rented room, grabbing my gear, and getting out of this postage stamp. As soon as you pay me the rest of the money you owe me, I am never coming back to Kentucky again. And speaking of which, I want extra for having to go into the fire the other night with Dudley Do-Right. You were paying me to get files and dirt, not risk my neck."

"I can be in the area in forty minutes. I'll have your money, plus a little extra for your trouble. Meet me at Route 563 about 20 miles south of your room. It's pretty remote. I'll be in a big diesel truck."

"You and everyone else in Kentucky," Mason said. "I'll be there. You just be sure you bring my money in cash."

#

The mysterious man in Frankfort looked out the French doors of his den. *I wonder where I can steal a diesel truck at this hour.*

#

June 6, 6:47 P.M., Mounton, KY

Jeb, Beth, and Naomi pulled into Hannah and Mac's drive for Thursday night dinner. Thursday dinners at Mammaw's and Pappaw's was the only night Jeb was off and Naomi enjoyed a later bedtime. Beth and Hannah disappeared into the kitchen to work on salads and side dishes. Jeb followed Mac around to the back patio to watch him grill some steaks, both of them nursing sweet teas. Naomi ran to the swings, it being too light this time of year for the big halogen lights Mac installed above the swings to be on.

"Did you hear?" Jeb asked his dad.

"Hear what?"

"KSP found Mason's truck run off the road and burnt to a crisp between here and Frankfort. Down a big hill out in the middle of nowhere." Jeb looked to make sure Naomi was out of earshot. "Neck broken."

"Before or after?" Mac speculated as he flipped the T-bones.

Jeb knew what he was asking. He'd been translating 'Dad-Speak' his whole life.

"Not sure," Jeb answered. "KSP matched some paint scrapings on the fenders which fit a dented-in, stolen diesel truck they found about 20 miles away. Also burned to a cinder. They found a body they *think* is Mason. Seems a big diesel truck forced him off the road, but the neck thing could have been after. Or it could have happened during the accident. Then the damned Dodge caught on fire. Burned up everything. Either way, someone didn't like Mason very much."

"Prints, fibers, DNA?" Mac quizzed as he loaded a tray with the steaks, each grilled to various family members' tastes.

"Nope. Somebody's been watching CSI or knows how we work. Naomi! Come to dinner."

"Does Beth know?" Mac queried.

"Nope. Figured I'd tell you first. She's got a lot on her mind these days with work, the upcoming baby, and ... did she tell you about Naomi's little dust-up at school?"

"Hannah did. Handled and done. Sounds like the Smith boy needs to learn how to take a punch."

"Dad. Kind of not the point. She talks like you. She acts like you, and now Naomi is inheriting your temper."

"She gave him a talking to and then only hit him once, right?" Mac smiled. "Sounds like she is taking more after her Mammaw."

"Who's taking after Mammaw?" Naomi out of breath, ran up to her Pappaw to help him carry the utensils.

After saying grace, Hannah looked at Mac as everyone was filling up their plates. "Did you hear about Mason?"

"Yepper. How did you?"

"The Church Ladies met here today. We're taking up a collection to help out Darlene and ..."

"What about Mason?" chirped Naomi between bites of salad.

"Nothing!" Hannah, Beth, and Jeb spat all at the same time.

"Well, I can tell you this," the six-year-old stated matter-of-factly in her best thirty-year-old voice, "by the way he acted at Ms. Darlene's fire, that boy is all buckle and no horse."

Three faces turned to stare at Mac.

"Okay, maybe that one's on me."

#

Bride & Prejudice

July 10, 3:49 P.M., Mounton, KY

It had to be white people. The very first visitors at the new front door.

"Can I help you?" After peering out the peephole, Felicia opened the hardwood door to view two white women and a little girl through the screen door.

"Hello. I'm Hannah MacDowell. This is my daughter-in-law, Beth, and my granddaughter, Naomi. We came by to welcome you to Mounton."

"I'm Felicia Harris-Williams. Uh, would you like to come in?"

Hannah held the screen door for Beth and Naomi to enter first. Beth had the day off and Naomi's 'school' was pretty flexible in the summer about attendance.

Beth handed Felicia a still-warm pie. "This is for you. I have to admit, I didn't bake it myself. It's from *Ginny's Diner*. Mom will never admit it, but Ginny makes the best pies in all of Mounton County. You'll meet him sooner or later."

"Him? Ginny's a man? Uh, thank you," Felicia hesitated, taking the pie awkwardly. "Excuse the mess. We haven't even made a dent in these boxes. It will be a month before we find our bed linens."

"Don't give it a thought," Hannah said smiling. "It's been decades since we moved here, but I remember to this day how long it took me. Mac was no help at all."

"Mrs. *MacDowell?* Are you related to Sheriff MacDowell?" Felicia asks. "The man who hired my husband?"

"That's my Mac. Just call me Hannah."

"Please have a seat," Felicia welcomed them. "Let me sit this down and move some of these boxes out of the way."

"Thank you, we don't want to be any trouble," Beth said. "If this is a bad time—Hey, who's this little guy?"

"Mom, this place is so—" A little boy with beautiful coffee-colored skin tore around the corner from the hall, and upon seeing the two white women and a little girl, abruptly tucked in behind his mother's leg.

"This is Gabriel. Can you say hello to these nice ladies, honey?"

"Hello."

"What a nice name," Hannah said to the boy. "Did you know there was a Gabriel in the Bible? He was an angel, too."

"No."

"Hey. I'm Naomi. I'm six now. How old are you?"

Gabriel holds up a handful of fingers spread wide. "I'm this many."

"I have scars on my belly. You wanna see 'em?" Naomi asked Gabriel.

"Naomi!" Beth admonished. "Sorry," she apologized to Felicia.

"Do you like to play?" Naomi asks, and after a nod from Gabriel, grabs his little brown hand in her little pink one and pulls him towards the front door.

"Gabriel! Be careful," Felicia called out.

"Don't fret none. They're as safe as houses in the yard," Hannah insisted.

"Really?" Felicia stared at the front door as if it would be the last time she would ever see her son.

"This is Mounton. Everyone looks after everyone else here."

"Then why'd you need another deputy?" Felicia asked.

#

July 10, 7:52 PM, Mounton, KY

"They just showed up without calling first. Who does that?" Felicia whined at her husband.

"Just the way they do things in a small town, honey," Davis related, loosening his Sam Brown belt and holster. Without a box-free chair in the bedroom in sight, he lowered it to the floor.

"You won't believe what they said when I ask them what they do."

"I'll bite. What?"

"Hannah is a *housewife*," Felicia spoke the last word as if it were a disease. "At least her daughter-in-law, Beth, is a nurse."

"Technically, honey, *you* are a housewife."

Felicia's eyes narrowed as she glared at her new husband.

Davis glanced at her as he pulled off his uniform shirt. "Okay, I see where I went wrong there. I can do better. *You are between career opportunities.*" Davis paused for effect. "Were they nice?"

"Oh, they were nice enough, but the 1950s called and they want Sheriff MacDowell's wife back. Do you know she has never had a job? Ever. He probably keeps her stashed away with his other hillbilly Stepford Wives."

"Yes, I'm sure he locks them away with his Klan robes," Davis chuckled. "How did Gabe like the granddaughter?"

"I guess he had fun. Do you know they played in the *front yard*, where anyone could come by and just snatch them?"

"We're not in D.C. anymore, babe."

"Really? I hadn't noticed. With all the black people around here, I feel right at home," Felicia snapped. "No, sorry. It's all the high-income career opportunities, personal development, and dental hygiene. I get this metropolis so confused with Washington."

"Didn't I tell you tell you all those details before we moved here?" A free throw and his wadded-up uniform shirt was in the hamper. "Three points. They keep all us colored folks locked up at night so we don't mess with the white women."

"Well, in a town this small, if you *did* mess with a white woman, it would be the gossip of every old bitty at the beauty parlor before you could take the condom off."

"Like I would wear a condom! The only way to get more black people in Mounton is to make them. Speaking of which ..." Davis kissed behind her ear.

She pushed him away. "Listen here, Deputy Cracker, you lock up your gun and help me with a few of these boxes or you'll *need* to find a white woman."

"Oh. Finding a white woman isn't hard. You just order one from the catalog," Davis opened a box on the chair. "The sheriff showed me. I was thinking, for a change of pace, I would get a hot woman this time, maybe one who's a little more opinionated. You know, shake things up a bit. Can I keep her in the garage?"

"Yes. Right next to where you'll be sleeping."

"Ha! Who'll have time to *sleep* with a *hot* wife around?"

#

July 13, 9:13 PM, Mounton, KY

A few nights later, Davis turned to his wife, "Felicia, can I ask you something?"

She knew it must be serious. He called her by name. Not 'Honey' or 'Babe.'

"Sure, anything."

"Was this a mistake? I mean, the move here? I don't want you to live somewhere you hate it."

Felicia curled up on the couch, staring at the blank TV. They haven't had the time to get the satellite hooked up yet.

"You have to be bored," Davis continued. "It is definitely different from D.C. Not necessarily in a bad way. Today, I had to help herd some cows off the road and back through a broken fence. On my shift in D.C. I would have spent the day on the perimeters of two different homicides. I know we wanted to move Gabriel away from the city, but if it's this boring for me, you must be halfway to Crazy Town."

"It *is* different. I've never lived in a place where everybody knows everybody else's business," Felicia said. "I know we moved here for Gabriel and even for your career. I love the fact I don't have to worry about a call about you never coming home. But I feel so *worthless*. I have a college degree and years of experience with no opportunities to utilize them here. For God's sake, I was an alternate on the Olympic archery team! The closest sporting goods store is in Louisville. I don't even *like* to shop, but I miss the *ability* to go to a real store if I want. Not to mention there is not another African-American family in all of Mounton."

"Uh, yeah. I looked into it. There is a black man in Mounton," Davis looks down. "He lives in a plywood lean-to, has a three-legged dog named Lucky, and drinks Sterno. The guy, not the dog."

"Well, *THAT* changes everything. Let's have him over for dinner next week. We can discuss black culture in Mounton."

"Perfect. I'll invite him tomorrow."

146

"I meant the dog."

"Me too." Davis asks, "Seriously, do you want to move back?"

Felicia thought about it for a moment, "Let's give it a few weeks and see if it grows on me. In a backwoods town like this, something is always growing on something else."

"Hey, if anything grows on you, I will be happy to help scrub it off."

"If you can find the loofah in one of these boxes, you are more than welcome to try."

#

July 14, 10:09 AM, Mounton, KY

The next morning, Felicia looked around the box-filled house. *How did my life get to this point?* She knew the answer. They planned it this way. Davis sent out dozens of resumes. After five years of raising their child in Washington, she and Davis decided D.C. was just not the right environment. Two weeks later, the call came from Mounton, Kentucky. The county needed another deputy to help with the influx of tourism. Was this something Davis would consider?

Davis and Felicia ran the numbers. The pay was good enough from Mounton County and the cost of living was so low, it would be a relative increase in their income, even without Felicia's job at the ad agency.

She never got to spend time with Gabriel because of her job. Their daycare costs were more than their car payments. Plus, if she was honest, job stress had taken a toll on both her health and her relationship with Davis.

After Mac hired him, in one of his many trips to Mounton, Davis purchased a foreclosed property they had both researched online and she had to admit, it was a big upgrade for them. The condominium seemed a little cramped and the house, while much older, was gigantic in comparison. The difference in the sale of their condo just outside of D.C. and the price of their house in Mounton would allow them to avoid a mortgage completely and just pay cash for the home in Kentucky. Decades ahead of their D.C. plan. While she had reservations about life in a small town, she didn't realize how dark the shadow of a mortgage was, until it didn't loom over them.

A peculiar concession was they would have to get married in order for her and Gabriel to have health benefits. Felicia's ad agency job covered her and Gabriel under her agency's policy, but the Mounton County Sheriff's Office only provided benefits for married families. There was a long late-night discussion, but neither she nor Davis could think of a single reason to avoid tying the knot. They had been living together for seven years and it just never seemed necessary. She insisted upon hyphenating her last name, but Davis officially adopted their, Gabriel, in the same ceremony.

Everything is so damned green here. Gabe will finally have a yard to play in.

Felicia looks at the boxes. Not one of them contains a mall, an archery range, a city, a career, or even other black kids for Gabriel to play with. When we moved here, all I saw was the upside. I never realized what we gave up. It's a great opportunity for Davis. Gabriel will not have to grow up in an environment of crime and murder, but why do I feel like a single lost grain of pepper in a very small pile of salt?

There was a knock on the door.

Felicia looked through the screen door to see a mob of white women in her front yard.

Felicia stared out at the women in her yard.

Gabriel came out of his room. "Mom, what—"

She turned toward her little man. "Baby, go back in your room and shut the door."

"Felicia?" The voice from the other side of the screen. A *white* voice.

"Yes?" She recognized Hannah MacDowell and Naomi at the door.

"Me and some of the ladies from the church thought we would come by and lend a hand."

"Doing what?"

"Why helping you get settled in, of course," Hannah explained, as she gestured back to the women on the lawn. Many of which, Felicia now noticed, carried covered dishes.

"You're very sweet Mrs. MacDow—Hannah, but I can take care of all this."

"Oh, pish. What are neighbors for, if not to help out? 'Sides, the sooner you get settled in, the sooner you can enjoy all Mounton has to offer. Speaking of enjoying, how'd your family like Ginny's pie?"

"To be honest, we're trying to raise Gabriel gluten-free," Felicia said.

"Well, then you're going to want to throw out about half this stuff. Is now a good time for some help?"

Felicia looked down the mostly empty street, the cars and trucks parked along the road, at all the white faces in her yard, and then at Hannah.

"Sure, come on in."

By the time Felicia showed Naomi back to Gabriel's room, the ladies had invaded. Covered dishes were stored in the kitchen and refrigerator, and the congregation gathered in the living room.

Felicia spent the day directing cartons to various rooms. The Church Ladies merrily unpacked the family's belongings after asking Felicia where she wanted them. Even Naomi helped Gabriel unpack his room. In the middle of the afternoon, Felicia stared at these women, working so hard without any expectation of payment or a returned favor. *We are definitely not in D.C. anymore, Toto.*

At 4 o'clock, Felicia collapsed wearily on the couch opposite Hannah. The other church women left as Hannah handed Felicia a cup of tea.

"And you thought it would take a month," Hannah smiled.

"I cannot thank you enough," Felicia said. "Please reiterate my thanks to the ladies."

"You can thank them yourself this Sunday at church."

"Uh ... Davis and I are not really churchgoers," she studied Hannah for a reaction. "I'm not even sure I believe in God."

"Oh, honey, it don't matter a bit," Hannah said. "He believes in you. 'Sides, a couple of hours on a hard pew is way better than unpacking for a month. You never know. You might like it."

"I guess we could try it. Once."

"Well, if not, no harm done. But don't think I'll stop asking. The Good Lord wants non-believers in church more than anybody else. Otherwise, we'd just be preaching to the choir. Speaking of which, how's your singing voice?"

#

July 14, 7:23 PM, Mounton, KY

"Wow. You unpacked the whole house in one day?" Davis crumpled on an uncluttered chair in their living room.

"No. The *ladies from the church* showed up and helped," Felicia said, kneeling down to wrestle a clean pajama top over Gabriel's head.

"You let *white folks* touch all our stuff? How will we ever get the *racism* out of our laundry?"

"Very funny, Mr.—" with a glance over at Gabriel, playing on the floor, "—Smartypants. And please don't use bad language in the presence of little ears."

"Yeah, Dad," Gabriel crowed, hugging his dad. "Some white people are cool. Naomi and I are going to get married."

"I thought you wanted to marry Mommy? Isn't Naomi a little ... old for you?"

"Nope. I'm this many and she's this many," holding out five fingers spread wide and then, with his tongue stuck out in concentration, raises just one from his left hand. "Besides, you already married Mommy." And with a giggle, scampered down the hall.

"Brush your teeth buddy! So, The Church Ladies arrived ... gasp ... unannounced and helped unpack everything?"

"I know. At first, I thought they were a lynch mob out to tar and feather us. Turns out it was casseroles. Don't even think about looking in the fridge, by the way."

"Not quite the Stepford Wives after all, huh?" Davis smiled.

"They were nice enough, but I still think Mrs. MacDowell came out of the womb with an apron tied around her waist and a rolling pin in her hand.”

“Don’t be too sure. Jeb was telling me at work about the sheriff organizing a posse a while back to take down some drug runners. The sheriff appointed Mrs. MacDowell as the designated sniper. She popped a van tire from several hundred yards away in a single shot with a scoped deer rifle.”

“Hannah? Hannah MacDowell? Betty Crocker?” Felicia leaned back against the bed, sitting cross-legged on the floor. “Wow.”

“But wait! There’s more. Evidently, she picked off an honest-to-God moonshiner from the church tower on a Sunday morning, at the end of ‘How Great Thou Art.’ Caused quite a stir.”

“No kidding?” Felicia digested this new view of Hannah. She then looked directly at Davis. “Uh, on the subject of church, how’s your singing voice?”

#

July 17, 5:34 AM, Mounton, KY

In the pre-dawn hours, Felicia sprinted to catch up to someone power-walking along the empty street.

“Beth?”

“Hey, Felicia,” Beth panted.

“Color me surprised to see someone in Mounton running,” Felicia panted. “Especially at this hour.”

“Yeah. Two miles every day. Seems like I ... am always fighting off baby fat. Now I am just trying to get ahead of the next one.”

“I know what you mean. It took me a year ... to get back into shape after Gabriel.”

“Good job. I would kill for your figure.”

“Thanks,” Felicia said. “When are you due?”

“Mid-September. I don’t know what possessed us to get pregnant for the summer. And by us, I mean me,” Beth laughed between panting. “Be pregnant in the summer. they said. It’ll be fun, they said. *They* need a hot watermelon shoved up their asses!”

Felicia laughed. “Do you know the gender yet?”

“No, we decided to keep it a surprise. But that hasn’t stopped Jeb and Hannah from workshopping names, both for a boy or a girl.

Hannah has some interesting ideas from the first few books of the Old Testament."

"Does Jeb have a preference on gender?" asked Felicia, wiping the sweat from her brow as she cooled down during their walk.

"Oh, yeah. He definitely wants a boy. Someone he can teach to shoot and play ball, pee off the back deck in the wintertime."

Felicia laughed. "What about you? What do you want?"

"I don't care as long as it's healthy and doesn't keep Naomi's hours. I swear she gets up before dawn just to think of new things to get into."

"I was wondering why you were out so early. You keep walking like this and the next kid will be a track star."

"With a taste for Cheetos!" Beth slowed as she laughed.

"Your mother-in-law is in pretty good shape. Does she run too?"

"Mom? Naw. Running a farm is as close as she gets. Almost single-handedly. She says it's enough work out for her. Mac's always on the job, and between the farm, helping with Naomi ... her church work, and helping reestablish this town, I have never seen anyone on the go the way she is."

"Doesn't she ever think about a job? A career?"

Beth slowed both of them to a stop and bent over to catch her breath.

"No, but I would love to be there when you ask her if running a farm isn't a full-time job."

#

July 21, 7:16 PM, Mounton, KY

"Did I hear correctly this morning? Did the sheriff tell me today you took a job with the town council?" Davis inquired of his wife when he arrived home.

"It's just part-time," Felicia explained. "They need some help marketing the tourism idea your boss came up with. Did you know they don't even have a website? They haven't listed any of the B&Bs online. I feel pretty confident I can increase their sales with just those two things alone."

"You know, I think the sheriff's wife suggested you to the council.

The way Jeb tells it, she might have done more than suggest."

"Well, the pay is next to nothing," Felicia disclosed, "but at least I get to use some of my skills. In D.C., I was a minute cog in a gigantic machine churning out ads about some overpriced product or another. I think I might be able to make a real difference here."

"Just don't make the website too 'black,' okay? Next thing you know, we'll be wall to wall in brothers and sisters."

"On the web, nobody knows what color you are."

"I'm proud of you, babe. I worried about the thought of you with nothing to do in this big house alone all day. You know I hid some of the bigger knives, right?"

"There's actually a little more," she continued. "Beth hooked me up with a man named Stemple and it seems he has an old cafeteria space for the mines they closed down and the land behind it. He will let me use the space to start a community center of sorts. I'll be teaching yoga, archery, and a fitness boot camp a few times a week. All it will cost me are some rubber mats for the floor. He'll pick up the cost of the archery gear. I'll do it while Gabriel is in pre-school so I will always be home when he is."

"My God, Felicia! What's next? Run for mayor?"

"No. I checked into it. You have to live here for a certain amount of time, so maybe next year. But I heard sheriff is an elected position, though ..."

#

July 23, 5:12 PM, Mounton, KY

"Hi, Mom. What's up?" Beth said walking into the MacDowell home, kicking her shoes off at the door.

"Not much," Hannah replied from her seat at the kitchen table with her laptop. "Naomi is in the backyard playing."

"NAOMI! GET YOUR STUFF! IT'S TIME TO GO HOME! Thanks for watching her. Jeb couldn't pick her up after school today. Some work thing."

"Yeah, Mac called home, too."

"What'cha doing?" Beth asked, peeking over Hannah's shoulders at the laptop screen. "What?! Why on earth would you want the recipe for a gluten-free pie?"

#

Care Packages

It took Betta Washington—no, Anesthesia, she reminded herself—several months to make all the arrangements asked of her. Once the box of burner phones arrived, she considered her needs and after some extensive research, prepared a quick estimate of costs. She padded the estimate generously, which she guessed The Voice suspected, but didn't comment on. After receiving a small FedEx box full of cash, she purchased the equipment and chemicals she needed from a variety of medical suppliers all over the country, under several aliases, so as to not attract attention. She purchased a prepaid debit card, also under an alias, to purchase the tranquilizer guns and sedatives from an online European supplier who had a reputation for providing quality products with a minimum of questions asked. She had everything shipped to the address of a courier company only to have them deliver it all to the outside of a public storage facility where she didn't even rent a unit. An errant paper trail leading to no paper at all.

The tranquilizer guns she packaged up as instructed into four separate boxes. Included in each box was a computer printout of instructions for both the weapons and the sedatives. The number of guns and darts varied for the different boxes. She then shipped all of them to a variety of, what she thought of as ambiguous addresses.

"What do I do now?" Anesthesia asked the commanding voice over the phone.

"An older RV will be delivered shortly. The main bedroom will be yours. All of the other sleeping options will be for our 'guests.' Set up the IVs and equipment as you see fit. Pack for an extended trip and stay with the RV. I will instruct you where to drive it."

"Then what?" Anesthesia barely contained her lack of excitement about the piecemeal instructions she was getting.

"Then we drop our guests off and you will make sure to keep them completely unconscious until we no longer need them."

"How will I know who is who?"

"It will be abundantly clear once you meet them," The Voice contended without humor. "What is most important is that the older woman, the child, and her father remain undamaged in any way. Those three are important to me in ways you cannot imagine. The others are useful leverage. As long as they are alive. Just keep everyone sedated."

"And then what?"

"Then, my dear Anesthesia, I will reward you for your services and some of our guests will be returned to their loved ones."

"Alive?"

"Does it matter to you?" the voice asked.

"Not particularly."

#

Diners Scarred

Ginny is the biggest man in Mounton, Kentucky. By far. It's very likely not his real name. Inheriting the diner from his mother, Virginia, Ginny built the small restaurant into a destination and staple in the growing tourist town. Word had gotten out to visitors far and wide: no trip through central Kentucky would be complete without a meal at *Ginny's Diner*. Resembling a tattooed, muscle-bound biker more than a diner owner and short-order chef, Ginny was also the gentlest, kindest man in the small mountain community. Until he wasn't.

"Shirley, I'm retreating to the scullery to achieve pastry perfection. You got this?" Ginny checked with the crone sitting behind the cash register.

The morning rush, a mixture of plaid-shirted locals and smiling tourists, thinned to five out-of-towners Ginny didn't recognize. Ginny's waitress, Peg, left after breakfast to give her mom a break from watching her two kids. She would return for lunch.

Shirley, the diner's ancient cashier, looked up from her knitting and peered over her ancient cat's-eye glasses at the three men sitting in the booth and the young couple at the counter. "No problem. Peggy gave 'em their checks before she left. The day I can't handle five customers is the day you can throw dirt on my grave, in the unlikely event you're still around."

"Give a yell if you need me." Ginny smiled. He has never heard the cranky old cashier raise her voice in his entire life. Shirley was an ancient crone back when his mom owned the place. It's rumored they built the diner around her. He ducked his head slightly walking through the door to the kitchen area.

The smiling couple paid Shirley and left, talking about their upcoming afternoon at the coal mine attraction. The three men in the booth watched them leave and rose from their seats.

Ralph Hickman and Mitch Northrup were bigger and thicker than the third, Josh, who was barely more than a teen. The older men looked as if they might have been in shape at some point in their lives, but that day had come and gone many moons ago. While their arms were thick with muscle, their waists were thick from too much alcohol and not enough exercise. Their hair was cut in the buzz-cut style popular 40 years ago, lending more evidence their glory days were long behind them. Josh's hair was too long and greasy, and his acne complexion, made him look younger than he really was. The older two treated him like a pet-in-training.

The youngest and smallest of the three hoods shuffled toward Shirley as the other two walked the length of the diner's counter to the opening at the other end. They quickly slid through the opening and into the kitchen, as the third moved to brush past the ancient cashier.

"Stay put, Grandma," Josh snarled as he tried to slip past her to the kitchen.

"I sure as hell ain't your granny, Snot Nose," not even looking up from her knitting.

"What'd you say to me, bitch?" Loud crashing noises emanated from the kitchen. He glanced at the kitchen door before turning back to Shirley.

Into the bore of a chrome-plated .44 Magnum revolver. A big one.

"You just stay right where you're at, Snot Nose. If Ginny has to deal with more than two of you, he may have to really hurt someone."

"How are you even holding that cannon up?" Snot Nose demanded. "It's bigger than you are."

"You want my arm to get tired?" as she lowered the gun to point at his crotch.

Right then, Mitch the Rat flew through the swinging kitchen door to crash headfirst into the back of the serving counter. Hard. The unconscious would-be robber slid to the floor.

"Okay. Ginny will see you now," Shirley motioned with the gigantic handgun for the thug to go into the kitchen.

The robber looked at the kitchen door, down at his unconscious partner in crime, and back at the 90-pound old lady holding the revolver.

"Uh. I think I'll stay here if it's okay with you," and as an afterthought, "ma'am."

"Smarter than you look, not'd take much. Sit your bony ass over in that booth," motioning to the table closest to the register.

He glanced at his fallen partner before stammering, "Yes, ma'am."

A long silence followed a last crash from the kitchen.

"Do you think he killed Ralphie?" the thug asked meekly.

"Depends. Was Ralphie armed?"

"Just a knife. Armed robbery is serious jail time."

The elderly cashier shook her head and slipped the Magnum back into the enormous handbag under the counter, in easy reach.

"Nah. There's only one left and Ralphie can't weigh more than 220. Ginny probably only bent him a bit. No need to break him. He hates making a mess in his kitchen."

Ginny elbowed the swinging kitchen door open, holding a hand full of zip-ties in his right hand while dragging the unconscious Ralphie by the collar with his other hand. He had zip-tied Ralphie's hands and feet behind him. Ginny hid his surprise of seeing the third man sitting timidly in the booth in front of Shirley.

"Any problem here?"

"Nope," Shirley chirped while redoing a stitch in her knitting. "Me and Snot Hose here were sitting having a little chat about quantum physics. Any problem in the kitchen?"

Ginny dropped Ralphie unceremoniously on the floor next to his equally unconscious partner. "No. The largest dilemma was in locating zip-ties. We don't have any long enough, so I had to zip two or three together to work. You call Mac yet?" kneeling to zip-tie Ralphie's nap mate.

"Do I look like your secretary? You want the sheriff, either call him yourself or wait an hour or two. Him and his boy of his will be in for their free lunch about then."

Ginny frowned at the young man sitting in the booth. "Do we need to put these on you or will you sit there quietly?"

The robber looked at Ginny and then over to Shirley knitting behind the register just inches away from the .44 Magnum. He lowers his gaze in either resignation or to look at his crotch.

"Actually, sir, I'd prefer if you put them on. I don't want any misunderstandings."

July 27, 10:52 A.M., Mounton, KY

"Dad, I don't think this one is breathing," Jeb told his father after they arrive. "Nope. I just saw his eyes flutter. He's good."

Ginny helped Mac and his son, Jeb, load the still unconscious robbers into the bed of Jeb's pickup. The third man assisted all he could, bound as he was, to get up into the bed next to his partners. Jeb watched over the prisoners as Mac and Ginny sauntered into the parking lot to talk privately.

"So, you're sure they were trying to rob you?"

"They weren't registering complaints about the eggs."

"Would it have made a difference?" The sheriff looked over at the two men in the back of his truck with probable concussions.

"Well, the result would have been the same. Luckily, the third guy enjoyed the eggs."

"All joking aside, is Shirley okay?" Mac's voice tinged with genuine concern.

"Well, she did miss a stitch in her knitting, and the last miscreant to make her miss a stitch may be on solid foods any day now, so all in all, I imagine she's fine. What's your proposed course of action for these chuckleheads?"

"Call the staties. Have them come get them," Mac said, rubbing his stubble-free chin. "They'll hold 'em over for trial. We don't have the facilities or manpower to hold them long term."

"I almost feel sorry for the younger thug. After his 'chat' with Shirley, I have a feeling his life of crime has come to an abrupt end."

"Yeah," Mac agreed, "based on what you two have told me, he technically didn't do anything. We can file for assault with a deadly weapon with intent, drunk and disorderly, public nuisance, escaping custody, and assault on an officer, but Shirley may have to press some of the charges on the kid."

"Do you honestly see *that* happening?" Mac smiled.

"No, but I would pay cash money to have seen the kid's face when Shirley aimed her artillery at him. Are you sure that piece is legal?"

Ginny laughed. "It's not only legal, but she has a concealed carry permit for it. You should see her knitting bag. I'd wager there's a howitzer in there."

"Well, charges aside on the kid, she will have to testify at the trial of the other two."

"Mac, I regard you as a brother and will assist you anytime you need me, but please, please, please let me be there when you inform her she has to relinquish her stool."

Returning to the truck, Mac walked up to his son.

"These are the ones from last night? Did you frisk them and read them their rights?"

"Well, him anyway. I patted the other two down, but he's the only one awake enough to acknowledge his rights. Dad, if the other two don't wake up soon, we may have to get these fellas some medical care," his deputy speculated. "What did he hit them with?"

"His fist." Mac turned to the only conscious robber.

"I've heard Ginny and Shirley's account of this and I find pieces of it hard to believe. Do you mean to tell me you three geniuses came in here to rob Ginny WITHOUT a gun?"

"Well, we thought the three of us could take him," said the young, but conscious, thief.

"Son, the three of you couldn't take Shirley, let alone Ginny," Mac held up a large knitting needle. "You're just damned lucky she only aimed a gun at you. That *was* her being gentle."

The young thug looked at the knitting needle until the lightbulb went on behind his eyes and he visibly slumped in the truck bed.

\#

July 27, 6:15 AM, Four and a half hours earlier in Mounton, KY

Jeb sat in the jail cell, handcuffed to a bed in the cell, and waited for his father to show up. He was in no hurry to face the sheriff. More embarrassing than being locked in your own cell, knowing the look of disappointment in his father was far worse. The good news was the cell was escape-proof. Almost. He tried every way conceivable to get out, just to avoid facing his dad, who would be coming on duty in a few short minutes. Shy of finding some other dumbass to trick into letting him out, he was stuck.

Eight hours earlier than that

Davis Williams, one of Mounton County's newest deputies had the afternoon shift that day. Of the four deputies, he was the only black officer in the department. Hell, he was fifty percent of the black male population in the town of Mounton. The other man lived in a plywood lean-to and had a three-legged dog named Lucky. Davis hated it when someone called him African American. Nobody used the term "Scottish American," or "French American." It was just silly. He actually preferred just being thought of as a "man." Which is exactly how Sheriff MacDowell and his deputies treated him. JAPO. Just another peace officer. It may not be true of all the citizens in the small mountain community in Kentucky, but his co-workers treated him like an equal, and for now, he would accept that first step. Besides, from what Jeb told him, the locals did not take to change well. The gas station changed owners twenty-five years ago and the residents still called it *The New Texaco*. Accepting a *brother* and his family may take a bit. But Davis was patient. He wasn't going anywhere. After a decade in D.C., policing in Mounton was so stress-free, it bordered on a vacation.

The call came in about 10:00 P.M. And as much as he hated to do it, Davis called the sheriff for backup. Seems three out-of-town drunks were tearing up *The Digger's Hole Saloon*, the local watering hole, and as confident as he was he could handle it, the sheriff's orders were to call for backup for anything like this. Davis knew he shouldn't count on any of the locals backing up the "Deputy Spook," so he called MacDowell. Mac scheduled Jeb, also a deputy, to cover the night shift in an hour, so he sent him to start his shift early. After a swing and a miss at Jeb, it didn't take long for the drunks to find themselves in Mounton County's only cell.

"So, what now, prints and pix?" Davis asked Jeb. Sheriff MacDowell had headed back home. "These are my first prisoners since taking the job here."

"Nah. The procedures in Mounton are probably a little more lax than D.C., so we don't fingerprint them unless we have to," Jeb replied. "Just collect their wallets and we'll submit their names to the Violent Criminal Apprehension Program database officer in Louisville. You don't even have to mark it urgent. All these fools did was start a bar fight. Given the hour, we probably won't hear back from the ViCAP database until morning. If nothing of importance comes back, Dad will more than likely let them go when they sober up. If anything pings, we can always charge them with drunk and disorderly, public nuisance, resisting arrest, blah, blah, blah."

Davis finished up his shift keying in the I.D. info into the station's only computer.

"Alright, I appreciate the help." Jeb suggested, "Go home to your beautiful family and get some rest. You have the 3:00 to 11:00 shift again tomorrow, right?"

"Yeah," Davis said, pulling on his coat. "Dawes went out of town, took the family down to Mammoth Caves. You'll be back on split-shift days in no time. Give me a call if you need a hand with the Dillinger Gang in there. I'm just a few minutes down the road."

"Buddy, *everything* is just a few minutes down the road here."

#

July 27, 5:17 AM, Mounton, KY

"Dude! I am gonna hurl!"

Jeb looked toward the smallest prisoner folded over in the cell and chewed his lower lip in worry. He knew it was against the rules to let a prisoner out of the cage without backup, but it was 5:00 in the morning and he didn't want to wake up his dad or any of the other deputies just to help with a guy recycling Jack Daniels. His dad and Davis shared his opinion the prisoners would probably sleep it off till morning, but now the young thug was up and moaning while clutching his stomach. The other two laid on two bunks in the cell faces turned away from their ailing partner. Jeb didn't want the other two prisoners locked in a small room full of vomit, nor did he want to clean up the cell floor. The detainee in question was the youngest and smallest of the bunch and Jeb figured he could handle him easily.

He locked his weapon in the gun safe, pulled an asp (a telescoping, steel baton), from the desk, grabbed the keys and moved toward the cell. He wasn't about to let the man take his firearm away. Taking a last look at the two prone prisoners, he unlocked the door and moved aside for the sick drunk to step from the cell.

"Out."

Jeb edged into the cell to assist the sick prisoner to the restroom. When he turned to grab the man by the arm, he heard a slight noise from behind and the lights went out.

Jeb woke an hour later, handcuffed to a cot, with his own handcuffs. The cell door was within reach but locked. His radio, asp, wallet, and keys were taken by the prisoners. His head was pounding and now *he* had the urge to throw up. Worse was the fear of his father arriving in a few hours and finding him this way. He had seen his father angry very few times in his life.

His mother once told him a story about a time before she and Mac were even married. His father, still in the military, ran up against a drunk private, twice his father's size. The drunk took a swing at Jeb's dad, while Mac walked Hannah back to her hotel. His dad's MP uniform more than likely inspired the unprovoked attack. MacDowell dodged the swing easily, but the next roundhouse clipped Hannah on the shoulder, knocking her down. His dad turned toward the drunk quietly, his face turned to granite. Faster than the eye could follow, he thrust his flattened hand toward the drunk, jamming him in the throat with the hollow between his thumb and index finger. The drunk gagged, clutched his throat, while his father calmly unclipped his radio and called for an ambulance and more MPs.

When the MPs arrived, they interrogated Jacob, "How did you know that wouldn't kill him?"

"I didn't."

The other time his father's temper burned into Jeb's mind was a few years later when Mac walked into the living room, just as young Jeb was angrily back-talking his mother. This was years before Child Services would have arrested Mac for corporal punishment, but it took two days for Jeb to sit down easily. He never sassed his mother again. Worse than the spanking was the way his father looked at him for the next few days.

As Jeb sat on one of the cell's two cots, handcuffed to the edge, he contemplated his future. Getting fired from the sheriff's office was a prospect. Hell, criminal neglect, malfeasance, and even real jail time were possibilities. Worse than any of those probabilities was seeing the disappointment on his father's face. Forty-three minutes from now.

July 27, 6:45 AM, Mounton, KY

"Jeb? You here?" Sheriff MacDowell called out to his son as he entered the sheriff's office. There was a possibility his son may be out on his last rounds, but unlikely since they had 'guests' in-house. The official SUV sat parked outside, but not Jeb's truck. Maybe Jeb was called out, but Mac had left strict instructions to call for backup, if for no other reason than to keep an eye on the prisoners. And he would have taken the department's SUV.

The silence was ominous. There were only two deputy desks, a smaller desk with the computer on it and a big oak number for paperwork. Jeb was at neither. Mac's concern grew until he glanced at the solitary cell.

"Hey, Dad," Jeb chirped meekly, handcuffed to the cot.

"Uh ... hey, Jeb, what's new?"

"Oh, you know. Same ole, same ole," Jeb said trying to lighten the circumstances with humor.

"Did we release the drunks?"

"In a manner of speaking."

Mac walked to the cell door and opened it with his own set of keys. He pulled a rolling office chair in to face Jeb, whom he left handcuffed to the cot. Thinking about this, Jeb decided it was not a good sign.

"Care to tell me what happened?" Mac asked.

"Not really, but I guess I have to," Jeb replied.

For the next 25 minutes, Jeb replayed the events of the night to his father as Mac's face slowly contorted into a grimace.

Several moments passed as the two men sat facing each other, one in handcuffs, the other lost in thought.

"Son, did I ever tell you about The Great Porno Robbery?"

"Uh ... no."

#

The Great Porno Robbery - Thirty-Seven Years Ago

Dingus Hemsworth and I couldn't have been more than a biscuit past 12 or 13 years old when he came up with the Great Plan. We was gonna purloin us some nudey magazines from the PX. Our daddies were stationed on Okinawa for a bit, on a base where they allowed families to live. After ya played on the beach some and talked to the few girls with daddies stationed there as well, there wasn't much else to get into. Boys being boys, and Dingus being Dingus, he decided we needed to further our education. He told me if I didn't go along, I was just a Nancy-boy chicken. So, of course, I had to do it. He was the distraction and lookout, being the brains of this heist, and I was going to make the snatch, pardon the pun.

So, the MPs hauled us away fifteen minutes later.

Dingus's daddy being the base commander and all, Dingus got a free ride and was immediately released to his daddy's custody. Knowing Dingus the way I did, probably meant he would be in trouble again by dinnertime. It was already 5:00 P.M. The MPs informed me they were now going to call my dad. I must have turned green at the mention as they just stared at me with sincere concern. I confessed to murder, arson, and grand theft to try and get them to send me to prison. For life. Anything, but do not call my dad.

But call him they did. And to their surprise, and my relief, he told them to keep me. The MPs fed me and made sure I had a cell all my own and left me there to ponder the day's events. I bet I didn't sleep two winks all night. I didn't know what prison was like, but I was well aware of my father's wrath and I was feeling like I would look pretty damned good in orange.

9:00 A.M. rolled around and my father walked into the MP station.

"Top," the senior MP hailed my dad with the shortened form of Top Kick. He was only a sergeant, but his reputation preceded him and far exceeded his rank.

The two of them stepped into the back office for a while and I assumed it was to discuss my permanent incarceration.

"So, what's your side of this?" my dad asked when he returned.

I tried to be a man and just face up to it. I'm not ashamed to admit there may have been a tear or two running down my face as I told him the whole story. I minimized Dingus's role because Daddy raised me to believe a man is responsible for his own actions. When it was all said and done, I looked down at the floor and waited for my judgment. At a minimum, a major ass whoopin' was not beyond the realm of imagination.

#

July 27, 7:42 AM, Mounton, KY

"Well? What happened?" Jeb was so engrossed in this story of his father's past, he temporarily forgot his handcuffs and predicament.

"Jeb, I said all that, to say all this," Mac drawled. "I'm gonna tell you what he told me ... 'Son, ya fucked up. Get over it.'"

Mac got up, unlocked Jeb's handcuffs, and pushed the office chair back to the desk.

"So that's it? You're not sore at me or nothin'?"

"Do you know where you screwed up?" Mac asked.

"Uh ... yeah."

"Are you going to do it again?"

"No, sir."

"Then you learned a lesson and we don't have to talk about it again. Especially not in front of your momma. If she ever finds out you let them three drunks hit you and cuff you to the bunk, I will have to hear about it. Forever. Nope. This is *old* news," Mac told his son.

"What did *you* learn from The Great Porno Robbery?" Jeb posed to his father.

"I actually learned a great many things," Mac began. "The first thing I learned from the MPs is you can uphold the law and still temper it with some compassion and kindness. Secondly, I learned my old man was smarter than I was, and to be a real man doesn't always mean being a hard ass. Thirdly, I learned Dingus Hemsworth wasn't much of a friend and a crummy sneak thief."

Jeb smiled but kept quiet.

Mac walked toward the front door of the station. "Whataya say we go find them desperadoes before they do something stupid like tangle with your momma?"

#

July 27, 10:45 A.M., Mounton, KY

The two MacDowell men patrolled Mounton for a couple of hours. Pretty thoroughly, given the town itself was only about four streets. It took them twice as long since they used Mac's Bronco to keep from alerting the trio if they saw the sheriff's official SUV patrolling. Jeb had set the station phone to forward to both their cell phones but not the sheriff's radio band. Before leaving, he checked the computer for the results of the ViCAP database search. The results hadn't come back in yet, so the two set out to find the wayward drunks, now accused of assaulting a peace officer and escape, on top of their other crimes. Before leaving the station, Jeb collected his handgun from the safe.

At about 10:45 A.M., Mac's cell phone rang.

"Ginny. Seems like there might have been little dust-up at the diner."

"Think it was our guys?" Jeb speculated.

"Don't know. Might've been. You know Ginny, he doesn't elaborate unless he can get in 43 syllables. Then you usually don't want him to. Let's go see."

#

July 27, 11:29 A.M., Mounton, KY

Mac and Jeb secured the three prisoners they had collected from *Ginny's Diner*, back into the cell at the station.

"Call Beth and ask her if she could come over and check these two out. Seems Ginny didn't care to be robbed today. Guess our boys here wanted a little spending cash for their way outta town. They're still unconscious. Like as not, they may need some real medical attention," Mac told his son. "I'll call Hannah and get her to look after Naomi for a bit after school. I'm sure she won't put up a fight about babysitting."

"Beth's on her way over and the ViCAP report came back. Seems like our friends in there have a laundry list of priors and warrants."

"Better call KSP to come pick them up," Mac suggested. "You can begin the paperwork on processing and charging these gentlemen. You can print and photo the thug still conscious. Get him some dry clothes. I think he may have wet himself a little at Ginny's place. And Jeb, if you want to minimize your little fracas here last night, I won't mind. No need to give the staties a chuckle."

"No, sir. As you say, I 'fucked up.' Might as well be a man and step up to it."

"Well, I also said to keep this from your momma. Aside from the language, the state troopers may get a laugh at your expense, but your momma will *not* see the humor in you getting walloped in the melon. I guarantee it. And while you are her baby and the father to her grandbabies, I will be the lucky devil to have to hear it. For a long, long time. You want to keep this quiet."

"So, now may be a good time to talk about getting another computer?" Jeb questioned with a grin.

"Don't push it, boy. You are still on son-probation. I may be your daddy, but I am also your boss and I suddenly feel the urge to change the duty roster. How does a month of night shifts sound?"

"Sounds like Mom doesn't need to know a thing about last night."

#

As he was dialing the phone for the state police, Jeb asked, "Hey, Dad, whatever became of Dingus?"

"Became a full bird colonel."

"Wow! Pretty impressive." Jeb's eyes opened wide.

"Not really. It was in the Air Force."

#

July 27, 12:01 P.M., Mounton, KY

"Hey, Ginny, what's shakin' big guy?" His first lunch customers greeted him as they entered the diner for lunch, tipping their hats to Shirley.

"Same ole."

"What's for lunch?"

"Today's special is shrimp gumbo. We were going to have beignets for dessert but I ran out of time," Ginny said in an apologetic tone.

"Piss poor time management if you ask me," Shirley grumbled under her breath.

"Come again, Shirl?" a regular customer asked, not sure he heard her correctly.

"Ya just can't keep that boy's head in the kitchen. His mother always had time to make dessert. He just can't handle any little distraction," Shirley ranted. "Hey! Has anyone seen my other knittin' needle?"

#

Great Calls of Fire

"Sheriff's office."

"Sheriff MacDowell, please."

"Speaking."

"Hi there, Sheriff. I don't know if you remember me. This is Devin Douvez. I'm the Commonwealth's attorney. We met at a law enforcement conference a few years ago."

"Hello, Mr. Douvez."

"Please call me Devin."

"Alright. How can I help you, Devin?"

"I'm not quite sure. Is there anything I should know about some of your recent cases we're trying here?"

"Nothing I can think of. Why?"

Bertrand hesitates. "I am noticing a few of your cases seem to be non-starters. Normally, you have a great conviction rate, but a few cases have come across my desk which seem to be ... what's the word I'm looking for? Hinky. When something is screwy with a case, I get itchy. The fact of the matter is, so many things are screwy right now, I am getting a case of psoriasis."

"This Jeb MacDowell on the speakerphone. What's so screwy, Mr. Douvez?"

"Like I told the sheriff, call me Devin, son. Well, frankly, it's your cases. I drew the Sylvester Reston case. The van full of opiates you guys caught them with: possession, intent to distribute, drawing down on you two. Remember?"

"Oh, yeah," Jeb remembered. "The boys from Chicago a while back. What about it?"

"A public defender friend of mine gets this anonymous letter in the interoffice mail. All it communicated was the case number and *Illegal Search & Seizure. Questions about how the vehicle broke down. Police harassment. Non-LEO weapons fire. Destruction of private property.* I don't think much of it. Maybe a family member with a semester of criminal law or a record and they don't want any attention from the authorities. I do a little research, but the PD writes some motions, pretty weak sauce to tell you the truth. But the next thing I know, we have to drop the case. Just isn't solid enough in the face of the questions posed in the email."

"We got those guys dead to rights. There was no harassment, and the non-law enforcement officer was my mom who fired a shot and blew out their tire while they held us at gunpoint," Jeb challenged defensively.

"Pretty much how I read it, too, but I scratched up an *L* and moved on. Until a day before yesterday, I get another of your cases. The diner robbers. I'm all set to talk to these guys' attorney, a different PD, about copping a plea when this time I get a late-night letter via interoffice mail. Same thing. Anonymous and pretty much untraceable. This file read, *Police brutality as proven in the photos. Register and cash untouched. Innocent man kidnapped at gunpoint.* Seems like there was another man there, who was innocent of any wrongdoing at all, kidnapped by a female diner employee at gunpoint. Well, maybe 'held against his will' would be more accurate. Seems like the diner robbers claimed police brutality and based on the pictures of their faces and bruises, they got a walk. They're threatening to sue the diner, you, and the county.

"Now I love a good robbery case and all, but this is starting to smell really bad. I get a hold of a guy down at the FBI office. You know Dave? Anyway, no prints on the letter. No DNA on the envelope gumming. Printed via computer with Times New Roman font. Multi-purpose paper you can buy in a million places. Bupkus. I know someone is screwing up these cases, but I am legally obligated to do everything I can to investigate all of this. Same thing again. More cases are dropped as 'unwinnable.'

"Even your murdering mayor case got tossed. Which is BS. At first, we had to drop it to second-degree murder since we couldn't prove he was lying in wait. The anonymous letter to his attorney mentioned *illegal search and seizure, lack of probable cause* to search his vehicle, which got the post-hole digger and DNA tossed out, and even political bias and election tampering. I have been in this game a couple dozen years and I can see holes you could drive a truck through."

"Even Jarvis? We got DNA, the weapon, motive, opportunity, and practically a confession. As for the diner, we never even touched those guys. The owner of the diner defended himself against two robbers with knives. The *kidnapping* was a little old lady at the cash register keeping the third robber from ganging up on the owner." As he spoke, Jeb looked at his father. "What is going on here Mr. Douvez?"

"I don't know, gentlemen. The DNA lab backlog is months away from catching up. The weapon is in question because of how it was found. As to motive, the victim was a union rep for a defunct mining operation, so plenty of unemployed and disgruntled men who had the opportunity could have killed him. 'Practically confessing,' was before you read him his Miranda rights. But now I smell it and out of curiosity, I check to see what else has popped up from your county. Turns out a few public defenders received letters similar to mine. Eager as public defenders are to clear cases, they followed up and filed motions. All of your cases got tossed."

"Hmph."

"Yeah, right, I know. Overall, it paints a picture of everything from sloppy police work to damn near criminal malfeasance. The reason I'm calling is, I know your reputation, Sheriff. I met you and you seem like a pretty squared-away LEO. If I didn't know better, I would say someone is trying to discredit you and your people. Like I said, either these cases were crap, to begin with or someone is stacking the deck for some very hinky reasons."

"Who do you think could be behind this, Devin?"

"Got any enemies, Sheriff?"

"None capable of this."

"Well, someone is taking an interest in you. Do me a favor and 'we never spoke' okay?

"No problem, Devin, I won't forget this."

"Please do."

July 30, 1:47 P.M., Mounton, KY

"Sheriff's office," Mac answered into his cell phone.

"Mac?"

"Hannah? Everything okay? Something wrong with Naomi?" Mac's mind raced with all the possibilities. Hannah almost never called him during the day. She was usually too busy with work of her own. His cell phone with enough signal to even take the call was a surprise.

"Naomi is fine. But something has happened. No one's hurt, but ..." Hannah began.

"But what?" Mac asked.

"It looks as though someone smashed up the tractor last night. I came out to use it to pull some of those big stump pieces and someone had trashed the motor."

"No chance it was an accident?" Mac knew the answer. Hannah would have never called him if she thought it was.

"No. Not unless an accident would have scattered the parts for forty feet."

Someone is trying to send a message. Who and what message?

"I'm on my way. Call the insurance company and get them started on this."

"I already tried them," Hannah moaned. "Seems they will have to investigate deliberate destruction to make sure we didn't do it to get a new tractor. It could take months to get it replaced. Tried to tell them it was our only tractor and we need it to keep this farm working. They were very sympathetic and said they would send someone out in a week or so and to not touch anything."

"They *do* know I'm the sheriff, right?" Mac fumed.

"They sounded like you being sheriff was why they were so suspicious. They sort of hinted someone may have said something about you to make them extra suspicious. Any clues as to why?"

More of the same message.

"No, baby. Just sit tight and we'll be right there."

"Mac," Hannah continued. "There's more. Some guy I never saw before came by asking for you. Looks like he was a process server.

Guess Adrian was right about his kids."

Boy, combine this with what Devin Douvez just called about and this was truly shaping up to be a special day. Not the birthday-sex-kind-of-special either. A little more in the farms-barely-making-it, someone's-sabotaging-your-cases, wrecked-tractor, and-you're-being-sued sort of way.

Forget the governor offer, I wonder what a rewarding career in the fast food industry would be like?

#

July 30, 4:37 P.M., Mounton, KY

"Did you receive the package?" the mechanically altered voice inquired of Neville Jarvis.

"Yes."

"The money and the included instructions for the trucks?"

"Yes. I know what to do. Could you please explain why we're doing all this? This 'need to know' crap is wearing a little thin," Jarvis complained.

"I could, but what I do, and how I do it, is for your protection as well as mine."

"Fine. We'll play by your rules. I guess it's better than life in prison, anyway."

"Correct, Mr. Jarvis. All the pieces are in place. It's time to make the opening gambit. Do you remember the chess game we talked about, Mr. Jarvis? Do you know what God's grandmaster does in his first few moves?"

"Uh ... no."

"He puts his pieces on the board. I have already reversed my opponent's past successes into failures and remade them into my own assets in this game. My knights, a queen, even a bishop like yourself. Even your own pawns. Then he removes his opponent's pieces from the board before he even knows he is in the game. Not only am I many moves ahead of him, but I am also making multiple aggressive moves simultaneously. The next move is to clear all his pieces from the board. All at once."

"I take it we're playing against Sheriff MacDowell?" Jarvis

assumed.

"Not WE, dear Neville, I. I am God's grandmaster. You are simply a single chess piece."

"Okay," Jarvis accepted, "When do we start making the real money?"

"We are on the cusp of enriching our coffers almost immediately," The Voice explained. **"This is a key component of our little game. It is not enough to destroy the opponent, we must also prepare to ascend."**

"Ascend? What the hell are you talking about?" Jarvis snarled into the burner phone.

"A part of the game even a bishop need not know, dear Jarvis."

"As long as we take care of that dumbass MacDowell and make a truckload of money."

"A truckload indeed."

#

Contacted the same as Sly, Ralph Hickman received puzzling packages full of burner phones and even more puzzling instructions. The Voice seemed to know a hell of a lot about Ralph and his friends and their curiously quick release from the state holding facility. The Voice even took credit when all the charges for their attempted robbery of the diner in Mounton vanished.

Ralph couldn't figure it out, even after the public defender had explained it to them, but someone suddenly dropped the assault, the robbery, drunk and disorderly, and kidnapping charges. Not one to look a gift horse in the mouth, Ralph and his two partners in crime did what any newly released prisoners would do: go straight to a bar. In their cases, their bar was in Lexington, Kentucky. A day or two after their release, Ralph had received the box of phones, some money, and a call from the mechanically altered voice. It didn't take long for Ralph to look at the box of phones, the strange dropping of charges, his lack of plans and options, and the packet of money, to agree to work for The Voice on the other end. He and his pals, all unemployed with no foreseeable prospects, and as The Voice had said, "possessed a certain moral ambiguity." Whatever the hell that meant. Ralph just knew this was easy money when they had none. *If this panned out, I would have no problem keeping 'Licia in that fancy private school my bitch of an ex-wife enrolled her in. Hell! I might even make a few of the alimony payments she was always bitchin' about. Ha! Who am I kiddin'?*

All paths led Ralph and his two partners to be in Mounton County at a certain location and time where they would receive further instructions. Instructions arrived in two cardboard boxes with three uniforms and an equal number of tranquilizer dart guns in the front of a garbage truck loaded with narcotics.

#

July 30, 5:15 P.M., Mounton, KY

"Sheriff's office."

"Sheriff MacDowell?"

"Speaking. How can I help you?" Mac looked at the caller ID to see the number was a Frankfort exchange.

"Sheriff, this is Samuel Jearns." It never even occurred to him to remind the sheriff who he represented or where they had met. He just assumed meeting him was memorable. "I need to speak with you about the discussion we had a few months ago."

"I remember." Mac had given very little thought to the offer of running for governor. Mac searched his memory as to which man Jearns was. Oh, yeah. Jearns ran Altria, funded by Phillip Morris. "I've been meaning to give you fellas a call."

"I'm glad I reached out to you then. I'm afraid, Sheriff, given all the negative press lately, we may have to look elsewhere for a viable candidate for governor. Being under investigation and with all the libelous accusations, which I am certain someone fabricated. I'm sure you understand."

Mac gave it a second to let what the man from Altria just told him sink in. After a deep, calming breath Mac told him in a forced drawl, "Yepper. I reckon I shore do, Mr. Jearns. We certainly can't have any unfounded accusations dirtying up the sterling reputation of Big Tobacco, now can we?"

"Now, Sheriff, there is no need to—"

"Mr. Jearns," Mac smirked on his end of the phone, "do you want to talk about fishin'? Cuz we're done talking about this."

Click. Mac set the receiver to the office phone into the cradle.

And that is why the telephone is the best invention ever made. With the push of a single button, you can put a stop to Stupidity.

#

Keep on Trucking

August 2, 10:14 A.M., Mounton County, KY

Syrus didn't understand it, but he followed Jarvis's orders anyway. He and his brothers "procured" four garbage trucks and cleaned them as instructed.

"But why just clean the insides?" Syrus whined to Jarvis over the burner phone.

"Because ... nobody looks twice at a garbage truck. And nobody would even think about inspecting the inside of a dirty truck. Garbage haulers and lack of inspections mean you won't need a commercial driver's license, a bill of lading, manifests, or even need to stop at weigh stations. They are better than invisible. They invite avoidance," Jarvis replied as though all of this was his idea and not The Voice's. "Did you leave the packages on the front seats of the particular trucks as you were told?"

"Yeah. What's in 'em? And why couldn't we use our semi?"

"You mean the semi used for a legitimate enterprise and the sheriff is familiar with? As to the packages, you'll find out at the proper time." The truth was, Jarvis didn't know what was in the boxes. He was just relaying orders as he received them from The Voice.

After the call from Jarvis, Syrus wasn't happy taking orders from the former mayor, but he and his brothers did as they were told. He had to admit the garbage truck hustle was pretty slick. They parked the four trucks at the assigned locations outside Mounton, where they were unlikely to be found for a few days. Then they went back to their shack to await more orders. Just as his brothers followed his lead due to recognizing his superior intellect, well, *superior* to theirs anyway, Syrus acknowledged Jarvis's leadership. He didn't cotton to it, but the money they had received so far spent easily enough. It wasn't much money, but it was more than Syrus had ever managed to finagle in any of his previous schemes. Leastways, he figured if at any point he didn't care for what Jarvis was selling, he and his brothers would just 'go to Plan B.'

#

179

August 5, 3:23 P.M., Mounton County, KY

Sly and his crew were on edge. They hated being in Mounton County, especially in a U-Haul moving van packed to the gills with drugs. The Voice had instructed and financed them to buy up all the product they could get their hands on, as long as the price was right. Then to rent a truck, under an assumed name, and drive everything down to a number of locations in Mounton County, Kentucky.

The big bruiser Sheriff MacDowell had thought of as "Kong" sat on the outside of the bench seat next to Grady Noble, Sly's other thug, and Sly himself in the driver's seat. His eyes, wide with apprehension, bounced from the view out the window to the rearview mirrors.

"Jefe, you sure we ain't gonna get popped for this?"

"Nah, man. I told you. We drop part of the shipment to four different trucks out in the middle of nowhere." Sly sounded as if he were trying to convince himself more than his boys. He wondered if the risk was worth the reward. The money would set their families up for a long time, but what would happen to them if they got caught?

Grady, jammed in the seat between Sly and Kong, looked at the GPS in his hands.

"The first truck should be around here somewhere," he glanced between the windshield and the GPS. "There! What the ...? It looks like a nasty, old garbage truck."

"Yeah, man. Dat's it," Sly affirmed as if he had known all along what to look for.

After parking the truck relatively close to the garbage truck, the three Chicagoans climbed out of the moving van cab and approached the garbage truck cab warily, guns out.

"Looks clear," Kong proclaimed.

Sly snatched open the driver's side door and spied the large box on the bench seat. Opening the box, he found a list of typed instructions and three uniform coveralls.

"Says here we are to unload a quarter of the product into the back of this truck, take these uniforms, and drop off the rest of the goods at three more trucks. Says to put on these work gloves so as to not leave prints." Sly lowered the paper and thought about what could go wrong. Finding no immediate flaw in the instructions, turned to his boys. "Okay. Let's get dis shit unloaded and get outta here. The longer we are in one spot, the more chance some yokel will stumble across us, up to our asses in Oxy."

"Sly, who is leaving these instructions and all this?" Kong asked.

"I dunno, hermano. But so far, everyt'ing dey said been right on da money. And da money been good." Sly didn't tell his compatriots about the small slice he had skimmed off for himself when purchasing the drugs.

"If you think it's okay, then it's okay with me. I trust you, jefe."

#

August 6, 11:17 A.M., St. Louis, MO

Syrus and his brothers unloaded part of their garbage truckload of narcotics, as instructed, to an unnamed group of men in Columbus. Syrus was uncertain about just handing over the drugs without getting any cash, but The Voice had said to, and after all, they were his drugs. It just didn't seem right. The 185-mile drive from Mounton had taken them more than half the day, staying about five miles above the speed limit. They paid cash for a seedy motel room with the garbage truck parked right behind their room, out of view of the highway. The Stampers took turns sleeping in the truck to guard it. The next afternoon they met with their contact in Cleveland as instructed and handed off the rest of the narcotics. The outsides of the trucks were nasty and gross, but while the insides still smelled of old garbage, they were clean enough to transport Saran-wrapped and Ziploc'd bags of drugs. Nobody would snoop too close to the smelly trucks.

Syrus didn't know others were handling nearly identical transactions in Cincinnati, Memphis, and Indianapolis by Ralph Hickman and friends, the Chicagoans, and Neville Jarvis. The resulting profits from the deals were astronomical. Hickman and his compatriots and the Stampers both thought they were the only conduits. Only Sly and his crew had a small idea of the quantities and economies of scale because they had dropped the drugs at the trucks originally. None of them knew the identities or schedules of the others. Jarvis knew of the Stampers since he had recruited them, but nothing of the Chicagoans or Hickman and his crew.

Every week at random intervals, the trucks left Mounton for various cities within 400 miles or so. In between, Sly and his crew would purchase drugs from Chicago and Detroit and deliver them to the trucks in Mounton, which were parked in different places each time. Soon, Jarvis was purchasing narcotics from Atlanta, so The Voice was not reliant on the Chicagoans as his only pipeline.

Syrus was oblivious to all the other details, and even though he didn't see the cash from the drugs, he knew this was a very profitable operation. He and his brothers were making better money than they ever had before, but before this was done, he intended to make it all.

#

August 13, 10:26 P.M., Indianapolis, IN

Ralph, Mitch, and Josh delivered the second half of a garbage truck full of Oxy to The Voice's contacts in Indianapolis. The first half of the load went to some equally shady characters in Cincinnati. The Voice hadn't given him any names and ordered him to not divulge his own. This was their second run to both Indianapolis and Cincinnati and Ralph had been doing some mental calculations on the retail value of the two truckloads. The cash they received was good, but nowhere near the street value of the product they were carrying. He grabbed a fresh burner phone from the glove compartment as Mitch drove them and the big truck back to its drop-off point in Kentucky where they had left Josh's car.

After a few rings and a few clicks, presumably, to initiate the voice scrambler, the hidden mastermind behind it all answered.

"Hello?"

"We handled Indianapolis and Cincinnati. We're coming back with the truck." Ralph's voice was weary from all the miles of the day and the ones yet to come.

"Very good, Mr. Hickman. Expect your compensation packets in the usual manner."

"Uh, yeah. 'bout that," Ralph started quietly, unsure how to approach the subject. "Seems like our *compensation* isn't quite on par, I guess you could say, with the risk we are taking, or the payday from all these *deliveries*. I got a family to support you know. Now that we got the trucks, the routes, and the general plan, what exactly do you bring to the party besides a creepy phone voice?"

"Oh, Mr. Hickman. I actually predicted you had the highest possibility of challenging my authority, but only by a slight margin. You don't actually have a *whole* family, do you? Your ex-wife left, but not before suing for child support," The Voice stated. Ralph didn't know where he was heading, but let him continue. "Now, let's see, what do I bring to the party? Well, I manage the transactions so neither you, nor our distributors, risk getting caught with the money and/or product, in the same location. I know the best personnel for distribution. I arrange for the product in the trucks. I provide all the up-front cash. I plan and arrange routes to avoid local entanglements. I arrange for distribution in secondary markets with less well-funded law enforcement and anti-narcotics capabilities. I coordinate not only you and your associates but several groups in similar endeavors. If those reasons were not enough, I have one more."

Ralph, feeling like a kid who had challenged his father: "What's else?"

"185 North Ashland."

Man, Ashland sounds familiar. "And what the hell is that?" Ralph was getting defensive and angry at losing control of the conversation.

"185 North Ashland, Mr. Hickman, is the address to Ashland Elementary School in Lexington, where your daughter attends school. Lovely girl. I could give you the address to your ex-wife's house, but I doubt you would care much about her well-being. But as derelict as you are as a father, I seriously doubt you would want any harm to come to little Alicia-Ann. But I could be wrong. If I am, please feel free to explore your options. You may also feel free to inform your compatriots I have similar addresses for them."

Shit!

"I will take your silence as acceptance of 'what I bring to the

party.' There is another item to discuss. If you make me speak this long, or candidly, on the phone again, without further discussion, I will hand this address, and many more, over to some associates who would rather enjoy visiting them. Do I make myself clear, Mr. Hickman? Do we have an understanding?"**

Grinding his teeth and looking sidelong at his two partners, Ralph whispered into the phone, "Yeah."

"I am afraid I will need you to say it, Mr. Hickman."

"Yes. We have an understanding." Whipped dogs had more enthusiasm.

"Now that we have had this conversation, you may notice your compensation packets slightly lighter due to this unseemly challenge of my value and authority. Good day, Mr. Hickman."

Click.

"Everything all good?" asked Mitch as he drove, glancing at his partner.

"Naw. Everything ain't all good. It's downright shitty," Ralph fumed.

"So, a 'hard no' on the extra paydays?" Mitch wondered.

"Yeah, not only ain't we gettin' any extra money, but this dickhead has us by the short and curlies. He's shortin' our cut for even asking. And if you think a shorter carrot sucks, wait till you hear 'bout the stick."

Ralph relayed the conversation to his partners. He usually wouldn't have been so open with them, but they had heard how he opened the conversation and he didn't want either of them to get any bright ideas and end up with Alicia paying for it.

Mitch stared out the windshield. Ralph bristled with anger. *Somebody somewhere needed to get hurt.*

Josh, who had sat quietly between the two men during the entire thing, began to wonder what he had gotten himself into, and more importantly, how he could get himself out. Suddenly, wasting time in school didn't seem so bad.

#

August 7, 6:53 A.M., Mounton, KY

"We had your basic night here," Dawe gave Mac and Jeb his report on the night before as they reported in for work.

"Not much here in the county itself. Couple of dead roadkill deer out on 44, which I am lovingly leaving for the day shift to clean up. Some fools stole three used garbage trucks out of Atlanta, and one from Nashville last week. Must have been real geniuses, because Waste Management parked a half dozen brand new ones they just purchased next to them, but our brain trusts left them alone, taking the old ones instead. APD and NPD put out BOLOs but doesn't sound like they are expecting anything to come of it. Probably a frat hazing. Cincinnati and Louisville police sent out an email saying Oxy busts are on an uptick. Herman Watson called in and complained about some strange lights on his hunting lease property, you know, down by 55 and Little Union Road. It was chasing off all the game. He's convinced it was UFOs. Do we have a UFO form? I couldn't find it."

"Bottom left file drawer," Jeb said with a smile. "It's right next to the Elvis sighting forms."

"Hey, don't be mocking The King. He's coming back. That explains it, though. I never go in to those drawers. I thought you kept all your profits from the meth lab there," Dawe laughed.

"Ow."

"Too soon?"

"Only if you expect a night off this month," Jeb replied.

"Louisville and Cinci have any explanations for the increase?" Mac questioned Dawe.

"Nah. My guess, people finally realized they're living in Cincinnati and felt the need to self-medicate."

"Too redundant," Jeb joked. "But thanks, Dawe. It's always a pleasure to come in and start our day with your overnight reports. They perk my day right up."

"Serve and protect, baby! Always been my motto."

"If you and Costello are through, we do need to get out and about. This county's not going to patrol itself, you know. Dawe, isn't Patty-

Jane expecting you home?" Mac said.

"I'll go home when I'm good and ready," Dawe stated with authority.

Both Mac and Jeb stared at the skinny deputy with dead-faced expressions.

"Okay then. Now I'm good and ready," Dawe stated, as he grabbed his hat from the hat tree by the door. Patty-Jane's ire was as famous as Dawe's affection for her. "Oh, and Jeb?"

"Yeah?"

"Have fun with them deer out there on 44."

#

August 7, 7:23 P.M., Mounton, KY

"You want us to WHAT?" Syrus Stamper hissed at Neville Jarvis over the burner phone.

"It's not what I want, it's what you're gonna do," Neville asserted with as much authority as he could. "At a pre-arranged time and place, you are going to kidnap Ginny Burton."

"Ginny? As in 'Ginny-who-owns-the-diner-Ginny'?"

"The very same."

"Neville, I gotta tell ya, up 'n till now, this has all been fun 'n games. The boys 'n I appreciate the cash, running truckloads of shit to Ohio and back is cool, but kidnapping is a life sentence. Kidnapping Ginny Burton is pretty near a death sentence. As tough as we may be, I don't figure the three of us could take the big sumbitch in a fight, fair or otherwise."

Syrus looked at his two brothers. Spence moved a toothpick to the other side of his mouth and almost imperceptibly shook his head no. Sonny watched a lizard climb up a tree. Neville wanted to talk to the Stampers and arranged a meeting out in the woods, several miles from their continually operating stills.

"Syrus, there won't be a fight. You just sneak up and shoot him with a dart from these tranquilizer guns. I have already loaded three guns for you. You just go to where I tell you and when you get the text on this phone, pop him." Neville explained it as if to an imbecile. Which may not have been too far from the truth in his opinion.

"I don't know ..."

"Trust me, Syrus. There's a big bonus in it for the three of you. This is critical to the plan. Just follow these instructions and deliver his big sleeping ass to this spot in the woods at this time. There'll be an RV there to pick him up," Neville insisted, handing him some directions.

"I guess," Syrus agreed. "Get close, wait for the text, shoot him, then drop him off. Don't sound so hard, I reckon."

Sonny made a grab for the lizard on the tree and missed.

#

Kids Napped

The texts went out almost simultaneously. "GO!"

#

"Hey, Dad?" Jeb called his father on the radio.

"Yepper?"

"Naomi's school just called and they need someone to pick her up. I guess she's not feeling well. They are trying to get a hold of Beth at the clinic, but I'm pretty close. I told them I would just swing by and get her. You okay?"

"Absolutely. Give her a kiss from Pappaw."

"Will do. If you hear from Beth, let her know. You think it's okay to drop Naomi off with Mom until Beth gets off work?"

"In what world do think Hannah would not relish a chance to spoil her only grandbaby? But, if Naomi isn't feeling well, maybe you should just take the day off. Not like there'll be a crime wave in Mounton today. I'll get the boss to okay some unscheduled time off. Oh. Wait. I *AM* the boss. Permission granted," Mac chuckled.

"Dad, would you do the same if Davis needed some time?" Jeb asked with a smile in his voice.

"Yepper. Not only would Davis be a better son, but Naomi would have a nice mocha color to her complexion."

The MacDowells were just finishing up their morning patrol of Mounton. Jeb wondered where Beth could be. She was inseparable from her mobile phone, especially when Naomi was in school. As he turned his truck toward the school, he promised himself to find her as soon as he got his little girl to his folks' home and in bed.

#

A few minutes earlier, Hannah received a call, telling her the school was unable to contact Beth or Jeb. Everyone in Mounton knew she was Naomi's grandmother. "Could she come pick up the sick little girl?" Hannah, dropped the phone into the cradle as she grabbed her Jeep keys and headed out the door toward the school.

#

Beth had just finished rewrapping the ankle of Little Earl Jackson when her phone beeped announcing a voicemail. His father, Big Earl, had brought the boy in a week earlier after an ill-considered jump out of a hay loft had twisted junior's ankle. With the crutches the clinic supplied and the wrapping, he would be back to jumping from inappropriate heights in no time.

After father and son left, Beth listened to the message. Unable to locate Jacob, could she come pick up Naomi at the school? Seems she was running a low-grade fever. After checking out with Bonnie Clayton at the front desk, who was the receptionist, billing department, and baked goods provider for the doctor's office, Beth climbed into her car to get her daughter. For the hundredth time, she cursed her and Jacob's timing for getting her so pregnant during the hottest months of the year. As her former military father-in-law might say, "Proper planning prevents piss poor pregnancies." Then again, he probably wouldn't. Mac doesn't say much.

At a little past 9:00 in the morning, it was already an unseasonable 90 degrees. Her car's air conditioner blew hot air for the first ten minutes, which would be just about be the amount of time she needed to drive to the town's only school. A quick glance confirmed the empty car seat in the back seat. The seat seemed like it had been there forever and all the MacDowells' vehicles had them. Looks like they all might need an extra set soon.

#

Ginny's call came telling him Mac's Bronco had broken down between town and the lake. As with large chunks of Mounton County, there was no cell service in the area, so a local called Ginny from a landline in town. Mac had stayed with his truck, waiting for a lift from Ginny. The caller claimed he had tried Jeb and Hannah but was unable to reach them. Mac gave Ginny as an alternative contact and the caller dialed the diner's number directly.

Ginny took off his overly stained apron, hung it reverently on a hook behind the kitchen door, and grabbed his bike keys. The caller hung up before Ginny could get his name or more info, but in

Mounton, everybody kind of expected everyone to know each other just by the sound of their voice.

Mac knows I'm on the Harley and he refuses to ride it. I can't imagine him wanting to ride bitch, no matter how desperate he might be. I guess I'll ask him when I see him.

"Shirley, the breakfast rush has declined, can you persevere if I withdraw for a bit?" Ginny inquired of the ancient cashier.

"I was handling things 'fore you could reach your little pee-pee," Shirley croaked.

And only a half dozen customers heard Shirley talking about my little pee-pee. Oh, yay.

"Our fearless constable finds himself stranded without functioning transportation, and requires a rescue operation."

"Tell him it's time to buy a new damned car," Shirley fumed.

"I will convey your fondest wishes."

"Hmmph."

#

Davis Williams was just sitting down with his second cup of coffee when the text came in.

HALFWAY TO THE COMMUNITY CENTER. CAR BROKE DOWN. CAN YOU PICK ME UP? - FEL

Davis looked at his phone for several seconds. It was weird the text didn't come from Felicia's phone. *Maybe she borrowed someone's.* It was weirder still she texted. Felicia hates texting. "It's just faster to call." He had never known her to sign *anything* as "Fel."

Davis shrugged as he dug his old Washington Redskins jersey out of the hamper. Davis loved the faded jersey, small holes and all. Felicia kept threatening to throw it out, but she knew it was his go-to comfort shirt. A pair of walking shorts and running shoes later, Davis grabbed his keys, wallet, and phone off the dresser and started toward the bedroom door. He hesitated a second and glanced at the small gun safe in the closet. In D.C., it was mandatory for all off-duty officers to carry. But this was Mounton. *What's the worst that could happen?*

#

Jeb pulled his truck up next to Beth's car in the back of The School parking lot. Calling it a parking lot was an insult to pavement as it was just dirt and a gravel patch. The dozen or so teachers and staff parked in front of the two buildings holding all of Mounton's students, grades pre-K through middle school. The front lot was closer to the doors, but the best parking borders the forest and provided some shade to keep those cars cooler.

"Hey, babe," Jeb started. "What are you doing here? I thought the school couldn't get a hold of you and even if they did, I told them I would pick up Naomi."

"They told me they couldn't get a hold of you," Beth replied.

Before the couple could discuss it further, Hannah pulled up in her Jeep Wrangler and parked next to them.

"This is ridiculous," Jeb complained as Hannah exited her car. "I could see it if there was a mix-up with me and Beth, but to call in Mom goes beyond gross stupidity."

The three stood there while husband and wife brought Hannah up to speed. "I pulled back here because I could just barely see your cars from the front." Hannah unfolded her arms and looked around.

"Kids, get in your cars—now!" Hannah snapped at her son and his wife. Hannah stepped between the woods and the pregnant Beth to shield her daughter-in-law and new grandbaby.

Beth turned, but before Jeb could move, red carnations simultaneously seemed to bloom on Jeb's chest and Beth's back. Jeb looked down at his chest, just in time to see a red bloom appear on Hannah's thigh. He pulled the dart quickly from his chest.

"Ow! Sunnuva ..." he managed to mutter before falling back against Beth's car door. Beth was falling as well, but even losing consciousness, she instinctively fell to her side to protect her unborn child.

Hannah pulled the empty dart with its red bloom from her leg.

"Mac—," she managed before she too succumbed to the tranquilizer's effect.

Sly and his posse walked from the woods on the edge of the parking lot, reloading the tranquilizer guns as they moved forward.

The MacDowell family had collapsed between Jeb and Beth's vehicles, making them invisible from the school.

"Vamanos, hermanos. We'll have to load them in the little mamacita's car. No point in having a nosy teacher scoping us," Sly told his subordinates.

After the Chicagoans loaded the three bodies into the back of the SUV, Sly grinned. "Looks like we bagged our limit of MacDowells. Three and a half with three darts."

#

At the same time, Hannah was being loaded into the back of Beth's SUV, Ginny pulled his Harley Road King up to the location the voice on the phone had told him Mac was waiting. No Bronco. No Mac.

Ginny threw his right leg over the back of the big bike, after heeling the kickstand down on the pavement. Kentucky doesn't require motorcycle helmets for adults, but knowing Mac's disdain for his bike, Ginny had worn it to give to Mac on the ride back. The muscular diner owner looked up and down the road and even through the trees to the lake. *Maybe he got the beast running and left. No. Doesn't sound like Mac. He would wait until I showed up at least.*

It was then the Stamper brothers stepped from the woods near a cliff bordering the eastern edge of Mounton Lake. With long guns in hand.

"What, pray tell, are you trio of hooligans conspiring about?" Ginny inquired.

"Shooting," Syrus answered.

"Nothing is in season. What are you shooting out here?" Ginny stepped toward the three as they approached.

"Fish in a barrel." The red bloom of a tranquilizer dart impacted Ginny's broad chest right in the middle of his Allman Brothers' tee shirt.

"Sonnuva—" Ginny bellowed as he launched himself at them.

The bear of a diner owner charged toward the brothers, half helmet still on. Two more tranquilizer darts bloomed on Ginny's chest as he bulled forward. Syrus was fumbling to reload his gun.

Just as Ginny reached the Stampers' position, they stepped aside.

Syrus noted the giant's eyes were glazing over. Three hundred pounds of muscle, tattoos, and hair roared past the astounded brothers to crash through the woods' edge out of sight.

"Get after him you mo-rons!" Syrus yelled at his siblings, recovering from his surprise.

Just as the three Stampers hit the shrub and woods, they heard a large splash.

The brothers emerged from the woods to stare at the drop into Mounton Lake, where their quarry must have fallen to his death.

"Aw shit!" Syrus spat.

#

"Mac would have come himself, but the issue, between you and me, is Jeb and Beth seemed to be missing. He sent me to pick up Naomi and make sure she's safe."

"Sounds like Mac," Eva Parton, the principal of the town school, agreed. "But he should have called ahead to let me know someone not on the list was coming to get her. I've never met you, but I heard he was changing up the roster there lately."

"My guess is he normally would have called, but with his family missing, he has a bit on his mind."

"I imagine. I'll call down to her class and have her brought up," the principal said. "I would normally not do this, but I guess since you are a deputy, it's alright."

The uniformed officer took Naomi's little hand and lead her to his police cruiser.

"I know you, don't I?" Naomi demanded. "Where are we going?"

"To see your mom and dad," the man in the uniform lied as he gently put her in the back seat. There was a wire screen between the driver and the back seat. Naomi looked at the seat belt he fastened with a frown.

"There's no kid's seat. There should be a kid's seat. It's the law. Where's Pappaw?" Earlier, the deputy engaged the door, window, and child-proof locks.

As he shut the rear door, he replied, "Well, honey, I don't know where he is right this minute, but I imagine very shortly, he will be beside himself."

#

"What do you mean he's *dead?*" Jarvis barked from the phone at Syrus's ear.

"Just what I said. We pumped three darts into him and he still kept running right at us an' he plowed right past an' fell plumb off'n the cliff into the lake. Ain't nobody can survive three darts. Not even a gorilla his size."

"Well, this is just dandy! This is NOT ... the plan. I told you to take him alive, ergo the tranq guns," Jarvis barked.

"If'n we hadn'ta shot him three times, he'd taken our damned heads off. *ERGO*, we would be deader than Dan'l Boone!" Syrus snapped back.

The line was quiet while Jarvis thought.

"Okay," he instructed. "Three tranq darts alone should have killed him. So at least he's off the board. You three hole up for a bit and wait for some instructions. I think you can safely kiss your bonus goodbye, though. I don't know how this affects things, but what's done is done."

Without waiting for a reply, he hung up.

Syrus squinted at the disconnected burner phone in his hand, his anger growing.

"What's done IS done ... for now."

#

Anesthesia met Sly and his team at the designated spot and the Chicagoans helped load the MacDowells into the RV. After strapping them down, they stood by and watched as Anesthesia hooked each of the three victims to IV lines with slow sedative drips. *He didn't tell me one of them was pregnant!* Anesthesia secured Beth and Jeb to the lowered dinette table-turned-bed. She strapped Hannah down to the jackknife sofa bed. Originally, the dinette bed would have been used for the big diner owner, but Anesthesia had heard from her enigmatic benefactor he would not be joining them. The bunk bed in the hall would secure Naomi. Neither she nor the Chicagoans introduced

194

themselves or addressed each other by name. The largest thug, the monster Mac thought of as Kong, started to speak once, but Sly cut him off. Once the three hoods had driven off to dispose of Beth's SUV, Betta drove the motor home to the next designated spot where she was to pick up Davis Williams from Ralph Hickman and his team. The drop-off, securing, and sedation repeated itself.

#

When the deputy pulled up in the silver police cruiser at the third designated location, Anesthesia momentarily panicked. She imagined the whole gig was busted with her in an RV with four drugged and strapped-down kidnap victims. Then she remembered this too was part of the plan. The deputy was pulling the screaming, struggling little girl from the back seat when Anesthesia stepped down from the RV.

"She's not supposed to see you!" the deputy scolded.

"Don't worry," Betta explained with a smile, pulling a loaded syringe from her scrubs pocket. Removing the plastic cover from the needle, she squirted a minute amount up skyward to remove the air. "This is Propofol, she won't remember anything. You, on the other hand, can remember all you want."

The deputy had to wrap both arms around Naomi in order to hold her still enough for Anesthesia to inject her. As soon as she relaxed, Anesthesia carried her into the RV and strapped her down in the bunk, and adjusted an IV for her weight and size.

"I'm not so sure about all this," The man in the deputy's uniform speculated from just outside the door. "It's one thing to go undercover and get the goods on a corrupt sheriff, but kidnapping a little girl seems ... wrong."

"The way The Voice explained it to me is," Anesthesia intimated, as she moved to the RV's first step to talk, "we are keeping the innocent ones, like this little girl, out of harm's way. Once this is all over, we return them to their loved ones. The not-so-innocent ones are part of the sheriff's support and removing them weakens him. In the meantime, they're all leverage to get him to surrender peaceably."

"I guess," he said, still unsure.

"Do you need to be somewhere?" Anesthesia purred demurely while touching his arm.

"Me?" the deputy smiled. "Nah. I'm off duty. Permanently."

"Then you got time for a drink?"

"I've got time for two. You got a name?"

"Yeah. You can call me Anesthesia."

"I bet you have a variety of ways to knock a man out," he said as he looked around the inside of the RV. "Whoa, looks like you've got a truckload of visitors."

"Don't mind these folks," Anesthesia breathed seductively. "We couldn't wake them if we tried. They're sleeping like the dead."

#

August 10, 6:37 A.M., Mounton, KY

Outwardly, Mac appeared calm. Inwardly, his emotional state could best be described as "freaked out." Getting to the station, Mac called in Patricks to cover the day shift so he would be free to investigate. Jeb hadn't come back after picking up Naomi from school yesterday and Mac hadn't heard from him, so he himself covered Jeb's evening shift. When he called home to let Hannah know he was working late, he got the antique answering machine. He left a simple message, omitting the part about not knowing where Jeb was. He called Jeb's house all afternoon to see if he was coming back and got their voicemail. Driving to Jeb and Beth's place revealed they were not only not home, but that their cars missing, and hadn't been home at all. Neither had Naomi.

To maximize his terror, when Mac got home that night at 11:15 P.M. on the 9th, Hannah wasn't home and didn't come home all night. This was the first time in 28 years of marriage they slept apart unintentionally. Not that he had actually slept. He made calls. He checked his cell phone voice mail. He watched the landline phone, willing it to ring. He cleaned his Colt. He dismantled and cleaned Hannah's deer rifle. Mostly, he just paced.

Panic was setting in deep.

When the light finally started to rise over the mountain, Mac showered, dressed, and after some thought, strapped on his Colt.

With a glance at the closet, he sighed and reached for his knee brace. He hated the "Robocop" look it gave him strapped over his jeans, but he couldn't let any weakness on his part endanger his family and friends.

He started his morning phone calls from a sheet Hannah had posted next to the phone. He called the doctor's office last night to find Beth had not returned yesterday afternoon after she left to pick up Naomi. She had also not come in this morning. Mac didn't even ask if they admitted any of his family. The staff all knew him and his family and would have called him first, had they been.

Naomi's school informed him Naomi was released to a deputy, but NOT Jeb, early yesterday morning. The school custodian reported Hannah and Jeb's vehicles, both well known, were in the parking area by the woods. But not Beth's.

Patricks had shown up by 8:00 A.M., started the morning patrol, and by 9:30 A.M., reported finding Beth's SUV ditched off the road in the woods past the lake. No keys, no signs of struggle, and all the doors locked.

#

August 10, 11:39 A.M., Mounton, KY

"Is this Sheriff MacDowell?" the distorted voice on the phone said into Mac's ear.

"Yepper. How can I help you?" Mac answered.

"The answer is very complex, Sheriff. I will be very direct since there is a small, but highly unlikely, chance this call may be traced. I have in my control all of your family and friends. If you do exactly as I say, no harm will come to them. Exactly as I say."

After a pause, Mac's voice cracked with emotion, "I hear you. What do you want? Money? How much?"

"It's not quite so simple, Sheriff. First, you are NOT to involve any law enforcement in this. Not the FBI, not even your own deputies. I have ways of hearing of this. If I learn of other any LEO's involvement, one of your friends or a family member, of my choosing, will die. Notice I did not say a

random one. I do not leave **ANYTHING** to chance."

"Got it. No law enforcement," Mac complied through clenched teeth.

"Second and finally, I will give you 24 hours to complete the task I have set for you. It will likely be unpleasant and distasteful, but if you fail to do it, a friend or family member will die. You will do this task and provide me video proof you have done it by noon tomorrow at the anonymous email address I will provide you. Every day you don't provide me with proof, another of your loved ones will die."

"Fine. Video proof by noon tomorrow. What's this task?" Mac snapped, his patience with the kidnapper giving into a rage with the repeated threats to his family.

"You will locate and sexually molest an underaged child." Click.

Mac sat at his desk staring at the phone. His mind was simultaneously frozen in shock and ricocheting thoughts at the speed of light.

He picked up the radio handset and called Patricks on patrol.

"Lawrence, you, Davis, and Dawes are the law enforcement in this town until further notice. Jeb is ... unavailable. Forget about Beth's car. I will take care of it. Everything else is business as usual for you guys. I am forwarding the 911 calls to your radio for the rest of the day shift," Mac instructed. "I haven't heard from Davis yet today, but I imagine he will be in for his afternoon shift as usual."

There was silence over the air as Patricks digested this confusing message. Jeb and the sheriff never missed their shifts. Patricks had only been on the job a few months but he understood the town's psyche: he was decades away from being accepted. Mac had never given Patricks a full solo shift. This was all damned unusual.

"Uh, where are you gonna be, Sheriff?"

"I have to go find a child."

#

August 10, 11:50 A.M., Mounton, KY

Mac drove out to The School. The building, such as it was, sat right on the edge of town on Main Street and Mac was there in minutes. Normally, he would have walked it, but today was not normal. Striding right up through the main doors, he brushed past the receptionist and directly into Principal Parton's office.

"Sheriff!"

"Ms. Parton, I need some answers," Mac turned, giving the rattled receptionist a look that told her in no uncertain terms, she should leave the principal's office and close the door. Quietly.

"Sheriff. Mac. Since you called this morning, I have been frantic with worry," Eva Parton stammered. Her normally pulled-back hair was showing a few rogue strands around her glasses. "Because you called about Naomi, and your wife's and son's vehicles are in the back parking lot, I checked with her teacher and Naomi didn't come in this morning. With no word from Beth, which is extremely unusual. I knew I shouldn't have let Naomi go with your deputy, but he seemed like such a nice, young man, and maintained you instructed him to pick her up. I even looked out the window and saw him put her in the back of a silver police car. It said POLICE right on the side in big letters. I am so, so sorry. What can I do?"

Mac fiddled with his mobile phone and held it up for Parton to see.

"Was it this man?"

"No."

Mac swiped across his phone again, displacing the photo of Patricks.

"How 'bout him?"

"YES!" Parton clenched both her hands to her mouth.

Mac looked at his phone. From his employment file, there was a headshot of former deputy Mason Wheeler in his uniform. The reportedly dead, former deputy, Mason Wheeler.

#

August 10, 11:56 A.M., somewhere in Mounton County

Mason woke, stretched, and rolled over on the queen bed in the back of the RV and saw the sleeping form of Anesthesia beside him. He had discarded his deputy's uniform in a pile wadded up at the foot of the bed.

He stared at her lithe form with its sinewy muscles under chocolate-hued skin. Her short hair, tattoos, and piercings made her even more exotic. And those were just the piercings you could see! Last night was unlike anything he had ever experienced. Granted it wasn't a marathon session, but Anesthesia had kinks even her rebellious appearance didn't foretell.

She must have been having a nightmare as she kicked the tangle of covers off her, and revealed even more luscious skin. On close examination, Mason could see what looked to be old cigarette burns and scars on her arms, now covered by tattoos. The tattoo artist strategically placed the designs to disguise the very old scars, but in the morning light, and on close examination, Mason could see them.

Who the hell did this to you, girl? They obviously weren't self-inflicted. Look at the lengths you went to in covering them up. This whole bad-girl, tattooed, piercing thing is starting to look like a giant Up Yours to someone. If that old saying about "Crazy in the head, crazy in bed" was true, then this woman was certifiable.

"You see something you like, or are you just window shopping?" Anesthesia yawned.

"I'm liking all of it," Mason said. "Where'd you learn some of that stuff last night?"

"You liked that, did ya?" Anesthesia smiled. "Let me go check on my guests and I'll come back here and show you things you ain't never seen before."

She rose from the bed, wrapped a light robe around her petite, nude frame and stepped into the RV's main cabin.

Mason, torn over his excitement to experience more of this psycho woman's repertoire and his concerns about the whole operation, realized that he had probably already seen too much.

Betta took a few minutes to check Hannah, Beth, and Jeb and headed back through the central hallway to look after Davis and

Naomi. A few things concerned her about the little girl, but until she spoke to The Voice, she didn't want to do anything about it.

She hesitated at Davis's bedside after checking his IV drip. She ran her fingers along the smooth skin of his arm. Damn if he wasn't a fine-looking man. Mason was good-looking in his own way. A little too skinny and pale for her tastes, but he seemed to enjoy her experimentation in the sack. He qualified as "definitely too little, too soon," but any port in a storm ...

Betta looked down at Davis's prone form and felt a twinge of excitement, knowing that Mason, who might be able to scratch her itch, awaited her. In a sudden impulse, she sank her fingernails into his forearm deep enough to draw blood. It was all it took to practically send her over the edge. Sedated, Davis hadn't reacted, but Betta was nearly orgasmic from that simple act of cruelty. She hoped Mason was up for round two.

#

August 10, 12:55 P.M., outside Mounton, KY

"Something's wrong," Anesthesia complained into the burner phone.

"What are you talking about?" The Voice insisted.

"The little girl is running a fever and she has some redness around some surgical scars on her torso. My guess is she had a kidney transplant. Two, by the looks of it. Quite a few months back," Anesthesia explained.

"We need to help her," The Voice was nearly pleading.

"It doesn't look like full-on kidney failure. It's more like a lack of anti-rejection drugs. Did you know about this?"

"Maybe. There was something in January about her getting a transplant which started the dust-up between the sheriff and the local judge, but I thought she was past all needing anti-rejection drugs."

"Shit."

"You need to save her."

"I'll need to increase her saline drip, she'll be more prone to dehydration and infection. Maybe I can score some

201

immunosuppressant meds from my contact, but I gotta tell you, we need it fast, and it ain't gonna be cheap," Anesthesia spoke into her phone.

Earlier, after another quick session in the sack, Betta had told Mason to stay in the back bedroom of the RV and to keep his mouth shut. After that, she double-checked on her guests. She noticed earlier that the little girl was feverish, uncomfortable, and showing signs of infection.

"Cost is no problem. Just save the girl. If something happens to her, Hannah will ... well, never mind. Just make her better."

"But wait, there's more! It's been a couple of days. If this goes on any longer, we're gonna have to do catheters. I can do them, but it's nasty and it will definitely cost you more."

"Fine. Go ahead. This may go another few days. Long before next week, we'll run out of hostages. But you better take good care of the little girl, and most importantly, save Hannah. I bought you another twenty-four hours, but no more."

"Did it occur to you to mention the daughter-in-law is pregnant?" Betta snapped.

"Is it a problem?"

"Probably not. I just need to use a different drip for her. Let me get on this immunosuppressant thing. I've got stuff to help with the fever until I get it. They're already on IV drips to avoid dehydration, but they're gonna have to get rid of the extra fluid somehow, so I can get the catheters going tonight."

"You just make sure you take care of my girls!"

#

August 10, 12:57 P.M., Mounton, KY

Mac sat in his Bronco, parked in front of the station. Someone, or more than likely *someones*, if they got Hannah, Jeb, and Beth all at the same time, had kidnapped Mac's family. Yet the voice on the phone used the personal pronoun "I." So, he's in charge, but there are multiple people involved.

He must have connections to the federal law enforcement community because they would know if Mac brought in the FBI. The

Voice said "*... if I hear of other LEO's involvement.*" So, he must be monitoring the station to report if his deputies started acting differently. Maybe listening to the sheriff's radio bands. And he used the expression "LEO." Only someone in law would be comfortable with the acronym for law enforcement officer. It's not exactly on *Law & Order SVU* every night.

Whoever this is, was probably the one who planted Mason in his office and turned the newspaper on Mac with files taken out of context. Someone who knows enough about police procedures to fake Mason's death. And provide him with a silver police cruiser. Mounton doesn't have *police* cars, they have SUVs and they are not silver. And they say SHERIFF in big letters on the side, not POLICE. If he has a crew on payroll, this was someone with some clout and deep pockets.

Okay. Let's start with the Watcher. Mac looked around. There was not much traffic, pedestrian or vehicle, especially in Mounton. And we have a winner. Young punk, greasy hair, bad skin, just sitting in an old, beat-up Corolla. Why would anyone just SIT on The Side Street?

Mac walked into the sheriff's office and right past Patricks, who had just come in for lunch, without a word. He pushed the door bar and barreled through the emergency exit in the back. It hadn't sounded an alarm since Kennedy was in office. Walking briskly, he passed behind the charred remnants of *Darlene's* and came up behind the old Corolla, staying in its mirrors' blind spots.

Gently knocking on the driver's window, he requested, "License and registration, please."

Josh shrieked in surprise and then tried to start the old Toyota.

Mac tapped his Colt on the driver's side window and merely shook his head no.

Josh slumped in the seat.

"I'm gonna need your license and registration, son. And I'm gonna need them now."

Posse'd

August 10, 5:12 P.M., Meeting Location #1 Outside Mounton, KY

Mac, Duncan, Darlene, and Felicia laid behind some brush on the edge of a small rise two dozen yards from a dirty garbage truck. Mac had instructed Shirley to leave the jail cell door open a crack. Although obvious, it was too tempting for Josh to not slip out of the cell and the back door with the non-functioning emergency alarm. Mac had deliberately not taken Josh's car keys when he frisked him. Duncan followed the Corolla at a discreet distance and Mac and his volunteers followed Duncan. Once they had the general location, Mac knew a hunting trail to get them closer undetected. Surprisingly, Darlene, despite her size, was extraordinarily quiet going through the brush and trees. The rest of Mac's impromptu posse stayed with the vehicles about a mile back. A radio call from the scouting team could bring them at a run. Mac's team watched from behind a small rise in the brush-covered ground as three men spoke to each other about 60 yards away. Mac recognized Ralph and Mitch from their attempted robbery of *Ginny's* a month or so earlier. Both carried semi-automatic handguns in their waistbands.

\#

"So, they just let you escape?" Ralph snapped at Josh.

"They didn't *let* me. The crazy old bat that questioned me just didn't close the cell door all the way. I snuck out when she left."

"And the first thing you did was come straight here?" Ralph's face was turning a bright shade of red. Between this idiot and the humiliating phone call from The Voice, this whole thing was too much for him to bare.

"Sure," Josh whined. "Where else was I supposed to go?"

"Go home. Go get a drink. Go to hell. But don't lead them here to us!"

"Ralph! Dude! No way anyone followed me!"

\#

"Do ye think they send out a training pamphlet beforehand to carry their guns all the same way?" Duncan smiled as he passed Mac his binoculars.

"I would say from *CSI* episodes, but I doubt those inbreds could spell it, let alone watch it." Darlene joked.

"They *do* have guns. A firefight would get someone hurt." Felicia worried, passing the second set of binoculars back to Darlene. "We have the numbers, or if you look at it a different way, just more targets for them to shoot at."

"Aye, and I'm guessing we could always jes' stroll up an' surrender and see if the boyos laugh themselves to death." Duncan was always the soul of sarcasm.

"You know," Mac smiled. "We might just at that."

#

Mac approached the garbage truck parked in the woods with loud, long, crunching strides. Ralph Hickman and his partners turned at the sound of his approach and stepped toward him, their backs to the truck.

"Boys, I am placing you all under arrest for the possession, transportation of, and intent to distribute, a buttload of controlled narcotics. If'n you put down all those firearms, I will read you your rights from this here card."

Ralph stared in shock at Mac standing at the edge of the woods.

"Sheriff, I gotta tell ya. Only a certifiable fool would come out here all alone."

"Walking up on us took some serious stones." Mitch laughed. He almost admired the man for his courage in facing down three times as many armed men. The missing Colt did not go unnoticed, but three against one? Even if he was armd, nobody was fast enough to outdraw three men.

Mac looked at the boys from Lexington and smiled.

"Ralphie—can I call you Ralphie? I never said I came out here alone."

The woods surrounding the garbage truck became deathly silent. Not a bird chirped or a leaf rustled until the unmistakable sound of a pump shotgun ratcheted behind the kidnappers. Simultaneously, a trembling arrow point pricked the skin on Ralph's neck. He immediately whirled and whipped out a Glock from his waistband, but the archer was already locked, loaded, and aimed the arrowhead just inches from his face, despite his still lowered handgun.

Mac moved forward slowly with his hands empty and palms down trying to calm the situation. "Now kids, there's no need for this to escalate. We can all play nice here. All we want is our family back. Nobody has to get hurt, or y'know... dead."

Mac looked at Felicia, her nerves pulled nearly as tight as her bowstring. Felicia still aimed directly at Ralph's head, but it quivered just a little more.

"Felicia, you okay there, honey?" Mac inquired.

"Yeah. It's just ... I never ... You know."

"You never shot a person before, right?" Mac beseeched the beautiful young wife of his deputy.

"Yeah. Sort of. Millions of targets, but never a real ... I mean ..." she whispered through clenched teeth.

"It's okay, darlin'. Taking a life is a forever thing. Ain't no takebacks," Mac comforted. "If you want, you can just put the bow down."

At this, Ralph started to smile. As soon as she lowered the bow, he would pop her, then go for the sheriff. His grip tightened on his Glock.

Smiling was the wrong thing to do. Felicia imagined Ralph's smile as he drugged and kidnapped her husband.

His finger tightened another quarter pound of pressure on the trigger. The hand with the gun started to raise.

"Screw it." The arrow penetrated his left eye and protruded out the back of his head before anyone could hear the *thwick* of the bowstring's release. As the head of the arrow exited the back of his skull, a small cracking noise could be heard.

Everyone froze and stared as the lead thug teetered back and forth before falling backward. On his head's impact with the ground, the arrow's head pushed back up through his skull, forcing three inches to emerge back from his eye socket, the gelatinous material of his eyeball clinging to the shaft of the arrow.

Duncan reacted first, ramming the barrel of the Ithaca 16-gauge pump shotgun into Mitch the Weasel's back. Mitch stared at Ralph, the arrow, and the viscera clinging to the arrow as he dropped his .45 to the ground, absently. Duncan shoved the thug forward toward the body, Mac, and Felicia. Josh proceeded to projectile vomit several feet in front of him.

Mac rushed to Felicia.

"Felicia, are you okay? Look at me. Felicia?" Mac gripped both her shoulders and tried to get the young woman to look him in the eye. She never stopped staring at the body at her feet. Finally, she lifted her eyes to meet the sheriff's.

"Mac, he was going to shoot me. Then he was going to kill all of you," she said in a flat, dry voice.

"I know, honey, but you didn't have to do it. Someone else would have handled it."

"No, Mac, you don't understand. He. Kidnapped. My. Man. And he enjoyed it. He was an animal and we needed to show the other animals how it is. He needed to die. Not just for what he did, but to show them," nodding toward Mitch and Josh, "what we will do if they fight. I don't regret I shot him. I regret I waited."

Mac stared at Felicia, holding her, knowing she was right. There was nothing he would not do to get his family back. These men needed to know. Better to put down one animal and save many. He turned and looked at Mitch.

"How can I help you, Sheriff?" Mitch squeaked as he watched Felicia notch another arrow. "Anything at'all. You jes' name it."

#

Three Hours Earlier

Mac sat in the chair in front of the office radio, mic in hand. His brown Stetson cocked back on his short-cropped, but graying head. Lines of worry and frustration creased his face. The transmitter's frequency dialed to the Kentucky State Police, but he hadn't keyed the mic yet. He had a few clues, but he needed help. The disguised voice on the phone claimed he would hear about any outside law enforcement immediately and there would be consequences to his family. Mac stared at the radio, torn between needing help and fear for his loved ones.

The door to the small station opened and a group of townsfolk, led by Shirley from the diner, entered. Mac eyed the ancient crone, her knitting bag clutched under her arm.

"Sheriff, Ginny din't come back to the diner this morning and I checked around and it seems a few other folks is missing, including all your family," Shirley croaked in a voice filtered through decades of unfiltered cigarettes. "Seems like somebody lured 'em out and snatched 'em. One of them Hendricks boys found an empty tranquilizer dart in the school parking lot. The kind you shoot at animals in the zoo when they act up. What are you intending to do about it?"

Mac looked at the people assembled. To Shirley's right was Felicia, Deputy Davis William's young wife. On the crone's left, Duncan, holding a pump shotgun certainly older than Jeb. Eaton Hendricks and his three boys crowded in behind Duncan, all armed with deer rifles. Ezekiel Thompson, Peggy Clay, and her boys stood at the back of the group. Darlene and Mr. Darlene filled the doorway inadvertently preventing others from getting in.

"To tell you the truth, I just don't know."

"Well then," Duncan brrrd, eyeing the brace on his friend's knee, "What would you do to get them back, ya wee eidjit?"

Mac looked Duncan in the eye and vowed, "I would do anything to get my family back."

"Hmph!" Shirley snorted. "'Zat include pulling your big girl panties up? Because if you don't go get them, we will."

Felicia quietly spoke up. "Sheriff, you said 'your family.' Davis and Ginny are missing too."

"Like I said," Mac stood. "I will do anything to get my family back. My WHOLE family."

The group nodded in agreement. Felicia lowered her head. Duncan smiled under his graying red beard. Shirley cocked an eyebrow.

"And how are we gonna get 'em back, Susie?" Shirley cackled at Mac.

"We?" Mac asked.

Shirley looked him dead in the eye. "You don't think you're man enough to get 'em back by yourself, do ya?"

"I can't ask you, any of you, to step into the line of fire. It's MY job to protect YOU. This is going to be tricky enough without me worrying about any of you," Mac said to the group.

"You don't worry about us none, sonny-boy," as she patted her knitting bag. "This town survived real well before we had a gimpy *pacifist* like you thinking you could protect us." Shirley spat the word "pacifist" the way a preacher says the word "whore."

Once more the group nodded its agreement.

Mac looked at the group. Friends. Neighbors. People he had known nearly his entire adult life. Mountain people. If you could find a more stubborn bunch in all of America, he didn't want to know about it. Right then, he wouldn't have traded them for a platoon of Army Rangers. Marines maybe, but never for Rangers.

"Okay, I guess if you're determined to do this thing, I guess the least I can do is provide you with some protection," he said as he walked over to the filing cabinet and pulled out a box of badges he handed out to the group.

"I'm sorry, Sheriff, but how will these protect us from bullets?" Felicia asked, holding up the badge.

"Aye, darlin'," Duncan explained. "They'll be protecting ya from something a wee bit more dangerous than bullets."

"What's more dangerous than bullets?"

"Lawyers."

Shirley looked at the "protection" before she pinned it on her omnipresent flowered housedress. "Well, at least it's not condoms."

Mac walked to the phone on the desk and dialed a number by heart.

"Mac! How can the FBI be of service to Kentucky's most famous unarmed mth dealer?"

Mac ignored the barb. The news stories about him were still making the rounds at various Kentucky law enforcement agencies.

"Bill, I need a favor and I need you to trust me on it. I hate to say it, but I need it fast too."

"Favors and trust you've earned a dozen times over. How fast will depend on what."

"I need to borrow some equipment. The 'how fast' is yesterday," Mac began.

After Mac explained what he needed, Dave laughed.

"So, you need some top-of-the-line-gear, can't tell me what it's about, and I can't let anyone in Bureau know I talked to you?"

"Yepper."

"No problem," Dave laughed. "You had me at 'I need a favor.'"

A Half Hour Later

After Mac updated the volunteers about the weird phone call he received and told them that Mason was alive and involved, he led the group back to the single cell in the back of the station house. The youngest of the three hoodlums from Lexington sat on the cot with his knees folded up to his chest and his arms wrapped around them as Mac and the townsfolk approached. It was the same cell he and his friends had escaped from earlier, before trying to rob *Ginny's Diner*. Mac had waited until Patricks went out on his afternoon patrol to lock Josh up in the station.

"I dinna know, Mac," Duncan continued. "Swearing us in by making us promise to uphold the law and not get dead seems a tad on the broad-stroked side to me."

Mac looked at the elder Scotsman, but it was Shirley who piped up.

"I like it. Gives us a whole lotta latitude between what we should do, can do, and will do," she croaked smiling, clutching her heavy handbag even tighter.

"Son," Mac summarized to Josh. "You're in a world of trouble. Five counts of kidnapping, transportation, distribution of drugs, and conspiracy. You're looking at federal time. Kidnapping alone is a life sentence."

"Aye, ye won't be seeing daylight till you're older than this beauty," Duncan chuckled as he put his arm around Shirley's shoulders.

"And you won't be sitting comfortably for a lot longer," Shirley chortled.

The young prisoner looked from Duncan to Shirley to Mac. "I want a—"

"Eh, before you finish your next sentence, Snot Nose, I would like to talk with you a few minutes," Shirley spoke through the bars and then looked at Mac. "Alone."

There didn't seem to be a question there for anyone to refute.

Mac looked at the little old lady, her giant knitting bag, and at the cowering prisoner on the cot. He pulled out a ring of keys on a retractable clip on his belt, selected the right key, and opened the cell. With a flourish, waved Shirley into the cell.

As the group started to filter out back into the front of the station, the young prisoner screamed out, "Hey! You can't do this!"

Shirley thumbed the house dress out at the collarbone showing off her new badge. "Oh yeah, I've just been sworn in as a deputy with a loose set of rules. And I have almost no scruples. So, buckle up, buttercup, we're gonna have us a chat."

While they waited for Shirley, Mac turned to Duncan, "Who's minding the store?"

"Aye, and herself would be Agnes. I had to resign as postmaster and appoint her since an officer of the government should nay be joining a posse. She'll keep the store and post office open and do a good job of it. I shoulda done this years ago."

"Looking forward to retirement?" Mac questioned his friend, as he reached down to tighten the strap on his metal knee brace.

"Nay. I'm looking forward to shootin' some no-count eijits for messin' with a Scot's family. Even a half-breed tourist such as yourself deserves better."

"Uh, thanks?"

Twenty minutes later, Shirley walked back into the front office.

"I don't know where the mutton heads are right now, but I know where they're gonna be in a few hours. Turns out his buddies are meeting with the RV where your family's tied up. Funny part is, you arrested all the shitbirds involved not so long ago."

"Shirley," Mac started. "You didn't ... you know?"

"Aw, hold yer water, Susie. All I did was start knitting and ask questions. I did 'xactly what you wanted. I think we shoulda roughed him up a bit, but I didn't, to spare your sensitive nature. On the funny side, Snot Nose took one look at them knitting needles and wouldn't shut up. Far as I know, he's still blubberin'."

#

August 10, 8:15 P.M., Meeting Location #1 Outside Mounton, KY

Ralph's body still lay cooling in the clearing where Felicia had dropped him. After a few hours of questioning Mitch and Josh, the Mounton group had all the information the Lexington contingent could provide. Surprisingly, Darlene and Mr. Darlene made an effective pair of interrogators. Darlene did all the interrogating and Mr. Darlene just quietly stared at them. His calm stare was almost as disquieting as her grilling. Every time a prisoner would start to ask for a lawyer, Mr. Darlene would grab his chin and slowly force his gaze towards Ralph's cooling corpse, deliberately still laying in the grass with the back end of a gory arrow protruding from his eye socket. A single look ended any requests for legal representation and started a whole new flood of details about the drug distribution scheme and subsequent kidnappings.

Felicia stood nearby and watched the questioning intently. Compound bow in hand. Duncan checked the truck for a GPS or other clues.

With Josh and Mitch zip-tied on the grass next to the truck, the impromptu posse moved off a bit to discuss their next move in private.

"Seems like we know what they were doing and how," Darlene said, "but not who's behind it or why."

"There's a lot of money to be made in the back of those trucks. All of the distribution points sit within 400 miles of Mounton and you can haul a lot of drugs in the back of one of them. I mean, who's gonna search a stinky garbage truck?" Felicia questioned.

"This is not about the money," Mac murmured quietly. "At least, not ALL about the money."

"Aye, whoever sits behind this invested a great deal of cash to get this all started," Duncan chimed in. "And why the kidnappings, particularly Mac's kin, and not ask for money, but a ridiculous request Mac could never do? Nay, this seems more ... personal."

Shirley snorted. "Who'd you piss off now, Nancy-boy?"

"I get why they grabbed the adults," Felicia said. "Don't get me wrong, I hate it, and they will pay for it, but they kidnapped everyone who, at some time or another, had helped Mac. Someone is trying to eliminate his resources."

"But why take Naomi?" Mac asked.

"To cripple you emotionally," Duncan stated. "Whoever this is doesn't just want to make money or remove any resistance in their way, they want to crush your soul. Weaken you. Distract you."

"Well, they did the exact wrong thing then," Mac growled in an almost whisper. "I have never been more determined, or more focused, in my life. Nothing in this world is more important to me right now than getting my family back safe and sound."

Felicia looked at the woods back in the direction of town. "I'm glad Gabriel is safe back with Peggy Clay and her kids. Besides everything else, it will be dark soon."

"Hee-hee!" Shirley chuckled. "Yeah, Darlene, I gotta give it to you. Convincing old Ezekiel Thompson he needed to stay back with Peggy and the kids to 'protect them' was a stroke of genius."

"It was a good idea to get him to keep an eye on the kids. He must be a hundred years old if he's a day," Felicia imagined.

Shirley hitched up her granny panties under her house dress. "Yeah, his old, tired, one-legged ass woulda just slowed us down."

#

August 10, 9:13 P.M., Basement of the Mounton Church

"Are ye aff yer heid, lad?" Duncan demanded of his friend. "Ye dinnae think the good parson was gonna agree to keeping yon scabby eijits in his basement do ye?"

"I asked Pastor Allen nicely and as long as it doesn't interfere with any services, he has no problem with it," Mac said, "It didn't hurt a good portion of his flock was standing behind me, armed to the teeth."

"Actually, it's not a bad idea. As a temporary holding cell. Windows' too small for anyone to climb out. Concrete walls. Soundproofed because of the Sunday school kids. And NO ONE would even *think* they would be here," observed Felicia.

"How sure you ain't still got a rat in the hen house?" Shirley posed to Mac.

"I think Patricks is a good egg, and I *know* Dawe is," Mac insisted. "But The Voice told me no law, including my deputies, and he may have a way of finding out, so for now, only we know any details."

Duncan looked around the basement of the church at the assembled townspeople. "An' ye trust these people?"

Mac didn't hesitate. "With my family's lives."

"Jes checkin'. Wanna make sure ye know what's what."

With the two living kidnappers zip-tied in the children's area in the basement, the Mounton townspeople crowded into the half of the basement that served as a kitchen, and sometimes dining area for receptions, out of earshot of their prisoners. Mac and Duncan locked Ralph's body in the gardening shed behind the church. Mac didn't think the August heat would do the body any favors, but at least this way it wouldn't be stinking up the church. He didn't believe Pastor Allen would fall down for bringing an arrow-pierced corpse into the church. Luckily, the basement had its own outside entrance, so the townsfolk didn't have to enter through the front doors. At Mac's suggestion, they also parked their vehicles at various locations around the small town so as to not draw attention to the church lot.

Duncan's General Store & Mercantile and *The New Texaco* were still open. *Darlene's* was burnt down. Shirley put a sign up on the door of the diner saying Ginny was out of town and the diner would open in a few days. It was unusual, but anyone connected to the kidnapping would accept the cover story for Ginny's disappearance.

Mac, knowing Davis was now missing as well, conference-called Patricks and Dawe and authorized unlimited overtime for the time being for both men. He told his remaining deputies he was under the weather and Jeb and Davis were in Frankfort to testify on an old federal case and the two remaining deputies should do the best they could. Both men were inquisitive and suspicious. Davis hadn't been on board as long as Patricks or Dawe, and neither knew of any federal case which would require both to testify at once. Mac had never taken time off unexpectedly before and he would never short-shift the town for manpower.

Mac broke off their questions by telling them they could temporarily deputize Bernie, down at *The New Texaco*, for any non-hazardous relief. He then hung up abruptly. Both deputies wondered why he didn't suggest Ginny or Duncan instead of Bernie. The whole situation was bizarre and completely out of character for Mac, but orders were orders.

#

The assembled Mounton residents looked to Mac, who was sitting on the kitchen counter.

"Okay. What do we really know?" Mac started.

"We have two of the hackit savvy heids in here and another out back," Duncan started.

"If by 'hackit savvy heids,' you mean those ugly shitheads, yes, then we have two tied up and one more *accounted for*," Darlene translated with only a brief glance toward Felicia. "We left their garbage truck in the woods, but unless they have an excess of dirtbags laying around, they may not have anyone to drive them and distribute their drugs."

"We ken from yon eijit," Duncan said, flicking his eyes toward Josh, but keeping his voice low, "what type of vehicle they have our people kept in and a general description of the bonnie hen that drives it. We also ken Mason still lives, but dinna have the wits or the bawsack to manage something like this."

"You know we only understand about half of what you say, right?" Shirley wheeled the big Scot.

"Mason, the mole in my department I fired, is who kidnapped Naomi," Mac uttered quietly.

"But they're all very likely alive," Darlene quickly growled. "The plan was to distract and punish you. So, it stands to reason they are keeping your family alive to hold against you."

"*Why* is the big question. The kidnappings, wanting to have a video of Mac molesting a child, a spy in the sheriff's department, the drug trafficking. It doesn't add up. We're missing something," Felicia added.

"I only have seventeen and a half more hours to send him a video or he kills someone," Mac seethed. He paused a long moment. "I can't do it. Hannah would never forgive me. I just can't."

"Aye lad, dinna worry. We'll get your family back."

Shirley, patting her knitting bag, looked over at the prisoners, and in a loud voice croaked,

"Because if we don't, I am going to knit myself a nice shitbird scarf."

Josh May, seventeen years old, peed himself. Again.

Shirley looked around at the townspeople and rasped in her usual grumpy voice,

"I am not cleaning that up."

After another hour of discussion and planning, Mac climbed down off the kitchen counter.

"Everyone knows their jobs? Great. Let's go."

"Wait. Who's gonna tell him?" Shirley snarled.

"Tell who what?" Mac turned to the ancient cashier.

"Who's gonna tell the pastor his counter has been hosting your sweaty ass for the last hour?"

Darlene laughed. "Two felons zip-tied in his basement, a dead guy with an arrow in his head is in his tool shed, and you think he's going to worry about his basement kitchen counter?"

"Hell, I am. You know, we occasionally have meals here. You never know where Susie's ass has been."

#

August 10, 10:45 P.M. Mounton, KY

Most of the "Mounton Posse," as Mac had come to think of them, were cruising around the county keeping an eye out for Mason, from a picture Mac had shown them on his phone, and most importantly, a class-A motorhome driven by an attractive woman. Not just any woman. According to Mac's sources, the only attractive African-American woman fitting the tattooed, pierced description with medical training in northern Kentucky was a Betta Washington. A disgraced anesthesiologist who had a criminal record and some very sadistic tendencies.

Given the low number of motorhomes in Mounton, any RV would

do. He had instructed them to "search casually." He didn't want to draw any undue attention from his two remaining deputies or the kidnappers. No more than two people per vehicle, stay in specific areas to not bunch up, and never go a mile or two above the speed limit.

Shirley and the youngest of the Hickman boys stayed in the church basement to keep an eye on their charges. Josh seemed particularly intimidated by Shirley's knitting bag. Mitch had seemed to mentally check out from the whole experience. Felicia used the church phone to call Peggy Clay's house several times and on the first call spoke with Gabriel. In the second call, she found out from Peggy that Mac had called once to go over security instructions with Ezekiel Thompson.

Despite Shirley's comments, Mac knew Ezekiel had proven himself a hell of a soldier during more than one hitch. He had given up a leg for his country and would give up more to protect little Gabriel and the Clay family. The centenarian seemed to have a new energy with his sudden responsibility. Mac figured it had been a long time since Ezekiel had a mission.

At 11:00 P.M., Mac popped into the sheriff's office to check on his two deputies during shift change. He had grabbed a few Kleenex from a box at the church for his meetings with the deputies.

"Boys."

"Sheriff! Didn't expect to see you in. Especially at this hour," Patricks said, genuinely surprised. The sheriff usually worked the day shift and rarely dropped in at night unless there was an incident he thought required his attention. Which was actually all of them.

"Just thought I'd check in with you fellas and see how you're holding up," Mac sniffed, holding the tissue up to his nose.

Dawe stared at his long-time boss quizzically.

"We're doing fine now, but I hope you're feeling better soon, or the boys get back from Lexington. Young Patricks here just finished a fourteen-hour shift and I intend to work until late tomorrow morning, so he can get some sleep. Patty-Jane said she can handle the boys getting to school for now, but she can be a handful if she doesn't get regular lovin'.""

"Tell her thanks. Did you call Bernie?"

"Yeah. He's gonna come in tomorrow when he gets off from *The New Texaco* and just patrol around. If anything happens, he'll call me or Patricks," Dawe explained.

"I almost forgot," Patricks exclaimed, leaning behind the desk to retrieve a box about two feet wide by three feet long. "You got a package. Marked personal. Came by same day shipping, but the return address says it's from the Bureau in Lexington, but no sender's name, which is damned strange."

"Great. I've been expecting something," Mac said.

"Anything else we can do, Sheriff?" Patricks inquired hesitantly.

"Yes. Forward all my personal calls directly to my cell phone. Hopefully, I'll have enough service to get them. Minimize radio traffic and everything is business as usual. The boys'll be back from Lexington soon and we'll have you guys back in regular rotation in no time. Consider me out of pocket for the next few days and do what you need to keep the flags flying."

Without another word, he walked out the door and left his deputies mystified.

"Did you notice?" Dawe asked Patricks.

"I'm not sure. What did I miss?"

"Aside from the fact Mac NEVER pops in to check on us unless there is an incident, he stressed the fact we are to *minimize* radio traffic and everything is supposed to be *business as usual*. He wants us to call in Bernie who has NO law enforcement experience. We can't afford a second-hand computer in this place and he authorized unlimited overtime AND extra help without taking a breath. Curious personal packages with an FBI address were sent here instead of to his home. Someone who looks suspiciously like a process server comes by asking about where he might find the sheriff. The Sheriff's Office normally serves papers here in Mounton. Did you notice he was wearing his knee brace? He *never* wears that thing. He didn't want his phone calls forwarded to his home landline, where he is supposedly sick, and reception is a hundred percent, but to his cell phone where reception on this mountain is spotty at best. He intends to be mobile. Oh yeah, the man hasn't taken a sick day in ten years."

"Maybe he never gets sick," Patricks guessed.

"Patricks, I've seen Mac report for duty with a 103 fever. His damned nose wasn't even red tonight. Then there's the big thing," Dawe said.

"What?"

"I asked when the boys would be back from *Lexington*. He told us on the phone earlier they were testifying in Frankfort, where the federal courtrooms happen to be. Not only did he not correct me, but he repeated Lexington back to me. I'm telling ya, rook, something is up."

"What do you think we should do about it?" Patricks questioned.

After a moment or two of thought, Dawe said, "Well, you need to go home and get some sleep. The man gave us some direct orders. I don't know about you, but I'm gonna do my job, patrol around a bit, and give it some thought. It doesn't do anyone any good for us to be wrong about this and fired. Maybe by the time you come in in the morning, we'll have some ideas on what the hell is going on in Mounton."

"Surely if there was something really bad, the sheriff would tell us, right?"

"Rookie, you really don't know the man too well, but that's exactly when he wouldn't. And don't call me Shirley. Have you met Shirley? That woman is as mean as a snake."

#

August 11, 2:42 A.M. Basement of Mounton First Baptist Church

"Mac? It's Duncan. I think I spotted the RV. They're at … … I'm watching like … … to do?" Duncan's broken sentences came in over Mac's cell phone. Mac looked at his phone. Two bars. *Damn this mountain!*

"Duncan! Where are you? You broke up. Say again."

"Mac, can you hear … … I kenna nay hear ye over the … … puddocks in the noggin loch." Click. The line disconnected.

Mac stared at the phone. Nine hours until he had to prove he molested a child or they kill someone he cares about. And he has no idea where his family is.

August 11, 3:08 A.M. Basement of Mounton First Baptist Church

Mac relayed his call with Duncan to as many as he could reach to come in, all the while opening a cardboard box and pulling out a large, tan Pelican case with the words "PROPERTY OF FBI" stenciled on it. He sat the case down with its writing against the wall.

Many of the townspeople were searching in areas too remote for a cell signal. Shirley, Felicia,Eaton Hickman, and his youngest boy were already there. The other two Hickman boys arrived as soon as Mac called, as their sector was close to town. Darlene and Mr. Darlene arrived shortly after Mac.

"Here's the deal. I want you all to go home," Mac declared.

"Oh, you can just stuff it, Nancy-boy!" Shirley growled.

"Ain't happening, Sheriff," Darlene's gravel-like voice agreed.

Mr. Darlene just nodded.

"No. Listen. Duncan seems to have found the RV, but the signal was so bad we don't know where they are. I would love to say this is so I can be a martyr, but I am just being selfish. I need you all to go home and catch a few winks or you will be worthless to help my family. Almost everyone here has been up nearly twenty hours, most of it worried to death, with a near gunfight right in the middle of it. You need some sleep. Even a couple of hours will help. Especially you, Felicia. This day has been tougher on you than most."

"And just what do you think you are going to be doing, oh fearless leader?" Darlene inquired.

"I'm gonna sit right here, watch our guests, who are technically my prisoners, try to get a hold of Duncan, or wait for his call, and stare at this map and see if I can figure out where he is."

"No." Shirley stood up to her full five-foot-tall height.

"Excuse me?" Mac asked.

"Listen here, Susie. I bet you ain't slept in two days. I know if Hannah didn't come home, you probably ain't slept a wink. Them slug-nuts over there are out like lights. 'Sides, I'm a deputy. Got a badge and everything. I can listen to your phone just as well as you can. If you don't get some sleep, you'll likely be dangerous to your family. Ginny ain't here, but his big, dumb ass would say the same thing. Get your scrawny butt home and sleep. Saw a few logs and we'll get back at it in a coupla hours. A shower wouldn't hurt none either."

The others waited for Mac to put up a fight.

"Nope. You're right, Shirl. Ginny would tell me the same thing. Now, he would have protested in hundred-dollar words, but he would have set me straight. I need to be at the top of my game. I'll make you a deal. I will go upstairs and sleep in the chapel. Upstairs, so I can be close if Duncan calls back in," Mac interjected.

"Well, if you sleep too long, don't expect God to wake ya up. He ain't no alarm clock, you know."

Mac shuffled up the stairs to the vestry. The others left by the basement back door a few at a time so as to not draw attention. Anyone watching a dozen people leave the church at 3:30 A.M. would raise some suspicions, but nobody was.

Mac didn't think he would be able to sleep, but he barely made it to the top of the stairs with his eyes open. Shirley was right. He was done in. The adrenaline of the day had fled and he was barely a shell. He piled some hymnals on a pew and was out before his head settled on them.

\#

August 11, 5:02 A.M. Mounton Church

Loch Ness!

Mac's subconscious had been grinding on the problem even while his body logged some much-needed rest.

Loch Ness! Loch is the Scottish word for lake. Duncan is by the lake!

Mac sat bolt upright in the pew and rushed down the steps to the church basement.

Shirley was sitting a half dozen yards from the prisoners, knitting, with Mac's cell phone on a stool next to her.

When Mac exploded down the steps, Shirley whirled on her stool, a gigantic, chrome-plated .44 Magnum revolver aimed right at Mac.

"Nice trigger discipline," Mac remarked.

"You goddamned fool. I coulda blown a hole in you Darlene coulda fit through."

"Nice language in the house of the Lord."

"If I was any quicker, I'da arranged you a personal meeting with Him. What are you doing up anyway?" Shirley moved over to where Mac was spreading a county map over the kitchen counter.

"Duncan said 'puddocks in the noggin loch.' I have no idea what 'puddocks' are, and I am assuming 'noggin' is one of Duncan's colorful adjectives, but 'loch' is Scottish for 'lake.' He found them somewhere near Lake Mouton."

"May not help much," Shirley huffed, looking at the map. "His section borders about an eighth of the lake and if I 'member my geometry right, we're talkin' dozens of square miles of territory."

"G.T.S.," Felicity said flatly, coming into the basement back door. Her dark brown skin, thin black hoodie, and jeans, compound bow, and quiver momentarily gave Mac the impression of a black ninja sneaking up on them.

"What? What are you doing here?" Mac asked.

"Couldn't sleep. No Davis. No Gabriel. House was just too … empty. Did get a buttload of housework done, though. When they come back, it'll be to a clean house."

"What is G.T.S.?" Shirley grumbled.

"Google That Shit."

"Why didn't I think of that?" Mac exclaimed reaching for his phone. Three bars.

"Probably lack of sleep, Nancy-boy." Classic Shirley I-Told-You-So.

In the time it took Mac to pull up Google and search on his phone, the Hendricks, Darlene, and Mr. Darlene came in.

"*Puddocks*... is a Scottish word for *frogs*," Mac read. "So, he is by the lake near where the frogs are loud."

"Collins Cove." Eaton Hendricks spoke up.

"What?"

"Collins Cove," Eaton continued. "It's up on the lake. Named for William Floyd Collins, an explorer 'round these parts about the beginning of the last century. I used to take the boys up there giggin' all the time. Collins Cove is jammed fulla frogs. If Duncan couldn't hear nothing for the sound of frogs croakin', I'm betting he's there."

"There it is," Mac blurted as he ran his finger over the county map. "Southeast corner of Duncan's section and there's an old logging road that runs around the lake's edge right to the cove. Eaton, I could kiss you!"

"Let me!" Shirley croaked excitedly, moving toward the farmer. Eaton backed up from the crone.

"Uh, ma'am, I'm married."

"Killjoy."

Mac looked at his people. His posse.

"Okay, if we go now, maybe we can catch them before they wake up and are alert."

"How are you planning on taking them without a full-on blood bath?" Felicia voiced.

"I have some ideas," Mac stated. "Eaton, you're a hunter, right?"

"Yeah, but my boy, Jesse, is a better shot." Eaton smiled at his oldest. The boy practically beamed.

"Good to know," Mac said. "Felicia, I need you to hang back."

"Mac, I'm fine," Felicia said. "I know I cracked a little before, but

Davis is still out there."

"No. This is not about Hickman, but we will talk about that later. I need you to do something special."

#

August 11, 5:50 A.M. Collins Cove, Lake Mounton

"It's about bloody time ye got here," Duncan told Mac as the two men shook hands. Duncan shook his cell phone in his hand in a fit of anger. "I've been trying this jobby-flavoured fart lozenge for hours, but it keeps saying "nay signal."

"You know we still cannot understand what the hell you're saying, right?" Shirley looked up at the red-bearded shop owner.

"Awa' n' bile yer heed, ye auld feartie!" Duncan smiled nicely.

"I hate it when mommy and daddy fight," Darlene told her husband.

"Duncan, if you're done bickering with the nice old lady with the giant handgun, could you tell us what the situation is?" Mac requested of his friend.

"Aye," Duncan pointed to a path toward the lake. "The RV pulled into the clearing by the road and a wee bit later, yon truck pulled up and I'll be dipped in shite if the Stamper boys dinna climb in the RV. About 3:15, the eeijits came out and sacked out in the truck. The big galoot sleeps in the bed."

Mac looked at the sky, then at his watch.

"We have about 40 minutes before the sky starts to light up, so we got to move now."

Mac knocked quietly enough on the side of the pickup to wake anyone inside the truck, but not loud enough to alert the RV.

"Up and at 'em, Atom Ant."

When he heard movement inside, he stepped back a bit. Syrus's scruffy head slid up above the window bottom, still half asleep. When he saw Mac, his eyes popped open and his hand started frantically shaking Spencer awake. Sonny still snored in the bed of the truck.

Mac waved his Colt in a motion to signal Syrus and Spencer to get out of the truck. As Syrus opened the driver's side door, Spencer opened the passenger door, looking around for a chance to make a run for it since he was on the opposite side from Mac. He looked down the barrel of Duncan's pump shotgun. Without a word, he put his hands up.

Mac pointed his pistol to indicate they should lay on the ground. Duncan covered them from a few feet away, just far enough a single blast from the Ithaca would do considerable damage to both men.

Mac looked over the side of the truck bed at the sleeping Stamper brother. Mac nudged him with the Colt a couple of times.

"Uh, hey, Sheriff Mac," Sonny said, rubbing sleep from his eyes.

"Hey Sonny."

"You here to arrest us?"

"Thought I might."

"Okay."

Sonny crawled to the tailgate and eased his bulk out. The leaf springs of the truck groaned as his weight slid off and the truck rose up a few extra inches. Sonny saw both his brothers laying on the ground next to the truck.

"Guess you want me down there?" Sonny asked.

"If you wouldn't mind," Mac replied quietly. He was glad the giant Stamper was acting so calmly. If Sonny decided to put up a fight, Mac didn't know if he and Duncan had enough ammo to put him down. Shooting him with the Colt may just piss him off.

"Keep an eye on these three," Mac instructed Duncan. "Eaton?"

Eaton and Jesse Hendricks emerged from the brush, rifles casually aimed at the ground.

Before Mac could take another step toward the motorhome, the door burst open. Helped by gravity, Mason half dragged/half carried the barely conscious Jeb down the steps. Mason held the handcuffed deputy by his collar. Behind Mason, Anesthesia dragged a mostly unconscious Beth out by her hair. Beth clasped both hands over her belly in a protective gesture. Both Anesthesia and Mason held handguns to their captives' heads. Mac and the Hendricks froze, guns trained on Mason and Betta. The semi-automatic Mason brandished looked like Jeb's service weapon.

"Well, it's the big man himself!" Mason laughed. "Don't you have a crack house or something to set up, Sheriff?"

Mac simply glared at the former deputy.

"You don't seem surprised to see me. Damn shame, after all the trouble someone went to fake my accident. Oh, well. Best laid plans and all. Before you even think about taking one of us out, what are the odds the other doesn't cap one of your kids here?

"You three!" Mason yelled at the Stampers. "Get in the RV. Now.

"Sheriff, this is how this going to go down. We're gonna drive this bad boy out of here and you're going to let us, without pursuit, or Jebby here is going to learn to breathe through his temple. If I see a single car behind us or hear any radio traffic, you're gonna need a new deputy, and a son. He's probably just as crooked as you are, so I got no compunction about cappin' his ass."

The rough handling and yelling started to awaken Jeb. He opened his not-quite-focused eyes. Syrus had made it to the driver's seat of the RV and fumbled to start the big rig. Mason and Anesthesia were walking their hostages backward. Spence was farthest away. Sonny had gotten to his knees but stopped moving.

Everything happened simultaneously. Jeb woke up enough to see Anesthesia dragging Beth across the clearing. With a scream, he lunged toward the women, breaking free of Mason's grip. Mason fired his handgun at Jeb. Mac ran as fast as his knee would let him toward Jeb and Beth to protect them, with his body if necessary.

The groggy Jeb tripped over his own feet and the shot meant for him missed and hit Beth square in the forehead.

Jeb looked up from the ground to see Beth fall. "BETH!"

Mac threw himself over his son's body to protect him from any gunfire.

"Shit!" Mason screamed. "Go!" he yelled at Anesthesia, as they both ran for the door of the motorhome.

In the shock of seeing Beth shot, the Hendricks were slow to get their rifles aimed and missed every shot directed at Anesthesia and Mason. Jesse blasted out a passenger side window narrowly missing Syrus in the driver's seat. Duncan fired several rounds of buckshot at the tires but hit just behind the moving vehicle's wheel wells.

Mason and Anesthesia scrambled in as the RV started to take off down the dusty logging road. Spence had made it to the door, but only managed to grab the handrails inside the coach as the lower half of his body dragged the ground outside the RV. Hands from inside the motorhome pulled him all the way in and barely got the door shut as the RV bounced down the road, leaving a cloud of dust and despair in its wake.

Jeb barely waited while Mac used his keys to uncuff him before he scrambled to Beth's side. The younger MacDowell sobbed and rocked as he held his wife's still form cradled in his arms. Duncan turned to cover the still-kneeling Sonny, but the bear-sized Stamper had not moved during the whole exchange. He just sat on his haunches and stared at Beth and Jeb. The Darlenes joined standing by the Hendricks, alternately staring down the road at the dust trail left by the big motor coach and at Beth. Felicia emerged from the bushes on the far side of the RV. She nodded to Mac, but he didn't see her.

Mac sat on the ground and stared at his son, his daughter-in-law, and her extended belly where his next grandchild would never be born.

Felicia ran to where the rest of the town folk waited, explained what had happened, and retrieved Mac's truck. Jeb refused to let anyone else touch Beth. He gently laid her in the back of the truck and then he climbed in and sat next to her. Felicia waited by the driver's side door. Mac still sat on the ground.

"Mac? Laddie. We need to go," Duncan placed his hand on his friend's shoulder.

"Why?" Mac petitioned his friend in all honesty.

"Hannah. And Naomi."

"Yepper." He stood without energy and handed Duncan the cuffs he had taken off Jeb.

Duncan looked at the cuffs in his hand. He walked over to Sonny. "Do I need to put these on ye, or will ye be a good boy?"

"I'll go." Sonny stood and started toward the truck.

"Nay, lad," Duncan said as he looked at Jeb. "I think it best ye go in a different truck."

Duncan stuck the cuffs and key in his back pocket. *I dinna think they would fit the big eijit anyway.*

#

August 11, 6:58 A.M. Basement of Mounton First Baptist Church

"Where's Mac?" Shirley asked, after hearing the story of Collins Cove.

"He and Jeb are upstairs with Pastor Allen," Duncan said solemnly. "We woke the parson so he could sit with the boys for a while. Beth is with them."

Once the volunteers had arrived back at the church, Duncan motioned Sonny over to the side of the basement where the prisoners were being kept. They found enough zip-ties to secure Sonny, his hands in front of him. Mitch still stared off into space and Josh was crying quietly.

"So, we captured one of theirs, freed one of our own, and lost one?" Shirley asked. "Not even close to being right."

"Two," Felicia said. "We lost two."

"Aye. Beth and the tad," Duncan said. "I dinna ken if Jeb will get over it, but if we lose Hannah or Naomi, I ken Mac won't."

#

August 11, 10:47 A.M. Mounton, KY

Mac came downstairs. The entire group turned to look at the man. Mac had always been whipcord thin, but in the last few hours, he seemed to have lost a dozen pounds he could ill afford.

"Jeb?" asked Duncan.

"Upstairs still. He ... needs ... more time."

"Aye. And you?"

"I am all cried out. Tomorrow may be different. I can't help but think if it wasn't for this damned leg, I might have gotten to Beth

229

before ..."

"Laddie, not even the good Lord above could've saved the lass."

"Well, I can't stop to worry about it this second. Right now, I aim to get the rest of my family back and God help anyone in the way."

"Sheriff, I'm awful sorry about your daughter-in-law and grandbaby," Shirley offered.

"I appreciate it, Shirley," Mac looked around the room. "I appreciate everything everyone has done. No man could ask for better friends."

"Mac, I think the Stamper boy wants to speak to you," Darlene approached Mac. "The big dumb palooka just keeps looking at you, opening his mouth, and then closing it."

"Bring 'im over and make sure the others can't hear what he has to say," Mac said.

Sonny approached Mac with his head down and his ballcap twisted in his gigantic hands, still zip-tied. When the pair were out of earshot of the others, Mac looked at the man.

"You wanted to say something, Sonny?"

"Yes, sir. I reckon I do. First off, I am powerful sorry 'bout what happened to Mr. Ginny. We was just s'posed to fetch him."

"Wait. What happened to Ginny?" Mac demanded, confused.

"I reckon he drownt in the lake. Tweren't nobody's fault he rushed over the hill. But our pappy always preached ya gotta take your comeuppance, so whatever you see fit to do to us, we probably got it coming," Sonny mumbled, his head hung low.

Ginny dead?

"Are you sure Ginny's dead, Sonny?"

"I reckon. I don't know for a fact. We shot him with three of them darts. One. Two. Three. And he charged at us like a bull if'n its tail was on fire. We ducked out of the way an' he ran into the woods and fell off the cliff into the lake. So, I guess I don't *know* it for a fact, but Syrus seemed to think so. Do you think he may be okay?"

Mac looked at Sonny, maybe for the first time. Yes, he was ...

simple. And he had definitely done some illegal things in his life, mostly at the direction of his older brother, Syrus. But despite his mental handicaps and his lack of sophistication, Mac did not believe the big mountain man was bad. He had just rolled craps on the genetic dice game of life.

His best friend was gone. Ginny had always seemed like such a good-natured force of nature, it didn't seem possible that the giant chef was dead.

"God Himself only knows about Ginny," Mac comforted the big man. "It's okay, Sonny. I know you didn't mean for him to die."

"Sheriff Mac, I'm powerful sorry about your family being took and 'bout Miz Beth. I didn't know'd it was gonna happen. I ain't all so sure Syrus know'd it either. Yeah, Miz Hannah shot Spence once, but she shot him in the arm and could killed him dead sure as I'm standing here." Sonny took a deep breath. He had probably never talked this much at one time in his whole adult life. "T'was mighty nice of her considering we was standing there aiming guns at you and your kin. So, despite shootin' Spence, I reckon Miz Hannah done right by my family. Ain't nobody s'posed to take a little girl. Ain't nobody supposed to shoot a purty girl like Miz Beth and kill her and her baby."

At the mention of Beth, Mac had to turn away. The loss of Ginny, the death of Beth and the baby, and the kidnapping of his wife and family were almost more than he could bare.

"Sheriff Mac, I cain't take back what happened to them as much I'd like to, but mebbe I can help get your family back," Sonny sniveled, his voice choked with tears.

"How?"

Sniff. The dim-witted giant wiped his nose on his sleeve.

"Mr. Jarvis told us we wuz s'posed to take Mr. Ginny to that RV, where he wuz gonna be kept asleep. Ya know, like a mobile home on wheels? Syrus thought it was a biggun with eight wheels in the back. One, two, three, four, five, six, seven, eight. Syrus claimed it had some fancy lights on it. I don't know where we was told to take him, but they probably ain't there no more no how."

Mac had already seen the RV, but didn't get a good look at it or the woman driving it. All he could remember was Beth laying in Jeb's arms.

Sonny continued. "It was s'posed to be driven by a purty colored woman. That Jarvis feller claimed she would nurse 'em or something, even though she had a crazy look in her eyes, a gold ring in her eyebrow, and drawings all over her arms."

If they sedated Ginny, there's a chance they sedated his family too. They could be all alive. It doesn't sound like The Voice ordered anyone harmed, he just wanted leverage against me.

"Neville Jarvis?"

"Yeah, he's the feller. Used to be mayor down here in Mounton."

Another piece fell into place. Neville isn't smart enough to organize all this, have enough cash or clout, or ... Mac couldn't think of another word ... EVIL enough. But he was rotten enough to be a part of it.

"I can tell you 'bout where we was taking them trucks in Ohio. Plus, Syrus thought some smart feller from outta state was in on all this. He weren't supposed know about 'im, but I reckon he did. Syrus is purty smart hisself."

"A smart guy?" Mac tried to figure out what the bear-sized Stamper could mean. *A wise guy?*"

"I reckon, he said something like he was sly like a fox outta Chi-cagi."

Sly. Chicago.

"Sonny," Mac said, "I appreciate your help and if it gets down to it, I will talk to the judge about your condolences and assistance. I don't know if it will do any good, but I will do what I can."

"Ah, Mr. Mac, you don't worry none about helping me, you jes' get yer family back. That young'un and her family need to be home safe and sound."

Sonny turned, hands still bound, cap in hand, to go sit with the others in the grass.

Duncan strolled up to Mac, his scattergun resting in his folded arms.

"Ya get anything from yon dumb gommy?"

Mac turned to his oldest surviving friend. "Gommy?"

"Aye, 'dunderhead,' 'simpleton,' 'iejit.' Ye would know if ye were a true Scot and could speak the damned language!"

"That *man* just may have saved my family. We have the names of four more players, probably a rung up the ladder from these foot soldiers, the location of their drug drops, a confirmed ID on the woman who held Beth, and my family is very likely alive. So, yes, I did get something from him.

"Also, Ginny's dead."

\#

August 11, 11:55 A.M. Mounton, KY

Mac's phone rang.

"Sheriff MacDowell."

"I'm glad to see you understand being near your phone. I heard about the unfortunate incident involving your daughter-in-law this morning. Had you tried not to be a hero, it would not have been necessary."

Mac gripped the phone tight enough to nearly break it.

"I understand you have recruited several of the locals to assist you. You are to dismiss them immediately. Since you did not actually engage law enforcement as instructed, we will consider Beth's passing as payment for your transgressions."

Mac closed his eyes.

"What happened to Beth was my responsibility."

"Of course, it was. Word is you have at least two of my pawns in custody. Possibly four. You will release them immediately or you force me to terminate another of my guests. If I can't confirm their release within the hour, your family will suffer."

"Fine." Mac turned to Duncan and nodded at the prisoners. "Cut 'em loose."

"What? Are ye daft boyo?"

"Just let 'em go," Mac snapped.

Back into the phone, Mac hissed, "Okay, they're loose. Now let my family go."

"I never said that was the deal, Sheriff. I stated if you didn't release my pawns, I would kill another of yours. I never promised anything about releasing yours."

"What. Do. You. Want?" Mac could barely get the words out through the anger.

"I have already told you my demands, Sheriff. This brings me to my next point. Since I did not receive the video proof I requested, I am afraid another of your entourage will pay."

"Wait! NO! What about Beth? Wasn't she enough?"

"Beth was merely the cost of defying me. Failure to provide proof of compliance will cost you another."

"No."

"Yes. But consider this: this sacrifice gives you another twenty-four hours to provide video proof of your acquiescence. You have until noon tomorrow. The price of today's failure cost you the life of ... the diner owner." Click.

Ginny.

August 11, 12:10 P.M., Mounton, KY

Ginny would pay the price.

The Voice doesn't know I know Ginny is already dead. He doesn't know Sonny talked to me. He's bluffing.

Duncan and the others stared at Mac as he relayed the conversation.

"So, he knows about some of us, but not the others," Duncan said. "We need to keep a low profile."

Mac shook his head.

"Just the opposite," Felicia agreed. "You need to be very visible. He needs to see you out and about doing anything but helping Mac. This will make him think he has control of the situation."

"Aye, like a sleight-of-hand distraction," Duncan agreed. "While he is busy watching the right hand, the magic is happening in the other."

"Yepper."

#
#

234

Trapping the Trappers

August 12, 5:15 A.M., East River Road outside Mounton, KY, Two Hours Earlier

"This is where the signal from the cell phone stopped," Darlene said.

"It must be around here somewhere, I'm still getting three bars on my phone," Eaton whispered, checking his cell. "The Salt River is less than a mile or so away. Past the river is nothing but woods and hills and Mounton Lake. The boys and I used to hunt here. These Find My Phone apps just aren't very accurate. Damned thing could be anywhere."

"No, it couldn't," Darlene grumbled. "The road ends here and there are no ATV trails into those woods. It has to be near this road somewhere. It should be *right here*."

"It is," Mason said.

Darlene and Eaton turned around to see themselves surrounded by Mason, Mitch, Josh, Jarvis, and the two elder Stamper boys. All with semi-automatics aimed right at them.

#

August 12, 5:15 A.M., SR55 and Little Union Road outside Mounton, KY

"That look like a damned UFO to you?"

"No, Shirley, I'd say it resembles our missing RV," Mac observed, peering between the bushes at the big motorhome hidden down in a low valley. Mac checked his watch. "It's about time. You ready?"

"Born ready," Shirley grinned.

"What year was that exactly, Shirley?"

"Let's just say Netflix wasn't a thing then."

"Were telephones?" Mac joked as he stood up and walked down the ridge.

"Far enough, homes," Sly called out from the door of the RV. The two Chicagoans crowded out of the RV after him, all with guns aimed at Mac.

Betta came out of the RV, stepping outside to back up the

Chicagoans.

"I gotta say, el sherif, you have some major cajones to stroll up on us AGAIN without a piece," Sly teased, looking around. "How many turistas you got backin' you up this time?"

"No tourists this time, Sly. Just a bunch of deputies locked and loaded with weapons aimed at you," Mac smiled.

Red laser dots appeared on the torsos of all four criminals.

"Don't worry about dat shit, cariño," Sly smiled to Anesthesia. "He pulled dat same shit this spring when he faked us out with a bunch of turistas holding cat pointers. We ain't fallin' for the same ole—"

Pop. Pop. Pop. Three shots cracked nearly simultaneously. Sly spun, dropping his handgun as he whirled in the air. A blast hit Kong, struck him in the shoulder, and knocked him up off his feet and back into the side of the RV. The third shot missed Betta by mere inches, blasting one of the RV's rearview mirrors into pieces. All the lasers immediately locked on to the only two left standing: Betta and Grady Noble, the remaining Chicagoan.

"As you can see, these are *NOT* cat toys," Mac explained. "I would heavily suggest you lay face down on the ground with your fingers laced behind your heads."

Grady dropped his gun as if electrified. With a practiced ease indicating it was not his first time, he was on his face, with his hands behind his head. Betta stared at Mac a long time before lowering herself to lay on the ground. Shirley, Jesse, and Tommy Hendricks, and Duncan stepped down into the clearing, keeping their weapons, fitted with FBI-supplied laser sights, night vision scopes, and suppressors, aimed at the kidnappers.

"Ballsy move, walking down here without a gun, Susie," Shirley jabbed at Mac.

"Fortune favors the bold," Mac told her.

"And sissy-merries, evidently." Shirley looked at Tommy Hendricks. "The mirror? Really?"

"She wasn't holding a weapon," the youngest Hendricks boys explained. "Didn't see any reason to hit her when scaring her would work just as well."

"Good boy," Mac told him.

"I got mine," Shirley grinned.

Duncan, leaning on his shotgun, was kneeling next to Kong. "If by 'got' you mean 'damn near blew his shoulder off with yon cannon,' then yes, you *got* him."

"This one's still got a gun," Jesse Hendricks exclaimed, keeping his rifle aimed nearly straight down at Betta. Mac removed the handgun from the back waistband of Betta's jeans and checked the clip. Her scrubs shirt had concealed it until laying down uncovered it. Mac nodded at Jesse, handing him some zip-ties.

"Shirley, you frisk her. Be thorough. Jesse, you and Duncan cover them as Tommy frisks the others," Mac ordered as he bolted for the RV door.

After climbing the steps into the RV, Mac aimed Betta's Glock ahead of him covering the narrow space. He first saw the dinette table converted into a bed which had presumably held Beth and Jeb, now empty. He ran to Hannah strapped down to the jackknife couch bed. A thin sheet covered her and besides an IV drip line, there looked to be a catheter running under the sheet.

Laying the Glock on the side of the bed in easy reach, he gingerly removed the IV needle from her elbow. Hopefully, removing the drip would start her waking process. He quickly unhooked the ratchet straps holding her down and stood, looking for Naomi. Picking up the Glock, he carefully slid the sliding pocket door open which separated the kitchen area from the bunk bed hallway. Strapped to the lower bunkbed was Naomi. The upper bunk held Davis. Thin sheets covered all of the victims. All of them attached to IVs and catheters, and restrained by ratchet straps. One of the hardest things Mac ever had to do was walk past his granddaughter with her tied down and IVs in her arms. He needed to clear the back bedroom first.

After clearing the rest of the RV, Mac quickly turned back to Naomi. She had an extra line in her other arm. Mac carefully removed the needles, unhooked the straps holding her down, but knew nothing about removing catheters, so he left her in place.

"Shirley!" Mac yelled out the open door of the RV.

"What now?" the crone barked.

"They're in here, but I need help. They have catheters we need to remove," Mac shouted as Shirley climbed up into the RV. Mac handed her some blue nitrile evidence gloves as she climbed into the RV.

"What do you expect me to do?" Shirley croaked. "Just because I'm old, you think I know about catheters? That's ageism. Why didn't you call Duncan in here?"

"Because I don't want Duncan's help pulling catheters out of my wife and granddaughter."

"Fine. I'll help. But if I do, I get to do Davis's too. I heard once you go 'deputy' you never go back!"

#

August 12, 7:04 A.M., MOUNTON, KY

"Dawe, are you there?" Mac voice crackled over the sheriff's station radio.

"This is Patricks, Sheriff. We both are." The two men were in the middle of the shift change between Dawe's night shift and Patricks' morning patrols.

"Great. I can't tell you any details right now, but I need you to put out a BOLO on a late-model recreational vehicle with Kentucky plates. Also, the Stamper brothers, the group from Chicago we arrested a while back, and a Mitch Northrop from Lexington, as well as Joshua May, also from Lexington."

"Aren't those two of the jokers who tried to rob Ginny a bit ago?" Dawe asked into the mic. "What happened to the third? Ralph something?"

"Mr. Hickman had an unfortunate ... hunting accident. He is no longer with us. Same for Mason Wheeler. Mason kidnapped Naomi, but unfortunately, he met an untimely passing before we could talk to him."

"What the hell, Mac?" Dawe asked. "What is going on? Are you talking about the Mason who used to work for us? I know he was spreading shit about the office, but you didn't kill him, did you?

238

Didn't he die in a truck accident or something?"

"Nope," Mac knew that Dawe understood very well they were on an open police band that anyone could listen in on. "Mason had an unfortunate meeting with some stray metal particulates in the air. Damned shame too. There were a few questions I would have liked answered. I hate dumping this on you boys, but I am out of resources right now. Put out BOLOs to the surrounding counties on all of those characters and the RV and let me know if anyone sees anything. I will fill you in on the whys and wherefores later."

With a click and some static, Mac signed off.

Dawe turned to Patricks.

"So, seeing as how *Ginny's* is closed down, for the time being, you wanna try the new *Waffle House* over in Yoder for breakfast? Patty-Jane's getting the boys off to school this morning, so I got some time to kill."

#

August 12, 11:15 A.M., East River Road outside Mounton, KY

Mason sent Mitch and Josh to check the road. When they came back, they were shaking their heads no.

"Where's the rest of your merry band?" he questioned Darlene. "I thought Little Sheriff Dillinger would send his whole gang. I guess he figured we would find the cell phone you planted and were tracking and use it as a trap. We made sure we put it where it would get a good signal. So, I guess you are the sacrificial lambs."

"A bit less like sacrificial lambs and more like bait," Eaton Hendricks told him, holding his rifle limply by the stock.

"What ya mean by bait, farm boy?" Syrus Stamper snapped. But Darlene answered.

"When the phone we were tracking never lost its signal, especially in this area, we kind of suspected you may be using it as bait. Syrus, I know you been fishin'," Darlene explained. "For different fish, you use different bait. The bigger the bait, the bigger the fish you aim to catch. I guess I figure I'm about as big o' bait as you can get in these parts."

"Dammit, Syrus, you only use bait in a trap!" Spencer snapped at his older brother. "I told you the minute we mixed up with them spics and negroes, this deal would go bad!"

Syrus was about to answer when ...

Shots exploded from different directions knocking Spencer Stamper and Mitch Northrup to the ground. An arrow thwipped by and penetrated Syrus in the collar bone. Eaton Hendricks, expecting the attack, punched the closest of the kidnappers, Josh, in the back of the head as hard as he could. Only Mason and Neville remained standing as Jeb, Felicia, and Mr. Darlene stepped into the clearing.

Mason grabbed Felicia with his arm around her throat, holding her in front of him as a shield, as all guns trained on him. In the blink of an eye, Eaton had his rifle to his shoulder and Darlene lifted her aluminum bat. Pistol pointed to the side of Felicia's head, Mason ordered everyone to drop their guns.

All of the newly minted deputies looked to Jeb, who was the most senior and had lost the most. After a long pause, Jeb lowered his weapon to his side. Eaton and Mr. Darlene dropped their rifles to the ground. The gun to her head had already caused Felicia to drop her bow.

"I didn't intend for this to get so far out of hand," Mason insisted. "But I am not going to go down for kidnapping while Mac the Knife is out there flaunting every law in the book."

Mason turned himself and Felicia in a circle, eyeing each of the rescuers. Neville Jarvis opened the door to the RV, getting ready to back up the steps.

"You too, Fatso," Mason snapped at Darlene. "Toss the bat or Whitney Houston here gets it."

Jeb coughed just as Darlene tossed the bat high in the air into the nearby woods. Mason turned in Jeb's direction after making sure the bat wasn't aimed at him but missed the giant rising up from the brush behind him snagging the bat in mid-air. The former deputy turned just in time to see Ginny hit a line drive with a solid "tink!" as the aluminum bat clipped Mason on the side of his head. While not a direct hit, the impact still lifted Mason off his feet and away from

Felicia.

Jeb aimed his lowered pistol at the unconscious Mason with absolute murder in his eyes.

Unexpectedly, Felicia stepped in front of his gun.

"Jeb, I know what you are feeling. But it's over. We got them. By now, Mac and his crew rescued your mom and Naomi and Davis and we don't need to do this. I thought killing Hickman would make me feel better, but it didn't."

Jeb kept the gun aimed right at Mason, even though the round would have to pass through Felicia to hit its target.

"He killed Beth. He killed our baby." Tears rolled down his face as he spat out the words.

"I know. I wanted them all dead too. But would Beth want Naomi to lose her only parent to prison? If you think so, then I won't stop you." Felicia stood aside, leaving Jeb a clear shot at Mason's prone form.

Jeb stood frozen for a moment. His right hand gripped his semi-automatic so tightly that his knuckles turned white. Sweat and tears poured down his face. With a single look at Felicia, he dropped the gun.

#

"GINNY!" Mac exclaimed as he forgot his natural stoicism and ran to hug his gigantic friend. The two teams had converged at the RV after Mac radioed their position. By mutual agreement, Darlene's team kept the secret of Ginny's survival to surprise Mac and Shirley. "We thought you were dead."

"Reports of my death were greatly exaggerated. Uh, you can let go now. You're embarassing me in front of the criminals."

"What happened? The Stampers swore they shot you with a bunch of darts and you fell off a ravine into the lake," Mac stated.

"For once our local ne'er-do-wells have spoken with veracity. I did indeed plunge into said lake. Thank God for motorcycle helmets. I washed up on the north end. After a day or so of narcotics-inspired beauty sleep, I started across the damned hill to follow Salt River to East River Road where I was hoping to hitch a ride into town. It's amazing how few people are willing to pick up a bedraggled, tattooed man over six-foot tall. Do you know how long it takes to traverse that hill on foot? I do. I just got in sight of the road and heard some shots and crept over to check it out, arriving in the proverbial nick of time."

"You're lucky it was summer. In the winter, you would have just broken down through the ice and froze to death," Darlene commented.

"However, it happened, I am just happy you're alive!" Mac beamed.

Ginny looked over at the diminutive cashier, digging through her oversized handbag.

"Shirley."

"'Bout damned time you showed up. I was havin' to do all the heavy liftin' for this bunch of panty-waists. Now that you're here, I suppose I'll have to tote your load too!" Shirley growled, not bothering to look up from her bag.

"I missed you too," Ginny said tenderly.

Everyone gathered around and clapped the big man on his back and shoulders, welcoming him back from the dead. Darlene gave him a Darlene-sized hug. Nobody noticed Shirley finding the tissue she was searching her bag for and wiping her eyes with it.

Ginny looked around the clearing, covered with wounded and unconscious criminals, and asked, "So, what did I miss?"

Shirley frisked Mason and went through his pockets. "Somebody wanna go get Jarvis? The keys to the damned RV are right here. He's in there sitting in a big metal box on wheels."

#

Arresting Developments

"Okay if I just barge right in?" Mac asked without slowing, as he stepped through the ornate doors to the den.

"Sheriff MacDowell?" the Commonwealth of Kentucky's District Attorney, Devin Douvez, bleated as he sat upright behind the enormous mahogany desk in his den. "What are you doing here?"

"To be honest, I just wanted to see your face."

"Well, it's nice to see you too," Douvez faltered, noting Mac's lack of firearm, "but aren't you a bit out of your way. I mean, Mounton County is about 30 or 40 miles or so south of here. Quite a drive at this time of day just to say hello. Besides, I thought I made it clear on the phone, I would rather people not know about us talking."

"I didn't come by to say hi, and we're not talking. I came for the arrest."

Bertrand stood abruptly. "What arrest? Did you find the people who took your family?"

Mac smiled. "How did you know they were taken, Mr. Douvez?"

"Aw, shit." Douvez's eyes flicked toward the bookshelf. He acted almost relieved not to have to keep up the pretense. "I know *you're* not going to arrest me and I don't think you're here to kill me. No sidearm." The thought crossed his mind because if their positions were reversed, Douvez would have shot MacDowell in a heartbeat.

"Besides, with all the negative press you've been getting lately and your criminal activity, even if you arrested me, I would be out by lunch and filing a lawsuit on you by dinner."

"You're right. I'm not going to arrest you," Mac smiled as he reached for the doorknob of the door he just came through. "He is."

Mac opened the door to let Dave Smathers; his FBI partner, Mike Sanders; and most of what Mac thought of as The Mounton Posse, into the den.

Dave handed several folded sheets to Douvez. "This first document is a search warrant for this house and your office, but just standing here, I can see a voice scrambler near the phone and several police scanners on the bookshelves. Is it tuned to the Mounton County Sheriff's Office frequency? And what looks like a scanner for the encrypted FBI frequencies, which, unless I am mistaken, only the FBI and the NSA are supposed to have. The second document is an arrest warrant which is required if we arrest you in your home, as you may be aware."

Sanders pulled a card from his suit jacket. "Mr. Douvez, as the Commonwealth of Kentucky's district attorney, I am almost certain you know your rights, but you also know, by law, I am required to read them to you. Mike, if you please?"

"You have the right to remain silent ..."

Jeb, who had been standing slightly behind his father with his jaw clenched in silent rage, stepped forward, pulled out his dad's 1873 Colt Peacemaker Single Action Army revolver from the holster strapped to his own leg, aimed it at Douvez's forehead, and pulled the trigger.

#

TWO HOURS EARLIER

"Jeb, are you sure you're up to this? I mean, with Beth and all ..." Mac looked hard at his son.

"Dad, I want to be there when we bring this sonnuvabitch in."

"Yepper, I get it," Mac agreed, pulling a Kevlar vest from a closet. "But if you're going, you're going protected. Naomi only has one parent now and Hannah would never forgive me if something happened to you."

"Are you wearing a vest?" Jeb asked.

"Nope. I'm probably not even gonna wear this sidearm. I'm just there to watch the show and see his face."

"Me too," Jeb confirmed, draping the heavy vest over the back of a chair. "We're not gonna need 'em. Dave goes in, serves the papers, cuffs him, and then it's all up to the justice system."

"Well, at the very least, take my gun. Your primary is still in evidence since it was taken from you and used in the commission of a crime," Mac pauses, remembering it was Jeb's handgun that killed Beth. "Your backup is being held for the shooting by the river. At least your mama can't say I let you go unarmed."

He unstrapped the gun belt from his waist and handed it to his son.

Jeb looked at the Colt. It was the first time he had ever held it. He strapped on the gunslinger-style belt and felt the weight of the pistol against his leg.

Jeb couldn't hear the slight rattle in Mac's pants pocket.

#

TWO HOURS LATER

Click.

The hammer fell on the Colt, clicking on an empty chamber. Dave jumped a step and snatched the Peacemaker from Jeb's grip.

"Aw, hell. Jeb, why would you ..." then it occurred to Dave that Douvez was responsible for Beth's death. "I'm sorry, son, but now I am going to have to arrest you."

"Hold on, Dave," Mac said, slowly taking the empty Colt from his hand. "What for? Douvez is alive and well and nobody here saw Jeb try anything, did they?"

The Mounton Posse all shook their heads as if rehearsed.

Mac folded his arms, still holding the Colt, leaned against a bookshelf, and looked at Mike Sanders. Dave watched Mac casually caress the Colt on his shirt sleeve, eradicating any prints.

"Didn't see a thing," Mike declared. "Can I finish his Miranda rights now?"

Bertrand, in shock from the near-death experience, screamed out, "I don't need my damned rights spelled out to me! He tried to kill me! I want him arrested!"

Dave looked at the Mounton Posse and back to Douvez. "I'm sorry, Mr. Douvez, but I don't have any evidence supporting such a claim. What I do have is a truckload of evidence you conspired to kidnap a half-dozen people, trafficked narcotics across state lines, and are complicit in the murder of Beth MacDowell. And despite you waiving the reading of your Miranda rights, we ARE going to read them anyway, because when this thing goes to court, you are not getting off on a technicality. If you would still like to waive them, we have a form you can sign."

"You have nothing!"

"Oh, Lordie, Devin, besides the physical evidence in this room alone, we have enough to convict ten guys like you," Dave shook his head in disgust.

"Like what?"

"Fine. I guess you're going to hear it from your attorney anyway, assuming you are not stupid enough to try and defend yourself."

"We couldn't trace any cell calls between you and your co-conspirators, which was pretty smart, but a little-known fact: since 9/11, retailers are required to notify the Department of Homeland Security when someone makes a non-resale purchase of a large quantity of burner phones. Call them silly that way. In an uncharacteristic spirit of cooperation, they notified us and we were able to trace the wire transfers through a variety of shell corporations landing at your deceased mother's childhood home. Coincidently enough, the serial numbers of the burner phone purchase matched phones we found on your co-conspirators, some still in the plastic bubble packaging. You purchased the RV with cash, another smart move, but registered it to the same address, not so smart. Mac also noted you used the term LEO over the phone, short for Law Enforcement Officer, which is not a common term outside the community."

"None of it points directly to me," Douvez denied.

"And then ..." Dave continued, "you hired Mason before he could even finish at the academy. It wouldn't have taken much for you to find out he was strapped for cash. Suddenly being a thousandaire, he did what any hillbilly would do: run out and buy a brand-new, expensive truck. Mac noticed his being ghostly pale and skinny as a rail leaned toward him not working on his parents' farm as he stated, plus he just bought a big new truck proving he wasn't dirt poor. Add his part in Mac's public defamation, and he was ripe to confess.

"Given there were numerous witnesses to him killing Beth MacDowell," Dave paused to look at Jeb, who just stared at the floor, "and after recovering from his last meeting with Ginny, even a moron like Mason could see the writing on the wall. He rolled over on you. He even admitted to pretending to be Jeb to the newspaper, even though we had Jeb and Beth's ticket stubs to *The Kentucky Castle* to verify his alibi. Did we mention Mac knew someone was listening in on the sheriff's band and totally faked everyone's getaway and Mason's death? Ironic, huh?"

Bertrand pressed his lips so tightly together, they actually trembled in anger.

"Once we had all the pieces, it was nothing to quietly get a warrant to laser mic your window and record your calls this morning, in an undistorted voice I might add, leaving instructions to your 'gang' on their burner phones' voicemail. Word for word, time-stamped matching to the second what we got from the laser mic. All about how to abandon the RV, what to do with the kidnap victims, and clean up this mess. You didn't know Mac already arrested them because he gave his deputies fake BOLOs over the radio.

"Mac called me days ago on my private cell phone and he and I have been working on this since. I managed the warrants this morning but was unable to get an FBI chopper on such short notice. Luckily, Mac has a friend who was able to bring everyone up from Mounton and drop us all off here."

Right on cue, Harlan, obviously hearing the conversation through an open radio, lowered the helicopter making it visible through the den's French doors.

"Just in case you were able to get to a car."

The hatred in Douvez's face was unmistakable.

"WHY? Why would I go to all this trouble? You have no motive, Smathers."

"There was the gubernatorial campaign. The power players in the state knew someone was running, but no candidates were trying to raise money for a campaign through the usual channels. They should know. They ARE the usual channels. The outlay of cash to pay your partners, we found out once they started talking, matched roughly the same amount as withdrawn from the shell companies' accounts, but the huge deposits you made matched the dates of the garbage truck runs. Great idea, using garbage trucks, by the way."

Douvez's mind was racing.

"Once this farcical shell company theory is disproven, all of this is just circumstantial."

Dave looked at the floor for a second and then at Mac. This part wasn't Bill's to tell.

Mac looked Douvez square in the eye, "I know about Hannah."

Douvez flinched.

"I've known for decades," Mac started. "Someone in her AA meeting thought it was important enough to break the anonymity. I think they were hoping I would hunt you down and give you what you deserve. But I didn't. Hannah wanted to keep it in her past and I respected her wishes. Every fiber in my body wanted to scatter your body over five counties, but she was strong enough to move on, so how could I do less?"

Bertrand sat down.

"Hannah has agreed to testify. After all, you kidnapped her granddaughter and killed her daughter-in-law," Dave spared his friend from continuing. "Even though the statute of limitations on her attack is long past, it goes to motive, state of mind, and a criminal pattern of conduct. You kidnapped her and her family to take what you thought of as yours and to remove Mac's support system. You tried to crush the soul, career, and will of the man who won her heart and who was the only serious competition you had for the governor's mansion. You planted a mole in his office and conspired to ruin his reputation and accomplishments, and implicate him in the burnt meth lab. You came up with this drug trafficking scheme to raise money for the campaign and use his recent arrestees to make him look incompetent or criminal.

"What you didn't count on was the people you kidnapped were not the ONLY friends and family a man like Mac would have. Something you may never understand. You kept all your minions isolated and in the dark, feeding them only the info they needed to do their jobs. Some of what you did was smart, but you use people like pawns and

Mac protects them like family. Big difference."

"We spoke with Jarvis," Mac told Douvez. "He claimed you thought of this as some sort of game. Chess or something. He thought you were God's grandmaster, playing me. Well, you weren't. I guess we both needed to learn you weren't playing against just me, you were playing against all of Mounton. And no matter how good you think you might be, not even you can beat so many good people at one time."

"You know, MacDowell," Douvez snapped at Mac as Dave cuffed him, "you need to do some math. I was with Hannah a little over 28 years ago. Even though he just tried to kill me, you ever wonder about Hannah giving birth to Jebediah so soon after your wedding?"

"Devin," Mac sighed shaking his head, "do you really think after what you did to Beth, Jeb would ever be yours?"

"Bertrand," Dave drawled, "all it takes is a single look at those two. Jeb is practically Mac's clone."

"I dare you to do a blood test!" Douvez ranted at Mac.

"I don't need to," Mac remarked quietly. "No matter what it would say, family is who takes care of you, help you, and even protect you from yourself. No blood test will ever show me anything else."

Mac lead Jeb and the posse back out the door as Mike read Douvez his rights.

#

And That's the Rest of the Story

August 17, 10:14 A.M., Lexington, KY

Darlene pulled up with a rented van to pick up everyone from the UK Lexington Good Samaritan Hospital. After their tranquilizing, drugged incarceration, and the effects of the kidnapping by Betta and her cohorts, the doctors thought it best if the victims stayed a day or two for observation and to purge the drugs from their systems. It took Harlan three trips to ferry everyone to the Lexington hospital. Jeb evaded the hospital stay long enough to attend Douvez's arrest but was immediately admitted once it was done. Felicia only left Davis's bed long enough to get Gabriel and bring him to Lexington. Ginny had refused treatment, despite being shot by three tranquilizer darts and falling into Lake Mounton. Two good meals and a gallon of water later and he declared himself fit. The doctor started to argue with him, but visually measured him from head to toe and pronounced him discharged as AMA, against medical advice.

Hannah insisted Naomi be put in her room. Despite the nursing staff's objections, Hannah moved Naomi into he own bed, so the two MacDowell women curled up next to each other. Between the drugs in her system, the chaos of the kidnapping, and the fuss at the hospital, Hannah was sure Naomi didn't grasp something bad had happened to her mother. There was going to be a tough conversation.

Mac and Ginny bounced between Jeb, Hannah, and Naomi's bedsides, but one of them was always at Jeb's. The young deputy hadn't spoken since his attempt on Douvez's life and while the doctors pronounced he was physically healthy, Mac did not care for the dark circles under his son's eyes.

Darlene dropped everyone off at their respective homes. Mac worried about dropping the still silent Jeb off with Naomi, but Hannah overruled him. Mac told Jeb to take as much time off as he needed. After hearing of Patty-Jane's complaints about Dawe never being home, Mac wasn't entirely sure Dawe was secretly enjoying his time away from home at the moment. Mac called Jesse Hendricks in to start as a deputy-in-training. Jesse was learning the ropes and helping out with patrols. Eaton was so proud, he could barely contain himself. Patricks happily passed Jesse the title of the FNG and finally started wearing jeans to work.

By law, due to suspicious circumstances, an autopsy had to be performed on Beth and her unborn child. The baby would have been a boy. No new details came to light, but the results added to the pile of evidence against her captors. Because of the autopsy, Hannah insisted the brief service at the church featured a closed casket.

#

August 22, 1:14 P.M., Mounton, KY

Jeb followed Beth's wishes to be cremated. Hannah, Jeb, and Mac spread her ashes on an overgrown shore of Lake Mounton. Felicia volunteered to watch Naomi as Hannah thought it best if Naomi wasn't traumatized any more about the lake than she probably already was. Mac collected Naomi afterward and walked with her around the MacDowell farmland.

"Mommy's not coming back, is she, Pappaw?"

"No, SweetPea, she isn't. Do you understand what that means?" Mac asked.

"I think so. Mammaw explained it to me. She said Mommy's in Heaven now. But she's watching over me."

"Of course, she is," Mac assured his granddaughter. "Have you ever known Mammaw to be wrong?"

"Well, she wasn't right about broccoli. I still don't like it."

"You will. Give it time. I have found out Mammaw is pretty smart about almost everything."

"Pappaw," Naomi started, "if Mommy is in Heaven, why is Daddy so sad?"

"He just misses your mommy, SweetPea."

"But isn't Heaven the best place you can be?"

"It is, baby. But right now, being here with you is a close second."

#

August 22, 3:11 P.M., Mounton, KY

Mac left Naomi at the swing set in the backyard to join Jeb and Hannah in the kitchen.

"Dad, Mom," Jeb starts, "I'd like to leave Naomi here for a while if you don't mind. I need some time to wrap my head around all this and I can barely take care of myself, let alone a precocious six-year-old. And the whole thing with Douvez ..."

"Son, of course, we'll take SweetPea," Mac reassured. "This must be incredibly hard on you. I can't imagine. How much time do you think you will need? Or do you even have any idea?"

"NO!" Hannah stated firmly.

"What?" both Mac and Jeb sat flabbergasted. Turning to face her, they thought Hannah would jump at the chance to take Naomi.

"I said no. Our little angel just lost her mother and baby brother and she is not going to lose her father to a raging case of self-pity. I hate what happened to Beth. Absolutely hate it. I would trade places with her in a hot second if I could, but Naomi needs to know she has a father who loves her and will always be there and you just need to suck it up, no matter how hard it is.

"Consider it settled," Hannah continued in a slightly softer tone. "You and Naomi are moving all your stuff in here and we will help you in any way possible, but we are not going to be her parents. She still has a daddy and he is going to step up no matter what. Parents step up. You should know by now when you become a parent, your life is no longer your own. Your number one responsibility, your mission, is to take care of your child."

Jeb hung his head down till his chin touched his chest.

"Yes, ma'am. I don't know what I was thinking."

"Well, you need to be thinking about what's best for your child. Lord knows that's what we're doing."

"I thought you were thinking about Naomi's welfare," Jeb asked.

"We are," Hannah continued, "but do you really think it's in your best interest to go off a pity-pout for a while? No, son, you need to take care of our little girl as much as she needs to be taken care of. If you protect your family, you'll get back tenfold what you give."

Jeb looked at his father, who just nodded.

"Don't look at me, I'm just barely figuring it out myself."

Hannah looked at the two MacDowell men.

"I don't know how you two have lasted this long without your family to take care of ya."

Mac smiled at Jeb. "What she said."

#

August 24, 11:11 A.M., Mounton, KY

Due to the drugs trafficked across state lines and the kidnappings involved the family of the sheriff and deputies, the FBI took over the investigation. Unlike movie cops, Mac wanted no part in the active investigation. He cooperated in every way and gave them full access to everything in his office, as well as hours of interviews. In the end, the FBI fully absolved him and his team of any malfeasance and criminal activity. They also exonerated Mac's impromptu but legally deputized, local posse.

No one formally mentioned Jeb's actions in Douvez's den. Douvez himself spoke very vocally about it, but no evidence was produced, no witnesses came forward, and so the matter was eventually dropped.

Sly and his Chicago cohorts, Syrus and Spencer Stamper, as well as Mitch Northrop, Josh May, Betta Washington, and Mason Wheeler, all cut deals for slightly lighter sentences by confessing their parts. Josh was the most forthcoming in his statement, but Mason's confession sealed Douvez's fate, as he was the only player who ever knew who was behind it all. Despite his relationship with Betta, he outlined her part in detail as part of his plea bargaining. Betta, in turn, gave an extremely damning account regarding Mason's part in Beth's death, the kidnapping plot, and more disparaging comments about his anatomy than the interrogators wanted to know.

Despite reduced sentences, the outlook for Mason and Douvez, in prison, as former law enforcement, was dire. Except for them, all of the parties involved were looking at a lengthy time at Big Sandy Penitentiary in Inez, Kentucky, once the trials were over. Sonny gave his statement, even to his own part in the crimes, but was released

into the sheriff's custody, after an impassioned plea by MacDowell.
The big downside to all of it is, all the convictions the
Commonwealth's Attorney, Douvez, had been involved with over
the past few decades, would soon be suspect due to his criminal
activity.

The FBI and Mac's office released a joint statement as to the
results of the investigation to every paper and TV station in
Kentucky, except *The State Journal*. FBI Special Agent in Charge, Dave
Smathers, privately suggested to avoid a libel and defamation of
character suit, it would be in *The State Journal*'s best interest to print a
retraction and full apology to the Mounton County Sheriff's Office,
and in particular, Sheriff MacDowell himself. *The State Journal* missed
the news cycle by a full day and was only able to print what they
learned from other news sources. By the end of the week,
MacDowell could have run against Clint Eastwood for sheriff and
still won by a landslide. Well, maybe not Clint Eastwood, but
definitely James Arness.

The trauma counselor recommended by the Kentucky State Police
released Jeb back to work three weeks after the shooting, but insisted
he continue to come to counseling once a week, as well as bring
Naomi to a family therapist for grief counseling.

The power brokers of Kentucky called once again to try to get Mac
to run for governor. With the scandals debunked and his popularity
soaring for rescuing his family, and busting a multi-state drug ring, all
while taking down a corrupt government official, the power brokers
stood convinced Mac was a shoo-in for the office in Frankfort.

"Gentlemen, I appreciate the offer, but I think I will stay right here
in Mounton. Since I ran for sheriff unopposed for the last twenty-
odd years, I don't imagine I will have any problem getting re-elected
again. Especially since the night fry-cook down at Ginny's still
doesn't want the job.

"My friends and family are here, and even when I wasn't the most
popular kid in the Kentucky playground, they stood by me. Which
could not be said for everyone. They need me and I need them. So, if
it's all the same to you, I'll pass. But thank you for the offer."

#

September 16, 6:14 A.M., Mounton, KY

Four weeks after the dust settled, Mac, Jeb, and Naomi were finishing up breakfast in the MacDowell kitchen.

"What're you fellas' day looking like?" Hannah asked while cleaning up the breakfast skillets.

"Pretty much the same ole," Jeb said. "I'm gonna help Dad patrol a bit, then come back and see if I can't get those stalls mucked out before Naomi gets outta school. Once she's home, I thought she and I would do a daddy/daughter project of painting outside of the barn. Doctors have still not cleared her to be around animal waste. Dad was talking about heading out to the Digger's Hole later to check-in. What about you?"

"Well, after dropping Naomi off," Hannah told them while washing the last frying pan in the sink, "I'm going to the community center and take some archery and yoga classes from Felicia. Beth said I might enjoy them and now's as good a time as any to try it."

"You taking yoga and archery? *Can I watch?*" Jeb smiled. It was good to see him able to laugh again. "Kind of *Hunger Games* meets Annie Oakley, huh?"

"Mammaw will get all bendy!" Naomi chimed in.

Hannah looked at Mac, still eating his breakfast.

"Do you have something smart to say, mister?"

"No, ma'am. I am just sitting here guarding my breakfast."

"Good. Give me your plate! I need a word with you in the bedroom, mister."

"Awww, Mammaw! You and Pappaw gonna get all lovey-dovey?" Naomi laughed while getting her pack ready for school.

Hannah glared at Jeb and Mac. "And just that quick, you two smut mouths have corrupted my angel!"

"At least I know," Mac leered with a lascivious grin, "I didn't sacrifice half my breakfast in vain. We don't happen to have any pie laying around, do we?"

"It's six o'clock in the morning, Jacob!" Hannah admonished.

"It's always time for pie. Did you bake it or Ginny?"

"I did," Hannah admitted.

"Well then, never mind. Let's go talk."

"Jacob! Are you saying Ginny's pie is better than mine?" Hannah demanded.

"Hannah, I would never say that," Mac pleaded innocently. "Not without strapping on a firearm."

"Get your scrawny, pie-eatin' butt back in the bedroom!"

"Honey, if you're done bein' silly, I want to talk to you about this money thing," Hannah announced.

"I've been giving some thought about the money as well," Mac replied, sitting on the edge of the bed.

"Me first. You know we had to let old George Walton go because we couldn't afford to keep him on anymore," Hannah began. She leaned against the dresser with both hands holding on to the edge like she was on unsteady ground. "Jeb has picked up some of the slack of what we lost with George. And I have this idea. What if we get an old buckboard, use an older mare, and hire George to give buckboard rides from town out to the mine? We're already feeding the horse and refurbishing an old buckboard wouldn't cost much over a biscuit. During the summer months, we could make a pretty decent amount of cash, and George would have a job."

"What would he do during the winter?" Mac asked his wife. "Man's gotta eat year-round."

"I've already convinced the town council we need a full-time maintenance man in the winter and early spring to help with snow removal, salting the roads, keeping up with the planters, and the gentrified downtown. He could work part-time six months out of the year giving rides and tours out to the mine." Hannah continued, "The Hendricks and some of the other farmers brought their tractors by and told me we could use theirs until the insurance company comes across. They even offered to help us put up the fall hay."

"Sounds like you've got it all under control. What do you need to talk with me about?" Mac wanted to know.

"Listen, I know we always talk to each other before any *major* investments, and I wondered what you would think about us boardin' and breedin' horses? We already got the space for 'em and a few more won't take up much extra room or feed. Daddy always raised some of the best thoroughbreds around. Not racing horses or such, but first-class stock. We've got most of his bloodline right out there in the barn."

"Sounds great," Mac smiled. "Between all the money the farm makes, the buckboard rides, and the little bit we'll get from the tourism profit sharing, we should make more than enough to build up the old cash flow."

"The way I figure it, if we have a good year, we'll have more than enough to rehire some extra hands to help out around here," Hannah beamed.

"Then I guess I should just give the county back the raise I just negotiated out of them?"

"What?"

"Yeah. Before they heard about me turning down the governor campaign offer, I went to the county and told them how much a governor makes," Mac stated, "and miraculously, they found enough money to bump my pay. While they couldn't match the governor's pay, I promised them I would not run for the office. I didn't tell them I had already told the money-boys to take a hike. Wasn't exactly a fib, but definitely more like an omission of sorts. I know how you roll, so if'n you want me to turn down the extra money, I will."

"You'll do no such thing! That's the first raise you've had in years and it's about time those old skinflints started paying you what you're worth."

"I didn't say they were paying me what I'm worth! Did I mention they threw in an extra SUV for the department? I reckon if I drive it at work, put gas in on the county's dime, and save wear and tear on the Bronco, I might get another decade out of it if I put it in storage in the barn."

"Jacob Andrew MacDowell, when did you become such a crafty old horse trader?"

"Well, I did get a new computer for Dawe."

"No kidding?"

"Sure did. Patty-Jane told me that was a good trade. Asked me what I could get in trade for a couple of unruly boys."

#

September 16, 4:14 P.M., Mounton, KY

Mac drove out to *The Digger's Hole Saloon* just before he finished his shift.

"Sonny." The sheriff greets the giant at the front door.

"Sheriff Mac. I wanna thank you agin for gettin' me this job. This is the first time I been on my own and Mr. Howdy's takin' real good care of me," the bear-like Stamper man grinned.

"No worries, Sonny. You did right by me and mine and it was the least I could do."

"Well, Ms. Hannah showed me how to spruce up. Even talked Mr. Ginny into giving me some of his old clothes. Ms. Hannah shore is a fine woman, Sheriff, if'n you don't mind my sayin'."

"Yepper."

Mac noted Hannah's influence. Sonny had scrubbed himself from head to toe and his beard was trimmed and neat, shaped in clean lines to accent his cheekbones. Cheekbones Mac never knew where there before due to the dirt and scruffy beard crawling all over them. The short beard also finished in a clean line just below Sonny's jawline instead of growing down his neck. His once-bushy hedge of wild hair appeared cut, washed, and pulled back into an almost hipster ponytail. When Sonny smiled, Mac could even tell Hannah had given him pointers about brushing his teeth and dental hygiene. Dressed in an XXXL black tee shirt barely stretched across his ursine torso, coupled with black jeans, the transformation was amazing. Had it not been for his unique stature, Mac might not have even recognized the man.

Sonny held the door open for Mac as the sheriff entered the bar. It wasn't dark yet, so the bar was mostly empty, but for a few bar stools. The smell of stale beer, old urine, and used ashtrays pervaded Mac's nostrils, but in a few hours, those would be replaced by the smell of fresh beer, new urine, and partially filled ashtrays.

"Sheriff!"

"Howdy." Mac greeted the leprechaun of a barkeep.

"How can I help you, sir? Anything you want. On the house!" the little red-headed man beamed as he swept an arm toward the rows of liquor bottles.

"I'm good. Still on duty. Just wanted to come by and see how things were working out."

"Outstanding! You recommended Sonny to me as a bouncer and the deal you and I worked out for him to work here and stay in the little apartment above the bar couldn't be better. He don't cost much, is happy to have the work, and it's like having a 24-hour security guard on the property. One look at him and any of these hard-cases even think of starting something and their common sense measures his height, reach, and biceps and the problem mysteriously seems to vanish."

"We *have* noticed a decline in your D&D calls to our office since he started," Mac asserted.

"Yessir. I don't think the boy has had to do more than check IDs since he started. Just the sight of him scares most of these layabouts half to death."

"Glad it's working out. I do have one more favor to ask."

"You name it, Sheriff. I'm already in your debt," Howdy replied with a smile.

"Do you know a woman named Peggy Clay? Two kids? Recently lost her husband?"

"I think I do remember reading something a while back. He got hisself killed after he left here, right?"

"She's been waitressing forever down at *Ginny's Diner* and is very good at it," Mac said. "I would consider it a big favor if you would interview her for a waitressing job on the weekends. She has two little boys and her momma helps watch them, but she could use a bit of extra cash now that she's on her own. Ginny will give her a glowing recommendation."

"Sheriff, if she is half as good as you say she is, and I know you wouldn't recommend anyone who would reflect badly on you, consider her hired. Damned if Sonny din't turn out to be worth his weight in gold and considering his weight, that's saying something. Since he's been on the job, regular folks come here now and it's not a drunken brawl every night. I could use the extra help. Send her by."

"Thanks, Howdy."

"Think nothing of it, lad. When you're a fellow my size, it's always a good policy to be friends with the law."

"Doesn't matter what size you are, Howdy. It's good to have friends, period."

THE END

About The Author

Paul K. Metheney was the featured author for dozens of sports magazines, has numerous short stories published in recent anthologies, a collection of his own short stories (*That Boy Ain't Write in the Head*), wrote *Posse Whipped*, and is working on another much-delayed novel or two. Paul defies genre-typing by writing whatever he believes will be a good story. From the supernatural and metaphysical, to alternate universe versions of 1963 and King Arthur, to a complex novel about a simple small-town Southern Sheriff.

Paul has over three decades working in advertising design, print, and graphic design. For the last thirty years or so, he has been working in the web design, SEO, PPC, social media, and marketing fields, including writing marketing copy for his client's blogs and social media on various subjects.

Despite a multifaceted nature, Paul is definitely 'what you see is what you get.' No hidden agendas. No having to guess what's on his mind. He is wide open. Usually TOO wide open if you ask his wife, Melinda. Paul is happily married to his one-time, high school sweetheart, loves riding his Can-Am Spyder motorcycle, sporadically smokes a good cigar, and is an avid poker enthusiast. Having sold their home and cars, Paul and Melinda are traveling the country, full-time, in an RV, exploring America and having adventures.

Paul can be reached at his site on writing, poker, travel, reviews, and all things politically incorrect at http://paulmetheney.com, on Twitter at https://twitter.com/PaulMetheney, and on Facebook at https://www.facebook.com/paul.metheney.

More from Paul K. Metheney

- *Concepts for Texas Hold'em* - making more money at the Texas Hold'em Poker tables in casinos

- *Posse Whipped* - a Southern sheriff struggling to save his town, all while protecting his most valuable law-enforcement assets... his family and friends.

- *Escape Claws* – What if werewolves were real? What if you were one?

- *That Boy Ain't Write in the Head* - the greatest hits of mixed genre stories: Sci-Fi, Alternate Universes, Time Travel, Supernatural, and More

- *Two Minds, No Waiting* - a collection of stories involving science fiction, time travel, alternate universes, and worlds beyond imagining by Steve Rouse and Paul K. Metheney

- *Beautiful Lies, Painful Truths Vol. I* - a Left Hand Publishers anthology of short stories focusing on the ironic beauty between humanity's love of Life and fear of Death, featuring two interconnected short stories by Paul K. Metheney.

- **Beautiful Lies, Painful Truths Vol. II** - a sequel to Left Hand Publishers anthology of short stories. Life seemingly brings joy, happiness, hope, and love. Death can end sadness, illness, suffering, and pain featuring a double short story by Paul K. Metheney.

- *Classics ReMixed Vol. I* - An anthology from Left Hand Publishers of short stories twisting classic stories and your imagination in all new ways. One story includes a Paul K. Metheney twisted version of Rapunzel.

- *Classics ReMixed Vol. II* - The sequel to the anthology from Left Hand Publishers' short stories warping classic stories with all new twists. Paul K. Metheney takes on Pinocchio and the Dark Knight in disturbing new ways.

Concepts for Texas Hold'em
By Paul K. Metheney

An easy-to-read pocket guide of concepts, notes, thoughts, and strategies on making more money at the Texas Hold'em Poker tables in casinos. From tactics to use at the table, to money management, to etiquette and terminology, Concepts for Texas Hold'em will steer you toward bigger profits from your poker sessions. Aimed at intermediate to advanced players, we skip over the basics of the game to tricks, tips, and thoughts on how to make the most from your play.

Maximize your wins in your casino cash games of Texas Hold'em Poker. Minimize your losses.

LHP - https://bit.ly/3r39YDF
Amazon - https://amzn.to/3AVTj7v

***

Posse Whipped
By Paul K. Metheney

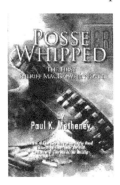

A Southern sheriff struggling to save his town from corruption, drug trafficking, moonshiners, and the economy, all while protecting his most valuable law-enforcement assets... his family and friends. As the sheriff protects his town and loved ones, a villain from his family's past assembles his own eclectic posse of criminals to destroy Sheriff MacDowell and everything he holds dear.

A down-home journey in to the hills of Kentucky brings you a sometimes humorous novel set in a modern-day western fight for survival, justice, and family. The spirit of the Wild West meets the 21st century in an adventure for the John Wayne in us all.

***

That Boy Ain't Write in the Head
By Paul K. Metheney

A Mixed Genre Stories: Sci-Fi, Alternate Universes, Time Travel, Supernatural, & More

A science-fiction author tries to save the world from alien attack, alien visitors that only eat cancer, a man travels back to his past, and a Secret Service Agent must protect the President from destroying the White House. These are just a few of the fantastic tales that await you inside.

This collection serves up Paul's best stories and an all-new menu of fresh tales to stimulate your literary palate.

The title of the book derives from a strip bar bouncer taking one look at Paul and saying
"That boy ain't right in the head."
LHP - https://bit.ly/3r0TAnn
Amazon - https://amzn.to/3AVTj7v
✳✳✳

Two Minds,
No Waiting

By Steve Rouse & Paul Metheney

Take two very disturbed minds. Add the ability to create any worlds or situations they like. And you have the recipe for a collection of science fiction stories like none you have ever tasted.

From alien saviors and attackers, to time travel, to fantastic tales that include unique teachers and hunted mammals. More than just spaceships and phaser beams, this collection contains alternate universes and superheroes. If you're ready to set aside your beliefs in what is or isn't possible, it's time to get your imagination rewired by ...

Two Minds, No Waiting!

LHP - https://bit.ly/3R9q5dI

Amazon - https://amzn.to/39jAjFm

***

Beautiful Lies,
Painful Truths Vol. I

Life asked Death, "Why do people love me, but hate you?"
Death responded, "Because you are a beautiful lie, and I am a painful truth."
~Anonymous

There's an ironic beauty between humanity's love of Life and fear of Death. Life seemingly brings joy, happiness, hope, and love. Death can end sadness, illness, suffering, and pain. We asked writers to "Let the title and quote take your imagination, your story, wherever it wants to go."
Join them now as an international blend of authors, both fresh and seasoned, bring you an exceptional menu of speculative fiction, mystery, realism, horror, and the supernatural. If your palate varies from the macabre to the dramatic, *Beautiful Lies, Painful Truths* provides an assortment of tasty treasures that will chill, delight, and give you food for thought.

LHP - https://bit.ly/2H1we86
Amazon: http://amzn.to/2reSyIe

***

Beautiful Lies, Painful Truths Vol. II

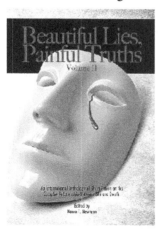

Most believe that Life promises light, bliss, and wonder. Death scares most with its shadow of mortality, darkness, and destruction. But what if those may be, if not lies, just facets of the entities that bookend our existence? Life does not mock Death, but feeds it. What would you do if faced with either?

An international galley of authors brings us a second repast of tales featuring the complex relationship between Life, Death, and humanity. From the supernatural to the sublime, belly to up a banquet of speculative fiction across a wide spectrum of genres. These stories will continue to feed your craving for the fantastic.

LHP - https://bit.ly/2HZW1Pn

Amazon: http://amzn.to/2ngBq0i

***

Classics Remixed Vol. I

An anthology of short stories twisting classic stories and your imagination in all new ways.

Alternate versions of stories you know taking you in new directions.

From much-loved fairy fables to time-honored tales, no genre or classic is off-limits. *Classics ReMixed Vol. I* spins and twists divergent versions of old favorites and stories we all know. Be prepared to have all your ...

LHP - https://bit.ly/2XLgkY9

Amazon - https://amzn.to/2M0qRLx

Classics ReMixed

***

Classics Remixed Vol. II

Continuing the anthology of short stories twisting classic stories and treasured tales in disturbing directions.

Once you read *Classics Remixed Vol. II* you will never be able to look a fairy tale or child's story in the moral again. No genre or classic is off-limits. The Brothers Grimm never knew what hit 'em. *Classics ReMixed Vol. II* unravels alternative versions of old favorites and stories we all know. Be prepared to have all your ...

Classics ReMixed again

LHP - https://bit.ly/3C6q5GP

Amazon - https://amzn.to/3aC5aeh

***

Please Review Paul's Books

If you enjoyed this book, please leave reviews at Amazon or Goodreads.com. All of Paul's other works are available at Amazon and the Left Hand Publishers' site.

Beautiful Lies, Painful Truths I Amazon: http://amzn.to/2reSyle Goodreads: http://bit.ly/2BobVCi	Beautiful Lies, Painful Truths II Amazon: http://amzn.to/2ngBq0i Goodreads: http://bit.ly/2slkBpP
That Boy Ain't Write in the Head By Paul K. Metheney Amazon - https://amzn.to/3AVTj7v Youtube - https://youtu.be/zpDkfvbzimw Goodreads - https://bit.ly/3E02x4z	Classics ReMixed Vol. II Amazon - https://amzn.to/3aC5aeh Goodreads - https://bit.ly/2vMBMDm
Two Minds, No Waiting by Paul K. Metheney & Steve Rouse Amazon - https://amzn.to/39jAjFm Goodreads - https://bit.ly/3pkLzH9	Classics ReMixed Vol. I Amazon - https://amzn.to/2M0qRLx Goodreads - https://bit.ly/2LZsIQI
Concepts of Texas Hold'em By Paul K. Metheney Amazon - https://amzn.to/3AVTj7v Youtube - https://youtu.be/zpDkfvbzimw Goodreads - https://bit.ly/3E02x4z	

***

Made in the USA
Monee, IL
28 November 2022

18785101R00154